SNAFU
LAST STAND

Dedicated to Frank Michaels Errington, for his long-time support of Cohesion Press, Australian writers and publishers, and the horror writing community in general.
Vale, Frank. We miss you.

Also From Cohesion Press

<u>Horror:</u>

SNAFU: An Anthology of Military Horror
– eds Geoff Brown & Amanda J Spedding

SNAFU: Wolves at the Door
– eds Geoff Brown & Amanda J Spedding

SNAFU: Survival of the Fittest
– eds Geoff Brown & Amanda J Spedding

SNAFU: Hunters
– eds Amanda J Spedding & Geoff Brown

SNAFU: Future Warfare
– eds Amanda J Spedding & Geoff Brown

SNAFU: Unnatural Selection
– eds Amanda J Spedding & Geoff Brown

SNAFU: Black Ops
– eds Amanda J Spedding, Matthew Summers & Geoff Brown

SNAFU: Resurrection
– eds Amanda J Spedding & Matthew Summers

Publisher's Note:

This book is a collection of stories from writers all over the world.
For authenticity and voice, we have kept the style of English native to each author's location, so some stories will be in UK English, and others in US English.
We have, however, changed dashes and dialogue marks to our standard format for ease of understanding.

* ● *

This book is a work of fiction.
All people, places, events, zombies, virus-ridden infected, various other creatures, and situations are the product of the authors' imaginations.
Any resemblance to persons, living, dead, or in between, is purely coincidental.

LAST STAND

Edited by Amanda J Spedding & Matthew Summers

COHESION PRESS
THE BATTLE HAS JUST BEGUN

Cohesion Press
Mayday Hills Lunatic Asylum
Beechworth, Australia
2019

SNAFU: LAST STAND

Amanda J Spedding & Matthew Summers (eds)

* •*

Anthology © Cohesion Press 2019
Stories © Individual Authors 2019
Cover Art © Dean Samed 2019
Publishing Editor: Geoff Brown

Set in Palatino Linotype

COHESION PRESS
THE BATTLE HAS JUST BEGUN

Cohesion Press
Mayday Hills Lunatic Asylum
Beechworth, Australia
www.cohesionpress.com

Contents

FOREWORD

Tim Miller

I f you are lucky enough to be someone who reads a lot, finding other readers who share your taste is a true gift. People, editors, even an A.I. (or at least a data-driven algorithm) who can recommend new books and stories with a high hit-rate of success are worth their weight in gold. While I was hunting for great short stories to become part of *Love, Death & Robots*, our Netflix animated anthology, I stumbled across a SNAFU collection and I was hooked. Reading one story in a collection and loving it isn't unusual, but after loving three in a row I knew I'd found something special. And the fact that the book was part of a *series* of short story collections was almost too good to be true. In the end, we found three of our eighteen stories in the various SNAFU collections and each story became the foundation of an ass-kicking animated short. And more SNAFU stories are already in the mix for future seasons of LDR.

Since I've read the anthologies, the editors, Geoff Brown and Amanda Spedding, as well as many of the contributing authors, have become valued collaborators. We had such a good time working together that when it came time to release a new SNAFU collection, they gave me the honor of suggesting a theme. My answer was instantaneous - last stands. Because I'm never happier than when I'm reading a great story filled with lost causes and final sacrifice!

My father's most beloved film was *Gunga Din* (spoiler, it ends badly for Mr. Din). As an avid reader of military history, *The Battle of Rorke's Drift* was a favorite one to study ('nother spoiler... it ends badly for a few thousand Zulus). The two poems I quote endlessly are *Invictus* and *If* (words to live by if

1

you haven't read them) as both share themes on facing dire circumstances and fighting on no matter the cost. And of course the films I choose to direct or develop – *Deadpool, Terminator: Dark Fate*, etc. – usually have elements of struggling against the odds. I'm drawn like a flame-bound moth to moments where characters must face death – or worse than death – and fight on regardless. It's not just about heroes – that would get boring – but the different ways in which characters face that *all is lost* moment are endlessly fascinating to me. Stories about that final, unforgiving minute offer dramatic tension that few other works of fiction – or real situations – can ever hope to reach.

I'm sure the roots of my fascination lie deep in a psychological need to know how I'd fare in that instant – coward, hero, or neither – but that's one bit of self-knowledge I hope I never learn.

The term 'last stand' seems to suggest events that are brutal yet brief, but, as you'll see, these tales come in all shapes and sizes. The ties that bind them together are how the characters face the end of everything they are, and the loss of everything they could become. Some of the stories are intensely personal, while others focus on the even larger canvas of the end of humanity. But each looks into the abyss in some way, and each finds a path to – and through – that moment. A moment that is, thus far, a universal experience for humanity.

And of course, the reasons why people choose to stand and die rather than retreat and live are fertile ground for drama and action. The more we identify with the beliefs, fears, and hopes of the protagonists the more dramatic their story becomes. So I've found that, more often than not, stories about choosing certain death travel down interesting roads to that big moment.

History is filled with stories of heroism and loss that are inspirational, aspirational or cautionary. And no doubt our future will generate many more before we reach enlightenment. Looking on the bright side, that means we'll continue to be shocked, amazed and moved by tales of sacrifice, loss and heroic last stands like the ones you're about to read.

This collection is truly a buffet of style, tone, and desperate action.

FOREWORD

Do you want a post-apocalyptic and heart-rending story about nanotechnology gone wrong? Try 'Canute'.

Maybe 'Katadesmos' is more your style, with marines facing a deadly plague of Sumerian gods, blending modern weapons and ancient magic in the dusty streets of Iraq.

Or how about a Zombie plague, or a Civil War voodoo tale?

Maybe an interdimensional *slug* infestation or alien invasion? No?

Well, then perhaps you'd go for a genetically altered slave revolt, or military bio-weapons gone berserk?

And if none of those excite you, please note that's not even *half* the great stories in this volume – I mean *fuck me* there's some cool shit in here!

So search the dead for any spare ammo, growl a terse farewell to your comrades and toss a prayer to any god who might listen – and enjoy the read.

Tim Miller - Los Angeles, 2019

BEAST TRAP

J.G. Grimmer

The shaman of Two Forest Clan awoke to the rich, meaty smell of slaughter. Four rapidly-cooling corpses, eyes wide, mouths open, lay around him. Their stinking insides coiled snake-like about their legs, gleaming in the flickering fire light – the shadows made them appear to be squirming on the cave floor.

Blood dripped down the cave walls. A smear of crimson painted a wide, sticky red swath out of the cave past the fire set at the entrance to discourage predators. The shaman uttered two sharp barks, startling the other hunters from sleep. They jumped to their feet, eyes wide beneath over-hanging brows as they took in the carnage all around them.

Their large, callused hands flew through the air, punctuated by high-pitched noises. Each trying to outdo the other in an attempt to explain the butchery.

Stone pointed to the clean-cut sides of the gashes that had opened the bellies of the four youths who'd accompanied them on the hunt in the hopes of earning their name. Stone's grunts and gestures asserted it was the work of a marauding great-fanged cat.

Club violently disagreed, making it plain the unnamed were killed by a spotted scavenger known to have dragged off the clan's kills in past seasons.

Stone snarled and smashed his large-knuckled fist into Club's face with a loud crack that sent the hunter staggering backwards.

Hair, Claw, and Hide joined in, insisting Stone was right. The shaman knew they banded together, as brood mates would – Rock and Horn were another matter.

Rock glanced between them, one shoulder sitting much lower than the other. Two winters ago, Horn had rammed Rock off a cliff, which only made Rock more determined to out-fight and out-kill everyone. Rock sided with Club.

Horn spat on the ground, his flat head jerking atop broad shoulders. His arms and legs were large and wide, resembling the dangerously unpredictable two-horned wooly behemoths who roamed the plains. He gestured angrily, certain the killer was a cave bear. He stopped suddenly, swallowing hard. The hunters fell silent, all eyes on their shaman.

Firelight cast his scarred hairless head red. His shadow, large and monstrous, stalked the cave wall. He stepped into their midst, thoughtfully twisting the hollowed-out bone that adorned his first finger – a claw bone from the cave bear that had ripped off one of his ears and clouded an eye during the third hunt of his eighteenth summer.

For three suns he laid thrashing and screaming in the grip of fever and strange visions; the clouded bear eye open, blindly staring and rolling in its socket before he revived.

From that day, he earned his clan name: *Ear*.

He was made shaman under the light of the Night Guardian and in the presence of the cave bear's massive fanged skull – Two Forest Clan's totem.

Ear slowly traced his fingers over the four puckered scars that carved his face, pausing at the hole that marked what the bear took. With his unblinking bear eye, he gazed upon Horn and the hunter grunted fearfully and looked away. Then Ear looked at each of the hunters with his good eye – the debate was over.

Our kin have been killed. Ear gestured at the white bodies, stark against the dark floor of the cave, blood billowing out around them. *Whether they died by cat, scavenger, or bear*, he paused, looking pointedly at Horn who meekly met his shaman's eyes, *does not matter. We will hunt it down and avenge this night of blood!*

The hunters nodded excitedly, thumped their chests, grunting their assent.

Pointing to the blood trail, *what of One Arm?* Ear asked; the elder male who looked after the young ones, imparting to them the use of tools and fire, and the Way of the Hunt. *He may not live, but we must find him and bring him back to Two Forest Clan.*

The hunters nodded as they covered the corpses with hides and armed themselves; Stone, Hide, Rock, and Hair with spears; Horn with his two fang-sharp nose horns, Club stood smacking his thickly-callused palm with his heavy-knotted namesake, and Claw with his curved long-fanged cat claws.

Finally, Ear picked up his thick club to which he'd attached an edged wing-shaped black stone.

At first light, with the fire burning bright and fierce, Ear led the hunters out to the grassy plains, following the blood trail.

The Guide of Light rose behind them like a fire in the sky, and the hunters moved warily but surely down the slope.

Ahead, the waving waist-high grasses glowed golden. The vista was soothing, but the hunters knew that slashing, tearing claws could erupt without warning.

Fat insects swarmed and buzzed around them, dipping to feed on the blood that trailed ahead, the grass flattened on either side as if by a storm wind.

Claw waved his heavily muscled arms about, making a raspy noise.

Ear went to him, cocked his head. *What?*

One Arm, Claw responded with excited grunts.

Ear looked ahead. All he saw was the flattened grass and blood trail that stretched until the shimmering air smeared the land into the sky.

The other hunters wore confused expressions as well.

Ear held his hands out to Claw, palms up. *Where – One Arm?*

Claw's hand jabbed out like a spear tip. *There – There.* Then he sprinted forward, vanishing into the grass, swift and impulsive like his namesake.

Ear yelped along with the other hunters and gave chase, calling after Claw to stop; reckless to run blindly and alone out here. Ear, who was just a step or two behind, suddenly lost sight of Claw, as if the grass came alive and swallowed him. Grunting his frustration, Ear and the other hunters continued on, their feet hammering the ground like a herd of charging bulls.

The grass whipped around them leaving bloody lines on their bodies with its sharp, serrated edges. Ear and the hunters knew every blade, rise, and furrow of these lands. A thin white tree came into view ahead and to one side of a low rise. Ear could smell the blood trail nearby. He turned toward it, and ran faster, pulling ahead of the others. After many steps, his feet were once more pounding the trail, kicking up dirt as he passed the dead tree.

The trail turned off into a blind corner ahead, and unable to see what awaited him, Ear slowed and touched the claw bone on his finger for guidance. Reassured by the bear spirit, he turned the corner where he came upon Claw, curled up and shivering, his bare chest covered in blood that was darkening and becoming crusty. The other hunters caught up and stood around Claw. They breathed easily – Two Forest Clan's hunters had chased prey longer and farther than this, but they were wary – Claw acted strangely.

Except for the blood, there was no sign of One Arm.

Claw's head snapped up, startling the hunters who stepped back; his eyes, shadowed beneath his brow and streaming with tears, darted frantically from one hunter to the next, until he met Ear. He stood. *One Arm, where did he go, Shaman? He was just here – then not.*

Ear knew Claw and One Arm were close. The old hunter treated Claw like he was his own child.

Ear gestured that he did not know how to answer.

Claw wiped his face with his hands. *One Arm just ahead,* he gestured.

Ear nodded. *We'll find him together.* Then he and the other hunters gathered around Claw and patted his shoulders and back, reinforcing the clan's bonds.

* * *

8

The Guide of Light was shining directly down on the hunters as they ran; strange insects followed, buzzing about the group and trying to keep pace with their blood-scent and sweat.

Ear slapped his head and bare chest so hard it left red marks. It did nothing to discourage the buzzing hordes.

Hide snorted and grinned at the shaman. He was covered from his wide shoulders to the middle of his muscular legs in the tanned flesh of a many-antlered stag he single-handedly cornered and killed. The insects completely ignored him, and most aggravating of all, neither Ear or the other hunters had ever seen his face and body dripping as theirs did – *ever*.

They reached the next rise and halted, Ear's good eye widening and blinking in surprise at what he first thought to be a dark storm cloud roiling over the giant carcass of a wooly great one. The jagged ends of its brutally splintered tusks pointed to the Light Guide.

As he drew closer, Ear saw the cloud was instead a living mass of insects known to feed on the dead. An ache, dull and slow, drew itself across Ear's heavy brow like stone scraped across bone. He tightened the grip on his club, which he raised, gritting his teeth and swinging it at the loudly buzzing swarm.

Stone raised his spear ready to fight. Long-fanged cats or vicious spotted scavengers would be close, guarding their kill. The others took a defensive stance around them and the massive corpse, ready to do battle.

The wooly great one's belly had been cleanly slit open. The beast's insides were gone, its belly splayed wide like the mouth of a cave. The Light Guide bathed the interior in a dull, bloody glow. The hunters gathered around the emptied carcass, their mouths gaping.

The agitated brood mates gesticulated fearfully, *what could have done this, Shaman?*

Ear touched the corner of his good eye and turned his hands palms up, *I have never seen this before.*

The insect cloud buzzing above their heads swarmed madly, its shape shifting constantly.

Ear and the hunters of Two Forest Clan felt the buzz in their teeth, felt it crawling all over them.

Rock, Stone, Club, and Horn, their faces twisted in shock and confusion, turned their attention to the beast's massive head that lay on the ground a few steps from the body. They chattered fearfully among each other, *why is there no blood? The ground should be thick with it.*

The wooly great one's head had been sliced from its giant body, its tusks snapped off; the pointed ends nothing but shattered pieces strewn over the ground. The stench of hide rotting in the heat closed around the hunters' throats like a choking fist.

Ear caressed the claw-bone on his finger – the bear spirit sniffed and stamped restlessly.

The belly-churning fear that silenced Ear and the hunters of Two Forest Clan was broken by the tooth-grating buzz of the strange insect cloud over their heads.

Then with a suddenness that caused Ear and the hunters of Two Forest Clan to jump, the swarm shot off in every direction.

The ache remained in the middle of Ear's protruding brow. It began to grow, as if the swarm had laid eggs in his head, which began to hatch. He shook his head violently, crouched, and bit his tongue. The pain caused the ache to leave as suddenly as the swarm.

Stone snarled at Club. *Claw led us into this place chasing One Arm!*

Ear turned at his raised voice.

Club growled, *One Arm dead!* He barked as he raised his hand to strike Stone.

Claw roared, *One Arm not dead!* He was joined by Hair and Hide who stomped the ground, snorting their agreement.

Brothers, Ear gestured, holding out his empty hands. *End this.*

Club lunged, ramming his thick, heavy namesake into Ear's belly.

Ear's breath exploded out of his body in grunt and spit, light sparked in his eyes. Breath returned in coughing, heaving snorts. Ear snarled and waded in – he would end it. He started with Club, smashing his fist into his jaw, spinning him around, then Ear viciously struck the back of his clan mate's head. Club fell hard and lay sprawled on the ground. Then Ear moved on to the others.

The land was spattered with blood and echoed with roars, screams, and blows.

The shaman of Two Forest Clan stood breathing heavy in the center of his moaning and bleeding hunters.

Stone lay flat on the ground, his jaw swollen; Horn panted hard, lips bloody but on his feet and showing his teeth. Hair sat up, grass and dirt stuck to his body, one eye swollen shut, while Hide staggered about holding his head. Claw stood breathing heavily, his face scratched, blood on his teeth, grinning. Club pushed to his feet, rubbing his bleeding mouth while moving it from side to side; and Rock, his face covered in bruises, lowered his head in submission to Ear.

Ear licked the blood from his torn knuckles, eyeing the others. All the hunters followed Rock's example and lowered their heads in obedience to their shaman. The dark emptiness of the hollowed-out great one's body loomed before Ear like an open mouth.

The Light Guide travelled across the sky and now shone in Ear's eyes when Stone approached, hands empty and palms up. Ear backed up baring his teeth.

Stone gestured, *my shaman, whatever killed the great one has left a stain on this land—on us. We lost our way, your might brought us back.*

Ear turned and looked at the group. Seeing agreement, Ear nodded. *Let's leave this cursed place,* he gestured.

The blood trail had now dried to brown. The contours of the ground becoming familiar as it led down to a ravine the hunters used to herd their prey.

Ear and Stone halted to scan ahead – the tip of Two Forest Clan's spear. The others fanned out behind while Horn took up the rear, disliking closeness with others.

Stone tapped Ear's arm, offering his water skin.

Ear nodded and drank. Its coolness felt good going down his dry throat.

Light would soon turn the land over to darkness. They had to keep moving. Without fire as a guard, the dark loosed swift things baring sharp fangs and wicked claws that promised a tearing, screaming, and bloody end.

The hunters moved forward with speed and purpose as their shadows lengthened in the dying light, all eyes and ears focused ahead and to each side, searching for movement and sound.

In the center of the blood trail ahead, Ear sighted a bloody flap of flesh with his good eye. He raised his hand as he slowed.

Stone issued a whistling sound, a perfect imitation of a bird call familiar to this land, and the hunters came to a stop, making no sound as they assumed defensive positions.

Ear crouched and picked around the meat's edges with a single bear claw – the same one that had scarred his face. He noticed the other side of the flesh was not bloody, but brown like weathered hide. When Ear flipped it over, he gasped and fell hard on his backside, eyes wide in horror.

The eye-less face of One Arm stared up at him.

Stone, who'd been standing point watching the trail ahead, rushed over.

Ear chattered in alarm, sliding himself backward along the ground, pointing when Stone came to his side.

Stone snorted explosively. His eyes narrowed, then widened, then narrowed again. He reached out and extended his dirt-covered finger before pulling it away sharply.

Rock came forward, curious. When he saw One Arm's face, mute, separated from his body he screeched and reeled back uttering meaningless sounds.

Club, eyes wary, inched closer. His face went slack, as though suddenly becoming boneless.

Hide and Hair ran forward then together skidded to a stop, showering One Arm's face in clumps of dirt and dried blood. Their wracked and choking sounds brought Claw running.

Hide and Hair turned to stop him, holding his arms and blocking his line of sight, grunting unconvincingly that all was well. The combined power of their grip, capable of crushing bone, had no effect.

Claw roared and broke through, falling to his knees in front of One Arm's face. A groan erupted from deep within his bare chest and echoed across the land. Eyes streaming with tears and mouth trembling, Claw gently brushed away the dirt and crusted blood from One Arm's face with his fingertips. With care he lifted it, pressing it tenderly to his face, massive shoulders shaking.

Horn's bellowing, snorting, and snarling shattered the air, silencing the mourning.

Alerted, Ear and the others turned.

A pale figure ran toward them, the landscape's growing shadows obscuring its features.

Horn roared his challenge, furiously waving two fang-sharp nose horns in warning. Ear and the hunters took position behind him, weapons ready.

The pale figure took shape as it closed in. Its protruding ribs stood out against dead white flesh, its bare legs churned over the ground, its one arm moving with a jerky flapping motion, like a wave of greeting – its face missing…

Shock and recognition froze Horn just as the faceless thing ran into then passed *through* him.

Ear watched, numb, as the thing they once knew as One Arm ran through the hunters, one after the other.

Unable to move, the last thing Ear saw was a skinless face and an open mouth filled with blood. As it passed through him, Ear's head was filled with snarling and tearing. Then his mind cleared. Ear turned and watched One Arm – *dead* One Arm – vanishing into the darkness of the ravine.

Stone produced a short clicking noise and thrust his spear into the long grass. A short piercing yelp along with a spray of blood spurted high and bright against the grass. While Stone gripped the spear, Hide and Club moved closer. As Hide stood ready, Club parted the grass with his knotted namesake.

13

The tip of Stone's spear had pierced the eye of a tawny slit-eyed cat, its long fangs jutting past a white whiskered jaw. Stone's thrust had killed it quickly.

Ear gestured. *What is* that *doing here?*

Shaman's right, Hide replied. *They pounce on prey from trees. Not hunt on the ground.*

Stone and Club nodded as Stone yanked the spear free with a wet pop.

The high grass around them came alive with the cackling of spotted scavengers, the snarling of other long-fanged cats, and the snorting of wooly two-horned chargers. The hunters closed ranks, barking their confusion at each other.

One, then another spotted cackler burst through the tall grass, their ugly flat faces marking each hunter as they ran past, just out of reach of spears and much too fast for edged weapons, before vanishing again.

Chest filling with fear and the droning ache returning in his head, Ear realized they were cut off. He yipped sharply at his hunters to move – *now.*

Stone charged over to Rock who sat on the ground rocking, oblivious to what was happening. He picked him up and struck him hard in the face, snarling for him to follow Ear.

The other hunters needed no prompting, pushing themselves forward with eyes wild and darting.

Ear set a steady pace. He did not walk, but he *dared* not run into the growing fang-filled darkness.

The snarling, cackling, and snorting of the beasts around them matched their pace, further unnerving the hunters. Ear struggled to keep from running faster, to end this.

Stone jabbed his spear at sleek and elusive shadows, and Club swung at snarls from the grass. Rock, Hide, and Hair grunted and roared at the darkness, trying to scare off the predators. Claw joined them, while Horn bellowed and kept looking over his broad shoulders.

The dull ache Ear felt in his head back at the gutted carcass became a squirming and thrashing thing pounding inside him to get out.

The trail narrowed and the sides of the ravine rose around them as the Guardian of Light died, splashing the sky red with its blood.

With a stab of unease, Ear suddenly realized that they were alone.

The beasts were gone.

*   *   *

As the sky darkened to the color of the bruise on Club's face, Ear raised his thick, muscled arm. The hunters stopped and listened.

Only silence.

No night birds chirped to the bright rock rising into the sky behind them.

No rustling from the undergrowth teeming with small, furry creatures.

No buzzing of insects in the night air.

No distant roars or howls from the massive sharp-clawed beasts of the dark, calling out to mates, or on the hunt themselves.

Ear fingered his bone ring warily, fighting the urge to piss.

The night held its breath.

A decision made, Ear gestured to his men to take their positions. Stone and Hide in front, Ear, Claw, Club, and Horn in the center. Rock and Hair turned to protect the rear.

Two Forest Clan's hunters moved silently forward, pushing deeper into the ravine. Overhead, the Night Guardian bathed them in soft light.

The hunters' thirst for revenge and the discipline of the hunt in itself barely contained their fear and panic. Ear sensed it in them, and himself. *This has been a strange hunt from the very beginning*, Ear thought. His eyes widened, and he barked at the hunters, *we've been herded here! We're—*

A large six-fingered hand shot out of the darkness, obscuring the Night Guardian's light. It grabbed Rock and Hair's spears and snapped them in half like twigs. Another six-fingered hand lunged from the darkness ahead, impaling Stone on fingers long and black. Hide's belly was sliced open by another in a spray of blood, his insides spilling out as Stone was lifted off his feet, eyes wide with shock and fear as he was yanked into the darkness.

Hair bellowed furiously before he was seized and smashed into Rock. The massive hand lifted both bodies into the air and squeezed. Blood streamed hot between multi-jointed fingers as bones crunched and flesh was mashed. The noise of the final squelch bounced back and forth off the walls of the ravine, and the remaining hunters felt a rain of blood and scraps of flesh splatter across their faces.

Something moved above them.

Claw, Club, Horn, and Ear watched in horror as the giant hand that had just crushed their brothers rose into the air, dripping.

The Night Guardian reappeared, illuminating a monster.

It stood as tall as the ravine was deep; its skin hard, black and glistening. It straddled the ravine on two long and thin four-jointed legs – like a jumping insect. Two of its spindly arms spanned the ravine's length, blocking the hunters from moving forward or back; while two more ended in six-fingered hands from which black knife-like nails extended and retracted like stone scraping against stone.

In the center of each palm, four glistening orifices opened and closed with wet snaps. Above the upper arms a grouping of scalloped segments led higher along a thin serpent-like neck to the thing's head.

The ache returned, echoing painfully in Ear's head. He twisted the bone ring, becoming frantic that the bear spirit had abandoned him.

Ear and the others shivered, gaping at the thing with fear.

It had no face.

Its head was as black as its body and made up of sharp-ly-angled plates that met in the center.

Claw and Horn whimpered. Club pissed himself.

The creature regarded each of the hunters in turn. Its breathing couldn't be heard. Perhaps it did not need to.

16

It froze as it peered at Ear, becoming a thing of stillness. Then turned its attention to the others. The black plates of its faceless head dully reflected the Night Guardian's light.

Claw screamed and turned; the cat's claws tied to his hands flashed, slashing Club's throat and plunging into the hunter's chest. More blood arced around the ravine, spattering Horn and Ear further.

Claw paused as the scream died in his throat, frowning and blinking at Club as the hunter gurgled and died.

Horn suddenly jerked, and moved slowly, his face red and muscles rippling with strain as he sunk his twin horn knives into either side of Claw's neck.

Red sprayed in twin fountains as Claw sank to the ground. Ear roared as he fought to stop himself from fleeing, before his body jolted and a dark and unnatural thought that was not his own invaded his mind. Ear swung his weapon, cleanly severing Horn's head. It tumbled through the air, trailing a scarlet arc, while the body crashed to the ground, blood spewing from the open neck.

Alone, head throbbing, insides shuddering, Ear found that he could not move. He stared at the monster with his good eye, searching for meaning.

Ear's vision darkened, shadows slowly resolving into an otherworldly landscape. A hazy silver sky filled with strange blue and orange stars. Two rocky orbs dominated the vision, one shattered in half, the other boiling and smoking as steamy red veins crisscrossed its surface.

Moving closer, Ear saw creatures like the one before him moving about the hellscape – massive numbers of them. Giant mounds dotted the vista, their sloping black sides marked with glowing scratches that hurt Ear's head. Demons of all sizes moved in and out of them.

Ear suddenly realized that this was the *demon's* home.

The demon, along with many others of its kin, rose into the sky, four arms and spindly legs hidden beneath swirling darkness.

It took Ear, screaming, into impenetrable blackness.

A blinding flash of light bloomed far in the vast black depths.

This, the demon whispered, *this is what attracted me. What filled me with hunger – the birth of your world. A new world to slaughter. To feast on.*

A blue orb appeared; then they plummeted, Ear screaming into the void before clouds, mountains, forests, and plains rushed by.

No. Ear whimpered.

Night.

The cave.

Fire burning bright and strong at the entrance. The demon passed through it without injury. *So easy*, it whispered to Ear. *The weak.* It slit open the bellies of the unnamed. *The lame.* It cut open One Arm's throat. Blood sprayed, covering the demon's head and body.

Good, the demon chittered as the blood was sucked under the plates of its head and into the mouths of its hands.

No! Ear gripped his weapon, knuckles white, muscle and sinews tearing against the hold.

The demon watched the sleeping clan for a few minutes, before dragging One Arm's corpse outside and along the trail. As it continued to withdraw, it painted the grass with One Arm's blood.

Farther down the trail, the creature startled a rogue wooly male, who charged. The demon shattered its tusks, sliced off its head, opened its belly, crawled inside and fed. *Good, this world – GOOD.*

The creature emerged from the carcass and lifted One Arm's body and studied it closely. A glistening black nail extended, and it cut free One Arm's face. The demon pressed it to its own, just as Claw had done, then dropped it to the ground.

The corpse of One Arm, controlled by the demon, as it ran toward and through the hunters, flashed in Ear's mind.

Another flash. The chargers, scavengers, and cats also slaved to the demon's control, herding the hunters into the ravine. Into the trap.

NO! Ear ripped free of the vision. Chest heaving, his whole body shaking with rage, Ear screamed and charged at the demon, swinging his club.

It slapped him away as easily as swatting an insect, sending Ear's weapon spinning into the night.

Pain, sudden and sharp, filled Ear as he crashed into the twisted branch and bramble covering the sides of the ravine. Blood ran down his back; Ear snarled and pulled himself up for another attack.

The demon hissed and smashed Ear to the ground, pinning him.

It thrust its head forward to within a breath of Ear's face. *Weak... easy... tasty... prey*, the demon taunted, purring like a great cat. *You-Your World. MINE.*

Rage, pure and powerful, coursed through Ear's body. Blood filled his good eye then poured down his cheek. His head erupted in pain as his good eye burst from its socket. Ear roared at the demon. To his ancestors. To his brothers. Bones crunched and snapped beneath his skin, bloodying it as they lengthened.

The demon screeched.

Ear's clouded *bear* eye awakened and, filled with fury, he shoved the demon off him. He pushed to his feet and watched as his body grew heavy and tall, hands doubling in size and palms turning black and becoming thickly padded. Sharp curved claws erupted from his fingers as coarse black hair sprouted across his rippling frame.

Pain tore through his mouth as it filled with sharp fangs. He ran his thickening tongue over them as a low growl rumbled up his throat and out his maw.

The demon struck, shrieking. Its claws raked across Ear's massive shoulder, leaving red gouges.

Ear shrugged off the blow. He wanted blood. He roared and lashed back, his claws reflecting the Night Guardian's light. He ripped off one of the demon's hands. It spasmed on the ground in front of him, long multi-jointed fingers twitching in the dirt.

The demon pulled back the long spindly arm and examined the dripping, tattered stump. It screeched, its insect-like legs pounding the ground. Its knife-like nails whistled through the air, seeking to rip Ear to bloody shreds.

Ear, now the monstrous black bear of his clan's totem, took a bone-snapping blow that sent him stumbling backward. Blood dripped from his nose and muzzle. He snarled and licked it away.

The demon rushed forward hissing, terrible hands lunging.

Ear growled and grabbed the grasping hands in his massive paws and twisted, his sharp claws gouging into the creature's hard black skin.

The demon shrieked. Cracks appeared and spread over its thin black arms, seeping thick black ooze. Its two hands hung limply, useless. It reeled backward unsteady on its four-jointed legs.

Ear stomped the ground, huffing explosive breaths that misted the night air. He raised his massive black-furred arms, his fury great and terrible.

The creature lifted its faceless head to the Night Guardian, black plates flashing in its eerie light. It looked at Ear; short guttural exhalations issued from under the plates –it was laughing at him.

Ear smiled, savoring the carnage to come, black gums stretched over his white fangs, drooling. He planted his black-clawed paws beneath him, ready to charge.

The air around the demon began to wave and shimmer.

His fur rippled, and stood straight up. Ear shook his massive head and snorted in confusion.

The demon hissed at Ear. Even without a face, Ear felt pure hatred washing over him. He returned it, and unleashed his own in a bellowing spit-flying roar that echoed through the ravine.

The demon's hand-less stump snaked serpent-like into the air and disappeared into its body.

Ear cocked his great head.

The two twisted, cracked arms rose, the dead hands lifting slowly off the ground; long black fingers trailing like wisps of mist slipped into the creature's body. Smoke-like grasping things swirled out of the air and began to wrap around the demon.

Ear snarled in alarm and bared his fangs. He charged, his giant paws pounding the ground. His head snapped forward. Pain, red and sharp, took Ear's breath away. He looked down. Four long black fingers pressed hard against his stomach. Ear roared in agony when the creature began turning its hand.

The demon laughed as it twisted, knife-like nails buried deep in Ear's guts. It laughed louder the more Ear shrieked.

Ear clutched its spindly arm in his paws and tried to pull it out – he paid for the effort with agony and blood.

So weak, the demon whispered, *easy prey for the taking – my never-ending feast.*

The bear spirit stirred to life, its rage boiled through muscle, heart, and guts. Ear raised his bulging arms bringing them down and striking the demon's arm with the force of a falling mountain, shearing off its nails.

The demon jumped backward, the air becoming alive with thick, black grasping things swarming over its body. *What-are-You?*

I am Ear.

The demon snarled, pain rippling through the air around it. *I am Bear.*

The demon flinched as Bear rose tall and powerful on his back legs and bellowed his fury like thunder.

The demon scuttled back, its form shifting and churning.

Bear stomped forward, growling, massive jaws snapping, claws slashing the air.

I am Guardian of Two Forest Clan!

A screech sounded as the demon sought the safety of the sky.

Bear glared at it. Hate boiled black and pure from his eyes.

For my brothers!

Bear dropped to all fours and charged. He leaped into the air, claws flashing, fangs sharp, roaring death into the night.

SKITTER

Anna Stephens

I t was called the Isle of Lost Souls, which was a fucking stupid name if you asked Syl. Island of nothing but stinging flies and stinking humidity, more like. Isle of itchy sand up your arse and no booze to speak of. Just a jungle-covered hump of shit on the far side of the Patient Sea.

But it was where the job was, so it was where Syl and the rest of the Iron Blades, under command of Captain Teg the Red, had landed that morning. She'd been with the company's hundred and fifty mercs for a little under two years, and during that time she'd seen some things and done some hard work. To her mind, she was due a rest, and guarding some rich bitch on her private island with the stupid name sounded good enough, despite the lack of rum or beer or, dead gods forbid, even wine.

The house was luxurious, befitting a businesswoman of some standing in Talannest's underworld. *Businesswoman, my sandy arse. She's a crook.*

Captain Teg's voice echoed in Syl's head, reminding her she was here to guard, not to think, which made Teg a fool.

But a fool in charge of the coin purse, she reminded herself as she walked another lap of the perimeter around the compound, spear couched on her shoulder. She didn't know what Lady Dagger – and wasn't that some shit – was fleeing. What could be bad enough that someone with a name like hers would need to lie low on a baking spit of land like this? What she did know was that if it was enough to put the fear in her, then Syl would do well to be wary.

The company had quartered every inch of the isle and memorised the fastest and safest routes between the compound and the shaky jetty where they'd tied up. Teg had them fanned out in the trees, sentries on all the approaches, and a concentrated force in and around the house itself.

He'd taken a liking to Lady Dagger, and was angling to get the Iron Blades named her personal muscle. Or maybe just to get his personal muscle up inside her; man panted like a dog every time she walked past.

Syl spat. Aye, the woman was pretty enough and unscarred, at least about the face and arms, and rich enough to tempt anyone, but there was a fire of madness gleaming in her eyes and Syl didn't fancy getting burnt.

But that wasn't the only thing unnerving her. It was too quiet. Island this big should have decent food sources, some of those tiny monkeys that went so nice with plum sauce, maybe even some pygmy pigs, but the biggest things Syl had seen while on stag, were birds. The jungle was too quiet and not just because a hundred people were crashing through it and disturbing the natural order. It was the quiet of something missing.

A loud skittering, like pebbles on stone, had Syl spinning and bringing her spear to bear, quartering the ground, the trees, even the compound wall for the source of the sound. She held her breath, but the noise didn't repeat. Bottom to top, right to left, she checked the ground, the trees and the wall again.

Nothing.

Dusk was lowering – time to light the fire pits out beyond the perimeter. Shit for maintaining night vision, but off-putting if you were aiming to creep around in the dark.

Syl patrolled on, spear ready this time. Strange noises in the trees just before dark. Bastard typical. Still, she'd report it to the captain and run the risk of being called a jumpy fuck.

* * *

Teg called her a jumpy fuck. He was a special sort like that.

"Reporting what I heard, Captain," Syl said. "And there's no game either, just birds and insects."

"And?" Teg snapped, smoothing the front of his uniform with sweaty hands. He was dining with Lady Dagger later.

"And I might be city-bred but I'm not stupid. Island this big should be teeming with life. It isn't." She changed tack. "Could be disease, Captain."

It wasn't disease, she felt it in her bones, but a feeling wouldn't sway Teg. Something that could give him the pox might, though. But the purse was striding towards them now with all the surety and swagger of a born pirate and Teg wasn't listening. Teg was panting. Syl rolled her eyes. Lady Dagger swept past with a hint of citrus and fresh sweat about her, long legs eating up the marble flooring. Teg trotted after her, gaze fixed firmly on her rolling arse.

The house within the compound's walls was ridiculous. Everything was fine ceramic, expensive silk, and hard, slippery marble. And yet it was a fortress in its own way, because the luxury was inside thick stone walls with small, high windows you couldn't wriggle a child through. The doors were iron-banded heartwood, same as the gates on the compound wall, which were twice the height of a man, and the house even had a well in its kitchen, capped with stone. As long as its occupant had enough food, they could outlast pretty much anything trying to get in.

Except murderous children, maybe.

Shut up, twat.

Syl escorted Lady Dagger safely to the dining room – or as safe as she was likely to get with Teg dry-humping her leg – and then hurried off to find the second in command.

"All quiet?" Porrin was asking Ollo.

"Too quiet," Ollo said and Syl's ears pricked up. "Something ain't right."

Porrin grunted. "Course not. When's anything ever go right for the Blades?"

"Second?" Syl saluted. "Second, I heard something in the trees not long ago. A, well a sort of—"

"Scampering noise?" Ollo broke in. Syl frowned and shrugged. "We're hearing it on all sides. Never anything to see. Just the sound."

"Maybe it's the lost souls," Porrin said, but his smile faded when theirs didn't rise. "Scampering don't sound so bad. Probably just a bunny."

Syl and Ollo exchanged a look. "It's more like skittering," Syl tried.

Porrin stared at her as if she was stupid. "Scampering, skittering, the fuck's the difference?" He gusted a sigh. "All right, show me."

Ollo led them out of the compound's north gate. They wandered for a while, looking for signs in the light of torches, listening at the trees thirty paces from the wall, but there was nothing.

"I swear, Second," Ollo began, but Porrin waved away the protest, and they followed Syl to the southern side of the compound. Again, the bare ground gave no clues.

"And you say this *skittering* has been reported all over?"

"Aye, Second."

"Well there's nothing we can—"

And there it was. In the trees to the left and right of them, a sudden rustle and rattle and... skitter. They closed ranks, spears ready, Porrin the Butcher somehow in the middle, and so the most protected when Syl had the least experience. *Not that I need protection.* She flinched as the sound came again.

"Is that..." She squinted, gestured with the tip of her spear. "Movement left."

The faintest hint of a gleam beneath the trees, as of distant firelight reflected in an eye or across water. There and gone, accompanied by that fucking sound that sent a primal fear slithering up her neck.

"Hold formation and head for the main gate," Porrin breathed. "Move."

From the north, screams.

●　●　●

By the time they reached the gate, the screams had crescendoed into howls before bubbling, coughing, and fading in such a way that it was clear whoever made them was no longer capable of making any noise ever again. Shouted challenges, roars to "stand to" from Teg and Kam in Porrin's absence, the heavy slide of bolts being shot and beams being dropped across doors. The trio broke into a sprint, but it was too late – the gate was locked.

Porrin pounded on it. "Three to come in," he bellowed. "Friendlies! Friendlies!"

Hissed conversation from the other side.

"Uh, Second," Syl said. "Mind keeping your voice down? We're out here and so're they, whatever the fuck they are."

"We can get over this wall easy," Ollo whispered. She propped her spear and sidled away from the gate, cupped her hands. "Up you—"

Something black flowed down the stone, made a sound like it was cutting meat, and vanished.

Ollo sucked in a breath and began to scream. Her hands were gone, severed at the forearms and thumped in the dirt at her feet. Porrin goggled as blood jetted up the wall. Ollo couldn't stop screaming. Syl punched from the hip, putting all the power of her shoulder, back and leg behind it. Her fist connected with the woman's jaw, snapping her head sideways so fast she was unconscious before she felt the impact.

"Cover us," she snapped at Porrin and dragged the medkit from Ollo's belt, snatched a roll of bandage and cut two short lengths from the end, tied them around the bleeding stumps tight as she could; no time for a proper tourniquet. The blood slowed, didn't stop. Likely Ollo was dead and just didn't know it. Likely Syl and Porrin were too because no one had seen what did it – just a shadow from above.

The voices on the other side of the gate ratcheted up into alarm and then screams.

There was another, smaller gate into the compound on the other side and they dragged Ollo between them in the middle of the path between wall and trees, expecting any moment something half-seen to lunge from the blackness and cut off their hands. *Why her hands? And how?* If it was a sword it had a bastard of an edge. But it hadn't looked like a sword.

The half-glimpse reminded her of something, but she didn't know what. *Monster*, her mind supplied, and no matter how much she tried to push away the thought, it settled in the depths of her brain and put down roots.

Ollo's feet were digging furrows in the dirt behind them and her bloody arm kept slipping from Syl's shoulder and they were slowing as the ground roughened.

Skittering from under the trees.

"They're coming," Porrin gasped. "Leave her."

"No," Syl wheezed. "Leave no Blade behind."

"Fuck the code! She's dying," Porrin said and his arm slipped from Ollo's back and he was gone, sprinting around the curve of the compound wall. His movement triggered movement to her left, and Syl stood very still with Ollo sagging off her shoulder as the unseen enemy rushed through the trees after him.

That's you fucked, Porrin my lad.

It was also between her and the gate, though, but with no other ideas in mind, Syl hoisted Ollo onto her shoulders with a grunt, spine crunching as it took the Blade's weight. Legs wobbling, she set off in Porrin's wake, expecting at any moment to find his dismembered body littering the path and dripping from the palms.

Syl could barely see through the sweat when the noise came again an instant before something hit her in the back. She went down like a fucking tree, face-first into the dirt with Ollo on top of her and then not. Gone. Like being tackled by a child, momentum and surprise taking her over, not weight, and maybe not strength either.

That's probably important. Syl gained her feet, spear in hand and feeling light enough to float without Ollo's weight. She turned in a circle, but whatever had taken her fellow Blade hadn't hung around. At least Ollo had been unconscious. At least there was that for when they clipped off the rest of the woman's limbs or whatever it was they were going to do.

Syl ran. The trail twisted, jungle receding until starlight and moonlight bathed her in silver and the fearful dark drew a little further back into the shadows. "Iron Blade friendly," she roared when she was on the final approach. "Open the fucking door!"

There was no hesitation this time. The gate opened and Syl hurled herself through into the compound. Barca was there and, for a stinking miracle, so was Porrin. Rage propelled her off the floor.

"Where's Ollo?" the Butcher demanded. "I tried to draw them away. What happened?"

The fucking balls on him. Syl's mind fizzed a hot blank, awash in outrage and sheer disbelief, but she could see it was a story he'd already fed Barca and he was Second and she was just a mid-level merc.

Her jaw was clenched so hard it was giving her a headache. "Taken," she grated and swallowed the urge to hurt him.

"You're lucky. Thirty seconds ago they were in that tangle opposite," Barca said, the old merc's tone steady. "They're already in the compound; we're holding here," he indicated the paltry walls extending around the gate, "until the route's clear."

Three of them, black as night, stutter-stop movement, fast and then still, beneath the trees. It was so familiar, that movement, tickling the back of her mind. A curve of blackness loomed into the open and starlight glinted from a wicked, recurved point, there and gone. Syl sucked in a breath, coughed it out. She knew that shape. She knew it, just couldn't bastard place it.

But she was nearly at the house, nearly safe. And then Barca began to scream. Out of nowhere, screaming. Syl's spear came up so fast she nearly stabbed herself as he convulsed and fell onto his back.

"Dead fucking gods," Porrin muttered, pressed against the inner wall. "Dead fucking gods!"

Barca's face was changing colour, purpling, swelling. His face, his hands and arms, everything she could see in the torchlit gloom was swelling up like a pig's bladder. His throat expanded like a bullfrog's and his screams became whistling wheezes as he tried to breathe, sausage fingers scraping at his neck, eyes red and slick as cherries popping from their sockets and then, with two wet squelches, really popping. Porrin shrieked like a frightened baby.

Barca's entire body inflated and his breathing was little more than a clicking whistle. Syl knew she should be watching the approaches but she couldn't look away. Great wet mouths opened in his flesh, the noise like ripping steak. Barca's mouth stretched wide, fat lips splitting at the corners and a tongue the size of a cow's pushed out, filling his throat. His back arched and blood and bulge leaked through shirt and jerkin and chainmail.

And then... he exploded. There was no other word for it. Barca came apart, the splits in his flesh widening all at once, lengthening, joining up until he was flayed by the pressure and his insides kept on coming through the slits, muscle and meat and organs pushing outwards until his chainmail couldn't contain it and they began creeping out of the neck and from below the bottom edge. Entrails, as if they were living, stretching and spreading like a nest of snakes.

Porrin fled the gatehouse.

From above, skittering.

Syl sprang over Barca's twitching corpse and followed the Second into the open.

There was absolutely no point in stealth – whatever was hunting them was fast and almost invisible – so they just ran. Syl's breath was whistling and she was running on the dregs of adrenaline, but she'd drunk the dregs of enough ales in her time to know they'll still get you pissed if you're determined enough.

Firepits and torches ringing the house, lit the pale stone orange – and the dark shapes crawling its surface. They vanished onto the roof just as she got her first clear look at them. Looked, but didn't comprehend, because they were normally the size of her palm, though lethal for all that.

Rock scorpions.

Rock scorpions the size of big fucking dogs, with pincers that could shear through bone and stingers – *that's what I saw, that's what got Barca* – that carried enough venom that people exploded. They were impossible, and yet they were there.

Either Porrin hadn't seen them or he was too far gone in his fear, because he didn't slow. He put on a last burst of speed and threw himself at the door, screeching. It opened and he fell in. Syl followed and the door nearly took off her foot it slammed so fast behind her.

She bounced up and looked around. Teg the Red was there. "The fuck is going on?" she gasped, grabbing him for support. "Did you see? Have you seen them?"

"Calm down and report," Teg snapped.

"There's fucking giant scorpions out there and Ollo and Barca are dead, sir," Syl shouted. "They're bastard everywhere. In the compound, on the walls."

"They're in the southern side of the house too – I said calm down! We've barricaded the door but we lost Three Platoon. Glad to have you back, Porrin," he added.

Syl's jaw clenched. *I could tell you a thing or two about shrieking, cowardly little Porrin.* She forced herself to calm and caught Kam's eye. The other woman's expression was that special type of neutral worn by grunts around arsehole officers.

"Listen up, Lady Dagger and forty Blades are at the inner sanctum, safest place available," Teg told them. "Five Platoon's in defensive positions and a squad in the room with her. Now, layout: corridors form a diamond shape with here, safe room, kitchen and sitting room at the four points. There's another corridor off from the kitchen – that's where the barricade is. Porrin, you've got protection detail. Rest of you, our orders are to clear the compound."

"The purse is giving us orders?" Kam asked as Porrin scuttled off.

"For what she's paying us, if the purse demands we strip naked and cover ourselves in honey, that's what we fucking do," Teg snarled. "There are ninety-seven of us – a squad in the kitchen, two in the sitting room, a platoon here and Lady Dagger's forty."

"Yeah, but... giant scorpions?" asked a voice back in the gloom. Lea, sounded like.

"Hold for how long?" Kam asked before Syl could.

Teg the Red shrugged. "Until we're told different. Syl, you're runner – check in on the other positions and tell them, quietly mind, to stand to and be ready to move. We go in an hour."

Syl saluted and left before she said something unwise. Hold the compound? Make a run for the bloody ship, more like. A way off this bastard island. What was the possible benefit in them staying? While she happily killed for money, Syl was less keen on being killed for it. And as far as she was concerned, this was one of those jobs where being killed was more than just an occupational hazard. It was a godsdamn fucking certainty.

Still, at least there were walls between her and the monsters. For now. She strode along the corridor into a wide sitting room. All the furniture had been hauled near the entrances, ready to be piled against the doors if needed. The windows she'd thought so high and small now looked like they'd fit a giant scorpion with ease. She eyed them as she passed through into another corridor leading to the kitchen.

They'd got a brew on and Syl took the proffered cup, dumped a big spoonful of honey in it. The house was far cooler than outside and without imminent death skittering towards her, all her aches and hurts made themselves known. She needed a breather. Instead she took the cup and made her way down the last corridor towards the kill zone outside the safe room. Sweat itched down her flanks, stung in abrasions on hands and face she hadn't noticed.

There was no cover along the corridor, which ended in small, tight pinch points before the secure room that a handful of soldiers could hold indefinitely if they had enough arrows. Fifteen Blades at and behind each pinch, and the rest in the safe room.

"All quiet, sir?" Syl asked after she'd been challenged, identified and allowed to approach. She and Porrin stared at one another in silence for a second, then he gave a grudging nod. "If the kitchen gets compromised, we'll be retreating along this corridor," Syl said, pointing. "And if the main entrance and sitting room fall, we'll be coming down that one. Don't shoot us."

"Those the captain's orders?" Porrin asked.

"Orders are to clear the compound," Syl said, evading the question. "That involves opening the door, so we might need to retreat in a hurry." She waited, but Porrin wasn't giving her anything. "If all's secure, sir, I'll report back," Syl said. He was a good Second usually, good in a straight up fight anyway. Didn't seem to have the imagination to think his way through this one, though.

"Aye, tell the captain we're holding. We've got his back."

* * *

They'd left only a squad in the kitchen and sitting room; everyone else, barring the purse's detail, was crammed into the vestibule, ready to clear the compound.

"Listen up," Teg said, tension thrumming in his voice. "Ground outside looks clear. Two archers in every squad – try and take these things down without getting too close. Rest of the squad, surround the target and use your spears. Watch the stinger, watch the pincers. They're fast and they can climb. Good luck."

The order did little to calm Syl's nerves. "Hold the fucking compound," she muttered. "Fucking bollocks."

"Stow it," Kam hissed.

The captain pressed his face to the grille in the door one last time, then removed the bar. He held up three fingers, other hand clenched around the top bolt. Kam knelt at his side, ready to slide the bottom bolt.

Two fingers.

Syl had spear, shield and a couple of knives, though the thought of being close enough to need one terrified her.

One finger.

Kam's hand began to draw the bolt, but then Teg was reeling back from the barred window with his hands clutched to his face. He collapsed and began to shriek, began to swell and thrash.

Men and women leapt away as he convulsed. Something hit the door from outside and it shuddered in its frame, rattling, only the latch holding it closed against the death outside.

Syl leapt over him, stumbled as her ankle twisted, and hammered the top bolt back across. The stinger came in through the bars again and she fell back from it. She landed on Teg. She… burst Teg.

The poison and the swelling had already killed him, he just hadn't known it yet, but still, to burst your captain was a new one. The man simply blew apart under her weight and a storm of screams echoed in the entrance hall as he rained down on them all.

Syl lay in his still-writhing guts and watched the door. It was shuddering under repeated impacts and the bottom bolt was open. The bar wasn't dropped across the middle. A single bolt was keeping them out and the Blades were too busy being horrified to notice.

"Secure that fucking door!" she bellowed as she slipped and skidded upright. From the back of her head to her heels she was wet. Something slithered from around her waist as she stood, and she refused to look down and see what it was.

Kam recovered first, hammering the bottom bolt across and lifting the big, heavy bar. "Help me," she yelled, and two Blades jumped in to assist, heads well to the side of the window to avoid the stinger. They slid the bar into place and the next impact barely rattled the door.

"Well, you can fuck any orders that say we go out there in the dark and take this compound," Syl said and spat into the mess at her feet. "We hold here until dawn and reassess then. We can't see them but they can clearly see us, so let's not give them the added advantage of wandering out there like a bunch of fucking amateurs. If Lady Dagger doesn't like it, she can go and kill them herself."

No one dissented, still trying to process Teg the Red's fate. Syl glanced down. Yep, he was that all right. And blue and purple and white.

"Don't give them a target. Keep an eye out, but don't go sticking your head through any fucking windows if you hear something. Hold the door and check in with the other positions on the regular. I'm going to—"

A pincer appeared in the window. It closed on one of the bars with a sharp click. Nothing happened. Syl breathed out. It came back, angled up this time between the bars. It flexed and a chip of heartwood snipped free.

Lea dragged her axe out of her belt. The pincer came back for another nibble and she let fly, shearing through the lower claw. A hissing and a rattle of legs thrashing against the wood and it withdrew, replaced by the stinger lunging through the bars again and again. It hit with such force it ejected a thin stream of venom and the Blades scattered, arms up to protect their faces.

"Right then," Syl said when it had withdrawn. "We've given it something to think about. Hold the door, send runners if anything changes, keep checking in."

"Who made you captain?" Lea muttered.

Syl spread her hands. "You want to go out there and die, be my guest. Far as I'm concerned, we're assigned to Lady Dagger, meaning we give the orders, not her. Any of you actually think fighting them in the dark is a good idea? Didn't think so. All I'm saying is what Teg would say if he was still alive or Porrin would order if he was here."

That last was a lie and they all knew it, but they also knew Syl was giving them a chance to live through the night, so they took it.

"I'll be back," she said, and Kam nodded.

"We've got this. Check the others."

Syl headed out on another circuit of the house.

● ● ●

The detail in the sitting room were holding firm, those in the kitchen likewise. Syl padded the long corridor back to the safe room. "Captain Teg is dead," she told Porrin. "There's no way that door's opening now." She didn't exactly tell him why and let him think the obvious.

"Are we secure?" Porrin demanded.

"Yes, sir." The thought of him being the new captain made her gorge rise; she wondered how long it'd take for him to fuck it up. Porrin wasn't built for this.

"You've got line of sight on the kitchen and the main entrance, sir. Suggest hand signals to stay in touch and keep the noise down. We're thinking we hold until daylight, assess the situation then."

"Agreed." He leant closer. "Did Teg say anything about the purse? This is her island – why would she bring us here when she knows what's infesting it?"

"He didn't have time to relay that intel, sir. I heard Lady Dagger was setting up her own crew – I did wonder why she wanted us as her protection."

"Getting rid of the competition, eh?" Porrin asked and his face tightened. "Bitch."

"Only works if she's got a secure way out," Syl pointed out. As one, they both swivelled to stare at the door of the safe room. Porrin nodded.

Syl rapped on the door. "Lady Dagger? Progress report. I regret to inform you that Captain Teg has been killed." There was a long silence.

"Oh, that is unfortunate," the woman replied. "I do hope his replacement is more efficient. The Isle is supposed to be my safe haven. Carry on."

Syl's eyelid flickered, and she dropped her voice. "Well she's there for now, anyway. Did anyone check that room before she locked herself in it?"

"Only the captain. But if we lose control of this house, I'm breaking that door down and sealing myself in with her."

"I hear you."

A clatter of noise from the roof cut them off and the Blades hunched lower on instinct, every eye turned upwards.

"Contact front!" came a yell from the main entrance and she heard the distant thumps as something hurled itself against the door again.

"Contact above," someone shouted from the kitchen.

"Secure the kitchen, Second."

Syl blinked. Second? He was naming her his Second? "Yes, sir." She saluted and sprinted for the kitchen. She paused at the fork: left was the kitchen, right was the short corridor terminating in a heap of stacked furniture. The barricade. Beyond, the door to the southern half of the house, where the monsters were already inside and those Blades who'd been stationed there had died horribly.

A chair high on the barricade fell with a clatter. Syl crept closer, one ear listening for fighting from the kitchen. There was the screech of table legs on slick, polished marble and the barricade began to move.

"On me," Syl roared, throwing herself at the barricade and nearly taking a chair leg through the chest. She tried to find something to push against but it was all moving, in increments true, but still moving. A gleam of light around the edge of the door swiftly darkened by moving shadows. Lea and six Blades hurled themselves against the furniture around her even as Syl's boots slipped on the ice-like marble.

"Kitchen?" Syl gasped, dreading the answer.

"Secure," Lea shouted.

More furniture fell and the gap widened. A pincer came through near the ceiling, and then another. A scorpion forced itself half-through the gap, clawing at the barricade as it scrabbled.

"Push!" Syl screamed. The tangle of wood shifted and settled, but the gap didn't close. Syl saw through it, saw the shadows and scrabbling legs at the bottom of the door too. Strong but not heavy; how many would it take to shove through? How many were there?

She risked a glance behind. The kitchen was right there, as was the long corridor to the secure room. Pull back to the pinch for a last stand with those defending it, or hide in the kitchen while the scorpions rushed the choke point and maybe sneak out the front door while they were busy? Busy slaughtering the rest of the company. "Hold," she roared again.

"Enemy above!" came a yell from somewhere deep in the house – the sitting room, maybe. The sitting room that was between them and the exit. Fucking bastard shit.

The corridor was too narrow for any more hands at the barricade, and Syl's boots were sliding again, slowly, inevitably, as the pressure on the door increased. The scorpion by the ceiling was jammed halfway through, but the fuckers got slimmer towards their back ends – it could pop free any second.

"I need a second line here," Syl shouted. "We're about to have incoming!"

Pounding feet and then soldiers skidding to a halt. "Dead gods," someone muttered.

"Enemy front, top right. Shoot the fucker," Syl screamed. Arrows thrummed overhead and clattered off the scorpion's carapace. It hissed like a kettle and thrashed harder, slid a little further through the gap. Another flight and another, but its armour was fucking impenetrable.

The door shuddered, a second scorpion at the bottom wriggling through – in – and into the barricade.

"Bottom right beneath the furniture, watch it," she shouted over the clacking of pincers hacking the barricade to pieces from within. If they let go now, they'd be swarmed. If they held on and could deal with the one inside, they still had a chance—

The second scorpion came in through the top of the door, clawed feet digging into the plaster walls as it ran at them.

The front line of Blades scattered, the second rank sending more arrows at the one overhead, but it was fast. Too fast. It dropped onto a man, pincer closing around his neck and severing his head without effort while its tail shot forward and stung another in the arm. Blood and screaming and monsters.

It reared up as the corpse collapsed and an arrow sprouted from its belly. Its hiss was more an alien screeching this time and it fell, claws and legs spasming. Syl jumped on it, foot coming down on its tail, and hammered her spear through the back of its head with every ounce of strength she had. The carapace cracked, and inside it was just meat, like everyone and everything else.

There was a moment of jubilation, and then the barricade burst apart and a tide of shiny black death skittered through.

"Fall back," she screamed, wrenching her spear free in a gout of purple ichor. The Blades turned tail and ran. Half of them sprinted down the long corridor towards the pinch point, hollering and screeching alarm; Syl and the rest went for the kitchen. Others were waiting for them and as soon as Syl slid through the door on her side, they slammed it, locked it and shoved the big, heavy kitchen table in front of it. It began shuddering in its frame an instant later.

Syl stood and leant her weight against the table, and not just to help it stay in position. Her heart was beating out of her throat. "Check our exit's clear," she yelled and a unit of four slid through the far door.

"If they take the area around the safe room, they've got a straight run for the main entrance and from there dogleg right to the sitting room and us." She paused at a scratching from the roof and more units slid into position beneath each small window, while those with bows took the centre of the room. If they legged it out of the front door they'd have scorpions raining down on them in seconds. From the look on the sweaty, big-eyed faces around her, the others had already figured that out. Holding inside was their best and only option.

"Attack on the front door, repelled," Lea said as she came back in with the unit. "Entrance is secure, sitting room too. The troop at the safe room can see movement, but it's staying back so far."

"So, we killed one. Seems like the only place weak enough to get an arrow through is their underside. Spear thrust with your weight behind it will get through their top armour too, but you've all seen how fast they are, and those tails are no fucking joke, so don't go in for heroics unless it's already hurt, right?"

The company nodded but they were scared. She didn't fucking blame them – she was close to pissing her drawers.

"Aside from the narrowing of the corridor and their shields, those at the choke point are completely vulnerable. They haven't got barricades or doors between them and the enemy. They don't have armour-piercing arrows and, while they've got an avenue of escape, that only lasts as long as one of the fuckers doesn't run up the walls and get behind them. We need to consolidate somewhere defensible."

"What about fire?" Lea asked. "Animals don't like it, do they? Burn the kitchen, pull back to the sitting room."

"Set another one at the pinch and we've cut them off and bought ourselves some time," Syl added, thinking it through. "Right, start shoving stuff that'll burn against this door, but don't light anything yet, eh? Get to it."

Syl stepped away as others began picking up chairs and tearing down curtains. The door was still rattling in its frame, but it wasn't budging, even though it wasn't particularly heavy.

"So… where have the rest of you gone?" she muttered. Her guess was along the corridor to the safe room at the centre of the house. More noise overhead; Syl glanced up. But no, there was no way onto the roof from inside, was there? They had to have taken the long corridor. The long, silent corridor, from which echoed exactly no sounds of battle.

"Lea, have you got this? I'll take word to the other positions. Porrin made me Second but he'll need to agree to this and agree to a fall-back position, so don't light anything without orders."

"Aye, Second," Lea said.

Syl scooped up a shield from the pile by the far door and ran through the short corridor to the sitting room, calling out her name well in advance. Door sentries let her in, and she took in the platoon – a few injured, the rest twitchy and nervous. She found Renn, the squad leader. "All quiet?"

"Aye, sir," he said. "Movement on the roof, though."

"Hold position and sing out if anything changes."

She hurried down the next corridor to the main entrance. If this was Lady Dagger's idea of a defensible property, the woman needed some serious lessons in layout, possibly accompanied by drawings in crayon and repeated smacks around the head. Straight fucking corridors everywhere – clear line of sight was one thing, but seeing them coming meant fuck all if there was nowhere to take cover.

"Kam, all good?"

"Yes, Second. We've got eyes on the corridor to the pinch – it's quiet. They're testing the door every so often, clattering up at the window as if they're watching us – and I'll admit that's got a few of us shitting ourselves – but looks as if they can't get through." Kam leant closer. "But then they don't need to, do they? There're others already in here with us and sooner or later we're gonna have to open that door to make a run for it."

"Well, we didn't lose anyone before tonight, so it might be they're nocturnal. Hold out 'til dawn and take a brisk walk back to the ship. But keep that to yourself. For now, make sure everyone's got a shield and if they haven't, make them one. We might be moving in a hurry. We might also be setting fires."

"Uh, right," Kam said.

Syl stepped around the defensive positions at the door and the mouth of the second corridor and advanced towards the choke point with her shield up and spear ready. It was still silent, and silence was not what she expected – or wanted.

The torchlight flickered, shadows leaping up the walls making her jump. She slowed halfway along – no one had challenged her and the red on the walls… might not be from the flames.

There'd been a platoon here and a squad in the safe room. No way they could've taken them all in silence. Syl reached the choke point, so much adrenaline in her system she could practically see in the dark. There was, indeed, a lot of red and it was, indeed, not firelight. Smears and splashes of blood, great artistic sweeps of it. Chunks and gobbets of flesh, the shredded remains of an arm, a few scraps of clothing and a lot of discarded weapons. And that was it.

Noise to her right and Syl spun and lunged, stabbing out with the spear at the opening door of the safe room. The newly-appointed Captain Porrin squeaked and drew back. "Get in," he hissed and dragged her into the dark.

Syl squeezed into the packed room, shield and spear pressed tight against her, and the door slammed shut, a bolt rammed home. Absolute blackness fell.

"Who's here?" she demanded. "How many?"

"Thirty-one," Porrin breathed, "and Lady Dagger. They were on the ceiling."

Syl shuddered. "And your plan?" Silence, pregnant with breathing and foul with sweat. "Sir, permission to set fire to the kitchen. If you can set a fire here too, we can block the approaches and buy some time. We—"

"It's probably safer to stay here," Porrin muttered.

"There's another forty-four of us – we'll all fit in here, will we?" Nothing but embarrassed shuffling. "Sir, they're out there somewhere. It's only a matter of time," Syl tried.

Porrin was shamefully silent. "Captain Teg's orders were clear," came the disembodied voice of Lady Dagger. "Protect me. He singularly failed to do that. Captain Porrin, on the other hand, is doing an admirable job."

"Hiding in a cupboard with you?" Syl snapped. "How long until they get in here, do you think? What'll happen then?" The woman didn't answer. "Porrin the Butcher, they Named you," Syl said. "Porrin the Coward'd be more suitable now."

"That is enough, Second," Porrin snapped with something like his old fire. "I am in command here and—"

"And your command, sir, is to let four-fifths of the company die while you hide," Syl said. "And if that's insubordination so be it. What're you going to do? Court-martial me? Leave no Blade behind, *sir*," she added, hoarse with anger. "Good women and men have already died fighting. More will die in what's to come and your intention is to hide and let them and then... what? Hope the monsters get bored and wander off?"

"As my Second, you'll follow orders," Porrin growled.

Syl turned blindly in the dark and felt for the door handle. "As your Second, my responsibility is to the company, *sir*. So I'll be out there with them trying to stay alive. I'll set the fire on the far side of the choke point – wouldn't want you cut off. *Sir*."

She wrenched at the door and stepped out. Shadows moved on the ceiling, flowed into the room she'd just exited. Men and women piled out of the door behind her and then something or someone slammed it shut, trapping the rest inside, Porrin among them, though not Lady Dagger. She'd moved remarkably fast.

Chaos, shouts and screams, thuds and desperate clawing at the door. Syl threw herself at it but it wouldn't budge.

"They're coming," someone shouted, and she spared a single look down the left-hand corridor. A tide of chitinous death on the floor and walls racing their way.

Syl kicked some of the discarded spears and shields into a pile, dumped her own shield on top and threw three torches into the mess. The fire was small but it was smoky and the best she could do. "Move," she bellowed, and they sprinted back down the corridor.

"They're coming!" Syl shouted as they ran. "Take position." She passed the slowest runners and saw the squad at the end of the corridor. "Shields up. Watch for stingers."

The words were garbled as she ran but they understood. Syl didn't look back until she was behind the corner squad. Smoke was hanging in the air, a grey haze, and so far nothing was coming out of it. "Leave a squad in the kitchen – do not fire it – and one in the sitting room and get everyone else here."

The Blades waited in tense silence.

No movement.

Smoke tickled the back of Syl's throat.

"Where's Porrin?" Kam whispered.

"Dead," Syl said.

"She left him," one of the survivors hissed. "She let the fuckers in and let them kill everyone. Heart of stone, that one."

"Stow it," Syl snarled. "I tried to get that fucking door open, so don't give me that. If you hadn't all been hiding in there…" She took a breath and gestured at the tall, red-headed woman standing with her back to the wall. "We got the purse, didn't we? Both Teg and Porrin were quite adamant about protecting this cunt, despite her not telling us about the local wildlife."

She stepped up close to the woman. "And why is that?" she murmured, heavy with threat. "Why bring us here, to an island you supposedly own, and not tell us what lived on it?"

Lady Dagger's smile was patient and tinged with condescension. "You think I'd put myself in danger to, what, destroy the Iron Blades? You're nothing to me."

"I'm guessing there was an escape hatch in that safe room, wasn't there?" She didn't wait for an answer, so close now her breath stirred the other woman's hair. "You're right, though: we're just another mercenary crew out of Talannest. But I've done my research, Lady. You're setting up your own company. Maybe you didn't want rivals. Maybe you'd prefer if the Iron Blades just... died. After all, you're the only one with a way off this stinking shit-heap. Kam, pat her down."

"Now wait," the purse began, but Kam didn't hesitate, pulling a total of five daggers from the woman's clothing and boots.

Syl gave her a humourless smile and distributed the weapons among her crew, keeping the fanciest blade for herself. Three daggers she had now, and she'd a feeling she'd need them all before the end.

She stepped in close again, her head tilted to one side. "Don't worry, Lady Dagger, we'll keep you safe. You're our purse, after all. But I'll make you a deal here and now: we'll only take half the coin due us and you can keep the rest. Think of it as selling us passage on that nice ship you've got at the jetty. What do you say?"

Lady Dagger licked her lips. "I say you have yourself a deal. And seeing as you're now in charge, you can call me Reba," she said eventually. "And may I say, Captain Syl Stoneheart, I'm impressed."

Syl blinked. "That's not my name."

Reba gestured at the survivors of the pinch point. "I think your own company Named you, Captain. I don't think you get a say in it."

The others were nodding. She'd been Named. Teg the Red. Porrin the Butcher. Syl Stoneheart. Fuck.

"Get a long weapon and shield and shut the fuck up, Reba," she snarled. "And stay where I can see you."

"Aye, Captain," Reba said with a small smile.

"Contact front," Kam yelled. "We lose this position, we've got no way out, Syl – I mean Captain."

"Aye, I know it. Deploy across the corridor mouth, shields up, second row I want yours overhead in case they come from above. Ranged weapons – try and pin 'em back. Renn, you had the sitting room – you're sure there's no way out?"

"There's a grille blocking the chimney breast, but it looked padlocked. We set a fire in there to keep 'em from trying it anyway."

"Then find me the fucking key. Go!"

Looked like the insects didn't know what to make of the shieldwall, for they'd slowed. Syl took a rolled blanket someone had found and lit one end; it flared up bright and smoky and faster than she'd expected.

"Gap," she yelled, and the centre two shields were yanked down. She tossed it, unfurling as it went, over the shieldwall. A scorpion reacted, reaching for it on instinct, and the burning material fouled its pincers. It thrashed, trying to free itself, and only succeeded in wrapping itself tighter. The mercs cheered as it burnt to death.

"Scorpion on toast?" Kam offered.

"Hold the celebrations," Syl said as more prowled closer. "They don't look happy. Now listen, we're going to get onto the roof through the sitting room chimney as soon as Renn finds me that key. We hold here until he does. Once we've got an exit, we're opening the front door and legging it into the sitting room."

"We're *what*?" Kam asked.

"They're already on the roof. We go up there, we're swapping one enemy for another. So, we open the door. Those on the roof and outside come in and we leg it up through the chimney. First one out drops off the roof and slams the door from the outside. Trap 'em and let 'em burn, take a stroll to the ship."

"Well, that sounds fucking awful, no offence, Captain," Kam said eventually. "But I don't see what else we can do," she added in response to Syl's glare.

"It'll mean a fighting retreat from this position against those already in and however many more enter," Lea said in thoughtful tones. "But—"

Two scorpions climbed the walls and came at them from both sides. Three more came at them straight. Stingers slammed into the overhead shields with shocking force and the Blades grunted, shifted tighter together. A pincer cut into an exposed leg, neatly snipping the foot off and the merc howled and went down, opening a gap. Syl threw herself over him, shield up, and knocked the claw away before it could drag the man out of the line.

She was crushed up against the wall and the oblong shield fitted nicely in with the others, so nicely she couldn't make space to stab with her spear. Hands dragged the wailing man from beneath her. The shield above her slipped sideways. Syl rammed her spear through the gap; the tip scraped off a carapace and then lodged in a leg joint. She shoved again and felt it give, felt the metal point slide into flesh. Angling the spear down, she tried to pin it, but it thrashed its way free and threw itself at the shieldwall again. Silly fucker. As it reared to try and climb the barrier, her spear and another rammed into its belly and tore it open.

"It's like platemail," Kam was shouting, "go for the joins at its legs and pincers, or go for the eyes."

"Above," Lea yelled. The shieldwall faltered.

"Hold!" Syl screamed as three Blades were dragged forward, shrieking. The line reformed, ragged and shorter than before.

"Got the key," Renn shouted as Kam formed a second wall, back to back with Syl's line.

The urge to call the tortoise formation and retreat to the sitting room was strong, but she had to get the door open.

"Take my place," she yelled and felt a tap on her back to indicate someone was ready. She counted to three and flung herself sideways, and another woman slid into the gap, shield punching into place and trapping a stinger in the gap. Venom spurted from it and across Syl's back and the woman's arm. A steady stream of curses as it burnt, but though it shook, the shield held steady. Syl drew her knife and hacked off the stinger.

She stood in the gap between the two shieldwalls. All of the surviving company except the injured were here and still they were close to being overwhelmed. If she opened the door now, they'd never make it to the sitting room. It wasn't going to work.

Kam wriggled out of the press, grey beneath the mahogany of her skin. One hand was pressed below her ribs. "Well, I'm fucked," she said as the blood pulsed steadily between her fingers. "How about I open the door and you lot make a run for it, eh?"

"Kam—"

"Don't," she said in a croak. "Just get ready to run."

"Leave no Blade behind," Syl tried. "We can hole up in the sitting room, think of something else."

"You the Stoneheart or not?" Kam snarled. "Save the company and make sure they know what a fucking hero I am."

Syl swallowed. "Prepare to disengage."

The second wall killed one scorpion and the other fled back towards its kin. On Syl's command, the rearmost line sprinted back to the sitting room, clearing the path. "All right, you lot," she shouted. "On my mark, you're going to turn tail and get the fuck back through that door. Do not stop, you hear me?"

"Aye, Captain," the shout came.

Syl met Kam's eyes. "You sure?"

There was blood on Kam's teeth when she grinned. "Fucking do it. They won't give me long, so be fast."

"You know it."

The lull came. "Break!" Syl bellowed and the three ranks turned and began to run, Syl at their head.

She felt the breeze as the door opened and more scorpions piled in, hopefully tangling with those already inside, slowing them, but soon enough that eerie fucking skittering rose.

"They're above," someone began before they were cut off. More shouts and the sounds of tearing mail, tearing flesh.

Syl hurled herself into the room and kept going to clear the doorway. The survivors piled in after her and then the door slammed – slammed on two Blades and a multitude of chittering, insectoid faces. They pushed the couches and tables in front of the door and Syl raced for the fireplace. Lea slapped a key in her hand. "Clear it," she said, chest heaving and Renn raked the fire out. It was quiet above. Might be they'd tempted them all inside.

"Everyone carries a piece of firewood when they climb – the smoke should stop any coming into the chimney from above. I'm going first. Be fast."

"And the injured?" Renn asked in a low voice as Syl was pulling on her gloves.

"Drag them close; we'll drop a rope and haul them up last."

She was gone before he could reply, because chances were, they wouldn't have time to do that and she didn't want to talk about how many more of the crew might die before this nightmare was over.

The padlock was sooty and greasy and very, very stiff and she worried the key would snap off in the lock, but then, squeaking like the gates of hell, the grille opened. She heaved at it, shuffled further up, legs shaking as she braced her shoulder and shoved it open.

"Pass me the firewood," Syl gasped. She met Renn's eyes below. "Let's go."

It wasn't yet dawn when they peeked over the edge of the chimney. The moon had set but there was just enough starlight and the roof was red. No black shadows moved across it. Carefully, they eased themselves out and onto the tiles.

Renn waved his firewood, signalling the next pair to climb, while Syl unfurled the rope looped around her and tied it to the chimney stack. She bellied towards the edge of the roof, hideously aware of the scrape of her chainmail over the tiles. She looked down. The main door was wide open and there were no mutant insects in sight.

She glanced back at Renn and nodded. He got his hands on the rope in case the masonry gave. Breathing shallowly, Syl dropped the rope over the edge and then threw herself off after it. Gloves smoking as the rope burnt through her hands, she slid down to the packed earth of the compound and ran at the door, praying that Kam would have released the latch so it would close. It did, slamming hard and locking. For how long, she didn't know.

Armed Blades began to join her, forming a perimeter around the rope. "Renn's collecting all the firewood," Lea said." When the last one's up, he'll drop it back down the chimney to buy us some time."

Syl grunted. "Good. All eyes."

Barely sixty of them on the ground, Reba included, when the silence was broken with yells to hurry. Moments later, chaos erupted inside the house.

"They're in," Reba said. "Nothing more you can do. Time to go."

Syl had the woman by the throat and pressed against the door, her face a whisker away from the barred window where a scorpion's tail could reach her. "You need to shut the fuck up right now before I knife you and leave you to die."

Reba must've seen the truth in Syl's sooty face. "As you say, Captain," she choked. "My apologies."

Syl let her go and took the woman's spear, leaving Reba once more unarmed. She trusted the woman less than a mutant fucking rock scorpion. Syl moved away from the wall, looking up at the roof and her back prickling, as though waiting for a dagger to be stabbed into it. "Renn?"

His panicked face appeared at the edge. "They're climbing the chimney!"

"Then throw the firewood down there and get your arse on the ground, soldier," Syl yelled. "Form up. We're heading for the dock and the ship. Support those who need it —" Renn slid down the rope into their midst " — and move out. On the double."

Bleeding, filthy, hurt and scared, the Iron Blades left no one behind. Apart from the dead or the doomed or the cut off or the plain unlucky.

Stoneheart.

They began to run, streaming towards the compound's main gate and then out of it and onto the wide, flat, open road to the dock. Sixty, from a hundred and fifty. Set up by their own purse, who'd so far come through this without so much as a lock of hair out of place.

Stoneheart, Syl. Be fucking stone.

The jungle was opening up, the sound of surf growing in their ears, when the rear ranks began to fall. She dodged to the side of the road, took aim and threw her spear with the last of her strength. It took a scorpion in the head, clattering off its armour but knocking it back and saving Renn.

"Move!" she screamed, and the company put on a final, desperate burst of speed.

Stone changed to wood beneath their boots and there was the ship. The line began to stretch out, the fastest pulling away to untie the ropes and hang up the sail, or whatever the fuck it was called. With water to either side and below the planking, the scorpions were cautious, which slowed them, and no more mercs fell to their claws or venom.

The company hurled itself onboard, and those who understood ships did what was needed. The sail opened with a crack, long poles pushed them away from the side, the wheel was swung over, and they began to move.

Syl stood at the back and looked to shore. There was no pursuit. When there was clear water between them and the jetty, she put her hands on her knees and threw up.

When she'd done that, she faced the company slumped on deck. Reba had the wheel. They watched her with the incurious, blank gaze of veterans just beginning the tumble from the adrenaline high into the depths of fatigue.

"Ships have rum, don't they?" Syl croaked. Reba looked back and nodded, pointed to the stairs down below. "Then let's drink it all," she said. There were a few smiles, no more, but that was to be expected. She staggered for the stairs, lurching as they hit a wave.

SKITTER

The scorpion fell out of the rigging above her. It landed on her head and shoulders and she went over backwards, slamming into the deck and splitting her scalp open. Her legs came up and she kicked it off her, one sharp insectoid foot slicing through her cheek and the bridge of her nose. Syl flipped onto all fours as the tail came for her, whipping forward almost too fast to see. The world slowed, shouts of alarm smearing through the dawn, the deck shifting as they hit another swell, the first of the sun gleaming from black carapace, black pincers, black eyes.

Syl caught the tail, caught it so close to her face that she saw the gleaming pearl of venom at the very tip. Her right hand scrabbled at her belt and then slammed down, past the raised claws and onto the scorpion's head. Her knife drove through its exoskeleton and into what passed for its brain.

The scorpion convulsed once, claws clacking wildly, and fell still.

The deck was silent. Syl didn't move, clenched tight. A single pair of footsteps advanced on her, hesitated, and then a hand touched her shoulder. "You can let go now, Captain," Renn said.

But she couldn't. The Iron Blades were her company and she had to see them safe. She'd never be able to let go again.

SEEING THE ELEPHANT

B. Michael Radburn

Isabella de Foyle rocked in her chair on the shaded porch, twisted cane of chestnut oak resting across her lap. Each sway tested the boards beneath her, the timbers as arid and furrowed as her lips. Some said she was a hundred years old; some said two hundred. But all said this: *Beware the Crossroads Witch.*

The hour was growing late as the auburn sun kissed the borderlands of Cyprus marshlands with their beckoning tapestries of Spanish moss and twisted limbs. Drawing on her corncob pipe with unblinking indifference, Madame Foyle watched the Union soldiers tramp past her gate beneath the heavy Louisiana sky. The men in blue – strangers in a strange land – kicked up a little dust as they passed. Horses with heads slung low pulled wagon and canon alike with an apathy born from the wheel ruts that led all the way back to Pennsylvania. The Yankee soldiers marched to their destiny, east towards LaFourche Crossing where the distant sounds of canon fire had only just fallen quiet.

"Go," she whispered in a voice like crushed autumn leaves. "Go see your elephant."

Seeing the elephant. She spat a black globule against the weathered boards at what the soldiers called their first battle. *Fools.* She brushed the faded Veve tattoo on her forearm, a pentagram with a knot of moon symbols in the centre. One of the young soldiers timidly made eye contact. She locked his gaze on her own, noted that the blotched birthmark on his left cheek was the shape of Texas. A smile peeled across her parchment face. There was something in the boy's soul that vibrated like air before a storm; a power of innocence, perhaps enough to overcome the darkness that was coming his way. *Watch this one.* She moved her attention to others, every man and boy a unique vessel, like the wiry man with the deep battle scar on his forearm, a ragged cross cut deep into flesh. *This one has seen the elephant, and yet returns for more. Such scars run deep.*

Madame Foyle spat as they passed; smacked her dry lips together. "Le Rougarou chasse ce soir," she whispered.

A murder of crows erupted from the crown of Cyprus's across the way, and the boy with the Texas birthmark made the sign of the cross as he marched on towards LaFourche Crossing and its elephants' graveyard.

The Crossroads Witch rested back into her rocking chair and stared towards the shimmering east where she could sense the full moon that dwelled just below the horizon. The black cloud of crows circled; flew on the cusp of an ill wind, day-two of the beast's blood-moon cycle. She drew on her pipe and spat more black. "Oui, le Rougarou chasse ce soir."

* * *

Will woke in the earthy darkness with a start. He gulped air like a drowning man who'd breached the surface of a deep lake. Confused, he flailed and kicked instinctively and scurried like a crab across the floor until his head struck the staircase behind him with a *crack*.

"Mama," he whimpered, his hand subconsciously brushing the birthmark on his cheek. The darkness didn't answer back; it offered no comfort. Will lay on the damp stone floor, steadying his breathing. *I'm alive.*

He lifted himself to a sitting position, every muscle aching and his ears still ringing from last night's storm of rifle ball and cannon fire. His eyes adjusted to the gloom with blessed relief as spears of filtered daylight pierced the boards overhead. *The night has passed... Dear God, the night has passed.* He remembered now. Bloodied and beaten, finding the root cellar doors at the base of the ruined manor on the shores of Lake Boeuf. Remembered crawling below as the screams of dying men filled the world above. Remembered the thunder of cannon fire, the stink of the dead and the dying. Remembered being afraid... and little else.

But now it was quiet – just his tempered breathing. He stood, and his left leg ruptured with pain. Using the banister as support, he blindly explored the wound above his knee, one finger disappearing an inch into his torn flesh. The pain bit again as he strained to fill the gaps in his memory.

The regiment had stopped before nightfall – that he remembered – and sheltered in the husk of this burnt-out manor. The air had smelt of the swamps, the ruins set on a finger of land that stretched out into the lake. Frustrated and afraid, Will pressed his fists to his eyes. They were to reinforce Colonel Stickney's men at LaFourche Crossing at daybreak.

And then it happened, delivered with the dusk, an ambush of confederate soldiers, the calm splintered by their Rebel yells. Earth and flesh exploding amidst the screams of men and barking orders from confused officers on both sides. The memory teetered at Will's peripherals like an unfinished book, lingering with the scent of shit, piss and sweat. What happened last night was greater than the battle itself; darker, a bloodlust fuelled by something in the night, dancing in the shadows. Discarded limbs, plucked like wings from a meagre fly, dust and blood rained down like rotten fruit falling from the tree, all to the whistled tune of grape shot cutting the air and cold steel bayonets lancing flesh. And… And a full crimson moon like a watchful eye bleeding into the lake.

The moon… The moon… Why is it the most frightening memory?

Will lumbered up the stairs towards the slivers of daylight, each step a new venture in pain. He forced open the root cellar door, collapsed on the bloodied ground, and inhaled the carnage before him.

The stench of salty copper filled the humid air – a slaughterhouse. The broken jigsaw of men hung from the manor's window cavities like a macabre butcher's shop display of limbs and human offal. The ground was littered with the shattered, empty bodies of man and horse alike, tents shredded, and wagons overturned. Bloodied uniforms shrouded the stained ground. A tangle of blues and greys – all brothers beneath their torn flesh.

An eruption of bile caught in Will's throat, all jerky and hard-tack biscuit from yesterday's march. He forced it back and began to traipse through the garden of dead. As he took in the horror, a mound of corpses rose, then collapsed. A bloodied soldier in grey was birthed from the carnage, his eyes full moons of white in a sea of red. He was an older man, stooped slightly, his beard matted with the congealed blood of the corpses that had been his refuge.

Will stood face to face with his enemy. *Dear God, he could be my grandfather.* He scanned the battlefield, the only movement that of the crows pecking at their feast. *Surely, we aren't the only survivors?* The shaky rebel then stumbled towards him, and Will stepped back instinctively, pain raking his wound as he looked around for a weapon. He reached for the nearest rifle, prying it from the claw-like fingers of a soldier who was now neither blue nor grey. Here, there was only red.

"Stop!" Will cried. It was more plea than order.

The old man raised his hands and opened his mouth to speak, but nothing came forth. He tried again with more conviction. "No, no, no," he rasped. "I surrender, Yankee. I surrender."

The old man fell at Will's splayed legs, his tears having traced crooked tracks through the mask of dust and blood. He clutched Will's boots tightly.

"You're real… you're alive and… you're real," the old man muttered in a heavy Creole accent.

"What-what happened here?" Will glanced from shattered bone to ruptured flesh, trying to understand the desecration, to fill the empty well in his memory. "How could we have done this to each other?"

"Oh," croaked the old man. "Look closer, Yankee. Grape shot and hot ball cannot do this."

Will frowned, studied each broken body that surrounded him. They weren't entwined as if in battle, but rather clustered in mixed groups, facing outwards as if surrounded. What began as a Confederate ambush, ended as a combined force fighting something… something…

"Was the Rougarou," the old man whispered. "Out there," he added, flapping his hand from the lake's shore to the thick canopy of Cyprus. "This is the place of the Crossroads Witch."

* • *

The old man said his name was Jean-Baptiste, but that Will should call him Old John. They sat-out the day in the manor's basement, a small fire boiling the last of Will's coffee, the flame's light little comfort.

"This Rougarou," said Will as he wrapped a scrap of cloth around his injured leg. "Who... What is a Rougarou?"

Old John grew restless at the name, his eyes darting up at the closed cellar door. "Both man and beast," he said in a whisper.

Will tightened the makeshift bandage. "Like a werewolf?" Will had read about them in his penny dreadfuls back home.

"Oh, no, Yankee." He began to rock on his haunches, combing his fingers nervously through his beard. "Not Loup-garou," he added. "I wish it were. Harder to kill Rougarou."

The torn bodies above them stifled Will's disbelief. He took the coffee pot off the boil and let it sit awhile.

Old John watched the steam curling like a ghost toward the battlefield. "Like the werewolf, Rougarou is a shape-shifter. Man... Animal... Something in between. Its cycle is that of the moon."

"Shapeshifter?" Will said, worrying at his bandage with trembling fingers. A collage of chilling possibilities paraded across Will's mind, the macabre procession scratching at his imagination. "What kind of animals are we talking about?"

"Oh," said Old John with a shake of his head, "the worst kind out here. Gators, bears, and cottonmouth snakes." He glanced again at the root cellar doors. "I've seen an alligator snapping turtle cut a hound dog in two with just one bite. Too many teeth out here, Yankee... too many teeth."

"Then we need to leave before nightfall," said Will. "Surviving another night out here is unlikely."

"Leave?" Old John stifled the laugh that trembled just below the surface. "To where? How?"

Will didn't think the option was that challenging. "Make our way to LaFourche Crossing," he said. "There are men there; soldiers. We can take the road through the bayou before nightfall."

"Oh no, Yankee. Don't you be thinking the Rougarou needs the night," said Old John. "It needs only the dark, and the swamps are mostly dark out this way. Deep in the lake where the sun can't reach, and in the shadows of the bayou no darker than the light of a full moon." He shook his head, clutched his arms around his shoulders like a spoilt child. "Be it by water or by road, both paths lead to death right now."

"We can't just wait here."

"One more night," pleaded Old John. "Then the cycle will be spent. We can walk out; *dance out*, if that's what you want, Yankee."

"Look what your Rougarou did to a legion of men last night," spat Will. "How long do you think it will take to dispatch an old man and a boy?"

"The boy is now a man," said Old John. "And this old man still has some fight left in him." He reached out and took Will's hand. "Out there, we have no chance. To fight for just one more night – in a place of *our* choosing – we might just make it until dawn." He patted the back of Will's hands. "Then, God willing, we can leave with our battle scars and stories for our grandchildren."

There was something jarring in Old John's rhetoric. Then it struck Will. "How many of these things are we talking about?"

"Oh," said Old John, "the Rougarou are many." He glanced at the noon-day light seeping through the board gaps above. "Like I say, Yankee," he croaked, "just too many teeth out here."

Will squared his shoulders and pushed back against the crushing weight falling upon him. "So, we will meet those teeth with cold steel and hot lead, Old John."

* • *

Isabella de Foyle hummed a Cajun song under her breath in time with the groaning boards beneath her rocking chair. She puffed on her corncob pipe, savoured the whisky-soaked tobacco, and watched the crows circle above the cypress trees. Her pipe smoke curled like ghosts in the afternoon light, keeping the mosquitoes at bay. Isabella was good at waiting. She had spent the day on her porch, anticipating the last cycle of the moon. *Not long now.* The sun was a shimmering red disk on the horizon, sinking into the waters of the bayou with every heartbeat. "Bientôt mes enfants," she chanted within the song, "Nuit du Rougarou," and cackled like a cold winter wind.

• • •

Desperate for every second of daylight, Will and Old John rushed around making preparations. By the time the sun had kissed the horizon they were ready. There was no shortage of weapons or ammunition left amid the carnage, just a shortage of men to shoot them.

They strategically placed mounds fashioned from the dead, arms and legs woven and intertwined in a macabre wall of flesh and bone bound in blood. Old John could not bear their gaze, and turned their sightless faces away. In the fading light, they lined the wall with loaded Springfield rifles paused ready to fire. Bayonets, their handles buried to the hilt in the earth, lanced the open ground between their fortresses of flesh and the marshland's edge.

Will and Old John each carried two Colts in their belts and good-sized skinning knives in their boots. Two 10-pound Army Parrott guns were at their disposal, loaded with chain-ball and dry powder. Will turned their barrels towards the swamp in a retreating line between the perimeter firing points they made and the sanctuary of the manor – their last stand. A timber torch burned brightly beside each gun, ready to set their powder alight.

Will rested against the wall of knotted bodies, never feeling so tired, his torn leg throbbing with his heartbeat. "How will I know it's Rougarou and not a man in the dark?"

"You will know," John said. "Fight well, Yankee, and we may see the dawn." He scurried across to the opposite firing point, took up the nearest Springfield, and watched the night creep from the bayou to saturate the battlefield. The blackness was both blessing and curse. It softened the carnage, concealed its worst, but also hid whatever else lay beyond its dark curtain.

Failure meant it would be the shortest night of Will's life. Success, and it would be the longest.

The moon began its climb, and a strange silence fell over the swamplands. It settled like mist in the hollows as the crows retreated to their cyprus roosts. Will retrieved his pocket watch, checking the time every hour as he waited. He began to wonder whether the Rougarou would come at all once midnight struck. Sleep tugged at his eyelids until three in the morn', as the moon began to descend once more towards the west. He stared deep into the bayou's shadows, wondering if the Rougarou were banking on his weariness before they struck. Then, as the darkness beneath the cyprus trees began to stir, his fluttering eyes sprang open.

"They're coming," cried John.

Will followed Old John's gaze, confused at first. A soldier in blue stood in the dim light. He was beckoning to them with a wave of his arm. *Reinforcements?* Will rubbed his weary eyes, a new hope burning in his gut, until the image cleared. *What was John talking about?* But then the soldier in blue became suddenly limp, arms flaccid at his side, head wilted above sagging shoulders. The lifeless marionette then collapsed in a heap to reveal the lumbering beast that had been taunting them with the cadaver. Bear and man moulded as one by the hands of the Devil himself.

Glass oil lanterns were gathered at their feet, and Will frantically lit his, six in all, and waited again. "Light 'em up," he cried.

The crows burst from the cypress woodland with a collective *caw*, black on black in the night. Will peered into the tangle of shadows they left behind. *So many shades of dark.* But then form and shape eased from the darkness. Old John was right about recognising the Rougarou.

Too many teeth out here...

Old John threw first. The lanterns arced into the night to shatter into fireballs at the perimeter. Will followed suit, realising that out here, light can be just as cruel as the darkness. The fires showed the approaching creatures for what they were. Monsters. Will couldn't tell where man ended and animal began… each a tangled nightmare of fur, scale, tooth and claw in their own right.

A shot echoed into the night as Old John fired his Springfield, jarring Will from his paralysis. He aimed at the lumbering bear creature, a broad target still shying from the flames. The ball hit the creature's chest, sprouting red and enticing a roar that vibrated through to the bone. Will and Old John moved from rifle to rifle, no time to reload the weapons, just shoot and move, shoot and move, before the flames dwindled and the creatures charged.

A wolf-beast paced the wall of flame, its red eyes darting from Will to Old John in anticipation. The alligator Rougarou stood, all muscle and scale, from its prone position at the bayou's edge. It winced when a bullet tore across its broad neck. Beside it, the razor-beaked jaws of the snapping turtle yawned widely in a piercing bellow.

"I'm almost done," cried Old John as he shot frantically. He had two loaded rifles remaining.

"Fall-back to the canon," Will yelled. "I'll cover you."

Old John fired, lead ball tearing flesh, but not enough to kill the beasts. He discharged his last rifle then fled to the nearest canon. Will shot at anything that moved. The darting wolf was the most elusive, all mischief and bloodlust in its eyes.

Will heard a vibrating hiss that preceded a guttural growl. *The alligator Rougarou.* It had circled around the flames, charging on all fours from the lake. Old John turned, defiant, and stood his ground, drawing both Colt's from his belt. The onslaught of gunfire halted the creature, but the rounds were barely breaking its leathery scales. Will did the same, fired each Colt in rapid succession. The creature snapped its gaze to him, stood upright, and roared an unholy barrage of sound that bore through to Will's heart. It lurched forward, its tail snaking behind as it marched towards him.

"*Run!*" Will cried to Old John, then glanced down at the two pistols. The chambers were empty in his left hand, one cap and ball cartridge remaining in the right. He holstered the loaded Colt and dropped the other; reached for the skinning knife in his boot. He just needed to buy Old John some time.

The creature glared at the blade, smiled. It stepped closer, and Will threw the knife the way his papa had taught him. He got lucky; the blade found a gap between the scales, sinking deep.

Then the creature exploded, forcing Will to the ground in a shower of wet gator meat.

"What in God's name..." He peeled a string of flesh from his cheek and looked towards Old John, grinning ear to ear at the smoking Parrot Cannon.

Will waved towards the second line of refuges, each with their course of Springfields lined against the corpse wall. "Take cover," Will yelled, then glanced back at the dwindling wall of flames.

The wolf's pacing increased, ready to charge. Will shuffled to the cover of the nearest firing point and snatched up a rifle. He took careful aim at the wolf when it paused, and took the shot. Its left eye burst like a ripe plum, and it thrashed about with a panicked cry. But it wasn't enough. The damned thing recovered, its remaining eye staring coldly into Will's. The pain seemed to feed its rage, and it crouched then bounded through the flames. Will managed three more hurried shots as it approached; too hurried, all missing. And the beast never missed a beat across the open ground.

It rushed towards the wall of the dead. Will fired his last rifle shot and ran towards the second canon where Old John stood paused with the flaming torch. Every step stabbed into the tearing wound in Will's leg, but he could hear the wolf's footfalls growing nearer. He glanced over his shoulder to see the thing stumble; the carpet of bayonets barely slowed it down.

"*Fire!*" Will cried as he ran. "Fire the damned canon!"

He knew why Old John had paused, bewildered. The barrel was pointing right at Will, and the ball chain would cut him in two.

The creature only had to reach out now and Will would be at its mercy. "For the love of God, John! Fire!"

He did.

Will dropped to the ground ahead of the blast; rolled onto his back and watched the wolf divide in a spray of crimson that rained warm on his face. More beast than man, its upper torso fell beside Will, its one good eye unblinking but as dark as its heart. That's when he saw the tattoo, the same as the old woman at the crossroads, a pentagram with a knot of circles at its centre.

* • •

Will stumbled to the cannon and collapsed against a wheel. "Thank you," he murmured, then saw the murderous stare that suddenly burnt in his companion's eyes. Utter exhaustion bound Will to the ground as Old John drew the long-bladed knife from his boot and stood over him.

"John?" was all Will managed to utter before the old man in grey clasped the handle tightly in both hands and thrust it down with all his body weight. Will closed his eyes and waited for the kiss of cold steel.

But Old John merely toppled across Will's legs. When he opened his eyes, the prone body of a snake-like creature sprawled just inches from him. Its silken scales glistened in the flickering torchlight, reptile and man blended in an unholy alliance, its thrashing tail slowing with its waning heartbeat. Old John had pinned its Cottonmouth head to the ground, jaws still open, paused to plunge its venom-wet fangs into Will.

Old John rolled off Will and onto his back with a trembling sigh. "Too many teeth out here, Yankee," he murmured with an exhausted breath.

Will looked back at the assorted creature's bodies strewn behind them. *We might just see the dawn after all.* His gaze eventually fell upon the familiar tattoo on the Cottonmouth's forearm. "But fewer now," he said. "I owe you my life, Old John."

"You owe me nothing" he said, and stood with a groan. He helped Will to his unsteady feet and dusted off his bloodstained uniform.

❦ ❦ ❦

Isabella de Foyle watched the flames dance in her kitchen fireplace, cane resting across her lap, sweat glistening on her brow. She clasped the pale pentagram etched into her forearm as another of her children perished, the pain like a cold hand clutching her heart. Every time it grasped without mercy, another fell; every time it squeezed, a piece of her spirit withered like fruit on an unkept vine.

"Fin à ceci, mon garçon," she called to the bear through the flames. "Avenge your brothers."

❦ ❦ ❦

Will watched the pacing bear creature through the flames as Old John surveyed their flanks. They crouched behind the last corpse-mound – all rotting flesh and stinking entrails – and its cache of weapons before the manor, Springfields in hand. The bear made eye contact, wrath burning bright within. But it did not attack. It roared and retreated into the shadows of the bayou with a final glance over its shoulder. Will prayed it had run out of fight.

"We got company," murmured Old John, rifle raised towards the lake's shore.

Will heard the gurgled snarl before he saw the monster stand in the dim torchlight between them and the sanctuary of the manor. It had blocked their retreat. *Perhaps there is more man than beast in these things after all.* He cursed the lack of prudence in their strategy. The creature's serrated beak yawned wide as it staggered from the water, claws extended, the jagged circle of its leathery shell prominent on its back. Old John had told him he'd seen an alligator snapping turtle cut a hound dog in two. Will shuddered. *So, what can this thing do to a man?*

Old John fired first, the ball bouncing harmlessly off its armoured chest plates. Will fired, missed, as the creature slumped to all fours, head partially retracted beneath the rim of its shell, murderous stare fixated on him. It marched towards

Will with a determined focus until the last Springfield rang quiet. The creature was only a yard away when Will tripped and fell. In a heartbeat it was perched over him, snarling in anticipation of blood. Will swiped his empty rifle at it, the timbre stock splintering across its ridged shell. Its beak opened wide as its leathery head extended towards Will's face, catfish and black water steaming on its putrid breath.

Then he glimpsed Old John. He had lurched in beside it, his Springfield's bayonet cutting the air and clumsily slicing Will's cheek, salty sweat stinging deep. Will's strength was waning as Old John speared his rifle's bayonet into the earth, then levered the creature's weight off Will long enough for him to scurry out from beneath. He struck the corpse mound, breathless, his heart pounding.

"Quickly, boy. Help me," cried John. He was pressing all his frail weight against the flailing creature, red faced and veins forming a tangled road map down his neck.

Will sprang to his aid, clutched the Springfield with white knuckled defiance, and the two finally levered the monster over onto its back where claws and snapping jaws flailed frantically into the air as it desperately tried to right itself. The creature's cries were the stuff of nightmares, latching on to Will's very soul. Old John stood wearily over it, extracted the blade from the soft ground.

"Don't stand so close," Will pleaded.

The thrashing claws were missing Old John by inches, but the man remained calm. "That's the thing about snapping turtles," he said, catching his breath. "As fierce as they be, they're no good on their backs." He raised his rifle high, trained the bayonet towards the creature's soft belly. The monster clutched the barrel and Will noticed the familiar tattoo through the scales on its forearm. *This was once a man*, he thought with an inkling of empathy. Then he saw the scar that ran the length of its left forearm in the shape of a jagged cross. *He was one of our own!* Old John plunged the blade into the creature's yielding flesh and its dying breath gushed out into the night, and with it, a little of Will's own.

The darkness pressed in, then for one glorious minute, it was so peacefully quiet.

"We should go, Yankee," Old John said with a spent tremor in his voice.

Will felt in awe of the man's courage. He surveyed the fresh carnage, drawing on Old John's resolution. "We did it," he murmured.

"All but one," Old John reminded him. "And our armoury spent."

Will thought about the final bullet left in his Colt, then pulled out his pocket watch one last time. "Barely an hour till dawn," he said. "The bear is gone. Perhaps we can wait it out." Will looked towards the blackened ruins of the manor, prayed that the bear Rougarou had not attempted to outflank them. The moon's cycle was almost spent, the promise of daylight teasingly close.

They staggered towards the broken walls, Will's torn leg weeping fresh blood. Every shadow drew Will's attention, every darkened corner a potential ambush footing for the bear. They opened the root cellar doors and felt their way down into the dank sanctuary. Will closed the doors behind them and slid the sturdy timber lock into place with blessed relief. The last spears of moonlight filtered down through the boards above. Will joined Old John at the circle where they first sat and shared coffee. They faced each other despite the near darkness, occasionally glancing up at the gaps for the first signs of daylight.

Every minute seemed like an eternity.

"How long now, Yankee?"

Will fished out his watch but struggled to read its face. Old John struck a match and held it high. The splash of light startled Will, and he remembered that out here, light can be just as cruel as the darkness. Dawn was only moments away, but the watch wasn't the only face illuminated in the dark. The bear creature towered silently over Old John's shoulder and slowly bared its ravenous jaws in a muted snarl.

Too many teeth out here, Yankee… too many teeth.

The watch slipped through Will's fingers and he drew the Colt from his belt, never more conscious of the single shot remaining in the chamber. *One round. Just one round...* His limited choices struck with a sickening reality. Attempt a kill shot at the Rougarou, spare his friend a painful death, or spare himself the same. His finger slipped around the trigger as the creature roared. Laughter, like crushed autumn leaves, echoed through the room. A single shot rang out.

MIDNIGHT IN THE HOUSE OF BATS

Josh Reynolds

Meyrick lifted the bottle and considered the dregs of amber liquid within. Barely more than a mouthful left. It was better than nothing. He knocked it back and tossed the empty bottle over his shoulder. It shattered on the floor of the cantina, and he turned and watched the shards wink in the reflected glow of the fire.

Outside, the bats were screaming. And the town – he didn't know its name – was burning. An accident, or maybe intentional. The end result was the same. By morning, it would be ashes. It didn't matter. The House of Bats had been opened, and Meyrick figured it was unlikely any of them would live to see morning.

The thought brought a cold sort of comfort. He'd been chasing death ever since he'd crawled out of the trenches. This was as good a grave as any, and better than some. He reached over the bar, groping for another bottle. Resigned though he was, he had no intention of crossing the River Styx sober.

"There must be hundreds of them out there," Razin murmured from the table by the window, where he and the others sat. The big Cossack had a bottle and a shot glass sitting in front of him. Both untouched. He was too busy watching what was going on outside, just like the others. Too busy watching the bats.

Only they weren't bats, were they? Not really. That was what Espinosa said. Then again, Espinosa said a lot of things that seemed like nonsense to Meyrick. Occult twaddle about stars and alignments and Great Cycles. He glanced at the occultist. Espinosa leaned forward, resting his pale and sweaty head on the table. He was a far cry from the dapper Brazilian who'd come to Campeche looking for guides and guns. Meyrick retrieved a bottle and popped the cork. "Didn't seem like that many to me."

"Maybe they got reinforcements," Fisher croaked. The American's vocal cords had been injured in a gas attack – or so he claimed. Meyrick had heard Fisher had actually gotten his throat cut by a *vaquero* in Rio de Janeiro some months after he'd mustered out. The keloid scars that marked the dark skin of his neck seemed to bear that out.

"The servants of Xibalba are legion," Espinosa said, his voice threaded and weak. "They will not give up until they have what they seek." The occultist hunched forward, coughing phlegm into his fist. His free hand was pressed to the bandages wrapped tight about his stomach. They had gone from white to pink, and on to crimson.

"Maybe we should give it to them," Pasqual said softly. The Italian was a mystery. All Meyrick knew about him was that he'd served in the army, and was a dab hand with the Thompson submachine gun sitting on the table in front of him. Razin had vouched for him back in Campeche and that had been good enough for Meyrick. "Let them have the blasted thing. What harm can it do?"

Meyrick took a pull from his bottle. "Ask Espinosa."

Espinosa shook his head and coughed again. "We cannot. We must not."

Meyrick shrugged. "There you go. Question answered."

Pasqual grimaced and reached for the bottle in front of Razin. "Why?" he said. "Why in the name of God did we have to take the thing in the first place, eh? Tell me that."

"You know why," Razin said, grabbing the bottle before Pasqual could. "You saw what we saw. We could not very well leave it there, could we?" He thumped a boot onto the crate sitting beneath the table. From inside it came the sound of scratching – insistent and determined. Razin thumped the crate again. "Quiet, you withered lump of gristle, or I will use you for target practice."

The scratching ceased abruptly. Meyrick laughed. "That bastard might be dead, but he's not stupid, is he?" He raised his bottle and drained half of it in one go.

"Not like us," Pasqual said bitterly.

"Speak for yourself," Fisher said. "I went to college."

They all laughed at that, even Espinosa. But there was a shrill edge to it. It was the laughter of frightened, exhausted men. They'd been a dozen strong when they'd gone into the jungle. All ex-soldiers like him. Men without countries, and in need of money. Men desperate enough to work for the pittance Espinosa had promised, and not ask questions.

A dozen men had gone in. Only five had come out. The bats had followed them the entire way. Picked off the survivors one by one until only a handful remained to stagger into town, bearing their burden.

Meyrick studied the crate as he drank. Espinosa had brought it especially, along with a number of other tools, most of which Meyrick didn't recognise. Strange books and equipment of glass and copper, all of which were now lying broken and scattered across the jungle floor, somewhere between here and there.

But they had the crate, and what was in it. He didn't like to think of that lanky, shrivelled thing in its golden regalia. He'd seen mummies before, in Egypt and Nepal. But never one like that. Never one that danced and moved to the drums of human worshippers. Never one that shrieked obscenities in an unknown tongue as a band of mercenaries drawn from the four corners of the Earth gunned down those worshippers in a haze of lead and blood.

It had almost clawed out Espinosa's guts before they got it in and shut the lid. It had killed Ewers and torn the fat Serb – whose name Meyrick could never remember – in half before they could blink. As quick as you like. It wanted to do worse to the rest of them.

Meyrick could feel its hate for them in general, and Espinosa in particular. There was a story there, he was sure, but he didn't want to know more than he already did. And he wanted desperately to forget what little he already knew.

He'd never been very good at that. He could still remember the way the mud had climbed up his knees, and the sound of rats gnawing at the split belly of a dead dray horse. He could still remember the way the sky burned and the ground shook. His hand trembled slightly as he took another drink.

He heard something scream and he whirled towards the door of the cantina, hand on his Webley. The bat came in, moving in that twitching, crawling way of theirs. It was as big as a dog and stank of dark places and spoiled meat. Razin and the others lurched to their feet, but they were too slow and the bat was too close.

It launched itself at Meyrick, and he slung the bottle into its face. Glass shattered, and the bat slammed into the floor, blinded and stunned. He stepped back and shot it, emptying the pistol into its hairy body.

He looked down as it lay dying. Just like the others, the body was mostly right, but the head was wrong. Malformed somehow – flat and ape-like, with a mouth full of teeth that seemed the wrong shape and size. Its face was the worst. Not a bat's face at all, but that of an old man, a withered ancient, with ratty grey hair and wide, staring eyes. The eyes rolled in their sockets and fixed on him. The mouth moved and sounds emerged. Not the whining of a dying beast, but something closer to words. One word. *Camazotz. Camazotz.*

Methodically, he reloaded the pistol and shot it again. When it was silent, he went to the bar and replaced the bottle he'd broken. For a time, no one spoke.

Then Razin called out, "Hey, Meyrick. What now?"

Meyrick looked at the Cossack. "Why ask me?"

"You are the only officer here," Razin said. "The burden of command is therefore yours." Meyrick laughed, despite himself. He and Razin had worked together before, in Bhutan. The Cossack was an artilleryman by trade, and a dynamiter by preference. He was never without at least one stick on him at any given time.

"What about Espinosa?"

"He is not a soldier."

"Fine." Meyrick took another pull from his bottle. "Way I see it we've got two options. Hole up, or make a run for it."

"I vote run," Pasqual said.

Fisher snorted. "Run where?"

Meyrick shrugged. "Up the coast maybe. Or farther south."

Razin poured himself a drink. "We would not make it past the town limits. Besides, what would we do with the box, eh?"

"Leave it," Pasqual said.

"We cannot leave it," Espinosa said in a strained voice. "We cannot."

Pasqual glared at the injured man. "What happens if we do?"

Espinosa's smile was grotesque. "We die, I imagine. And not just us – everyone. Our friend there is fated to usher in a new, darkling age of this world. He will cast wide the twelve gates to Xibalba, and empty the Six Houses…"

From inside the crate came a horrible and rattling hiss that Meyrick knew was laughter. Or as close as the thing inside could manage. It said something, its creaky voice muffled. Meyrick felt a wave of nausea at the sound. Espinosa closed his eyes and shuddered.

"The remaining Houses, I should say. The House of Bats has already been emptied." He swallowed and hunched forward. "The Camazotz are here, and they will not cease the hunt until our heads are hanging in the court of the gods."

A shriek sounded from outside. A wagon rattled past the window, frightened horses pulling it. Bats clung to the animals, gnawing at their necks and flanks even as the terrified beasts galloped blindly down the street. There was no sign of the wagon's owner, though given the heaving crowd of bats in the back, it wasn't hard to guess what had happened to them.

"We shouldn't have come here," Fisher whispered, his hand on his revolver.

Meyrick took another pull from the bottle. He wasn't sure what he was drinking, only that it burned. "I'm open to suggestions."

"I can send them back," Espinosa said.

Meyrick turned. "What do you mean?"

"Close the passage to Xibalba. I meant to, before, in the jungle, but…" He pulled his hand from his stomach and studied the red that stained his palm. "I was otherwise occupied. And by the time I'd recovered my wits…"

"We were halfway to here," Fisher finished for him.

"What else could we have done?" Pasqual said. "We were being chased by those goddamn monsters. They just came boiling out of the night sky like… like…" He trailed off and looked away, wiping the sweat from his mouth. "This isn't our fault."

"No. It's his," Razin said, giving the crate another kick. The thing in there laughed again, and this time no one had the courage to silence it. The dead could afford to be patient. It could wait them out. Eventually, the bats would get them. Eventually, it would be free. It knew it, and they knew it.

Meyrick looked at Espinosa. "I thought you needed those damn tools of yours. You know," Meyrick gestured. "The ones we lugged out there." The ones they'd left behind he thought ruefully, when the bats got too close. The way they'd left behind the horses as bait. Meyrick could still hear the animals squealing as the bats tore them apart. All to buy time.

He pulled a rag out of his pocket and mopped at his face. It was hot. The fires, he thought. All those fires put out a lot of heat. It had been hot in the jungle as well. As if the beating of the bats' wings had stirred up the flames of Hell.

"Yes… but there is always more than one way to do these things." Espinosa winced. "Unfortunately, it requires time – among other things."

"How much time?" Meyrick said. No horses left to use as bait now.

Espinosa grimaced and closed his eyes. "An hour, maybe more."

Pasqual popped open his pocket watch. "Midnight, then. As long as the bats are preoccupied with the town that should be easy enough."

Espinosa gave a wracking cough. "They won't be." He clutched at his stomach. "Our friend in the box will call to them when I begin, and they will come. All of them. Every damned one of those things will be trying to get into this cantina the moment I speak the first word of the binding ritual."

Razin chortled and reached down to retrieve his Chauchat from the floor. He cradled the light machine gun like a child, and gave it a fond pat. "Then we must prepare a welcome for them, yes?" He pushed his chair back and stood. "I saw a hammer and some nails in the storeroom when we checked this place. Fisher, break up some tables and board up the windows. Pasqual, get the door."

"And what about you?" Meyrick asked. He blinked sweat from his eyes. He could taste smoke, and the heat – God, the heat. The others were feeling it as well. And it wasn't just the fire. He thought of asking Espinosa about it, but something told Meyrick he didn't want to know the answer.

"You two can help me," Espinosa said, trying to stand. Meyrick caught him before he could fall. Espinosa nodded his thanks. "Get the crate. Bring it to the centre of the room."

Razin dragged the crate out as Meyrick helped Espinosa across the room. "We need... salt. Yes. As much as you can find. Alcohol as well."

"What else?"

"Blood." Espinosa gestured with a bloody hand. "But I will provide that."

Luckily, the cantina was well-stocked. Meyrick found a bag of salt in the storeroom and grabbed several bottles of the cheaper booze from behind the bar. He and Razin followed Espinosa's whispered instructions, drawing a circle of salt around the crate first, then a circle of alcohol.

The air rippled like a desert mirage as they worked, and Meyrick wondered what the weather was like in Xibalba. The thought made him laugh, and he had to force himself to stop when Razin gave him a curious look.

Espinosa painfully situated himself between the two circles.

He was panting by the time he sat. "A knife..." he rasped. "I need a knife."

Meyrick drew the blade from his belt and handed it to the occultist. "Careful with it. You're already bleeding badly."

Espinosa offered a pained grin. "I am aware of that." He slid the knife beneath his bandages. Hissed and withdrew the blade, now stained red. Carefully, but quickly, he began to draw a sigil on the floor.

As he did so, the air in the cantina became even more stifling. Meyrick licked his lips, trying to summon the saliva to spit. "What does this entail?"

"Mostly chanting."

Meyrick blinked sweat from his eyes. He needed a drink. "What should we do while you're doing that?"

"What I hired you to do," Espinosa said. He was pale, and sweating profusely, but he continued to scratch sigils on the floor. "When – when it is finished, our captive must be destroyed. Fire is the traditional method."

Meyrick nodded, but didn't reply. He was watching the crate in horror. It had begun to shudder, as if its occupant were pounding on the lid. He could hear the thing whispering. Outside, the wingbeats of the bats were like thunder, and they shrieked in time with the thing's whispers. The noise was just shy of deafening. He drew his service revolver and cocked it. "What if it gets out?" he said loudly.

"The circle will contain it."

"If it doesn't?"

Espinosa closed his eyes. "I leave it up to you. I will likely be dead at that point. Either way – destroy it."

Meyrick frowned. Again, he was struck by the notion that there was more to this than he knew. "I never asked how you knew about this thing."

Espinosa didn't look at him. "Do you truly want to know?"

Meyrick considered it. "No. Not really."

Espinosa gave a strained smile. "I never thanked you, Mr Meyrick. I'm sure you're the one who insisted the others carry me out of the jungle." He paused. "Which begs the question, why did you save me?"

Meyrick shrugged. "Seemed the thing to do." He opened one of the bottles and took a drink. It was too warm, but he drained half the bottle regardless. "As a rule, I'm not really in favour of letting the world end."

"A good rule." Espinosa gestured for Meyrick to stand back. "Now please, leave me to my work and see to your own."

Meyrick joined Razin at the window. The Cossack retrieved a cigarette case from inside his coat and flipped it open. As he selected one, he chuckled, "Rorke's Drift, yes?"

"What?"

"A last stand. Very famous. English. Like you."

"More like the Alamo," Fisher said. Razin looked at him, confusion on his face.

"What's the difference?"

"Everyone died at the Alamo," Meyrick said, taking a cigarette. Razin laughed again and lit it for him.

Pasqual whistled. The Italian stood near the barricaded door, his Thompson in his hands. "Listen – it's gone quiet out there."

Meyrick joined him. The street outside was silent, save for the moans of the dying and the crackle of flames. The frenzied cacophony of moments before had ceased. He could not say when it had happened, but he knew it portended nothing good. He glanced at the others. "Fisher – cover the back. Razin—"

"I will stand here, I think." The Cossack hefted his Chauchat as if it were no more burdensome than a rifle. Fisher drew both Colts and cocked them.

Meyrick didn't bother to argue. The Cossack had never been one to follow orders unless it suited him. None of them were, really. That was why they'd wound up here in the first place. Maybe if they'd been better soldiers, fewer of them would have died in the jungle. Maybe if they'd been better, they wouldn't have been in this situation in the first place. It would be some other unlucky bastards up to their arseholes in giant bats.

Behind them, Espinosa began to chant. Slowly at first, and then more rapidly. The words were in no language Meyrick understood. But the thing in the crate did. It began to scream – a noise eerily reminiscent of the sound the bats made – and pound on the inside of the crate. The scream grew louder and louder, as if it were trying to drown out Espinosa's faltering voice.

"Can't we shut the damn thing up?" Pasqual shouted.

Meyrick didn't reply. Through gaps in the boards nailed across the door, he saw black shapes creeping across the rooftops and hop-scuttling out of doorways. The bats were answering their master's call. They rose into the air with a sound like leaves caught in a typhoon wind and swooped towards the cantina.

Meyrick took aim and fired. Pasqual followed suit. He began to shout a prayer in his native tongue as he swept the weapon across the ranks of scuttling bats. A cloud of screeching bats descended onto the cantina's roof. They tore at it and the clay brick walls, desperately trying to reach their master. The cantina was sturdy enough to endure a mundane storm, but not this. Their shrieking rose to almost unbearable pitch.

The windows gave way first. They collapsed inward and a bat the size of a mastiff tumbled into the cantina, wings flailing. It bounded towards Meyrick on folded wings, hopping like one of the tiny vampire bats so common in the jungles.

He fired again and again as it leapt towards him. Wings beat at his head, and he glimpsed a mouthful of sharp teeth riddled with strands of flesh snapping at him. Then the barrel of Razin's gun battered the creature to the floor. The Cossack stamped on it, bellowing obscenities, before turning his weapon on the others squirming to push through the windows.

The Chauchat roared.

The bats screamed.

Fisher shouted and his Colts thundered as more man-faced bats spilled into the cantina from the back. Meyrick took aim at one and plucked it from the air with a shot. The small size of the cantina hampered the creatures – made it all but impossible for them to get airborne for any length of time.

Pasqual shouted a warning, and Meyrick turned and saw the bat he'd shot springing towards him. It crashed into him with bone-jarring force and he fell. The bat rode him down, screaming and snapping at him. It gibbered obscenities in what might have been Spanish or Portuguese before he slammed his Webley into its face and threw it off of him. He emptied the pistol into it, and staggered back against the bar, heart hammering.

Espinosa was still chanting, his voice now hoarse and thin. A bat crawled towards him, hissing, and Fisher blew its brains out. Meyrick started to reload but paused as the crate split. A ragged fist, shrunken and bound in filthy tatters, stretched upwards. Meyrick froze as the dead thing hauled itself free of its prison, one lean limb at a time.

Time slowed. A golden mask, wrought in the shape of a snarling bat, turned towards him. From behind the mask, a sour gaze burned into his own. Hell-spark eyes flashed, and it was as if all the air were ripped from his lungs at once.

It was, or had been, a man, but like no man Meyrick had ever seen. A man, with limbs shrunken to withered sticks, and torso scooped to a hollow fold. A man, stretched and twisted all out of joint, as if some power had sought to reshape him in its own image. Whether it had failed, or succeeded, he couldn't say.

The air grew hotter, and Meyrick felt as if a great hand had settled upon him, forcing him back. The dead thing straightened and stretched out a gangling arm towards the door to the cantina. Claw-like fingers, loose at first, stiffened and curled into a fist.

Time resumed its proper course and wood splintered as the door was broken apart. Bats spilled in, roaring as one as they attacked in a whirlwind of leather wings and sharp teeth. Pasqual screamed as they swarmed over him, his Thompson swinging wildly and spraying the room and its occupants.

Meyrick threw himself flat. Bullets dug into the floor around him, but none struck home. Fisher wasn't so lucky. A bullet caught him in the back of the head, spraying his brains over the bar. He pitched forward, Colts slipping from nerveless fingers. Shots punched into the dead thing as it watched with cold patience, but it barely flinched.

Meyrick looked up and saw Razin stumble against the table. At first, he thought the Cossack had been hit as well. Then he saw that Razin was trying to reload the Chauchat, a bat clinging to his back and tearing at his flesh. More of the creatures were converging on him. Meyrick took aim, but his pistol clicked empty. Cursing, he ejected the spent brass, trying to reload as he clambered to his feet. "Hold on, Razin – hold on!"

He snapped the Webley shut, then above the cacophony he heard Espinosa cry out. The occultist had collapsed, one of Pasqual's bullets having struck him earlier. His blood was running freely, carving red lines through the circle of salt. The dead thing crouched, watching the blood do its work. Meyrick realised in horror that it had been its plan all along.

Espinosa rolled over onto his back and locked eyes with Meyrick. The circles broke, and the dead thing leapt and finished what it had started in the jungle.

Its too long fingers dug into the red wounds and forced them wider, fingertips digging into muscle and fat, digging for the occultist's heart. When it found its prize, it gave a shriek and wrenched the crimson and pink knot of muscle from beneath Espinosa's ribs in a welter of gore. The occultist died staring at his own heart, crushed in the unyielding grip of his killer. It had taken only seconds.

Meyrick cursed and put a hole in the dead thing's shoulder, knocking it off the occultist's body. It was on its feet in moments, roaring. It glared at Meyrick, and a single long stride took it to his side. Crumbling claws caught him by the throat, and it lifted him into the air.

Meyrick screamed as he emptied the Webley again, this time into the thing's chest and face. The gold mask was sent clattering to the floor, and the dead thing screeched as it hurled him across the room. It clutched at its face as if injured.

Meyrick rolled across the floor, the wind knocked out of him. He lay for a moment, panting. His pistol was gone. Bats circled and crept towards him, their eyes alight with fierce hunger. There was a bellow and one of the bats was smashed to the floor by a powerful blow.

"Up," Razin growled. The Cossack was bloody and battered, but still on his feet. He grasped the broken barrel of the Chauchat like a club and brandished it at the remaining bats. One screamed and sprang, and Razin smashed it from the air.

As Meyrick hauled himself to his feet, a guttural cry pierced the din. The bats retreated slowly, gibbering in frustration. The dead thing stepped forward. Its exposed features were little more than a skull wrapped in frayed hanks of colourless hair. It spoke, and though Meyrick could not understand it, its words made his stomach turn.

Razin glanced at him. "What now?"

"We improvise," Meyrick coughed. He spied one of Fisher's Colts on the floor nearby. "Got any of that dynamite handy?"

"One stick."

"That'll do."

The dead thing spoke again, the air shuddering at the touch of its voice. It stretched out a hand, as if beckoning them near. The bats hissed and snarled, their man-faces twisting into leers.

"What do you think it is saying?" Razin asked, as he surreptitiously slipped the stick of dynamite from his coat. Even if the thing saw it, Meyrick doubted it would understand what it was, or what it could do.

"Maybe it's asking us to surrender." Meyrick calculated the distance to Fisher's weapon. The bats would be on him seconds after he reached it.

"They did not surrender at Rorke's Drift, did they?"

"They did at the Alamo," Meyrick said. "Didn't do them much good."

"Stiff upper lip, yes? That is what you English say." Razin paused. "Hey, Meyrick?"

"Yes, Razin?"

"You were a good officer."

"Yes. Too bad you were all shitty soldiers."

Razin laughed. Still laughing, he lunged at the dead thing, swinging the barrel of the Chauchat towards its head. At the same moment, Meyrick threw himself towards Fisher's revolver. Bats converged on them both. Meyrick leapt and rolled, narrowly avoiding the snapping jaws and flailing wings.

Even as Meyrick snatched up the revolver, the dead thing caught Razin's wrist and sank the claws of its free hand into the side of his head. The Cossack roared and shoved the stick of dynamite into the dead man's belly with enough force to puncture the tattered flesh. Meyrick swung the revolver up.

The dead thing growled and snapped Razin's neck. It dropped his limp bulk and looked down. What might have been a quizzical expression crossed its leathery features as it reached for the dynamite.

Meyrick fired.

The pistol had more kick than he was used to, yet it was all but impossible to miss at this distance. Explosions were different, up close. Rather than a gout of fire and a distant reverberation, it was a moment of white heat, stretching in all directions at once. There was a sound, like someone screaming, that rose up and up and up into inaudibility. Then the heat lifted him, almost gently, and cast him backwards, through the bar with bone-snapping force.

The world juddered to a halt for a time. But the pain brought him back soon enough. Things were broken inside him, and the skin of his face and arms felt raw, like he had been dragged over hot coals. He could barely move, and he couldn't catch his breath. Every time he tried, it felt as if something sharp was going into something soft. There was blood in his eyes, and he could smell smoke. The cantina was burning.

Through the gutted roof, flames painted the night sky in vivid hues of red and orange. Meyrick could hear bats screaming around him in what he hoped was pain. He fumbled for the pistol just in case, but his blistered fingers encountered only shattered glass, and a few intact bottles.

As he fell back, a cloud of winged shapes rose into the fire-lit sky and flew away. He wondered if they were heading south, and whether the dynamite had been enough. Espinosa hadn't specified the type of fire needed. As the world started to go dark at the edges, he dragged one of the bottles over.

There was time for one more drink, before he crossed the river.

LEAPFROGGING

Buck Bloomingdale

I f it wasn't for Private Jacobi's dog tags, nobody in the squad would've been able to identify the corpse. His body had been split open from groin to neck, and his entrails draped across the jungle's canopy like Christmas lights.

Sergeant Rourke had been a doctor before Pearl Harbor, and had been examining the body for nearly fifteen minutes. As far as Rourke could tell, Jacobi's entire intestinal tract had been pulled out through his ass.

Carmichael had seen plenty of cruelty from the army of the Rising Sun: men filleted, staked, burnt alive. But nothing like this. He glanced toward Felder and Keene guarding the perimeter, both smoking their USMC rationed cigarettes. Felder scanned the jungle with his Browning Automatic Rifle, hands knuckle-white around his weapon, a slight tremble to the smoke dangling from his mouth.

Rourke tossed Jacobi's dog tags to Carmichael. "Taxi up, and put out those smokes," the sarge barked. "Might as well draw a goddam bullseye on your face."

Felder's cigarette sizzled as it fell into a puddle. Keene looked at his smoke like he was saying goodbye to an old girlfriend, and very slowly stubbed it out.

Carmichael frowned. "What gives with that?"

"You don't smell it? There's shit everywhere."

The kid was right. Jacobi's large intestine must've been slammed into a tree where the two men stood guard. There was shit plastered on bark, clumps of it staining the undergrowth. Even little brownish-green flecks on Keene's boots.

"Fuck this island."

• • •

The sun had crawled down from the sky and brought night to the thick jungles and swamps of Iwa Kame. The island was about the size of a deer tick on the globe and wasn't even originally part of the island-hopping operation – or 'leapfrogging' as the men called it – planned by General MacArthur.

Iwa Kame was the perfect hiding place, and why General Yamashita was rumored to use it as a munitions depot.

Rourke, Felder, Keene, and Carmichael were part of a small recon force of eighteen that landed seven days prior to finding Jacobi's body. Now it was just the four of them, plus Privates Dawes and Vaughan, who waited back at camp.

The faces of the dead flashed in Rourke's head as he trekked through the jungle. They hadn't gone in a blaze of gunfire or with a blood-curdling scream; they had simply disappeared one by one. A few, like Jacobi, had been found ripped open.

The shifting sun painted tangled shadows against the foliage. Birds squawked and fluttered, fleeing their hunts and heading back to the nest. Insects tunneled underneath the squad's carefully placed boots. The jungle was alive around the silent men.

Rourke noticed Keene's finger never left the trigger of his M1 Garand, and on a few occasions, the kid aimed through his iron sights. Rourke himself stayed composed, iron clad, yet his eyes shot frantically to any rustle in the undergrowth, twig snap, or flicker in the canopy. He hoped the men didn't notice. It didn't help that he could still smell Jacobi's shit on the underside of his boot. A constant reminder of what could happen to any of them. *What will more than likely happen to all of us.*

He watched Felder hack through the vines with his machete. The man was strong as an ox and had voiced no complaint about taking point, but when he raised his arm for a particularly thick vine, the blade trembled so much it looked as if it would jump out of his hand. Felder brought the machete down and let out a scream.

"Shit! No! No!" His cries echoed back to the men.

Rourke rushed forward, dropping to a knee and aiming in every direction. His sight narrowing, fixing on any glint of movement. Carmichael slid beside him, laying prone, mumbling something to himself.

Felder turned to them, his face white. "I cut my hand. Bleeding pretty bad."

Rourke saw the man wasn't lying. A thick trail of ichor ran from the gash in Felder's palm and down his arm, staining his uniform, and making them easier to track.

Keene walked out from behind the tree he was using to hide, dropping his gaze when Rourke gave the kid an encouraging nod. Carmichael kept mumbling. Rourke couldn't help but notice his words, even as he watched Felder's blood drip from his body and mark the undergrowth.

"Hail Mary, full of grace, the Lord is with thee... Hail Mary, full—"

"Double time back to camp," Rourke ordered. "Move!"

Camp. Rourke stifled a laugh. Shortly after Jacobi had gone missing, they came upon a series of caverns in a hill side. Rising Sun flags, ceremonial swords, and broken radio equipment adorned the walls, along with blood-stained handprints and a few piles of rotting human meat. Rourke had told the men the Japanese soldiers committed suicide, but it was a lie. It didn't matter that there were no bodies. They set up base in the cavern anyway.

When Rourke's sunken sleep-deprived eyes spotted the familiar camp, nothing else seemed to matter. Despite the lack of a warm bed, fresh food, or any real safety, it was still home for now. Anything was better than the vast unknown of the marshes and jungle. Every single man quickened their pace, ignoring the pain in their bodies as they double-timed it up the embankment to the cave.

"Honey, I'm home," Carmichael sang as he entered.

"You're lucky I didn't shoot you," Dawes replied.

Vaughan was asleep but Dawes stood guard, his M1 Garand poking over the ridge of the cave and scanning for movement. He was a big boy, a former Maine logger who looked the part. Rourke let him stand guard not because he was the best soldier or the best shot, but because he wasn't afraid. None of the other men, not even Rourke himself, could make that claim.

"Found Jacobi," Rourke told him.

"Like the others?" Dawes asked.

"Like the others."

He nodded slowly. The two had been close. Jacobi came from a family of Maine lobster fisherman and the two had formed an instant connection over their love for The Pine Tree State.

Rourke gave him a minute to grieve then returned to giving orders. "Somebody wake Vaughan, he's got the next shift. We'll prep some C-Rations and that last fish Jacobi caught. Everybody get some rest."

Rourke tried to appear strong for the men, but in all seriousness, they were fucked. The food was dwindling and three days ago, through binoculars, they had watched the boat that brought them here slowly sink. All the radio men were missing, probably dead. The situation was FUBAR.

Still, they were Marines, and Rourke refused to let them give up. Sometimes it had gotten ugly, like when he was forced to punch Vaughan, the mouthy Italian, in the face after the private had questioned Rourke's ability to get them out of this quagmire. In truth, he didn't know how he'd do it, but he needed them to believe that he would.

*　.*

Vaughan's shift was almost over, but he knew once Keene relieved, he still wouldn't be able to sleep. Ever since he'd found the first body, he couldn't catch a wink of sleep when darkness fell. Ridgeman had still been alive when Vaughan discovered him, and the exertion of screaming had pushed his organs even farther out. With every yelp, a little blood spurted from where his groin should've been. That night had been a starless one, just like tonight.

There was a shuffling noise, the sound of scraping. Vaughan pointed the M1 Garand wildly around the jungle, looking through the iron sights and praying to see whoever – or whatever

– had killed his friends. He was nauseous, a cold sweat on his brow, but he did his best to ignore it. Fear had no place in this assignment.

It took longer than he liked to realize the noise was coming from within the cave – it was just Carmichael shifting in his sleeping bag.

"You awake?" asked Vaughan.

"What does it look like?" Carmichael replied. Always the smart ass. It was an admirable trait, considering the circumstances.

"I gotta shit," continued Carmichael. "I mean I'm prairie doggin'. Been backed up near three days, and I feel like I'm about to explode. Has to be that fish Jacobi caught. I thought it smelled funny. That fucker is dead and still playing pranks."

Vaughan tried to maintain a whisper as he glanced over at Rourke. Even asleep, the sergeant looked alert.

"Use the hole in the corner. The Japs dug it, and if it wasn't used for shittin' before, it is now. Dawes dropped a turd the size of squirrel in there yesterday."

Carmichael shook his head and stood. He looked to make sure everyone was asleep before replying. "I need privacy. Besides, once you boys see my gear, you won't be able to hold back your jealousy. Might slit my throat in my sleep out of envy alone."

Vaughan laughed. "No matter how big your junk is, our graves are all gonna be the same size. Stay in the cave, man."

Carmichael gave him the finger as he pushed past, heading down the sloping hill that was the cave's entrance. Vaughan shook his head as Carmichael sloshed through the marshlands just on the other side, then ducked out of view.

With Carmichael gone the silence was deafening. "You stupid son of a bitch," Vaughan muttered. "Why the fuck would you let him go outside? Sarge is gonna have your nuts for a necklace—"

Something snapped outside. It could have been Carmichael tripping on a log, but it was loud enough to be something worse. "Carmichael?" Vaughan whispered, knowing his voice wouldn't reach outside the camp. *CRACK!* Another noise, followed by a wet tearing and low gurgling.

Vaughan glanced back at the slumbering sergeant. His mind told him to wake his commanding officer, but he was frozen. The noise from outside grew louder, more distinct. *Shit.* It was the sound of teeth gnawing on gristle.

"Fuck, fuck, fuck," Vaughan repeated as he glanced once more at his sarge then left his position without waking Rourke. Rounding the corner of the cave, and entering the outside world, his eyes took a minute to adjust to the night.

At first it was just a dark mass, standing at around seven feet tall and blending in seamlessly with the jungle around it. Vaughan didn't make a move for his rifle, instead tracking the silhouette. His eyes found what must've been an arm, then arrived at the gruesome heap that used to be Joseph Carmichael.

Vaughan pulled the M1 Garand to his shoulder and fired, not even bothering to look down the iron sights. The muzzle flash lit the surroundings, and for a split second, Vaughan thought he was looking at a giant turtle chewing on an intestine, blood dribbling down its beak-like mouth.

● ● ●

Rourke awoke to the first gun shot. By the sixth, everyone else was up and racing toward the cave opening. "Goddammit," Rourke spat as he realized Vaughan and Carmichael were missing. A shriek that must've been one of the men tore through the camp.

Weapon in hand, Rourke ran from the cave just in time to see Vaughan being split in half at the waist, a clotted rope of guts dangling from his torso. The creature's arm was shoulder-deep inside the soldier. Rourke unloaded his Thompson submachine gun into the beast. The weapon crackled, the muzzle breathing fire, but by the creature's reaction, the bullets must've felt like bee stings.

The thing pulled its arm out of Vaughan, dragging the man's spinal cord with it and whipping it around like a medieval flail.

Felder was to the right of Rourke, firing his BAR relentlessly. The bullets skipped like rocks off the water below, empty shells ricocheting off the cave walls.

The whirling spinal cord hit Felder in the face, knocking him back. The creature got a brief reprieve from the gunfire as Rourke reloaded. Keene was trying his best but struggling to hit the thing, hands shaking as they were. Dawes had only grabbed his sidearm. It wasn't doing much, but Rourke didn't think any of the guns were.

The creature's long, scaled arm hefted Vaughan's corpse with one hand and launched it at the cave entrance. The corpse hit with a splatter, raining guts down on the soldiers' position. Their enemy seemed unconcerned with their presence as it chewed. Fractured moonlight illuminated long fangs and row upon row of sharp teeth gnashing down on Vaughan's offal.

Rourke's Thompson clicked empty again, but this time he didn't reload. The barrage of gunfire was doing nothing. He realized though, that the creature wasn't even attempting to advance. *Maybe it can't leave the swamps?*

"Cease fire!" he ordered. Nobody listened. "Goddammit! Cease fire! It can't leave the water! It can't come up here!" The cacophony of gunfire morphed into the echo of empty shells ricocheting off the ground.

The creature just stared up at them, examining the soldiers from below. Chomping down on the glistening red meat that was once Vaughan's leg. Tendons snapped. The thing was almost smiling as it cracked a bone in half and slurped out the marrow. It knew it would kill them eventually. It didn't mind waiting. This disturbed Rourke more than if the thing had just charged, screaming, clawing, tearing. That level of patience was terrifying. This was a beast older than any of them could understand. And Rourke still couldn't quite tell what it looked like, with only a glimmer of the moon.

"Fuck this," Dawes muttered, and chucked a frag grenade.

The creature didn't move, just stood over it, rolling the grenade around with a taloned finger. Then *BOOM*.

Shrapnel exploded in every direction. The creature's head shot up, and it shrieked, sounding not quite animal but definitely not human. Rourke saw a liquid fly out of its head. *Not blood. It's something, but it's not blood.* The creature retreated into the stinking water of the thick marshland.

Rourke knew seeing the beast was a double-edged blade. Knowing what he was up against meant he could find a way to kill the monster. But recognizing their enemy was not human, or animal, but something of a different world entirely, pulled one's mind out of the rational world. He looked at Keene; tears streaking down the young soldier's face, and knew this realization would drive some of them mad if they had the time to focus on it.

"We need to move. Now. This point has been compromised," he ordered, clenching his teeth to prevent them from chattering.

"We have to bury them," Keene begged, cracking Rourke's cold demeanor for an instant.

"I'm sorry, son, but we can't help them now. We help ourselves." Rourke had tried hard to get Keene to overcome his fear, but now he needed the kid to step up. "We establish a new camp, gather munitions. Continue the mission."

"Hell yeah, Sarge," growled Felder as he reloaded his BAR.

"Dawes take point," Rourke ordered before noticing the soldier was already in front, using rags and kerosene to create a torch around a broken Japanese flag staff. "Could be a way out down there."

"And what if there's not?" whispered Keene, flames reflected in the kid's eyes.

"We'll come back up here and kill that motherfucker." He strode into the cave, and the men followed, disappearing into the darkness.

* * *

Three hours they'd been trekking through this goddamn cave when Keene's flashlight caught a glimpse of something. The light reflected off a shining boot, but Keene paused when he realized there was a leg attached. He moved the flashlight up the body, spotlighting the sheathed sword on its hip, a lifeless hand clutching the hilt. The light moved up the arm, collar patches indicating the dead man was an officer.

"This one's still intact..." he muttered as the light grew close to the dead man's face —

It blinked. Keene leapt backwards, raising his rifle. "Shit!" he cried, pulling back the bolt and chambering the first round of the magazine.

The officer's hand clicked the blade free from the sheath. Dawes pulled his sidearm and flanked the living corpse. "You want the honors?" he asked Keene while pulling back the hammer of the pistol.

"Stand down," Rourke ordered, shouldering his weapon. He stepped in front of his men, blocking their line of fire then turned, raising his hands to the Japanese officer in a motion of caution. "Easy... easy..." he reached for his canteen, an offering of peace. The officer slowly removed his hand from the sword and accepted the water.

"Sarge, what the fuck...?" whispered Felder, a look of awe and distrust marking his features.

Rourke turned to him slowly, keeping one eye on the not-dead officer. "He's the only survivor. Maybe he knows something we don't."

"That man is the enemy. Fucking Rising Sun, *Sergeant*."

"*Private*, if we don't make it off this island – don't stop that *thing* – then everyone who sacrificed their life here died for nothing. Jacobi, Ridgeman, everyone."

Dawes shook his head. "We get the intel. Then we kill the prick."

"I speak English. Quite well, actually." The Japanese officer pushed tentatively to his feet, extending the canteen to Rourke. "I am Captain Nagisa Tanaka of the Imperial Army, but I agree with your commanding officer, that does not matter now. We are all ghosts. Already dead."

Dawes spat on the floor in front of Tanaka. "Speak for yourself."

Rourke once again inserted himself between the men. "Sergeant Rourke, USMC." He pointed at the soldiers as he recounted their names. "Dawes, Keene, and Felder."

Tanaka placed the sheathed sword against the wall, indicating that he would not use it against them. "There were many more of you?"

Rourke grimaced. "Yeah... many more."

Tanaka looked at Rourke with what appeared to be genuine sadness. "When the noble sun was in the sky, I ventured back to the swamp to try and find their bodies. To keep the demon from eating their souls. I brought back what I could find. Not many. Then I came here. It cannot follow."

"What is it?" Keene asked, curiosity seeming to win-out over hate.

"It is called a Kappa," Tanaka said, his voice barely above a whisper, as if by speaking its name, it would appear. "A river monster and demon from folklore that preys on fishermen, feeds off of a hidden organ called the 'shirikodama'... located just past the... the anus." Tanaka shook his head. "They enjoy wrestling and are known to feed on cucumbers as well."

The men just stared at Captain Tanaka, and while Rourke didn't know what to make of any of it, he was grateful for an explanation, no matter how insane it sounded.

"There is only one way to kill them," Tanaka continued. "Their heads are shaped like bowls and cradle a life-giving water. They are only vulnerable once the bowl has been emptied."

Rourke began pacing. He scanned the room, looking for something, anything, that would give them the upper hand. He was not a religious man by nature, but was about to start praying when he spotted a flamethrower tucked away in a corner of the cave near one of the dismembered bodies Tanaka had dragged in. He traced a line with his eyes, from the weapon to the torch in Dawes's hand.

"We're going to kill it, Tanaka," Rourke said, eyes locked to the Japanese captain. "Face the wall and we'll quickly and mercifully release you to your fallen soldiers. Or, fight with us in the swamp. In the demon's home."

Tanaka reached for his sword. "Not much of a choice, Sergeant."

Felder and Keene stared open-mouthed at their sarge, but it was Dawes who spoke the truth of it. "Shit, boys. Five is better odds than four against this thing." He nodded once to Tanaka, turned, and headed back the way they'd come.

Tanaka and Rourke slowly fell to the back of the group. They walked in silence for an hour before Tanaka's quiet voice finally spoke.

"Sergeant, what was your mission on Iwa Kame?"

Anger surged through Rourke as he shot out his retort. "Are you a spy, Tanaka? Hoping to gather enough information for another air raid? Kill some more innocent civilians?"

Tanaka frowned and kept pace with Rourke; it was another half hour before the man responded. "The Kappa is not what I fear most on this island. The Imperial Army is my greatest fear. The source of my deepest pain. My unit was sent to Iwa Kame on recon, in hopes of creating a defensive position. We were given intel that an American landing force was nearby. There was no landing force. They knew the demon was here. They wish to weaponize it. My men were a test. We walked into a trap set by my own general."

"A munitions depot," Rourke replied, glancing at Tanaka. "We were sent to destroy one of your munitions depots."

Tanaka inclined his head. "Bad intelligence, probably leaked by the Imperial Army. No depot."

Rourke smiled despite the situation. "I gathered that."

"I owe no allegiance to an Empire that treats its own people this way. I chose to starve rather than commit hara-kiri." Tanaka stopped, and after a few steps, Rourke turned to face the captain. "You have no reason to trust me... but trust that I will die to defeat the monster."

Rourke was starting to like Tanaka.

●　●●

With the few hours of daylight left, Dawes and Keene planted their remaining land mines. It was hard to guess which spots would be most effective, considering the Kappa didn't think with the strategy of a soldier, so they figured an unpredictable approach was best. They placed some close together, and others farther apart.

Felder set up his BAR in a perch and got busy preloading every magazine he had. He set his frag grenades beside him so they'd be ready to throw, and his sidearm nearby.

Rourke carried the flamethrower to the flank of the ambush area. Pouring the gasoline from the weapon, he created a very literal kill zone. He hoped that when the time came, the men wouldn't hesitate. Hoped that he himself wouldn't let fear seize him. The Kappa wasn't afraid of anything and would certainly return to finish the job it had started. But that lack of fear could be used against it. Tanaka wasn't afraid to die either, so he sat waiting, the water soaking his clothes and sticking to his skin, a katana by his side, waiting for the Kappa to appear.

All hope of making it out alive had dissipated. This was a last stand, a last shot at killing the creature. A last shot at revenge.

They sat in silence, aiming down their sights, waiting for the monster to rise.

• • •

Night returned, flooding the sky with darkness, but their focus hadn't wavered, not for a second, not—

The Kappa launched itself out of the water, its greedy jaws set on Tanaka. Felder opened fire, his BAR pelting the creature, pushing it back from the Japanese captain. Keene fired his Garand, the bullet casings coming out hot and hissing as they landed on the water.

Tanaka ducked out of the way, narrowly avoiding the razor-like claws that swung after him. Dawes appeared from the cave, a torch in his hand, sprinting to the leftmost flank of the Kappa, flames dancing in the darkness. The creature swiveled its head and pursued the man, but Rourke ran alongside him, peppering it with his submachine gun. The bullets cut a red-hot path in the night. They slowed the creature enough that Dawes was able to get the torch to its desired location and drop it in the pool of gasoline. It had pooled in a little trail, and when fire-touched, it *whooshed* to life, encircling the Kappa.

The monster charged Dawes, unleashing a roar of frustration at the soldier. Dawes dug into the ground and let out a roar of his own. He charged the beast, the six-inch blade of his Ka-Bar catching the light of the fire.

The Kappa's arm smacked against Dawes, knocking him towards the fire and onto a landmine.

The explosion tore through the night, and Dawes rained down, now a mess of blood and flesh. The blast propelled his innards into the flames. The smell of burnt flesh filled the air.

"Dawes!" Keene yelled, but the creature was concentrated on Felder as the private reloaded his BAR.

The Kappa grunted, almost like it was catching on to the plan.

With the fire blazing, the soldiers could finally see the Kappa in its entirety. It looked like an anorexic turtle, standing on its hind legs, impishly bouncing around, taking joy in the hunt.

It charged Rourke, but the twin explosion of two landmines knocked it off course, and a bucketful of the water went flying out of its head. Rourke unloaded into the Kappa, and while they were now knocking the creature around, the bullets still weren't piercing.

"Keep hitting it!" Rourke yelled over the gunfire. "There's still more of that shit in its head!"

Keene's final magazine clicked empty. He rushed to Felder's position, lobbing grenades wildly as he ran. They exploded in quick succession, some hurting the monster, but most horribly off target.

Tanaka raced forward, his katana ricocheting off the Kappa's legs, doing little damage. The creature raked its claws down the Japanese soldier's face, blinding him, blood spurting from his forehead and cheek in quick gushes. He dropped his sword as Rourke's Thompson ran dry. With only a few bullets left in his Colt .45, Rourke tried to make them count, but his shots to the torso did little more than make him the next target. The Kappa jabbed its knife-like fingers deep into Tanaka's stomach as it stalked toward Rourke. The Japanese officer began to shake uncontrollably, a mixture of piss and gore running down his uniform.

"Man the gun," Felder roared, and raced down the slope towards one of the mines. "Come and get me, you stupid son of a bitch!" He kicked at the rough ground where the mine was planted.

The mine and exploded, sending Felder's shredded body back towards the cave, but the explosion had been enough to knock the remaining water out of the Kappa's head. It also knocked Rourke, defenseless, to the ground.

Keene picked up the BAR and charged. He would die to protect Rourke, who had stood by him despite his repeated cowardice. He emptied the rest of the BAR's clip into the Kappa. The bullets penetrated the reptilian skin of the Kappa. Black ichor leaked from its wounds. The creature turned to him, picked him up by the head, and palmed his skull. Keene screamed as it squeezed its hand into a fist. Pain erupting like lightning.

Blood and gray clumps of brain dripped through the creature's fingers and onto Keene's limp and lifeless body, dangling in the air. Opening its palm, ivory flecks of shattered skull sank into the swamp.

"No!" Rourke screamed.

Keene's efforts had lasted only a few seconds, but it was enough time for Rourke to locate Tanaka's katana in the bog. He charged the Kappa. Locking eyes with the beast. For a brief moment he saw recognition in the thing's eyes. Rourke leapt as its claws swept towards him, but it wasn't enough. The claws punched deep, and warm blood flooded from his body.

He drove the katana up into the Kappa's chin. The blade scraped against the creature's bones before erupting through the top of its bowl-shaped skull. The creature howled, vomiting buckets of its black blood. Rourke twisted the blade farther into the beast, until the hilt was nearly inside the Kappa.

The creature stared into Rourke's eyes as it died.

Rourke smiled.

* * *

Tanaka was the only other survivor, though his wound was substantial and the light was already dimming in his eyes. Rourke assessed his own injury. He wouldn't last much longer than the Japanese officer. Using the last of his adrenaline, the sergeant dragged Tanaka up the embankment.

Rourke propped the man up against the side of the cave and took a seat beside him. Both were too weak for words, but Tanaka nodded slightly, a hint of a smile on his face. Their own blood had been spilt, but they'd done it. They'd sent the river demon back to hell.

Rourke fished two cigars out of his pocket. The effort to light them made his leg throb, but it was worth the pain. He gave one to Tanaka, who happily accepted. Rourke noticed the blood of both men was flowing down into the swamp. Mingling with the blood of all the fallen soldiers. He puffed his cigar.

The smoke was sweet.

It tasted like victory.

FIREFALL

Mike Barretta

Vandenburg AFB
July 28, 1974

I s this it?" whispered Corporal Nelson. "Are we a go?"
"Secure yourself," hollered Deck Sergeant Bolin. "We don't
have time for a fucking Q and A." The sergeant pushed past,
barking orders for his Ballistic Marines to get their crap together.

"Shit," said Nelson. "It's real." He moved to his designated
seat to stow his weapon.

Captain Michael Kristoff climbed the short ladder from the
upper troop deck to the flight deck. He opened the hatch and
climbed up to speak to the pilots off-channel. He stepped back,
secured the hatch, and slid the rest of the way down. He spun
about, surveying the troops strapping into the crash couches of
Ballistic Assault Vehicle *Atlas*. He keyed the boom mic attached
to his helmet. "We are go. This is not a drill. Sergeants, secure the
troop decks and make ready for launch." He pushed past troops
too slow to get the hell out of his way. "Take a seat, Nelson.
You're going into space."

"Yes, sir."

Captain Kristoff strapped himself in with smooth efficiency
and rattled his weapon secured in its brace. He tugged on the
pack under his seat. Items adrift would be fatal during launch
and re-entry.

Nelson broke into nervous sweat. He tightened his harness
until pain bit into his shoulders, which, according to his instruc-
tors, was the minimum level required to ensure survival. He
liked the idea of going into space. Who didn't? All the pulp
stories had made it sound amazing, but the US Marines had a

way of sucking all the fun and glamour out of every activity it engaged in. Here he was, right out of high school, strapped in and weapon at the ready, set to defend his country against the alien hordes.

It was almost funny, until you saw footage of an alien horde moving into a town and fucking eating people. They hit isolated places, made literal mincemeat of the local police forces and the odd farmer with a shotgun, and left before any real opposition could arrive on scene – hence the Ballistic Marines. Their mission was to descend out of the sky on a pillar of fire and negotiate vigorously. *Very vigorously.*

"Remember your jobs. Kill everything not human," said the captain, reiterating Nelson's thoughts.

Captain Kristoff pressed his hand to his left ear to cut out the noise of marines securing themselves for launch. All three decks reported secure for launch. The lights dimmed as the *Atlas* switched over to internal power.

Nelson glanced up. The countdown clock started, red LED segments flickered off and on. The sharp tang of ozone from live electrical equipment filled his nose. Servos whined. The fresh air intake secured. They would be breathing each other's farts for the next thirty minutes – the time it took to cross a continent. A trembling vibration, like a waterfall, rattled his bones. *The deluge system.* Hundreds of gallons of water flooded the pad to keep it from getting burned up when the engines fired.

"Oh, fuck," said Private 'PJ' Patrick James. "This is fucking it."

Thumps and bangs resonated as the fueling umbilicals and service gantries severed and retracted. Everything was louder and more urgent than the simulator. Intense. High pressure turbo-pumps screamed. A liquid oxygen fuel tank chilled the wall behind him. The cold seeped into his spine and he shivered. Explosive volatiles, super-cooled cryogenic fuels, high-speed rotating equipment, and pissed off Deck Sergeants surrounded him. Two hundred and seventy marines and two flight crew were about to be blasted to a place where a person would boil, freeze, and suffocate, more or less, at the same time. And if lucky, they'd be dropped into a zone where they were considered a tasty snack.

"How the hell did I get here?" asked Nelson, unaware he was transmitting on the tactical channel.

"Volunteered like the rest of us," said PJ.

A few snorts and chuckles sounded across the channel.

"Hey, Nelson." PJ grimaced. "How the hell do I get out of this chicken shit outfit?"

"Shut the hell up, PJ," Nelson responded. "You're scaring the ladies."

"One minute," Captain Kristoff yelled over nervous laughter.

The deck quieted. Each Marine retreated into himself to imagine the worst-case scenario. If everything went perfectly and he wasn't blown up on launch, or burned up on re-entry, he'd soon be dancing with an alien raiding party. Pretty much every scenario he could think of was worst case. The LED clock indexed down to his doom. *Fucking aliens.* Who the hell knew why they came? Bizarre shimmering portals, breaches in space and time, would just flash into existence, and they would pour forth looking for a feed. Lost civilizations and vanished places littered Earth. Easter Island. Anasazi. Roanoke... maybe the alien bastards had a hand in their loss.

Deck Sergeant Bolin roared. "Marines! Brace, brace, brace!"

Ignition.

The engines exploded into a shrieking banshee scream that made thinking impossible. His teeth rattled. Eyesight blurred. Vibrations shook his bones. The hold back bolts securing the ship to the pad fired and the ship lifted free. Nelson, and the other two hundred and sixty-nine marines on all three decks tightened their stomach muscles and pushed their heads deep into the cradles. Powerful rolling waves of vibrations wracked the ship. The aerospike engines throttled to full power, pinning him down with crushing G forces like a bug on a board. The *Atlas* leapt off the pad, climbing fast into clear skies as if it was fired from the barrel of a cannon. Every wrinkle and crease in his uniform bruised his body. Anybody who had anything in their back pocket would regret it. He gasped for air, taking small sips between grunts. His vision tunneled out, graying at the edges as if viewing through a long tube. Across from him, a Marine lolled in his seat like a boneless rag doll. Too late for that poor, dumb bastard.

"Staging," bellowed Deck Sergeant Bolin.

How the hell that man can speak is beyond me.

Engines throttled back to something less than deafening. Acceleration eased. Explosive bolts fired like shotgun blasts. External tanks captured by the hypersonic slipstream shrieked murder as they peeled back from the fuselage like a blossoming flower. He filled his lungs with air, taking in a deep gasping breath. The engines throttled up to max. With the excess mass shed, the *Atlas* accelerated even harder. Nelson's vision shrank back to a tiny bright spot as blood pooled in his lower body. His legs and abdomen burned with lactic acid fatigue from tensing. His heart pounded like a triphammer and he bore down pushing blood back up to his head so he wouldn't lose consciousness. His vision widened a tiny measure. The G-meter next to the mission clock read 7.5. Blood ran from the nose of the limp Marine across from him. Some people weren't built for this shit. The high-G centrifuge trainer and low-G Vomit Comet could only weed out so many. A couple of pussies were bound to get through if they were dumb enough not to quit.

The main engine cut off. Freefall. Let the puking begin. Nelson's stomach gurgled, and his inner ear tried to make sense of the situation. If he hadn't strapped in, he'd have bounced around the deck like a beachball in a windstorm. He sucked in a normal breath through his nose and regretted it. Bubbles of blood and urine floated up from the deck. His stomach turned.

"I think that guy shit his pants," said PJ.

"I think that guy is dead," said Nelson. A bubble of blood oozed from the limp Marine's nose and broke free, taking flight, wobbling in the air currents. Someone retched to his left, and the sour smell of puke filled the deck.

"Congratulations, marines, you're all fucking astronauts." Bolin sniffed the air and looked around. "Fuck me! Keep your cookies down, you apes. Hoover that shit up. You don't want to be anally probed with puke all over you, do you? Now pay attention to the briefing."

"Anally probed," PJ hissed. "No one said anything about anal probing."

"It was in the brochure," said Nelson. "Now shut the fuck up."

"Marines, this is what we know." Captain Kristoff paused, making sure he had the eyes and ears of those that had survived the launch. "Three portals have opened at Crooked Creek, Montana. Aliens are engaged in hostile operations against US citizens. Survivors are evacuating to the regional high school, and our mission will be to drop in, advance to the school, and relieve the citizen defenders. We are being supported by the *Hector* and the *Achilles* on this mission. This is contingency ops. We are making it up as we go. Am I clear?"

A chorus of affirmatives clogged the tactical channel. Not much of a brief, but every operation involving the aliens was contingency ops. The aliens moved too fast. In and out. If you took a moment to make a plan, it was all over. Nothing left to do but the singing and the digging.

The ship tumbled as it reoriented itself for re-entry. Nelson felt a little green, but not as bad as PJ, who had plugged his mouth into the vacuum hose, making horrible animal noises as his body convulsed.

"You okay?" Nelson asked.

PJ unplugged his mouth from the hose. "Imma kill me some alien sumbitches for making me feel this shitty."

Before Nelson could respond, Captain Kristoff continued over the tac channel. "Marines, we don't know why they've come. All we know is they take our people. That ends today. We drop in, and fuck them up. Stand by for re-entry. Oo-rah."

"Oo-rah," chorused the marines.

* * *

Crooked Creek, Montana

"We shouldn't be here," Marilyn whispered. Halcyon light glazed the lake's surface. Dragonflies skimmed the water, their legs cutting trails along the surface. The lake at the park was beautiful and semi-isolated. The perfect spot for privacy.

"We both have study hall." Jason smiled. "It's not as if we're missing anything."

Marilyn smiled back. "Oh, I know what you're missing. You talk me into anything."

"Anything?"

"Almost anything." She kissed him.

A rippling boom, sharper than thunder, shook the ground.

"What was that?" asked Marilyn, sitting up in alarm.

A bright flash, followed by two more, blinded them. They blinked away purple after-images.

Jason swore, and the blood drained from his face. "We have to leave," he said, jumping to his feet.

"Jason, what is it?" Marilyn looked around as Jason fumbled for his keys.

"It's them, Mare. We have to go!" He took her by the hand and pulled her to his car – a perpetually out-of-gas 1962 Chevy Impala.

Instead of romantic playing hooky on a warm Spring day, this now seemed like a foolish and fatal idea. The town's invasion sirens wailed. A warm spike of adrenalin flooded her body and she stumbled.

"Come on, Mare. Get up. We have to get back to the school."

Civil defense engineers constructed regional schools like fortresses. Anyone who heard the siren or the special ringer built into every phone would move to a shelter.

If they could.

Mare clung to the seat as Jason sped along the narrow road that circled the lake, the car floating through the turns on its soft shocks. The sound of distant thunder rumbled. An ominous, continuous sound of superheated air expanding away from breaches in space-time. The sky burned with the queer alien brightness of sunlight diffused through fog. They hit the smoother roadway to the school and Jason punched it, swerving around a bloodied man staggering away from a rollover accident. Someone else – man or woman, Mare couldn't tell – lay crumpled in a boneless heap at the side of the road.

"They're coming," screamed the man.

"Stop," said Mare. "Jason, please stop. We have to help." Her heart hammered in her chest as the cold chill of shock settled in.

He drove on.

Jason had made the right decision and she hated him for it. Nothing to do for them. Gunshots echoed. They neared the school. Panicked crowds converged, some dragging luggage. A delivery truck slammed on its brakes and swerved to avoid rear ending stopped traffic. A bicyclist went under the wheels and was kicked out a bloody pulp.

"Oh my God," said Marilyn. "Oh my God."

The town's invasion siren cut off. The school's claxon, powered by an emergency generator, continued to ring. Jason clipped the corner of some farmer's field, mowing down rows of corn. The car burst from the corn field onto school property strewn with cars. A mindless mob pounded on the blast shutters of the front door. Jason drove through the parking lot and over the curb onto the grass. The car fishtailed, flinging clods of dirt in a dark, rooster tail. He rounded the school, front to back, to the only other exterior door. He slammed on the brakes and leapt out, pulling Mare out his side of the car. Mr Simmons stood his post by the narrow firing slit window of his chemistry class. He carried one of the school's M-14 civil defense battle rifles.

"Mr Simmons! Open the door!"

"I can't!" he yelled through the thick glass, glancing around for a solution. "The school is locked down. I'm sorry. Get to my Jeep. Keys are in the ignition. Go!"

"Mr Simmons, please! They're coming. Please, open the door," pleaded Marilyn. "I can't. I'm sorry. Go, dammit. Just go."

A man staggered around the building wild-eyed with incoherent terror. Blood streamed from a loose flap of skin on his forehead. "They're here," he screamed. "Oh Jesus save us. They're here." He stopped screaming, brushed down his shirt then looked to the sky as if he had just had an epiphany. Then he put the barrel of a snub-nosed revolver into his mouth and pulled the trigger.

Mare screamed as Jason dragged her away and around to the teacher's parking lot avoiding the crowd pounding at the front doors.

"Mare, get your shit together," said Jason. "We're still in this."

"Okay, okay. I'm good." She was anything but good. She scanned the doomed crowd looking for her parents. Any fool knew the principal was prohibited by law to open the shutters before the all clear sounded. And he wouldn't. Mr Corwin had vacationed at Alice Springs in Australia when that town was wiped off the map in an attack.

Gunshots barked, and a round of screaming began. They weaved between parked cars working their way to Mr Simmons' Jeep. A hand shot out from under a vehicle, snagging her ankle and pulling her to the ground.

"Under here. Hide with me," a panicked voice urged. "They're coming."

She kicked free. *Run, hide, fight.* That was the mantra drilled into her, and everyone else, since grade school. As far as Mare was concerned, there was still time to run.

The ground shook, and tumultuous shrieks filled the air. Everyone knew that sound. It was them. Dust clouds rolled out of the corn fields surrounding the town. Gunfire and the high-pitched whine of alien weaponry pierced the air. The parking lot exploded. Cars spun in the air, flipping end-over-end. A gas tank detonated, and vehicle parts and broken glass rained down.

Keys dangled from the ignition of Mr Simmons' Jeep, and Jason had the engine kicked over and into gear before Mare was even in the seat. A stowed AR-15 hung from the roll bar.

"Check the glove box," Jason said. He worked the clutch.

Mis-shifted. The gears ground against each other. He corrected and the Jeep lurched forward, building speed.

As she opened the glove box, the Jeep hit a bump and the contents exploded out. Manuals, an unsheathed filet knife, loose bullets, no-shit actual gloves and a M1911A1 .45 caliber pistol. She fished the gun from the floorboards and racked the slide back to chamber a round. The heft of the .45 reassured her, and she tucked the weapon into her waistband at the small of her back.

Jason plowed through the rustic split rail fence that wrapped school property and jumped the curb onto the road. The top-heavy jeep tilted, and she grabbed the head rest and pulled herself back in. It carved a slalom of shredded rubber before regaining traction on the asphalt.

Jason looked up at the rear-view mirror. "Fuck!"

Mare turned, dread winding through her. A tall, black centaurian nightmare galloped after them. The speedometer read sixty. The creature gained; its long legs eating up the distance.

"Shoot, Mare. Shoot!" Jason yelled, jamming his foot down on the accelerator.

Mare spun about, knees on the seat. She slit the canvas top of the jeep with the filet knife, freed the AR-15 from its rack and stood, bracing herself against the roll bar. Her hair whipped in the wind yet an eerie calm settled over her. This was it. She could choke on her fear and die, or deal with it. She sighted down the length of the weapon, concentrating upon the front sight, aligning it with the galloping creature's center of mass. She fired a few quick rounds, gouging black, viscous chunks from the creature.

The alien stumbled, lowered its axe-shaped head and reached for its own weapon.

"Faster," she screamed, firing again. She missed as Jason swerved around a wreck. Mare steadied herself and fired once more, hitting the creature in its upper torso. It let out a raptorial squeal inappropriate for its size.

"Shoot the damn thing!" yelled Jason.

The creature closed the distance, making it impossible to miss. Clawed feet chewed up the asphalt. She fired as fast as she could pull the trigger. Rounds hammered into the alien, most sparking off its armor but some cratering its flesh. The alien raised its own weapon and fired. She heard the weird shriek of the alien projectile, the heat of its passage scorching her face. The alien fired again and the tires on the left side of the Jeep blew out. It veered violently and dug into the soft dirt at the edge of the road. Tires shredded, throwing chunks of rubber into the air. The Jeep dropped into the shallow drainage ditch and rolled, catapulting her into the cool spring air. *I'm flying...* Tall cornstalks embraced her, wrapping her up and cushioning her fall back to Earth. She hit the ground and rolled, arms and legs flailing.

Mare lay still and took pained shallow breaths. She tasted blood. Smelled the crushed cornstalks. Surprised that she wasn't busted up much more than she was. Her head throbbed as the alien approached. It chittered and squealed.

Run. Hide. Fight.

Run. Put distance between you and the alien. They had tried that. Failed.

Hide. She lay still, calming herself. Running now was not a viable option. To run, was to be seen, was to be heard.

Was to be caught.

She froze, concealed by the cornstalks.

"Oh, Jason," she whispered. The Jeep lay on its side. Jason hung in the seat and stirred. He moved his head and saw her. *Run,* he mouthed.

The alien stepped into view and she fought the urge to vomit. It moved around the Jeep, and its head swiveled, scanning the terrain and assessing threats.

She held her breath. God, they were big. And terrifying. A ten-foot tall centaur of sharp angles embodied the worst attributes of reptile and insect. Their taut ebony skin glistened like oil on water. Two parallel rows of black hemispheres, spider eyes, receded at an upward swooping angle across a face like an edge on hatchet blade. A horizontal split formed a bladed mouth used, not for eating but communication and as an extra appendage. Two muscular, multi-jointed arms, affixed at the upper torso, ended in clawed three-fingered hands. Most terrifying was the boneless cilia ringing the puckered sphincter on its chest.

It slung its weapon, gripped the Jeep's roll bar, and pulled it upright. The busted radiator hissed and pinged, dribbling green fluid.

Please stay still. She bit her lip. *Play dead.* Sometimes, they left the dead alone.

The alien ripped the door off the jeep, reached in and sliced the seatbelt. Long, thin fingers like spider legs wrapped Jason's torso. The creature pulled him away, held him up to its eyes. Jason screamed, and the alien screamed back. It shook him hard and smashed his head against the Jeep's mangled roll bar, spraying blood in arcs across the flattened corn stalks. Jason's pulped head rolled on his shoulders. The creature crab-scuttled up onto the embankment. It secured Jason's body in its mouth and twisted his left arm off. Marilyn took a hitch of breath as Jason's bones snapped and tendons severed. The chest sphincter unpuckered, revealing a gullet lined with spiraling rows of silver, razor teeth. The teeth whirred like machinery coming to speed. The cilia curled inward and crammed Jason's arm into its maw. She covered her ears to silence the sound of the alien's mastication.

"No, no, no," Marilyn whispered.

The alien picked Jason apart, shredding him like bloody string cheese, feeding in his head last, like a ball fed into a muzzleloader. The alien's lower torso flexed in waves of peristaltic ripples as it devoured him. Finished, it turned away, walked back towards town. It cocked its tail and defecated, spraying the road with pungent fecal matter.

Goddamn those things to hell. She spotted the AR-15 in the dirt and pushed herself upright ignoring the pain of her pummeled body. She reached the gun, ejected the nearly-empty magazine, reversed it, and reinserted the full mag taped to empty. She drew back the weapon's charging rod and let it snap free.

The alien turned. Its body rippled with tension.

Her vision blurred and pain flared in her skull. Alien telepathy did that when near. From painful headaches to complete incapacitation.

It let out a hungry shriek and sprang at her, arms outstretched. She fired into its face. Its head bucked under the impact. Black fluid and chunks of flesh sprayed the air. The wounds glassed over, part of the creature's fantastically efficient healing process. She dove aside and rolled. Claws raked the air recently occupied by her head. She scrambled to her feet, reacquired her target, and fired repeatedly into its torso. The creature reached for its own slung weapon, but one of her shots shattered its hand. Another round shattered a leg joint and the creature buckled to the asphalt leaving a greasy smear and exposing the brain hump between its shoulders.

"I got you," she screamed, sending more rounds into the hump. "I got you!"

She felt the thing's pain as it shuddered into death.

Exhausted, she dropped to her knees; shock and adrenaline prevented a complete collapse. She sobbed. Jason was gone, ground to paste in the belly of monster from another world.

"You're dead! You're fucking dead," she screamed.

Her head burst with painful light. She choked out a scream as a massive hand crushed air from her lungs. Mare dropped the rifle as another alien hoisted her high and plunged her deep into a foul capture bag.

* * *

The *Atlas* fell through the atmosphere. Frictional heat burned the air to white hot plasma, ablating the heat shield. The engines ignited, slowing the ship's plummet.

"Funny thing," yelled PJ. "You always have enough fuel to get to the crash site." "Shut the fuck up, PJ," said Nelson.

Best case, a plume of white-hot plasma burned through the ship and boiled him to mist, tearing the ship into scorched aluminum confetti. Second best, they cratered into the ground at

18,000 miles per hour. Third best, they made it to the surface to fight the aliens.

"On target men, remember your orders," said Captain Kristoff over the tactical channel. "The school is south of our LZ. Do not become disoriented."

The aerospike engines throttled to a powerful throaty roar, braking for a landing that wouldn't shatter bones and pulp organs. Landing skids thumped down. The ship hit hard and rocked violently as if it was going over. The suspended crash couches snatched taut on their cable risers. Nelson bit his tongue and tasted blood.

The engines shutdown and the deployment light turned green. Deck Sergeant Bolin was on his feet first as if rocket propelled. He pulled his pack out from under the seat, flung it over his head while sliding his arms through the straps in one smooth motion. He freed his weapon, slung it on his chest and then pulled a red lever inside a safety box. Three hatches arrayed equidistantly around the perimeter of the deck exploded free. Sunlight and smoke wafted in. Inflatable slides rolled out like fat tongues. Captain Kristoff was first out, vanishing over the edge like he had just stepped off a cliff.

"Hit it, grunts," yelled Bolin. "Stand clear of the blast zone. We are one great big target."

Nelson repeated the sergeant's procedure without any of the man's grace. When it was his turn, he leapt into the slide and slid seventy feet to the ground. He hit the bottom, rolled clear into a semi-crouch, and unslung his weapon in one fluid motion. The ship emptied in just under thirty seconds. Death by alien had a way of concentrating the mind. Everyone was razor sharp.

The school, like a medieval fortress, lay ahead. The ground was hot and scorched black from the landing. Flattened corn stalks burned around him, and distant shrieks and screams rent the air. They had taken a wrong sub-orbit and landed in hell. The town burned. A greasy, gray pall shrouded the standing buildings. Bodies, and parts of bodies, lay strewn about the LZ.

Without an obvious target, he ran for the nearest cover, the skeletal bleachers of the high school football stadium. He dove under thin aluminum benches that would tear like snot-soaked tissue if hit by alien weaponry. Another Marine slammed into the ground next to him. He had expected PJ.

"Who the fuck are you?" asked Nelson.

"Private Miles, second deck. I got turned around."

"Fuck. Well, Miles, we're all going that way." He pointed to the fortress-like bulk of the regional high school.

Alien and human gunfire sliced the air. Heavy rounds punched holes in the bleacher's aluminum seats, but it was sporadic and undisciplined. Probably stray rounds meant for someone else, but still a good enough reason to keep your head down.

"Keep low, run fast," said Sergeant Bolin over the tactical channel. "Form up on me. Move out!"

Nelson spotted the sergeant and ran to keep up, PJ angling in from the right.

The gunfire increased, but it was still sporadic and distant. Aliens stalked the school's roof, holding civilians aloft and flinging screaming students to other aliens below.

"You gotta be fuckin' shittin' me," said Nelson to himself. Such a sight did not process. There was one reasonable response to such atrocities. Something snapped inside, and murderous warmth filled him. Heavy machine guns on his left opened up, chewing into the aliens at the base of the school.

"Let the big dogs bark," Bolin yelled. "Then it's our turn."

Nelson wiped burning sweat from his eyes as he waited. Light from multiple breaches filtered through the heavy smoke to create flickering, overlapping shadows. The effect was unnerving, like a horror movie's special effect.

Two bright lights, like meteors, appeared overhead and fell from the sky.

"Fuck yeah!" Nelson roared. The *Hector* and the *Achilles* had arrived. Cheers rang out over the tac channel, before a purple beam lanced the sky and the *Hector* exploded, blossoming into white-hot light. Fragments, trailing smoke, spiraled out of the sky. Cheers turned to cries of horror and curses. Flaming debris and burning fuel blanketed civilians too slow to get out of the way. The remains of *Hector* hit the ground hard and exploded again. Pillars of smoke rose into the sky. Even at this distance, the heat was palpable. Hot bits of metal and carbonized marines pattered like rain.

"Fuck, fuck, fuck," Nelson swore. Two hundred and seventy dead marines. Just like that. Beams lanced out bracketing the *Achilles* and missing. The surviving Ballistic Assault Vehicle vanished behind a horizon of corn. He hoped they made it.

"The dead don't need us," said Bolin. "Alpha element, flank left, use the parking lot for cover. Bravo go right and haul ass. You ain't got much to hide with. Charlie is up the middle. Go!"

Nelson, part of Charlie element, advanced up the middle, moving from car to car in the parking lot. Doors hung from broken hinges and roofs were peeled back like jagged flower petals to reveal blood-soaked upholstery and scraps of people. He crouched behind a tire and peered over a fender. The school's tower mounted guns were silent, smoking ruins. A squad automatic weapon opened up and chattered viciously, shattering brick and hammering aliens. One tumbled from the roof, landed hard and snapped its legs. It screamed like tortured animal.

Nelson advanced, keeping tight enough to Bolin to cover him. PJ kept pace right behind.

"That is my fucking dream car," PJ said suddenly.

Cherry '69 Mustang, pretty if you dig out the headless corpse. He moved closer to Bolin.

"Nice of you to join me, Nelson." Bolin smiled viciously. The sergeant assessed the situation. This wasn't his first rodeo with four-legged monsters from another world. "Right up the middle, across that open ground. Access ladders to the roof," said Bolin. "Then we drop in and kill the bastards in the school. Ooh-rah."

"Ooh-rah," said Nelson. *Open ground. Fucking hell. The smart thing to do would be to dig a hole and hunker down until the bad things went away.* "Let's go lay some pain on these motherfuckers, Sergeant."

"That's the spirit," Bolin said.

A migraine exploded in Nelson's head. He spun, saw rippling cornstalks and the black gleam of alien heads. "Contact," he screamed. He shouldered his weapon and fired. Three aliens burst from the corn and onto the short grass. They hit the parking lot at full speed, leaping and snaking around cars. An alien swiped Private Miles, splitting the Marine in half. His upper torso spun through the air over the cars; ropey intestines unspooled from his body. Most of private Miles landed face-up on the long hood of a Dodge Charger, his mouth making gasping fish noises.

Concentrated fire chewed into the aliens, bringing them down. They screamed like scalded birds as Marine bullets tore into their flesh. More burst from concealment and returned fire with rounds heavy enough to rock the parking lot vehicles on their suspensions. The aliens jinked so fast it was hard to get consistent shots. Another squad automatic weapon opened up and swept the area, cutting the monster's legs out from under them. They screamed in rage and fell like broken, twitching horses.

Nelson took disciplined shots, putting his marksman skills to use by shooting the aliens in their brain humps.

Bolin whooped. "Fuck yeah, Nelson. You're giving me a hard on."

Nelson's head burst into white-hot agony again. Blood spurted from his nose as he turned to target the source of his pain. An alien loomed out of the corn, and all he saw was the big bore of the gun that would vaporize him. A thundering roar cut through the cacophony of the battle, and the alien exploded.

A screaming shadow passed over him. He looked up and followed the three AH-56D Cheyenne attack helicopters as they strafed the battlefield, vaporizing the alien horde with 20-millimeter depleted uranium rounds.

"Where the fuck did they come from?" PJ yelled.

"Who the fuck cares" Nelson shouted back.

Bolin cupped his hands over his ears and screamed over the roar, "Copy that." He turned to Nelson. "National Guard Cheyennes on deployment about a twenty clicks out. We got lucky. Designate targets with red smoke. Danger close, those are Army pilots, so marines and aliens look alike to them. Let's move the fuck away from this killing field."

Charlie element advanced to the school, letting the helicopters do their bloody work. At the far end of the corn field, the helos pitched up and rolled in hard on new targets. Rotors sliced the top of the corn rows and the Cheyenne's guns screamed like buzz saws. Hellfire missiles rippled from their stub wings. Aliens exploded into gory fragments. Purple lances rose in defiance, the same kind of fire that took down the *Hector*. One beam speared the lead helo, and it exploded mid-air. The second and third jinked back towards the parking lot, bunting lower, pushing down until their bellies dragged through the top of the corn rows. More beams split the air, hitting both.

"Cover," screamed Nelson. He and Bolin sprinted at an angle away from the doomed national guard choppers. Both helos hit the ground, breaking apart and tumbling. Ruptured fuel tanks exploded, and severed rotors flung away, scything marines down. Three marines vanished under a roiling wall of flame and wreckage. One emerged ablaze and screaming. He fell to the ground, legs kicking.

Nelson caught his breath. The flames from the burning wreckage created a barrier that would provide cover.

"War is hell," Bolin said.

"You're a real prick," Nelson responded.

"Least of my sins."

Bolin, Nelson, and other surviving marines crossed the parking lot, taking advantage of the time the helicopter pilots had bought them. They reached a breakaway ladder and climbed. They reached the top as three aliens emerged from a hole blasted into the roof. Seeing the marines, the creature's tossed their capture bags over the edge and shouldered their weapons. The marines moved quickly, energized by their disgust. Concentrated fire cut the monsters down before they get a shot off. One alien reared like an outraged stallion, bullets slamming into its exposed belly and splitting it open. It toppled over the edge, its fucked-up arms pinwheeling.

* * *

The bag was slick with blood and smelled of copper. Mare battled the urge to vomit. Near as she could tell, three others, their bodies contorted beyond human limits, shared the bag. Probably dead. In the darkness, her hands found someone's face and she touched it gently and brought her lips down to its ear. She spoke softly, but whoever it was did not respond. The alien resumed its run and she bounced against its flanks cocooned by soft broken bodies. She heard wood splintering, the soft pop of a small caliber weapon and desperate screaming. The bag opened relieving the suffocating heat. The screaming stopped and the alien thrust another victim into the bag.

"Hello," Marilyn whispered. "Hello?" She was desperate for human contact.

A child sobbed in raw terror.

Her hands sank into warm viscera and gore as she searched. She found the child's arm and pulled it closer. The child let out a blood-curdling scream that tapered off into sobs.

"I'm Marilyn. I'm with you." She wrapped her arms around the child and pulled it close. "It's okay. I'm Marilyn. Who are you?"

"W-William. I want to go home."

"I do too, William."

"Stay with me?"

"I will." She squirmed to find a better position, pulling the child close. The alien moved, picking up speed, and she slammed against its armored torso. She became aware of a sharp pain in the small of her back. She reached behind, and slowly pulled out the .45.

* * *

"Don't shoot the bags," Nelson ordered.

With the roof swept clear, Nelson dropped into the school through the same hole the monsters had blown into the building. He took point, leading three other marines, including PJ, into the east wing. Emergency lights illuminated swirls of gray, gun smoke and shattered brick dust. It collected in his nose and coated his tongue. Blood and water from burst pipes slicked the linoleum tiled floors. Notebook paper and textbooks soaked up the mess. Hand lettered posters advertising prom hung in tatters.

"School's out," PJ whispered.

"Forever," another Marine responded.

"Can it," Nelson snapped.

Armored interior doors and barrier gates hung off hinges. The dead and dismembered, both alien and human, littered the hall. The civilians had put up a hell of a fight.

They worked in silence, using hand signals to clear the rooms. Each one was an abattoir. Scrabbling claws and loud bangs echoed ahead. Nelson peered around a corner. A trapped alien, hunched over to keep from grazing the ceiling, rammed its body into a steel-reinforced classroom door. Nelson held up two fingers and pointed. PJ and another broke cover and crossed the hallway junction.

PJ looked to Nelson, who nodded.

"Here kitty, kitty, kitty," PJ called.

The alien whirled about, facing them. Rounds smashed into its upper torso, spraying the walls with that black shit they used for blood.

The alien returned fired with a volley that shattered sheet metal lockers and vaporized the brick behind them.

The alien reloaded and the marines returned the sentiment. Bullets stitched the creature's upper torso and found gaps in its shattered armor. The alien chittered madly, trapped at the end of the hall where its speed meant nothing without room to maneuver. Nelson's head throbbed from being in such close proximity to the thing. He could feel its utter indifference and contempt for humans. Hate rolled off the thing in ugly waves, threatening to swamp his mind. He would have ordered grenades, but a squirming silver bag of hostages lay at the monster's feet.

"Cease fire," Nelson called. He looked at the alien, focusing on the empty black hemispheres of its eyes.

Surrender, he thought at it.

The alien, standing in puddle of its own blood, hissed. Black blood drooled from its mouth in thick viscous strands.

It understood. Fuck me, it understood!

The alien hurled its empty weapon at them with enough force to drive it into the brick wall behind the shot-up school lockers. The creature seized the bulging silver capture bag and threw it with same force. The bag hit the wall and burst open, gushing blood, severed limbs and pulverized bodies onto the floor. The creature rammed the classroom door hard and the anchor bolts on the hinged side pulled free from brick. It vanished inside.

The marines advanced to the classroom door. Nelson peered in and pulled back.

"No humans. Southeast corner. It's pounding on the armored window." Nelson smiled. "Grenades." The marines grabbed their oversized anti-alien fragmentation grenades, pulled the pins, and lobbed them in. The explosion rocked the classroom, dropping suspended ceiling tiles and fogging the air with dust and black blood.

Nelson entered. The alien lay in a black, bloody sprawl, panting like an eviscerated dog clinging to whatever shreds of life remained. Spider-leg fingers grasped and clutched. The chest cilia surrounding its maw waved. PJ pointed his M-16 at the creature's surviving eye.

"No, here." With the tip of his own rifle, Nelson guided PJ's gun barrel to the hump on the alien's back.

PJ fired and the alien's head erupted into a fountain of gore, exposing brains like gray cauliflower florets.

Deck Sergeant Bolin barked suddenly through the tactical channel. "Nelson, report."

"Secure. The East Wing is secure."

"About fucking time. Take your men and assume firing positions on the roof. Three more breaches have opened up and the fuckers are streaming in! The school is now our fort. You get me?"

"Got you," Nelson murmured. A blood-soaked teacher staggered out of classroom closet. The man's eyes bulged with wild fear. Nelson grimaced at the sight of the coward and squared off on him. "Round up anyone you find. Gather any weapons and get to the roof to reinforce our positions."

"Yes, yes," the teacher responded, but Nelson wasn't sure he understood. The teacher stood statue-still, eyes glazed over with insanity.

"Move! Take charge," bellowed Nelson, a bit surprised at his own surety.

The man flinched and ran.

"That guy is about one-sixty pounds of alien chow. Don't expect too much from him," PJ said.

Nelson exited the room. His team followed him up a stairwell and into the dismal light on the roof. He bellied down in an empty sector next to a Marine wearing the flight patch of the *Achilles*.

"Fucking *Hector* bought it," the Marine from the *Achilles* spat.

"Old news," PJ said.

"Blown right of the sky. I had friends on that bird."

"Fuck," Nelson cursed.

"Town is fucking gone man. These fuckers have a hard on for Crooked Creek. We found a holding pen. Hundreds of people, like cattle for the slaughter!"

"Stay sharp," Nelson murmured. He removed himself from the chatterbox and picked a more peaceful corner of the battle. He surveyed the terrain. The trampled corn field was a hellscape of scorched crops and broken bodies. Toxic black smoke billowed, coating everything in a dismal gray. He retched at the scent of burnt meat. Alien chittering and high-pitched shrieks of horror surrounded him. A few untouched stands of green corn stalks waved in the fields. Evil shadows sprinted for cover through smoke from burning fires.

"They're regrouping," PJ noted.

"Command has closed the LZ due to the loss of the *Hector*," Captain Kristoff stated over the tactical channel. "No one knew they had that capability."

"Good news is the captain is still alive." PJ grinned. "No one knew he had that capability."

"Shut the fuck up, PJ," Nelson barked. He rolled onto his back and took a quick inventory of his ammo. PJ sidled up to him.

"Not the time for slap and tickle," Nelson said.

"Just bringing the party." He held out a silver hip flask. "One more nip left."

"Where the fuck did you find that?"

"Teacher's desk."

Nelson took it, unscrewed the cap and swallowed the warm whiskey. He handed the empty flask back and PJ flung it over the edge.

Movement. The school was about to be swarmed.

"We could use some artillery right about now," PJ sighed.

Nothing better than artillery to turn monsters into mulch.

The aliens appeared out of the dust like a nightmare cavalry charge. Rider and mount fused into a single obscenity. They weaved back and forth, leaping like gazelles over the torn apart cars, moving with frightening speed and spraying the school with gunfire.

The marines scythed them down in a tumble of flailing limbs and hideous screams. The monsters crumpled, falling over each other, but they kept coming. M18A1Claymore mines detonated and high-velocity steel balls shredded them further. Still, they came. The first ones reached the base of the school, and Nelson and PJ dropped grenades over the sides. The grenade's explosions sprayed alien chunks into the air.

A clawed hand slammed down at the edge of the roof. Its owner screeched a hideous sound and pulled itself up. Nelson jammed his rifle into the alien's mouth and fired. Bullets exploded out the back of its head and it fell back, taking two of its comrades with it. Another clawed hand snapped forward and snagged his body armor, PJ shot the alien and it fell backwards, taking Nelson over the roof's edge with a yell.

He landed hard amidst the tangled pile of destroyed alien bodies. Weaponless, he rolled clear and sucked in a breath clotted with dust and vaporized flesh. He pried a weapon from the dead grasp of a Marine and fired into the bulk of a charging alien. His men leaned over the edge exposing themselves to fire. They hosed down the aliens to give him a chance. He risked a glance over his shoulder. No way back up. The only option was forward into the bloody melee.

He limped deeper into the parking lot, seeking some sort of cover and firing at targets as they presented themselves. Nightmares emerged out of the fields, heedless of their own destruction. The sky glowed with the opening of multiple breaches that spread in an arc from the north to the west. There had never been so many before. Bullets snapped and whirred around him. He was in the center of the kill zone. An alien head and torso loomed over the car he sheltered behind. The alien scrambled to reach him while attempting to bring its own weapon to bear. Nelson jammed his rifle's barrel into a chink in the creature's armor and fired at full auto. The creature screamed and pushed back. Its torso split. Slimy, black organs gushed out in steaming flood.

"*Ulysses* is inbound for civilian evac," Captain Kristoff screamed over the channel. "Clear the courtyard. They are coming down in the school courtyard."

Nelson grimaced. The courtyard? Fucking hell. They'll need some crazy ass pilots to plant a ship in the school courtyard, especially under siege. He scanned for better cover and spotted specks on the horizon, tiny dark dots, blooming into strike aircraft that moved way too fucking fast.

"Heads down, alpha strike inbound," Kristoff roared.

"Oh, fuck me," Nelson cursed. "Fuck me." He ran across the parking lot, exposing himself, heedless of the heavy alien projectiles pinging the air around him. He dove into the drainage ditch surrounding the school parking lot and scrambled into a buried culvert, low-crawling for his life. He reached the dark, cobwebbed center, and felt something with multiple legs tickle his neck. Nelson opened his mouth and covered his ears.

The tactical channel screamed. "Take cover!"

* • *

Six F-108 Rapier's flew so fast they outran their own sound. Their supersonic shock wave left a blasted trail behind them. Each strike aircraft carried a narrow diameter thermobaric bomb, the most powerful explosive outside of nuclear weaponry. They overflew his position, and he felt the shock of their passage a good four feet underground.

Aerosolized explosive and powdered aluminum mixed with atmosphere oxygen, and the sky exploded. Both ends of the culvert burst with light and heat. The ground compressed around him, and the air in the culvert was sucked out. Concussion waves sledgehammered his body and the ground heaved, rattling him like a pea in a can.

The air returned, and Nelson knew he was alive because he hurt so bad. He spat blood and dirt and scrambled towards the flame-colored light at the end of the culvert. Acrid, hot wind hit his face as he emerged into a chiaroscuro of flames and dark, swirling ash wrapping cars smashed flat by the hand of God. Ruptured gas tanks burned. The school still stood, but all its armored windows had been blown in and the wall closest to the strike had collapsed. The thermobaric bombs had crushed the alien assault. Their ruptured bodies lay everywhere. Limbs curled in like dead spiders.

The flickering, actinic glow of the breaches smeared the sky. They were still open.

"Anybody? Can anybody read me?" he gasped into the tactical channel. The world had a muffled quality. *Blown eardrums.* He stopped, bent over, and coughed up bitter blood. He spat into the ash.

"*Ulysses* is inbound," Captain Kristoff roared over the channel.

Some crazy bastards were bringing down an evac ship in a Hail Mary play. Every ballistic assault vehicle was a throw away. One launch, one landing. Mission complete when boots hit the ground. But for the *Ulysses* to have fuel for another takeoff, it would need to launch empty. There would be no resupply or reinforcement. Not everyone was going home. Certainly not anyone wearing a uniform.

He looked up and saw an alien galloping down the road towards the school, a silver capture bag dangling at its side. *No fucking way.* No fucking way this thing was going to gallop down an American road with Americans in its lunch sack. He ran an intercept angle to meet the creature and make it suffer. Every step shocked his body with a lance of pain that ran up his spine like a lightning strike. He leapt over fire and twisted metal; his boots crunched through pulverized roadbed and broken glass. He stood exposed, without cover or fear, blocking the filthy monster's path.

The alien raised its own gun.

Nelson fired first. At this range, the bullets would be not much more than an annoyance to the creature, but it would spoil its aim. He fired short sharp bursts. The ground popped around him as the alien's own bullets sought him out. A single round would vaporize his torso and blow him apart, but he was beyond caring. He shot low and the creature buckled, one of its forelegs bent the wrong way and shattered. Shards of bone burst from the alien's leg and it screamed as its hindquarters pitched up and over its upper torso. It somersaulted and came to rest in a burning corn field.

Nelson limped to the dropped capture bag and slit it open with his battle knife. He had low expectations, figuring that there would be nothing but pulverized humans inside. He was right about the pulverized people, but the soft gore had cushioned two survivors. The bruised and bloody faces of a teenaged girl and younger boy gazed back at him. She rose, soaked in blood, .45 in hand. She lifted the weapon and fired over his shoulder until the hammer fell on an empty. The alien, he had assumed dead, dropped. Its flanks heaved with wheezy, wet breaths. Hate and loathing rippled off it. Nelson's head pounded with the nearness of the thing. He shot it in the hump to end his pain.

Fuck you.

123

The girl tried to step clear of the capture bag and its gory contents and slipped. She stumbled and he caught her with his free arm. She dropped her empty gun and wrapped her arms around him holding tight. He lifted her clear of the body parts and set her back down. She held tight and he let her.

"Thank you," she breathed into his neck. "Thank you." He could barely hear her. Her lips on his neck felt like kisses.

A boom of thunder, and the short, sharp crack of air compressed beyond the speed of sound signaled the arrival of the *Ulysses*. The empty Ballistic Assault Vehicle fell through the sky suspended by the ferocious thrust of its aerospike engines. It dropped into the school courtyard. Not something typically seen in Montana.

"Not much time left, darlin'," he said to the girl. "That's your ride." She slipped free of him. He shouldered his rifle and scooped up the blood-smeared boy. "Let's go, sweetheart. She took his hand and held tight.

They ran across open ground and climbed the rubble of the school's collapsed wall. Two marines, covered in ash and filth, set up a heavy machine gun. Others stacked slabs of concrete and broken brick for cover. More breaches had flashed into existence. They would come. Nelson stepped over the dead and wounded that lined the school corridors. He ignored barked orders and dragged the girl to the Ballistic Assault Vehicle.

The *Ulysses* filled the scorched courtyard. *Fuck. Damn good piloting.* He didn't see any fresh faces, clean uniforms, or crates of ammo. A female crewman stopped him at the boarding ramp to the lower deck.

"Is that their blood? Are they green?" asked the crewman.

He gave her a puzzled look.

"Any injuries," she clarified.

Nelson shook his head. "Negative." It made sense to evacuate uninjured. Injured could not survive the launch stress of a ship designed to deliver strong, healthy marines into a combat zone.

The crewman frowned at the boy. "He's too young. Too small to secure. He stays."

A death sentence. No one was leaving this corner of hell except by the *Ulysses* and even then, doubtful. The *Ulysses* was probably destined to become a spectacular fireball in the sky.

"I'll secure him."

"I said —"

Nelson raised the muzzle of his rifle and poked her under the throat with the barrel. "He's green," he whispered. He would be damned if he would go through all this bullshit to let this child die.

She stared at him for a long moment.

"Well, one of us has to fucking blink," said Nelson. "And I have the gun."

"Go," the crewman murmured.

He pushed past her into the lower deck. Chaos. It was full of stunned or crying kids from middle to high school age. Too many for the number of seats. Crew struggled to make order and secure the kids.

"Climb," he motioned to the girl. "To the top."

She went up the ladder, and he followed. The boy clung to him like a shell-shocked koala. The top troop deck, his deck, was only half full. *Full on crazy hadn't quite reached this level. Kids. Makes sense to take kids. Less weight.*

He found two seats next to each other. "Sit," he ordered her. She sat and tried to make sense of the straps. He pried the boy away from his body and strapped him into the seat, taking as much slack out of the straps as he could. The boy did not struggle. He just stared. He turned to the girl and cinched the straps until she winced.

"What's your name?"

"Marilyn," she replied.

"Marilyn. Pretty name." He ripped his nametag and unit patch from his uniform and handed the lot to her. "Remember me, please. Can you do that?"

"I will," said Marilyn.

"I've got to get back to work."

She reached out and grabbed him by his combat harness.

She pulled him close and moved her hands to the side of his face and held him there. She craned her neck forward and kissed him as best she could. "Thank you," she whispered.

* * *

Nelson, PJ, and Bolin crouched against the far wall of a classroom hoping that when the *Ulysses* launched, they would not be buried alive or burned to death. He slumped letting his muscles relax and uncoil. *How long had it been since I was in sunny California? Four, maybe five hours? Hard to tell.* He touched his split nose. A riot had broken out when the *Ulysses* sealed its hatches, and he had taken a brick to the face from a civilian left behind.

"The only easy day," said PJ

"Is yesterday," finished Nelson. Exhaustion enveloped him in its warm embrace. Through the blown-in windows the sky glowed with weird energy of new breaches forming. The aliens were not finished with Crooked Creek.

"Brace yourselves," screamed Captain Kristoff over the tac channel. "*Braaaaace!*"

"Damned if he ain't still alive," said PJ. "I'm starting to like the son-of-a-bitch."

"Good Captain," agreed Nelson. "Best one we got."

"Only because all the others are dead," said Bolin.

The *Ulysses* launched.

The school's thick concrete walls vibrated like the epicenter of an earthquake. The air pressure shifted violently, and the heavy classroom door, braced with desks and wreckage, blew open. Dust, debris, and scalding water vapor exhaust blasted through the room. Nelson covered his eyes and prayed. The shriek of engines faded, and Nelson found himself not vaporized for the second time that day.

Bolin recovered first. He stood from behind his barricade of desks; waved dust from his face. "All clear, marines, back to your firing positions. This ain't fucking over."

Nelson pushed up from his huddle and leaned against the wall. Fatigue soaked his muscles. If he could, he would just drop to the floor and sleep. Maybe dream of a girl he knew.

"You okay?" asked PJ.

"Yea, fine," said Nelson.

He followed Bolin and PJ to the roof. A naked civilian, burned so badly his skin sloughed off in ragged sheets, screamed with incoherent pain.

PJ shot him. "A mercy," he explained.

"Yea, mercy," Nelson murmured.

Up on the roof, he looked out over charred fields at thousands of aliens galloping through newly opened breaches, their horrific screeching filling the air. They charged, shoulder to shoulder, spraying the school with their weapons. They reached the boundary of the kill zone, and Nelson opened up on full auto, firing into the crushing mass of aliens. Everyone else followed suit. There was no need to conserve ammo.

Bullets slammed home, blowing off limbs and punching holes into monstrous bodies. Sappers hit their clackers, and the last of the claymores detonated, shredding the aliens to fragments. The monsters bunched up, trampling each other, crushing their brothers into screaming piles to reach the marines.

"Semper Fi, motherfuckers," screamed Nelson. Most of PJ lay dead beside him. Bolin was gone, lost somewhere in the smoky haze.

He looked skyward. The *Ulysses* was just a point of light, soaring up and away, penetrating the high cirrus clouds. Another bright star flickered and fell towards them. And he thought of the last, best kiss he'd had from a pretty girl. He stood, exposing himself to enemy fire. He didn't care. No need to care anymore. His weapon clicked. Empty. He drew his knife, hoping there was time for one last kill.

"Firefall," said Captain Kristoff, a hitch to his voice. "It's been an honor."

The falling star grew brighter, and then the world filled with a brilliant, penetrating light.

KATADESMOS

Amanda Dier

C lear!"

"Clear!" Neil called back, keeping an eye on the room around him.

"Good out here!" Heisman called from the door out into the street.

The rest of the squad filtered back into the main room as Neil started checking the pile of crates at the edge of the room for anything that even remotely resembled an incendiary device. Nothing. Just crates of what Neil could only assume were guns, drugs and supplies.

A smaller crate on the top of the pile caught his eye, and he carefully lifted the top, feeling for any catch between the lid and an IED buried somewhere in the box. He should have asked someone to spot him, but they were all busy and he was driven to know what was inside. His armpits grew damp as he wiggled the wood, but the lid came free with nothing trailing behind and he set it aside. The box was devoid of weapons but the stone tablet within indicated another crime. Archaeological theft.

Neil cautiously removed the tablet, not wanting to damage it, although the chipped sides gave testimony to either prior rough handling or immense age. Carefully carved creatures cavorted along the top of the tablet, chief among them being a four-winged angel with a lion's head. Some of them, especially the angel, looked familiar, but Neil couldn't place it. He wanted to put the tablet down, but his fingers tightened around it, and an unpleasant feeling sat deep in his stomach, weighted like he'd swallowed a brick.

"What's that?" Sergeant Aken came up behind him and started rustling through the box.

"Old tablets I guess," Neil said.

"Didn't know hadji liked this kind of stuff," Aken said doubtfully.

"It is weird." Neil glanced to the dead hadji on the floor next to them. "Most of the time they destroy this stuff out of spite. Wonder why they kept it."

"Just guns in here," Parker grunted, foraging through a nearby box.

"Anything weird?" Aken asked.

"Nah, looks like Neil got the spooky box," Alvarez said with a grin.

"Bullets in this one," Baker called.

The team medic stepped back from examining Heisman's shoulder. He'd taken a close shot that had hit the wall and sent shards of wood into his neck and shoulder.

"Lucky he wasn't a better shot," Hill said, nodding back towards the old AK on the floor next to the body.

"Good," Aken said. "Let's mark this house for pickup and move on to the next."

"Can I see that?" Hill asked, grabbing the tablet from Neil's hands, turning it over and leaving red smears on the clay surface.

"Jeez, Hill, can you not get blood on everything?" he snapped, snatching it back.

Hill rolled his sandy, bloody fingertips together. "My bad," he said, but Neil was focused on the tablet.

The front of the inscribed clay had changed. Gone was the rough surface with a few smears of red. All the letters of whatever dead language it was written in had filled with shining red, the exact shade of the blood Hill was still tacking between his fingers. Sheer malevolence radiated from the thing, and Neil wanted badly to put it down but found himself unable to let it go.

"Uhh, sir?" Neil said, frantically gesturing at Aken. "Hill did something—"

A screech rent the air outside, and Heisman slowly eased back from the door.

Aken stomped towards Neil, clearly intending to take the tablet, but most of Neil's attention was focused on Heisman now.

"Shut the fuck up," Aken hissed. The rest of the men were rapidly falling silent as Heisman carefully, but quickly, shut the door to the street. The air in the front room was suddenly stiflingly hot, and Neil had to resist the urge to pull his collar away from his throat. Crackling had replaced the silence left after the shriek in front of the house. The smell of hot sand and dust filled his nose, and the air was drying out. Fast. It was always uncomfortably dry in Iraq, but the air smelled almost burned now.

Baker leaned to look outside, moving a lot quieter than he had before.

Heisman's face was white, his eyes anxiously looking past them to the other door at the back of the room. Parker held his rifle at the ready and stepped through it to re-check the rest of the house.

"Mother fuck," Baker whispered, peering around a curtain into the street. "Fucking Satan," he said.

"The fuck is out there?" Aken snapped.

Baker gestured to the sergeant, who stalked forward, his gaze promising punishment in Baker's near future.

Neil crept to the other window. Both men were glued to the dirty glass and watching something outside. Aken's hands were clenching and unclenching around his radio and sidearm. Tension flooded the room. Hands slammed against magazines, making sure they were seated, accompanied by the cloth-on-cloth sound of his teammates checking their spares.

Instead of the large group of men with weapons Neil had expected, a being crafted of air and fire drifted down the street, gazing listlessly from side to side. Neil's first thought was an honor killing, that someone had been lit on fire and left to die, but the movements were too smooth for that.

"The fuck is that?" Aken said.

Neil didn't want to be a smartass, but he'd been reading the books his culture-oriented wife had sent him, and one of them had been on the mythology of the region they were freeing.

When he was able to video-call in the morning just as she was going to bed, he'd watched her read Middle-Eastern fairy tales to her still-flat belly.

"I think it's an ifrit," he said quietly.

"A *what?*" Aken hissed.

"Uh... a genie, sir," he said, trying to keep a straight face. "Fiery appearance, pretty malevolent, usually lives in a cave—"

"You're telling me that thing out there is from Aladdin," Aken spat.

"Does it look blue, sir?" he shot back.

Hill joined Neil at his window while Heisman moved to watch the back of the house, looking like he'd rather be anywhere but here.

"When I'm not sleeping, I'm reading, and sometimes I read about fucking folklore. It's basically an angry demon."

"Does it grant wishes?"

"Why? Did you want to go out and ask it?" Neil said.

"You could ask it for a bigger dick," Baker suggested helpfully.

"Or a dick in general," Parker whispered, coming up behind them. "Everything's still good upstairs, by the way. What are we looking at?"

"Bloor thinks Aladdin's outside," Hill said.

Neil ignored him and just pointed at the ifrit.

Parker sucked in a breath. "Is that fucking *fire?*"

Neil stood back from the window and sighted down his ACOG. The magnification didn't give him much more detail, but he was clearly able to see the terrifyingly surreal sight of fire and cinders buoyed on an impossibly fast air current somehow contained within the vague outline of a human body.

"We're going to ignore it," Aken said.

"The ifrit," Neil said, just to make sure he was hearing Aken correctly.

"I mean... it's closing in," Baker said, wiping sweat from his brow. "What if it wants Neil's tablet?"

For a split-second Neil thought about putting the tablet on the front step, but he didn't want to let go of it. He patted down his jacket and realized the inscribed clay was just small enough to fit into one of the pockets of his vest. He dumped the translation packet that had been inside and replaced it with the tablet. Somehow he didn't think the ifrit would respond to 'Do not resist' in modern Arabic.

"It's coming this way now," Parker warned.

"Amazing, now it knows where we are," Heisman groaned.

"Hill, why did you have to touch it with your fucking tampon fingers?" Neil asked, kicking him in the ankle. Hill ignored him.

"Do we shoot it?" Baker asked, stroking the barrel of his M4A1 like he might a dog.

"What part are we supposed to shoot?" Hill asked, sweat glistening on his upper lip.

There was no clear face on the ifrit, and Neil wondered if there was a brain in the head at all.

"Head and center of mass," Aken said. "If it looks like a human, aim for the most important parts."

Baker went upstairs to take position in a second-story window with his SAW and the rest of them sighted on the creature that seemed unbothered by the baking sunlight pouring down over the street.

As soon as Baker reported that he was in position and aimed down at the thing, Aken told him to blow it back to whatever cave it crawled from.

A hail of bullets smacked into the street around it, and the ifrit froze as the green tipped rounds and occasional tracer passed straight through it like it was made of shadow, not fire.

The SAW's chattering ceased and the ifrit slowly turned its face up to the room where Baker had fired from.

"Sitrep!" Aken yelled.

"It's looking at me, sir." Baker's voice drifted back down the stairs. "I would definitely fucking say it knows we're here."

Following the sound of his voice, the ifrit started moving towards the door of the house again.

Neil heard the scrape of something heavy moving over the floor behind them. Heisman was throwing his entire body weight against a crate to shove it across the floor.

"Block the windows," he grunted, and Neil and Parker dashed to help him.

Aken stayed by the window, counting down the distance as the ifrit neared the building. They managed to completely cover the windows with only three yards to spare.

A smell like burning wood filtered past the crates, but the door remained intact. Above them, a brief *whoop* sounded. "It can't get through the door!" Baker yelled, and the relief in his voice was obvious.

Neil sighed in relief and felt the knot in his belly start to ease just a little. Baker was a quiet man who didn't seek to fill the silence by talking, and Neil had rarely heard him yell.

A burst of rounds firing above made them all jump, and Baker started calling, "It's looking up at me! Can this thing fly or am I—"

A bellow that was unmistakably Baker's set a chill in Neil's blood, and he pounded up the stairs through increasingly hot air and found the upstairs room that overlooked the street filled with greasy smoke. Flames surrounded a rapidly charring human figure in the corner, and there was yelling behind him. Shots rang out but nothing changed. The flames raged on and Baker kept screaming. He didn't even seem to be pausing to draw breath anymore. Hands pulled Neil back through the door and down the stairs. Men surrounded him on all sides as they all fought to get down the stairs and away from the impromptu barbecue. Baker's screams had climbed the register into a high, thin whine that Neil barely recognized as human.

"Come on," Aken yelled. They reorganized into formation with Neil covering the rear.

"Fuck, fuck, fuck," Alvarez chanted.

They scrambled out the back door that led into an alley, watching for any movement that meant either hadji or the ifrit. Inside the house, Baker's screams abruptly cut off. The sudden silence was suffocating.

"What the fuck?" "Where's Baker?" "What's on fire?" all scrambled together until Aken fired a single round into the ground.

"Shut the *fuck* up." The sergeant looked pissed. His face was pale with a greasy sheen, and Neil's stomach dropped as he saw the tremor in his sarge's hands where they held the rifle close to his chest.

"Baker's dead," Aken said shortly. "Neil's Aladdin got him. Radio's still out so we're going to get out of this block, back towards somewhere with better reception so I can get some help. Now form up."

No one argued, and they started moving south down the alley. Protruding mashrabiya coupled with a sun that was rapidly lowering in the sky cast the alley in shadow. The still-bright opening of the main street lay ahead of them now as they worked their way down the curve of the alley.

Bright red blood glistened in great splashes on the walls, darkening in some places... or it could have been shit smears. It made Neil uneasy and he raised his arm to tap Aken on the shoulder. A gibbering noise from one of the open windows caught everyone's attention, but before anyone could pinpoint the sound, a skeletal woman lurched out of a dark doorway and started swiping at Aken.

Each slash left rents in his jacket, and Aken stepped back and smashed his rifle butt into her face. The woman fell backwards silently, then rose with unnatural speed and no hint of injury on her twisted visage.

She came at Hill now, hands extended to reveal fingertips that narrowed to bone-white claws.

Neil didn't bother to explain what she was. His M4A1 thundered in his hands and the night spirit dropped after multiple rounds punched through the head and torso.

"Jesus, Neil," Alvarez was repeating over and over as the ringing in Neil's ears slowly wound down.

Neil dragged the clawed hand out from under the body with the tip of his rifle.

"That thing wasn't human," Hill whispered, flinching when Neil stepped on the wrist and made the fingers curl into a loose fist of blade-sharp bone.

"What's this one called?" Aken asked, running his fingers over his jacket, clearly feeling for blood or skin tears.

"Uh, Lilith? I think," he said. "No. Lulu. Lilu? Fuck." Neil shrugged and it felt like he was letting everyone down. If he'd only known more, maybe Baker would still be alive. The tablet weighed a thousand pounds in his pocket. If he could just look at it again...

"Keep moving," the sergeant hissed. "We'll head for one of the walled compounds that's on the river north of Purple Heart Boulevard."

As a group they made their way to the end of the block, and Neil popped his head around the corner. There was no sign of the ifrit, but billows of smoke were coming from the house they'd originally holed up in.

Aken led them north and east towards the Tigris River. Neil couldn't think of the exact compound Aken must have in mind — there had been so many — but hopefully they'd be able to reinforce it and hole up until the rest of the platoon arrived. There were no actual extractions. Not in Baghdad.

On edge was how they normally operated, clearing buildings and watching for an attack, but never blind panic. This felt close, though. Neil didn't want to be roasted to death like Baker had been. He started at every instance of heat or light, even if it was just the heat of sun-warmed brick pressing through his pants or the glare of sunlight through a narrow opening.

Every street seemed to bristle with menace, and every living hadji they saw was a potential enemy until either the soldiers or the local had ducked out of sight. Neil didn't care so much about the dead ones that littered the street, half crushed into a paste on the ground.

The team had just entered another back alley when the second Lilu attacked. Aken didn't hesitate this time, and opened fire, blowing it apart. They didn't stop to examine the corpse this time, double-timing it into the street leading to the Sarafiya bridge.

The ground started to rumble, and they swayed on their feet as a gargantuan rhino lumbered into view. Snorting in rage, it dropped its head and charged, shoving cars aside effortlessly. Its ridiculously long horn was already slick with blood. Had it been hunting the streets of Baghdad since Hill had touched the tablet?

Alvarez's shout snapped the team out of their shock. They moved, looking for an escape.

Aken hung a right and dove down a narrow passage. Neil followed, and a glance over this shoulder found everyone else piling in right behind him. The alley was blind, ending in a high wall. They all crowded against it, desperately scrambling as the rhino pushed its immense, armored bulk into the mouth of the alley.

Roaring, it strained and bellowed at the soldiers, trying to reach them with its horn.

"How do we kill it?!" Hill screamed.

"I don't fucking know," Aken yelled. "Shoot it!"

They turned as one and went full auto, opening up at the bulky head that was getting dangerously close to impaling them. Their bullets did nothing against the rhino's armored hide, and only seemed to piss it off more. The masonry was starting to crumble around its bulk as it forced itself further into the alley. The team reloaded, but no one fired another shot. The weapons they had were useless against this thing.

Neil glanced desperately at the doorway they'd passed on the way in, but before he could consider it Hill shoved past him in a desperate bid to escape. Aken hollered at Hill to stop just as the rhino's horn punched through the medic's vest and out his back, spraying the team in blood. The rhino lifted its head, and Hill's body slid further down the horn, his scream pitching higher and higher. Before Neil and the others could react, the rhino snorted and retreated out of the alley, taking Hill with it. Out of sight, there was a *crunch* and Hill's screams faded to gurgling, then silence.

Neil stood dumbstruck until he was pulled into the doorway Hill had died trying to get into.

They regrouped in one of the inner rooms that didn't have a window for the rhino to see them through.

Three bodies littered the floor. All were men, unarmed and looking like normal hadji. He'd have thought they were regular victims of the assholes preying like wolves on the civilian population except for the deep slices on their bodies and the fear etched on their faces. A bullet hole to the face just made you dead. These men had suffered. Like Hill had suffered, whimpering and skewered and utterly trapped.

Impotent fury swirled inside him. It clawed at his stomach, filled his throat with bile and his ears with Hill's desperate screams. No matter how many bullets he'd shot at the thing, it had still been alive to kill Hill.

Roaring overtook the screaming in his ears, and he bent and vomited onto the floor. He hadn't eaten anything, had barely drank any water that day, but his stomach kept heaving until he was spitting out stomach acid with nothing else left to give. The thin liquid spattered the floor and the tips of his boots, leaving trickles through the thin layer of dust.

Neil's hands fumbled at the top of the pouch that held the tablet, and he pulled it out with trembling fingers, studying the intricate carving for clues. The rhino was there along with a slight figure that could have been the lilu, and on the other end of the assemblage hovered the ifrit, with carefully impressed swirls filling in its body. Between those, however, were three creatures Neil could only guess at.

The four-winged angel with a lion's head, a grotesquely tall humanoid figure with obscenely long arms, and then rounding off the trio was a donkey with the head of a lioness and a massive, drooping belly that touched the ground between its feet.

He described them for the others and hoped there was nothing else missing from the tablet that would be making an appearance. Several of the monsters from the stories he'd read had been poisonous, but no matter how he tried he couldn't remember the names or descriptions.

"You don't remember anything else?" Aken asked. "Fucking anything? Speed, weapons, do they come on flying fucking carpets?"

"Just the poison," Neil said. "We could stay out of hand-to-hand range just to be safe," he suggested, but it felt lame, even to him. Poison was probably the least of their worries with a fucking tank with a horn running around. They could all be stacked up on it like a shishkabob with room to spare.

Aken's shoulder wounds seemed freshly clotted and free of infection or anything that any of them recognized as poison now that Hill wasn't around to ask. Neil kept expecting to hear Hill make a stupid remark as he probed the deep cuts on Aken's shoulder with fingers that were far from tender, but the air around them lay still and silent except for their rasping breaths. The air wasn't hot like it had been before the arrival of the ifrit, but Neil couldn't stop imagining what was next. The finger-bladed woman had come silently without warning. Would the next attack be a poison miasma? A hail of arrows that turned the sky black with sheer numbers? His throat was tight; was that an invisible cloud of poison or the fact that they were now two men down? The bodies on the floor had swollen wounds to their faces and arms, but was that rot or something more sinister? Something pathological?

Would Neil live to meet his child?

Aken swatted Neil's hands away. "We go out, head left, follow the street around to the right for a little bit, and make another right," Aken announced. They all formed up behind him: Neil, Heisman, Alvarez, and Parker.

"The building I'm thinking of is on the left with a stone wall and blue glass in the front windows. Get in and check all the rooms, close off any doors to the outside. Neil, you're with me. There's a gate in the front and we're going to use it to close off the courtyard from the street."

Weapons at the ready, they moved quietly out into the street. Nothing moved. They advanced as quickly and as quietly as they could, following Aken's directions carefully. Shadows lurked in every corner, deepening as the sun sank closer to the horizon. Once he thought he saw naked women with freakishly long hands, but they ducked out of sight before his roving eyes could really focus on them. They passed two more bodies in the streets, but both were women in burqas and no one wanted to strip them to see what kind of wounds had killed them.

Neil realized with some relief that he was starting to recognize some of the buildings around them now. They'd gone door to door only a week ago, clearing houses and rooting out insurgents. Most of the people they'd seen had been innocent, cowering away and begging shrilly. Weaponless. Defenseless. He wondered where they'd gone.

He'd pointed his rifle into the faces of so many merchants, so many women and children. There was no way to tell who was hiding a rifle under their robes, who had explosives concealed in a vest underneath the heavy fabric of a burqa or chador. So they'd threatened all of them, watching hands and eyes for signs of intent or bodies for sudden, purposeful movement.

And now they were all missing and the neighborhood of Utafiyah was a godforsaken ghost town. Distant screams made Neil hunch lower to the ground as they moved, and once he heard a distant *whump* and saw smoke billow up a dozen streets over. The screams cut off one by one, but the smoke continued.

The rolling gate of the compound Aken had chosen sat ajar as they rounded the last turn. The door still hung open from where they'd kicked it in a week ago, and there were no fresh tracks in the dust and rubble that littered the yard. It appeared to be as empty as it had been after they'd cleared it. They split into two groups, and after the others were out of sight clearing the house, Neil tried but couldn't keep his breathing from speeding up again. What if another lilu was in the house killing them one by one? Or worse, a pack of them. A night demon for every member of the team.

Neil cleared debris from the gate's path while Aken pushed it closed before they locked it as best as they could and Neil jammed rock into any gaps, trying to block it up.

They followed the path the others had taken up the marble-paved driveway and closed the front door behind them. Then Heisman and Parker shoved an ancient bed that took both of them to move across.

"Any other doors to the outside?" Aken asked.

"Just a kitchen door and we have a stove and some furniture in front of it," Parker said.

"Windows?"

"Still boarded up from the last time we were here," Heisman replied.

Neil left the tablet propped against a wall in what used to be the living room and followed Alvarez up the stairs.

They posted up on the roof, watching the street in front of the compound, the alley behind it, and the two properties with busted walls on either side for any sign of movement.

The sun was getting low when Aken came up to switch with him, and all three scanned the horizon.

"Think Aladdin's gonna glow in the dark?" Aken said.

"I hope so," Neil said. "Make him easier to spot."

Aken nodded jerkily. "I tried the radio again. We're at least a full kilometer from where we were and it's still nothing but fucking static."

With a nod, Neil headed downstairs. Parker was alone in the living room when he got down there, fumbling with what looked like a cell phone, the tablet, and the last of the available sunlight.

"Taking pictures for posterity?" Neil asked.

Parker held up the phone. "It's a satphone," he said by way of greeting.

"Dude, that's an iPhone," Neil said. "It's not gonna send shit out here."

"The sleeve turns it into a satphone," Parker said, pointing to the case that Neil realized had an antenna on it that looked like it had been stolen from a 90s brick phone.

Neil stared at it, the glimmer of an idea giving him the first hope he'd had since Baker ate it.

"I need to borrow that," he said abruptly, grabbing for it.

Parker resisted his tugs.

"Need to call my wife," Neil said shortly. "She's a college professor that specializes in cuneiform studies."

"And?" Parker grouched back.

"I knew about the ifrit and the witch-thing. Where do you think I learned that? My fucking wife. You think I can identify all this stuff? She'll probably be able to tell us what kind of praying might make them go away."

"I tried that," Parker said, slapping the phone in his hand. "Jesus ain't listening. See if your wife is."

Neil texted the photos Parker had taken to his wife's phone number, both front and back, and then the lineup of monsters at the top of the tablet.

He called, and Stacey picked up instantly. Any time on the phone was rare, and she was good about answering numbers she didn't recognize now.

"Neil?" she sounded uncertain.

Neil pressed it to his ear like he could magically transport through the phone line and reappear back in Illinois.

"I don't have much time to talk. Did you get the pictures I sent?"

"No... yes! Wow, what are these? Ooh, is that Pazuzu? And Sumerian cuneiform?"

"Yeah. Listen hon, I don't have a ton of time. Need you to look for anything useful in that and identify the things on the top."

He checked his watch. 1913 Iraq time. That meant 1113 at home, just before noon.

"So, University of Chicago?" Aken said.

Neil jumped. He hadn't even noticed his sarge come down from the roof.

"Yeah," he said, covering the mouthpiece on the phone. "She teaches Sumerian to kids who want to be archaeologists."

"Lucky us," Aken said.

Neil nodded.

In his ear, Stacey started rattling off identifications.

He scrambled for his pocket notebook and started writing, with Aken and Parker peering over his shoulder.

Lilu – female night demon, probably the woman from earlier

142

Edimmu – demon, dark, poison claws, sneaky
Karkadann – rhino thing with the long horn, horn is poison
Ifrit – Aladdin
Pazuzu – four-winged dude, invoked against Lamashtu, has lion head and bird feet
Lamashtu – Donkey body, lion head, hates pregnant women and babies.

Aken's lip curled. "You couldn't get a list of weaknesses?"

"We already know we can shoot the Lilu," Neil pointed out, covering the mouthpiece again. "And I guess Pazuzu might end up fighting Lamashtu. That might take those two out of the fight, right?"

Aken shrugged. "Aladdin is still made of fucking fire, bullets didn't touch the rhino, and I don't know what the fuck Eddy-moo is."

"Maybe we'll get lucky and bullets will work on it too?" Parker suggested hopefully.

Aken shrugged. "I don't want to count on that. Find out everything she knows about these things. I'm going back upstairs. Let me know what she says."

"Babe," Neil said into the phone. "There's some weird stuff going on here. I gotta go. Text this number back when you find something in the writing?"

What she sent back a few minutes later wasn't a text message, but a bunch of crossed out translations and notes at the bottom in precise handwriting.

It's a trap tablet. It's a prayer to Lamashtu and Pazuzu along with a few other types of udug (demon) that they were sometimes associated with, and if you bleed on it then it summons them.

"Fucking Hill," Parker muttered under his breath.

She'd circled something in Sumerian at the end of the notes. The phone rang.

"The thing I circled?" she said. "The key word here is *ma-la-a-ne-ta* which breaks down into 'her male companion' but the thing afterwards is confusing because the ancient Sumerians didn't exactly do love when they did marriage. The word for love also means to mark off land, so this is probably her male lover or husband. But uh, Lamashtu wasn't exactly a positive character in ancient Sumerian myths so maybe it means Pazuzu?"

Neil almost put up a hand to stop her and then remembered she couldn't see it. "Ok, so now what?"

"We're still working on that," Stacey said, and he groaned. "I'm sorry!" she snapped. "Mahmood is checking some translations he already has of similar tablets but they're taking a while to find. What's going on, Neil?"

"Okay, okay, okay," he said soothingly without actually answering her question. "Just uh, let us know when you find anything."

Yells and rifle fire burst out from upstairs, and he grabbed his gun from where it had been sitting next to the tablet.

"Be right back," he said hurriedly, ignoring her panicked calls as they echoed from the speakerphone.

Neil got to the roof in time to see Heisman's gun absolutely wreck the head of a tall, androgynous figure that was black even against the encroaching night.

He watched Heisman kick the slumped body off the edge of the roof, and Aken lowered a visibly injured Alvarez to the ground.

"What the fuck was that," he moaned, clutching at his bleeding throat.

"Bloor's wife said it was an Eddy-moo," Aken said. "Was that the poison one?"

"I think so," Neil said. Bile rose in his throat, pushing fear in front of it as he scanned the night for more things his wife had described and hoped nothing that wasn't on the tablet was making its way towards them under the cover of night.

"I got movement out in the street," Heisman snapped, and Aken stood, leaving Alvarez against the wall while Neil watched the back alley.

"Is that a donkey?" Aken hissed.

"That is one ugly motherfucking donkey," Heisman replied, as Neil risked taking his eyes off the back alley to look.

Wrathful eyes stared up at them from a lioness face that seemed like it had been badly affixed to a donkey's body. A heavy, dragging stomach that looked like it had been overfilled and then popped like a balloon hung between its legs, and it stood proudly in the street like one of the green lions outside the Chicago Art Institute, unmoving but with a distinct feeling of menace.

Neil saw something flying through the air towards it and winced. This was either going to be very good, or very bad.

Heisman's grenade exploded with no effect, and Lamashtu stood unharmed in the rubble-strewn street below. It wasn't stalking towards the gate or trying to jump over the walls, but watching it stare without blinking was unnerving.

"Get Alvarez downstairs," Aken said.

Neil grabbed Alvarez's arms and dragged him down the stairs, trying to keep from bumping him too bad. They reached the bottom and he went to check the cuts on Alvarez's throat with a flashlight.

"Alvarez? Hey dude, can you lift your head up?"

The other man didn't move.

"Fucking Alvarez, come on dude," Neil pleaded. He was not doing this again. "Alvarez… Juan, come on. Please."

Grief closed his throat, and all he could do was shake Alvarez's shoulder. *Dude, please.*

Alvarez never moved, and when Neil felt for a pulse at his throat, there was nothing there. The man was dead. Red streaks covered his badly swollen throat, and the edges of the wounds were almost splitting under the pressure.

Edimmu, he remembered. *Poison claws.*

He dragged Alvarez into an upstairs bedroom and laid him out beside the bed, then thudded back downstairs, praying his wife had figured something out. Parker handed him the phone and went upstairs to replace him.

"Fuck," he heard distantly from the roof.

Aken came downstairs, despair warring with rage in his eyes. "He bled out?" he asked.

Neil shook his head. "Poison," he said quietly, not wanting his wife to hear.

Aken sucked his lips in, and he reached for his radio. "I'm trying again," he said. "We're down three now."

Neil nodded.

Compartmentalization was a bitch. He ignored the fact that his friend was dead in favor of the reminder that these monsters were getting more dangerous and that they still didn't have an answer for how to stop them. He had no idea if he would ever make it home to see their baby born, or if it would grow up in his shadow. A Gold Star baby.

"Utu," Stacey said suddenly, and he realized that he had the phone sandwiched between his shoulder and his ear. He wondered when that had happened. He wondered why he cared.

"'Utu'?" he echoed, feeling stupid from exhaustion.

"Utu is the god of the sun," she said quickly. "This says something about Utu's warmth and justice, and I can't imagine why this would be in here near the end if it didn't represent the end to the curse."

"What does that *mean*," he hissed.

"Dawn," she said. "Until dawn, I think."

"This is probably where I tell you that I love you, and I hope you and the baby are ok," he said. "Things are fucking weird here."

He told her what the day had been like, explained that things were happening that were hard to rationalize, and that he'd been sending pictures of a tablet for a reason. Normally he wouldn't give two shits about it, but today wasn't normal. Today was the furthest thing from normal he'd ever fucking seen. Stacey didn't question him, didn't call him a liar. He'd always liked that about her, that she didn't call him on anything that sounded a little too weird to be true.

"I love you," he said. "I gotta go tell Aken about the time thing."

The sergeant almost laughed when he told him what Stacy had said. "Dawn?" he said. "It's fucking 2030. Dawn is in like nine and a half *fucking* hours. How the fuck are we supposed to hold out until then?"

Neil looked hopefully at the radio and Aken's face closed up.

"It's bricked," he said. "I'm not even getting static now."

"So we're on our own," Neil said bleakly.

Aken fished a wad of chew out and hurled it into a corner. "Fuck yeah we are."

He spat again a few seconds later, and both of them startled as a roar echoed from the alley behind the house.

"Fucking not this thing again," Aken said.

They booked it up to the roof to see Heisman's light trained down on what Neil hoped was the same rhino that had gotten Hill. Having more than one of these things roaming the streets with a built-in weapon that could maybe take out a Bradley would be a disaster. He couldn't see blood on the stupidly long horn, but that didn't mean it hadn't been the same beast.

The rhino paced up and down the alley. Its horn made it unable to turn, but it did a good job sweeping the entire width of the alley with its horn, making it clear they wouldn't be able to escape that way this time.

"Fuck this," Aken said.

"Sir?"

"I'm done with this thing," Aken said.

He stomped back down the stairs to the ground floor and out to the kitchen door that opened into the alley, Neil close on the man's heels. "Fuck this thing, and fuck this stupid country and its *myths*," he spat, pulling the stove away from the alley entrance.

The sergeant opened the door just as the rhino pounded past, and he whistled. The noise made the karkadann stop in its tracks and it bellowed loudly as it struggled to back up enough to trample him.

Aken didn't give it the chance.

Two grenades rolled under its heaving flanks, and Neil back-pedaled into the house. Aken followed him a second later and they both dropped to the ground away from the door seconds before a pair of loud explosions shook the walls.

Aken struggled upright and back out into the alley.

A smell like cooked meat wafted back into the room, and Aken shone his light down the alley. "Yes! Fucking roasted you, motherfucker!"

Neil started gesturing for him to come back inside but the alley behind Aken lit up like a bonfire, and before he could even call out a warning flames filled the doorframe.

A pair of smoldering arms wrapped around Aken, and he started screaming. Like Baker, it was a noise Neil had never heard from him before. Angry roars, loud cussing, and barked commands had all been part of his daily noise repertoire, but never this pain-filled *shrieking*.

Neil didn't want to risk trying to shoot it, terrified the bullets would go through it and hit Aken, and he looked around frantically for anything to use on the ifrit.

The water had no doubt been cut weeks ago, and he searched frantically through cabinets and a small room off the kitchen. Aken's screams rattled Neil's bones, before hope shone in the form of a familiar red canister in a dusty corner.

Aken's screams stopped when Neil yanked the ring out and scrambled back to the door. The stream may have been weak, but he ventured into the searing heat of the alley to spray Aken and the ifrit with white froth from the extinguisher.

The ifrit shrieked, a high, thin wail that sounded like a kettle boiling, and it vanished beneath the weight of the foam, leaving Aken's charred body to collapse into the dirt of the alleyway.

Neil rushed over. Most of Aken's torso had been charred where the ifrit had pressed up against him, and there was nowhere Neil thought he could touch his sarge without causing pain. Carbonized cloth came off in pieces along with the flesh beneath it, and he carefully lifted blackened ballistic plates out of the mess that had been Aken's vest.

Heisman dropped to his knees next to him. He didn't say a word, he just helped Neil scrape off the worst of the foam and start checking Aken. Above them, Parker called that they were clear.

"Neil," Heisman's hand was gentle on his shoulder. "Neil."

Neil kept scraping, hoping if he could just peel off enough clothing, wipe away enough suppressant foam, that he'd find unburned flesh beneath it and Aken's hands would soon be shoving him away. He'd tell him to pick up his rifle where he'd dropped it next to them and man up and watch the fucking street.

"Neil!"

"What?" It came out as a yell.

"He's gone, man!" Heisman said. "He's fucking gone. Come on, help me get his... help me get him inside."

Neil didn't want to look at Aken's face, but he forced his gaze to the left, made himself look at the man he'd failed. Aken's face was twisted in a rictus of pain, red where the heat from the ifrit's arms had burned him and peeling lower towards the chin. Neil could smell burned hair and swallowed his gorge, fighting not to look past Aken's face to the mess of the back of his head.

Shaking legs beneath him, Neil rose to his feet and grabbed Aken's ankles and started dragging his body back into the kitchen while Heisman watched the street. They shoved the oven back across the door and left the body in the kitchen.

He checked his watch again. Nearly 21:00 hours. Dawn felt like centuries away. Rage filled him.

He picked up the phone again, listened to empty air for a few seconds, and the frustration of not having an answer exploded out of him. "We're fucking dying here, Stacey!" he screamed into the phone, and he heard her stifle a sob.

"I'm sorry," she cried. "I don't... it just says to wait until dawn!"

"MotherFUCK!" he bellowed into the room, and Parker's phone went quiet in his hands.

He couldn't hear anything and wondered if she'd hung up. She'd done that a lot on his first tour when he'd never known what to say and they'd been on-again off-again.

In the silence he could hear pages flicking and frantic muttering. He was starting to bristle again, preparing himself that another attack could be imminent from either the windows or upstairs when a quiet voice spoke.

"I have an idea," she said. "The Sumerians often invoked Pazuzu against Lamashtu. If I can put together an amulet of Pazuzu and we string together some kind of petition for him to arrive and protect you as the father of my child, it might help."

On any other day Neil would have laughed at her. The idea of any supernatural enemy arriving to fight on their behalf was as ludicrous as the idea of Jesus himself coming down in a robe and sandals to duke it out with Allah in the streets of Baghdad. After everything he'd seen today, though, he was willing to give it a shot.

"Do what you gotta do," he said. "I'm going to put the phone in my pocket. I'll let you know if it works."

Whatever she said next was lost as he tucked the phone away.

He and Heisman returned to the roof and after they'd dragged Alvarez's SAW and all of his ammo back up, they closed the hinged door that rose from the staircase and Neil stood on it. The roof was where they were staying until either dawn or Pazuzu came. All three of them would protect each other, no matter what new monsters came.

The streets below were dark as pitch now, but when they shone the light out front, Neil could still see the dim form of Lamashtu still standing in the dirt. *What is she waiting for?*

A scuffle sounded from down below, *inside* the courtyard. All three checked the walls of the house and Neil's heart rose into his throat as their flashlights illuminated multiple pale forms closing through the darkness. Lilu were climbing the walls, using their clawed hands as leverage.

Gunshots rang out through the night and Heisman joined them on Alvarez's SAW in chattering bursts as they fought to keep the clawed women at a manageable distance.

"Don't let them get above the second floor," Heisman shouted.

Neil slapped another magazine into his rifle and let loose with another volley, focusing on their heads. It wasn't standard procedure, but headshots saved ammo and sometimes a lilu would take out the one below when it fell.

There was a growing pile on the ground beneath them and Neil let a stubborn spark in his chest bloom that maybe the three of them would get out of this alive.

The SAW stopped. Heisman cursed. A scream ending in a gurgle tore through the air.

Neil pulled his gaze off his temporarily clear wall to see a lilu perched on the edge of the roof, fingers impaling Heisman's throat and chest.

Parker turned and shot her, and she tumbled away into the darkness. Heisman's body slumped to the ground as he struggled to breathe.

Neil turned back to his section of the wall and tried to ignore the bubbling breaths behind him until they stopped. He knew he'd pay for it. Even if they got out of this, he would hear those gasping breaths in his nightmares until it made him eat his gun.

Flecks of something hard were starting to hit his face, and he realized they weren't tears.

"Sandstorm!" he yelled, and he pulled his goggles down from where they'd been perched on his helmet. Smears marred the surface but he couldn't risk taking a hand off his rifle to wipe them clean. Eyes narrowed, he peered through them to the ground below, wondering where all the lilu had gone.

"Any on your side?" Parker yelled, straining to be heard above the cacophony of the growing storm.

"No," Neil called back.

Deciding it was worth the risk as the wind increased, he pulled his shemagh up and tightened it across his face. The loosely woven fabric created an instant shield although the wind buffeted the cloth close to his nose to the point where he could smell and regret all the times he'd used it to wipe up sweat and other bodily fluids off his face and forgotten to wash it afterwards.

He pulled the phone out and pressed it to his ear, wondering if the sandstorm had anything to do with Stacey's prayer, but all he could hear was syllables he didn't recognize coming from her mouth in a frenzied chant.

A braying howl echoed from the street below.

Pazuzu was coming.

Neil and Parker trained their flashlights out and down. Lamashtu was still in the street, but she'd been joined by a winged figure that strongly resembled the angel on the top of the tablet.

The two stood staring at each other with their lionesque heads. Stacey had mentioned something about the two being lovers, but Neil couldn't imagine how. Lamashtu's horribly bowed legs jerked in a backwards kick that swirled darkness through the air towards Pazuzu, and he flew backwards out of its reach. Lightning lashed down from the sky in single bolts, bypassing the higher roofs to batter the ground below, leaving spots of black, fused glass.

Her lion's face snarled spittle towards Pazuzu that changed midflight into what looked like a throng of rats. They swarmed not only the god but skittered unerringly across the street and up the walls towards the two men on the rooftop.

Neil used his rifle like a bat, hitting the oversized black rats off the edges of the roof when they were within reach. A few managed to get past and left burning bites behind where they managed to chew through the fabric of his pants. Yelping told him that Parker was suffering similarly.

"Turn!" he yelled, and Parker spun in place. Neil squashed the rats with the butt of his rifle, breaking their spines or just knocking them off and stepping on them where they lay stunned. They swapped and Parker cleared rats off of him while they both kept an eye for anything worse on the horizon.

More rodents kept coming, a veritable flood from the street below. Roaring from who he could only assume was Pazuzu turned the sky above them black. It blotted out the few stars that had been visible and resolved into a rain of locusts that poured down and attacked the rats as quickly as they came.

Neil dared a look over the edge of the roof at the gods, and while he could see that Pazuzu was bleeding where he hadn't been before, so was Lamashtu. Some of her gray fur had been burned off in glossy patches or eaten away, and around them, rats and locusts tumbled in the street.

The rats were larger but the insects outnumbered them, and Neil watched in fascinated horror as the locusts quickly ate the rats down to bones that crunched under Lamashtu's hooves and Pazuzu's taloned feet as they circled one another slowly.

Pazuzu's mouth opened, exposing long fangs. His mane seemed to double in size in the air that was abruptly so dry that Neil could almost feel the build-up of static electricity. A growl started low in Pazuzu's throat, clawed its way up Neil's spine as it built into a roar.

The sandstorm that had been circling now came in earnest, focused on the middle of the street.

Lamashtu screamed that horrible bray again as the sand closed in on her, tearing at her body. Chunks came off only to be whipped away by the wind in a spray of blood.

Neil swallowed the cheer building in his throat, but Parker didn't. He whooped and hollered as the sand and the wind ground Lamashtu down to nothing, pounding away until not even her bones were left.

Pazuzu was now the only one standing in the street, and as Parker threw an arm around Neil's shoulder, his attention turned to them. Another roar shook the night and Pazuzu vanished, only to reappear next to them in a swirl of sand that made both men stumble in shock. His wings hadn't even moved.

Parker fell to his knees in front of the god.

Neil would have to get him for that later, find some joke to make about Parker having *that* in front of his face. Pazuzu was butt-naked, and though his hands were replaced by lion's paws and he stood on bird feet, his body was all human.

"Thank you," Parker cried.

Before he could say anything else, some of the sand that still swirled around them narrowed into a thin band, leaving a cut on Parker's cheek.

"What—" Neil gasped.

More sand drove at Parker and he started to scream. Neil put his hands up to protect his face, only to realize that no sand was coming at him. Just Parker.

He lowered his arms and found two more lion-headed demons were standing either side of him. Their human arms were extended before Neil, and crossed as though to ward off Pazuzu, and he watched in horror as the sand wore away Parker's skin, exposed tendon before it shaved it away, and burrowed down towards bone. Blood welled up and was swept away as quickly as it came, leaving wet muscle glistening between gusts of sand and wind before it dried out.

Stacey's prayer in Sumerian echoed in the sand-choked air and tickled in his ear, and he remembered what she had said, and thought about the intent. *Protect the father of the baby in my belly.* It was so narrow-minded. She hadn't thought to include anyone else in her petition, and so these lion-headed demons were only protecting *him*. Parker was fair game. And no matter how much Pazuzu hated Lamashtu, he was still considered a demonic god, fickle and destructive at his core. Parker strained against the weight of the wind-laden sand preventing him from moving forward and Neil watched, horrified, as Parker was flayed just like the dark goddess.

Pazuzu stared impassively as Parker's screams faded, as he bled out through a thousand tiny cuts and abrasions. His balaclava was long gone, face stripped to pink muscle and white tendon. His lips were shredded, exposing his teeth to the air.

Neil screamed at Pazuzu, begging him to stop, but the god ignored him and watched as Parker pitched to one side. His one remaining battle buddy was no longer screaming.

Pazuzu's stubby catlike fingers finally jerked in a complicated motion Neil couldn't even begin to understand, and the scrape of sand slowly stopped.

Parker hadn't quite been worn away to nothing like Lamashtu, but all that was left was a sand-buried, flayed body wearing tattered BDUs in a pile at Neil's feet.

The ancient god barely twitched, but the sand that had been lazily circling them all was abruptly falling from the air like rain, leaving a thin layer over Neil and everything around him. The sheer blackness that was the Baghdad night sky returned, and the stars sparkled overhead, a cold witness to the suddenly empty roof. No lion-headed demons or gods stood with him now, and there was nothing around him but sand and death.

Beneath it – almost at the edge of his hearing – hovered the staccato heartbeat of his unborn child, now promised to gods and monsters.

THE THROAT

Alan Baxter

Jack Warren had every intention of running for his life, but his foot shot sideways in the pool of viscera that only moments before had been digesting Tom Johnson's last meal. The rest of Johnson had been carried away. Instead of turning tail, Warren faceplanted in the warm, recently spilled entrails of his friend. He sat up, brought his assault rifle to bear, inadvertently lifting a loop of Johnson's intestine over the barrel. Through the gore pouring down his face, deafened by automatic fire exploding all around him, Warren had a moment to see the giant creature bear down. The size of a small car, fat and rounded, thick muscles rippled under taut, maroon skin. A huge, blood-red maggot, it powered along the jungle floor at uncanny speed, rapid peristaltic movement undulating its flesh. Its seemingly blind face split open, half a dozen interlocking tusks separating outwards and tipping forward to reveal a wide circular mouth forested with row after row of diamond-sharp teeth disappearing down a deep, wet gullet.

Warren got off a short blast of fire, then the thing's lower right tusk, as long as his forearm, punched into his face between the eyes.

The beast didn't slow.

The sharp bone burst from the back of Warren's head as it slithered on as fast as a fit man might jog. Warren was lifted and swept along, his corpse dragging at the fat worm's side like a rag as it plunged through thick foliage. The creature shook its front end like a wet dog shaking its head, then bent up in the center even as it moved on, and Warren was flipped up and into the wide round maw. He vanished, a momentary extra bulge in the thing's rapidly pulsing body.

"Fall the fuck back!" Jimenez yelled over the roar of 5.56mm fire, aware of the fear evident in his deep, strong voice. The squad backed up as one, between the trees dotted across the valley floor, firing as they went.

Behind the dark red maggot that had swallowed Warren, hundreds more surged up and over the bullet-lacerated bodies of their brethren. They moved like an undulating sea, rushing forward at frightening speed, sometimes rolling, no particular concern about which part of them was up. Hundreds of rounds ripped through the air to meet them, tracers flashing through the gloom under the canopy, bursting ichorous green splashes from the fat sides of the creatures. The first few shots seemed to barely slow the things, but enough firepower eventually split them open to burst and leak and writhe on the leafy ground. But still more came.

"Spread out!" Jimenez called, and the squad fanned wide, crossfire ripping the giant maggots to shreds. The gulping worms consumed their own kind in massive swallows even as they slid over them, growing with everything they ate. "This is for Warren and Thomson!" Jimenez screamed, his rage incandescent, and every assault rifle echoed his sentiment.

Crimson flesh and thick green blood slicked the jungle floor, but still the wave of maggots rolled on, an all-consuming tide.

"Where's the end of it?" Gemmell yelled.

Jimenez's squad of eight was already down to six and he had no intention of losing any more.

"Grenades!" he barked, and the rack and pump of mounted grenade launchers sent explosives flying. Designed to pierce armor more than 50mm thick, the sudden wall of explosions had the desired effect and tore the flood of maggots to shreds. Among the smoke and sizzling meat, a strange quiet fell.

"The fuck was that?" Ichiro asked in his low, quiet way.

"Warren and Thomson, gone," Shackleton said, her voice almost as low as Ichiro's.

"I told my little girl this was a routine investigation," Jimenez said firmly into the momentary lull. "I told her I would be back for her birthday on Saturday. I have every intention of riding a fucking pony with my little girl this weekend. Does anyone have an objection to that?"

"Maybe the fucking pony," Salisbury said, her face split in a grin.

Jimenez barked a laugh. Given he was six foot seven and close to three hundred pounds, she had a point.

Their laughter was a mask, a shield against the sudden and horrible deaths of their friends, and Jimenez knew they needed it. He opened his mouth to call them to order but was interrupted by Ichiro.

"More coming," he said, field glasses at his eyes. "A lot. And by a lot, I mean a fuck ton."

"What the hell are they, Cap?" Haversham asked, his posh English accent incongruous as always among the rest of the squad.

"The fuck I know? They never told me anything about this."

"What did they tell you?"

Jimenez scoffed. "Not a whole lot, it turns out. We need to find where they're coming from. This time we'll be ready. Stay wide, we move forward and meet them."

"Fast, giant, carnivorous maggots?" Shackleton asked, her eyebrows riding high under a short, dark brown bob that poked out from the edges of her helmet. "Seriously, Cap?"

Gemmell, the only squad member bigger than Jimenez, looked from her to his captain with eyebrows raised. If Gemmell was spooked…

Jimenez raised his hands. "You want boring, go work for the DMV. You want excitement, stick with me. We lost Warren and Thomson to a surprise attack. Let's not lose any more. Stay sharp."

12 HOURS AGO

"What kind of experiments?" Jimenez asked.

The bald man behind the desk, gut straining the buttons of his suit, made a rueful face. "I'm afraid I can't tell you too much."

159

"But it ain't legit, or the Army would go in, the government. You guys are covering your asses, that's why we get the call. So, Mr Cantrell, if you want me to put my team in harm's way, I need intel."

Cantrell pursed his lips for a moment. Jimenez folded his massive arms across his chest and sat back, immovable. Cantrell sighed. "Very well. Honestly, I don't know much about the finer details, not my department, but our organization has been financing some cutting-edge scientific research."

"Deep in the Amazon jungle?"

"The sort of research we'd rather no one else knew about. Let me put it this way: the facility in question is called the DDS, which stands for the Department of Dimensional Sciences. They explore interdimensional interstices and universal nexus points, so I'm sure you can imagine the interest that might garner from certain... authorities."

Jimenez raised his eyebrows. "They explore what the fuck now?"

Cantrell carried on as if Jimenez hadn't spoken. "We've lost contact with our facility down there. I imagine it's been overrun by rebels, something like that. The jungle is a lawless place. Something simple, but nonetheless dangerous. We need your team to go in, clean up, and secure the facility. That's all."

"Clean up and secure, huh?"

"That's all."

"You got any more details of the possible threat?"

Cantrell shook his head. "The facility is situated in a narrow valley. It's steep-sided, a waterfall at one end, so it's a gorge, a deep, rocky dead end. You can only access the valley from a pass between high cliffs at the northern end, but otherwise it's sheer rock faces all around, narrow at the pass, wide at the other end where our facility is built. Good for security, for privacy, but obviously bad for visual access. Our satellite imagery can't see in there."

"What else aren't you telling me?"

Cantrell smiled. "Astute."

"Yep, and I have a cute ass too. What are you holding back?"

"There's magnetic interference of some kind. It's been steadily building since we lost contact, further hampering our attempts to see or hear from them. We assume some equipment has gone on the fritz. So we called you."

"To clean up and secure."

"Precisely. You'll be in and out in no time."

Jimenez nodded. "That right?" Cantrell wasn't so good at hiding his lying ass behind that condescending smile. If this went bad, Jimenez would come back and cut those smiling lips off the asshole's face, maybe eat them with eggs for breakfast. "It's my little girl's eighth birthday on Saturday, and I ain't missing that."

"Captain Jimenez, it's only Wednesday. You'll be fine."

NOW

"Here they come!" Ichiro had already moved to one side and hunkered down with ammo packs to either side.

They'd made it another half a mile down the valley. The others picked their spots in time to see the front of the next assault appear between the trees. Weapons fire thundered again as they began decimating the oncoming wave.

"Interesting observation," Ichiro shouted over comms. "They can't climb. The valley slopes up either side, getting steeper until it meets the cliff walls. Every time they try to go up the valley sides, they reach a certain incline then just roll back down. It doesn't slow them, but it keeps them on the valley floor."

Jimenez nodded. "Okay, that's the first good news we've had since my wife woke me early this morning with crude intentions."

A HE grenade from Shackleton blew a wide gap in the advance, then she said, "Well, that was only good news for you, Cap."

"Yeah, not us or even your poor wife get any joy from that," Gemmell said, dropping to one knee to change out mags.

"Not true, witches and warlocks." Jimenez gritted his teeth and managed to gun down three maggots in a row. More slowed briefly behind to swallow their dead. "When I'm satiated, I become a much kinder captain to your sorry asses. You should all send my wife a thank you note and some chocolates."

"I'll send her one of those *With Deepest Sympathies* cards people use for funerals," Haversham said in his posh accent, then his words turned to a furious roar as he went full auto for several seconds.

Jimenez sucked in a breath. "Focus, people! We can't let any of these fuckers get by us. If they get out into the wider jungle, they'll run rampant and cause a whole lot of damage. We came here to find out why the base lost contact, but we find ourselves in a containment situation. If they get past us that's a whole lot of fucked up-ness, agreed?"

"Yes, Sir," they chorused.

The squad moved in a synchronized dance, covering each other, crossfire holding the wave back. Crimson meat fell and blood surged up, and still more came.

"Die, fucking maggots!" Salisbury screamed, her voice high.

Rounds streaked through the hot air tearing chunks from the worms. Their long, bony tusks snapped and spun away, thick green blood sprayed and splattered as red flesh was torn apart, but the maggots were unperturbed. They might momentarily slow as one of them fell, but the wave bunched and then surged over the top. Grenades flew, pumped and thrown up and over the front ranks. Chunks of deep scarlet flesh tumbling in geysers of green viscera burst into the air, along with rocks and earth and thick, waxy foliage. As the bodies piled up, the worms stretched their maws wide and swallowed the crimson barricade of their dead, barely slowed by the process. Their bodies pulsed and flexed, contracted and extended, growing as they swept up the shallow incline.

As Jimenez quickly switched in a fresh mag, he looked up through the trees. In the distance he saw swirling dark clouds of indigo and purple, forks of bright lightning arcing and crackling inside. *What the fuck is all this?* he had a moment to think, then turned his attention back to carving up the inexorable worm tide.

1 HOUR AGO

"We're getting interference in readings." Barnes's voice was tinny in Jimenez's earpiece.

Jimenez made his way to the cockpit, past the team strapped into webbing on either side of the heavily customized Boeing C-17 Globemaster III. His plane was his pride and joy, deftly liberated from a drug lord in Nicaragua with a personal fortune more than the GDP of some countries. Not that it was any good to the guy now, given he was in several pieces and long eaten by bugs, no doubt.

As Jimenez passed, he glanced at the webbed stacks of cargo locked into place between them: twelve cases of old Spanish CETME Model L assault rifles, six cases of M67 frag grenades, two-thousand pounds of C4 in stacked M112 demolition bricks, eight long cases, each holding a 50-caliber M2 Browning, about three tons of various caliber munitions for everything from semi-automatic handguns to 50-cal, a few cases of mortars and surface-to-air rockets, and, at the back, an armored jeep. He really needed to figure out what to do with this bonus stash from the recent Honduras thing. It was all worth a small fortune if he could only find the right market for it. "What kind of interference?" he asked Barnes, leaning on the back of the pilot's seat.

"Not sure, but instruments are glitching. Probably the magnetics you were warned about." Barnes looked back over his shoulder, gave a shrug. His face was still tanned from the recent leave he'd enjoyed, three weeks on a Caribbean island with the young woman he'd just married.

Jimenez thought he wouldn't mind a few weeks on a white sand beach himself right about now. "How close are we?" he asked.

"Almost there, but I'm reluctant to push too far if we don't have to."

Jimenez nodded. "You want us to drop early?"

"If possible, Cap. You're about a half hour's hike from the target right now, maybe less."

"Good enough. Loop here, we'll drop, then you head back

to Manaus. I'll radio in if we need you back. You might need to bring a chopper to lift us out."

Barnes nodded. "Good luck, Cap. And happy camping."

Less than two minutes later the team were parachuting towards the dark green canopy, two pallets of supplies ahead of them.

On the ground, Jimenez said, "Remember the philosophy, witches and warlocks?"

"Expect no trouble," the squad said in unison, "but bring all the ammo you can carry!"

"You got it! The camping gear and food can stay here until we get back. Arm up and move out."

"Back in time for supper?" Gemmell asked.

"You got it," Jimenez said. "Barnes can cook us up one of his world-famous hot chilis for dinner. Then Haversham'll read you a bedtime story. His lovely voice'll put you right out"

"How about *Winnie The Pooh*?" Haversham asked, and the way he pronounced Pooh made them all laugh. "Heathens!" he muttered, though he grinned along.

They set out south, expecting no trouble, but armed for a war.

NOW

Jimenez's ears rang from the thunder of gunfire and grenades. The stink of burning meat and the acrid stench of their blood drifted on the breeze blowing up the valley. But they'd stopped the carnivorous tide again. The squad stood panting, checking gear. They were already dangerously low on ammo, but how many more of these things could there be?

Over the tops of the trees, at the distant end of the valley, the mass of dark, bulging clouds he'd seen earlier had grown. More lightning crackled and burst through it. The wind pushing the stench up the valley increased, driven ahead of that unnatural storm.

"Will there be any more?" Salisbury's voice held a tinge of panic Jimenez had never heard before as she echoed his concerns. She was a badass, usually unshakable.

"Don't know."

"Also," Ichiro said, "do you think these *are* a kind of maggot? Or a kind of worm?"

Jimenez frowned. "Both and neither maybe. Does it matter?"

"Maybe. A worm is a worm, but a maggot is the second stage of something else. Something bigger. Egg, then larva, then what?"

"Well, fuck me, thanks for your cheery observations, Ichiro. Let's just murder the fuck out of any we see and then we don't need to know, right? Come on, let's move."

As they jogged on, Jimenez turned his attention to the most immediate problem.

We don't have anything like enough ammo for another fight like that.

Salisbury's tone of panic was borne of the same knowledge, and the rest of the squad would have realized it too. He switched his radio channel over, hoping for the best. "Barnes, you copy?"

"Go ahead, Cap," the pilot said. "You finished already?"

"Not even close. You still airborne."

"Yep."

"How long to get back here?"

"Get back, Cap?"

"I need an ammo drop toot sweet."

"Holy shit. And there was me planning to masturbate and nap when I got back. Okay, I'm turning now. I'd say about an hour to get back to you?"

Jimenez shook his head. "Can you engage the warp engines and make it quicker? And fuck the interference, I need you right here. I want the ammo dropped on top of us."

Barnes's voice gained the clipped edge of determination. "Shit, okay. I'll do all I can, Cap. On my way."

As they moved further up the valley, the winds from the storm became buffeting and the air beneath the clouds looked dark and electric.

"Let's get up the valley side," Jimenez said. "I want to see this place before we get any closer. We need to know what's down there. And how many more maggots might be milling around." Surely what they'd already fought had to be the last of them. How many could there be in a finite space?

They explore interdimensional interstices and universal nexus points... He shook the thought from his head and ran on.

As they made their way up the steepening incline of the valley side, they spread out into pairs. Jimenez and Gemmell on point, Ichiro and Shackleton behind, with Salisbury and Haversham bringing up the rear. Once they got a few hundred yards up, able to see over the trees to the end of the deep scar in the landscape, they stood in stunned silence for several seconds.

"Jesus fucking Christ," Haversham said eventually.

Jimenez tore his eyes from the spectacle in front of them to glance at the Englishman's pale face. Haversham was no prude, but Jimenez had never heard the man swear before, which was more than unusual given their company. But if there was ever a time to start cursing, this was it. "What the fuck is that?" he asked, returning his gaze to the sight before them.

They stood on a steep, rocky scree some five hundred yards above the valley floor, cliffs at their backs. Ahead, the highest part of the dead-end tear in the earth towered above them, a waterfall tumbling down. In the depths of the valley's end, it seemed physics no longer existed. Evidence of the secret facility was visible, the last few buildings broken and burning around a massive hole in the ground. But 'hole' was nowhere near description enough.

A massive circular rift, wet and glistening, plunged down into the earth. A seemingly living thing, a giant pulsating gullet some hundred yards across. The top of it slowly but continuously prolapsed up and out, folding over itself as it rose. As it curled into the valley, it immediately dried and crumbled, forming a kind of caldera of its own meat. The sides of the quivering gullet were covered with wide rings of rounded pustules, one ring every few hundred feet going down the energetic vessel. As the throat bulged up and crumbled down, another ring of pustules reached the crater's edge and they all burst, hundreds more maggots born, twisting and writhing as if burning on a hot plate before they sensed their purpose and surged up the valley.

The waves Jimenez and the squad had just fought were one thing, and even should there be another, the odds were maybe not insurmountable, especially with an ammo drop. The squad could finish that many. And now that next wave had indeed been born, hundreds more carnivorous crimson worms writhing into existence over the edges of the vomiting throat.

But down its glistening depths were ring after ring after ring of swollen pustules, mile after mile, as far as they could see. Already hundreds more maggots were in the valley, sliding and surging up towards the pass that would release them into the wider world, and there were millions more in the throat, a galactic maw endlessly puking out destruction. In the farthest depths of it a swirling void emanated a bone-chilling cold and absolute blackness, leading to who knew where or what.

Jimenez rocked with vertigo at the sight of it, as though its very presence could pluck him from the valley side and send him falling into eternity forever. Above it all, the unnatural storm raged and roiled, dark blue and purple clouds rippling with white lighting, the static making their hairs stand on end. Jimenez recalled Ichiro's question: *Egg, then larva, then what?* Apart from the devastation they might cause in the wider world in this form, what might they become next if they got out?

"There's no way we can contain this," Shackleton said, her voice shaking in shock and terror. "No one could contain it. It's only a matter of time before they overrun everything."

"Is it getting wider?" Gemmell asked.

"Yes," Ichiro said. "Very slowly, but it's widening with every wave, I think. How big might it get?"

"There's not really anything to stop it growing," Haversham said. "I mean, look at the thing! What rules could ever govern that?"

"Get back down!" Jimenez barked. "We have to get in front of that next lot of maggots before they reach the pass. We have to hold this place, stop any of those fuckers getting out of the valley."

"Cap," Haversham started, "this is—"

"Now!"

"Yes, Sir!" As one, the squad turned back and began to run.

"Ichiro," Jimenez said, "we still have those mines?"

"Yes, Cap."

"Okay, you and Shackleton get directly down and lay mines. We need to disrupt the front of the next wave as much as possible. Then fall back to us. With any luck, we'll have an ammo drop by the time you get there."

Ichiro and Shackleton peeled off to the left while the rest ran on, talking quickly as they ran.

Jimenez switched channels again. "Barnes, we need you now!"

"I didn't stop for a wank. I'm just a few minutes from the valley, coming in low. Ammo crates ready to drop. Where do you need 'em?"

Jimenez looked down into the valley and saw Ichiro and Shackleton start laying mines. The wave of maggots was barely a hundred yards behind them.

"They're too close!" Gemmell yelled, even as Jimenez came to the same conclusion.

His gut clenched. "They're buying us time," he said. "Mad, beautiful bastards. *Run!*"

The squad pounded on, trying to get as far ahead of the wave as possible.

"Barnes, you're gonna see the valley light up in a second. Drop the ammo five hundred yards before that."

"Yes, Sir. What the fuck is that storm I see ahead?"

"The target, pilot. Drop the ammo, then turn tail and radio in an airstrike. I don't care how you convince whoever you need to convince, but break into government channels and get us a strike. We need big fucking ordinance right under that storm. The end of this valley needs to disappear in fire and rock. We'll hold it in until then."

"Will we?" Gemmell asked.

Jimenez threw him a desperate look. "We have any choice?"

168

Gemmell didn't get to answer because the mines went up, explosions of noise and dirt and red flesh filled the air.

As the squad hit the valley floor, they heard the distant roar of the C-17's engines. Moments later the big plane powered over them. Jimenez spotted the white domes of the ammo crate parachutes dropping between the trees a couple of hundred yards further ahead. They tried to run faster.

"I hope that drop was in the right place," Barnes said over the comm. "My instruments are fritzed and I'm doing everything by eye and feel."

"It's bang on target," Jimenez said. "I'm sure your new wife is very happy with your ability to hit the button. Now get that strike in."

"No chance Ichiro and Shackleton would have survived that, is there?" Salisbury asked as she skidded to a halt beside the ammo. White silk fluttered down around them as they smashed open the crates and filled their weapons, pockets, and webbing with as much as they could carry.

"What the fuck is that swarming up the valley?" Barnes said, voice crackling with interference. "It's like a thick red sea, flowing up against gravity and–" He fell silent as the squad turned and spread out to meet the maggots.

"And he's seen the... whatever the fuck that is down there," Gemmell said.

"The fuck is happening here?" Barnes yelled.

"Call in all the damn strike!" Jimenez ordered.

"It's Ichiro!" Salisbury said, pointing between the trees.

Shackleton was nowhere in sight, but Ichiro, battered and bloody, limped along some two hundred yards away. He paused, looked over his shoulder, and stopped.

"What's he doing?"

The man stood tall, saluted, then bowed low from the waist. He moved as quickly as his injuries would allow, laying a line of mines across the valley floor.

"Ichiro, no!" Salisbury yelled.

The crimson wave swelled up behind and Ichiro turned to face it. He lifted his arms to either side as it engulfed him, then the valley lit up with noise and fire again. Red meat sailed and sizzled, green blood sprayed.

The squad howled their rage and started crossfire containment again. The scream of the C-17 engines came directly overhead, Barnes flying back the way he'd come.

"We need support!" Jimenez yelled. "Did you make the call?"

"Cap, there's no time," Barnes said. "Even if you carve up this wave of whatever the fuck it is you're fighting, there'll be another one less than thirty minutes behind it. And again and again. And that hole in the fucking world is growing."

"That doesn't mean we quit, pilot! We might be a band of scumbag mercs, but we fight the bad guys, right? We have to hold this valley."

"Fall back!" Gemmell yelled, and he dragged an ammo crate with one hand while continuing to fire with the other. The squad matched his active retreat, bullets flying, tracers flashing.

"Exactly the point, Cap," Barnes said. "There's no way you'll contain this until help arrives unless those fuckers stop being born."

The C-17 screamed overhead again, once more heading down the valley.

"Barnes, the fuck are you doing?"

"Making good use of that unexpected gift from Honduras, Cap. Otherwise you guys will never make it out of there, and if you don't make it out, those fuckers will. Two-thousand pounds of C4 and all the rest, plus the mostly full fuel tanks of our bird here, should close that ugly hole, right?"

"Barnes, no!"

"You tell her I'm a fucking hero, Cap." Barnes's voice was tight with emotion. "Tell her at least we had Martinique. See you in Valhalla, you fucks!"

The C-17 engines howled to a pitch Jimenez had never heard before, then a concussive wave rocked up the valley. Fire and smoke mushroomed up above trees then the shockwave hit them as the sound of the explosion blew the hearing out of their ears. The thunder of gunfire slowly came back as they kept up the fight against the advancing maggots.

"You mad bastard!" Jimenez yelled, and only hoped it had been enough. If that throat had indeed been blown back to wherever it came from, perhaps they had a chance. The crack and boom of falling rock echoed up to them as they fired in retreat, but still the carnivorous wave kept breaking. They had to stop it.

Gemmell dashed his hopes immediately. "We can't hold them back with just four of us, Cap!"

And the big man was right. Down to four, they couldn't cover enough ground and the maggots threatened to flank them.

"Fall back to the pass!" Jimenez said. "Grab whatever you can carry and run like fuck!"

They gathered what ammo they could and bolted.

"That rocky pass was only about sixty feet wide," Jimenez yelled as they sprinted. "It's high-sided and much easier to defend. If we can contain the maggots in this valley, and if Barnes has successfully prevented any more from coming, we have a chance."

"Every wave is bigger than the last," Haversham said. "How big is this one? Did another get out behind it?"

"Who fucking cares? We fight until we can't any longer."

There was a scream behind, and Jimenez turned to look. Salisbury had tripped, tree roots catching her feet as she had tried to run and carry a grenade case with her.

"Don't fucking stop!" she shouted, as the dark red tide mounted behind her, tumbling through the trees.

"On your feet, soldier!" Jimenez yelled.

Salisbury shook her head, gave him a smile that said it all. No time. She pulled a grenade pin with her teeth and hugged it and the box containing twenty more to her chest as she fell into the shadow of the advancing worms.

Jimenez stared. *I don't deserve these people. The world doesn't deserve them.* "Incoming!" he roared, and then the grenades went up.

The blast took Jimenez, Haversham, and Gemmell off their feet, the heat of it scorching their backs. The stench of cooking maggot filled the air as they scrambled back up to run on. Haversham yelped in pain. A chunk of tree wood, sharp and ragged, stuck sideways from his thigh. He couldn't stand.

Gemmell ran back, leaving the ammo crate he'd been dragging where it was, and got a hand under Haversham's arm. As he heaved up, Haversham shook him off. "Don't be a fool! You can't carry me and fight."

"Get up!" Gemmell shouted at him, but Jimenez saw the amount of blood coming from the leg wound. Haversham would bleed out, even if he could stand. They had no time for field dressings.

With a lump in his throat, Jimenez barked an order. "Gemmell, to me!"

The big man looked back, desperation in his eyes. Haversham nodded, then caught Jimenez's eye. "A fucking honor, Cap," he said.

"Fuck!" Gemmell grabbed up his crate again and ran back, leaving Haversham where he lay. The red tide was almost on him.

"Go! Stop them!" Haversham yelled at Jimenez and Gemmell, then turned and fired from the ground, sweeping full auto left and right into the surge of maggots as they came over the burning corpses of their brethren. One maggot scooped Haversham into its tooth-filled maw and still he fired, blowing it apart even as it tried to swallow him. As it flopped wet and dead over him, he tried to scramble back, but another worm, bigger than the first, swallowed the lot and Haversham vanished down its wet throat, his weapon still barking fire.

Jimenez's teeth threatened to crack apart, he clenched them so hard. His entire squad wiped out, only he and Gemmell left. They had to stop this.

They reached the start of the narrow rocky pass that led down into the gorge and started to clamber up its steep incline.

"We need to get high enough to hold here," Jimenez said, gasping for breath as he scrambled up. The rock would bottleneck the worms. If they could only hold this ground, not let any maggots past… But four of them hadn't been enough down on the valley floor, so would two be enough even here? Regardless, they had no choice.

He sensed a lack of movement beside himself and paused, spun around. Gemmell was fifty yards back, scrabbling at a crack in the rock face. Sheer gray stone towered above him on either side.

"Get up here!" Jimenez yelled, the surge of thick red death was almost on Gemmell's back.

"You have to mop up the last of 'em, Cap!" Gemmell called up, and raised a detonator in one hand.

"Gemmell, no!"

"We've got to get them all, right?" Gemmell said, a grin on his wide face. "Like the fucking Pokemon."

Jimenez forced a smile and nodded. "Gotta catch 'em all!"

The thick tide of maggots rose up, forced atop one another in the rapidly narrowing pass, dropping Gemmell into their shadow. As Gemmell slammed his thumb down on the button, Jimenez turned and scrambled up the rocky slope.

The explosion knocked him down, sharp stones carving up his face and palms, but he crawled on. Deep, booming cracks echoed behind as the rock above the blown-out side split apart and fell in. Rock dust, smoke, fire and green blood roiled into the air as the low end of the pass became blocked by a new wall of fallen boulders.

Jimenez found a high point and turned, feet braced wide as the remaining maggots came boiling over the top of the rock wall blocking the low end of the pass. Clearly there were still enough pressed up against it that others tumbled over them like water filling a vessel, and flooded past the top edge. But Jimenez had the high ground and the way up was narrower than ever now. And he had a lot of ammo.

He lobbed grenades over, dozens of maggots at a time blown to smithereens, the wave falling briefly back before surging up and over again. Jimenez raked them with fire, moving forward as he went, sending the fat red bastards tumbling back down into the pass. In moments he was standing atop the newly made wall shooting down into a mass of red flesh and green ooze at anything that moved.

* * *

Captain Jimenez sat across from the sweating Cantrell, fury seething in his gut. "Well?" he asked.

"You did a fine job," Cantrell said.

"What does that mean? It hasn't come back?"

"Correct. You said you went back and could see no trace of the… the…"

"Let's call it the throat, shall we? Because honestly, who knows what the fuck it really was."

"The throat. Okay. Well, you're right. It seems your pilot's amazing sacrifice did sever its connection. There's nothing moving down there, no trace of the base or anything else. And the magnetic interference has ceased. Whatever you met down there, it's gone. You beat it."

"Beat it?" Jimenez asked, stunned at the man's audacity. "It very nearly beat us. They're all fucking dead, Cantrell!"

Cantrell held up both palms in a gesture of surrender. "I'm sorry. But so is everything else. We can't thank you enough."

Rage bubbled through Jimenez's veins. "You knew this was more than some rebels breaking into a lab to steal tech, didn't you?"

Cantrell licked his lips. "We suspected it might be more than–"

"They saved the fucking world!" he yelled. "And they will never be credited for it." He stood, leaned over the desk. "Fuck you!" And he punched Cantrell right in his smug face, sending the man backwards onto the floor, chair and all, howling in shock and pain. Jimenez pulled a pistol from his jacket and shot over the desk, right between Cantrell's eyes.

"I got a fucking pony to ride."

BREACH

JW Stinson

"Next stop sub-level B3. Doors closing," the automated voice said.

The elevator was filled to capacity. Captain Tracy Rex – Trex – knew this was a one-way ticket for the twenty fully armed ex-military hurtling two hundred and fifty metres into the depths of the earth. Trex's second-in-command and head of recruitment, Colour Sergeant Reaper, wouldn't have it any other way. She traced her finger over the double helix insignia on her forearm. The words *BSS - Biotechnology Security Solutions* embroidered around the multi-coloured logo. An ex-soldier for hire. Keeping her service rank was a throwback to a time when she fought and killed for her country, services that were needed now.

"Captain. It's time." Reaper's voice snapped Trex from her reverie. "Listen up Team Five. Your briefing starts now." Reaper's firm voice, deep and authoritative, commanded everyone's attention. Her 2IC was the best she ever had, making her first twelve months of her new posting the smoothest of her career. That was until the resident biologically-engineered super creatures, all of whom were bred to be apex weapons, breached their containment.

Trex faced each of the seated warriors. Eighteen sets of eyes searching for guidance or reassurance. Technically they were security guards, but every one of them had the heart and experience of warriors.

"Teams One through Four are inbound. Sixty mikes. We are the first and only line of defence until they get here." Trex paused to let the weight of that sink in. "The whitecoats didn't tell us much. But we do know those mad scientists created three

175

variations of ungodly abomination. The worst will be on or near the top of the complex – demons, they call them. We'll work our way up. Time is not our friend. Power is failing everywhere. Automated controls are not responding, and if we don't get this situation under control by the time it goes offline, all emergency exits will open. That will give those abominations unbridled access to the surface. To our city. Our homes, our families. So nothing, I repeat, *nothing*, escapes to the surface. Let's get it done."

Reaper's voice filled the elevator. "Three sub-levels of hell. Each a maze of narrow corridors wrapped around clusters of labs and offices. Two lobbies connect the levels. Those areas are equipped with ceiling cannons that are currently keeping the creatures from reaching the main door on the upper level. Those weapons will be black on ammo in the next fifteen minutes. The plan is simple. We breach into the lowest floor – B3 – clear the level manually, and lock down each section. Then we rinse and repeat, moving up to B2 then B1."

Trex offered some last words of reassurance, "Stay together. Watch each other's back and we *will* get through this. I'll be right there with each and every one of you. When the complex is safe, the security system will open the main doors on B1. We do not leave until we take back this complex."

Bing. "Welcome to Sub-level B3," the automated voice said.

"All right girls and boys, let's fuck shit up."

● ● ●

"Squads Bravo, Charlie, Delta breach now!"

The teams of four powered through the doors into the first three rooms of B3. Shoulders down, weapons up, grouped close and moving with the grace that only comes with years of real-world application.

"Squad Zulu," Trex whispered, "shadow us in. Hard point our turns and safeguard the fallback position. Hold the corridor until we've cleared the rooms. Reaper, you're with me. Scox, August, on me too." The command squad – Alpha – moved through the doors, Trex on point.

In the dimly lit corridor, the fluorescent lights flickered and went off, and the team was plunged into darkness.

Trex led Alpha into the fourth room off the hallway, squad leaders emulating the manoeuvre and searching the nearest labs. Alpha's weapon-mounted torches illuminated smashed computers, crushed desks and destroyed laboratory equipment. The crunch of boots on glass confirming the extent of the devastation.

"This place is fucked," whispered Scox.

"Room's clear," Reaper reported. His posture softened but his weapon remained at the ready. "The holding pens next door look empty. But this door is still intact. Whatever was in here must be on the move."

The radio burst into life. "Trex. Zulu actual. We've got movement up ahead. Something's in the shadows."

"Squads report," Trex said into her chin mic.

"Bravo. Place is drenched in blood. But clear."

"Charlie. Same here."

"Delta. Yeah, we're— Contact! Contact! Engaging! Two, no three hostiles incoming!"

Automatic gunfire erupted from the room across the corridor, brilliant streaks of muzzle flash punctuating the darkness.

Roars and howls rose over the sound of gunfire. The doors leading to the holding pens in front of Alpha rocked and shook, groaning in protest against thumping pressure from the other side. Squeals and bellows reverberated through the metal structure as Alpha squad swivelled to meet the threat.

Metal screeched, and the doors began to buckle. Muscular, black furry limbs started peeling back the metal like tinfoil.

"Contact!" Reaper called, firing into the unnatural mass of black fur. Scox and August responded with their own salvos.

A force like a truck suddenly smashed into Trex, catapulting her into the wall opposite. Pain spiked through her shoulder as she slid to the floor. Three hulking creatures had ploughed through a wall nearest the corridor.

"They're in the room," Reaper yelled. Non-stop firing, guttural screams, and desperate shouts of the other guards filled the confined space. The lights flickered back to life increasing the field of vision, and Reaper switched his fire between the three monsters in the room and the others crushing at the door.

Trex rose, targeted the mass of monsters, and fired. With skin as dark as night and tentacles flailing, they looked like a depraved blending of killer octopus and oversized gorilla.

"Guard down!"

"Badger's bleeding out!"

"Medic!"

The desperate shouts and calls over Trex's earpiece cut deep. *We're losing this fight.*

The tentacled creatures filled the tight space, rampaging through desks, machinery, even ceiling tiles.

"We're cut off!"

"They've blocked the exit!"

The calls from her squad intensified. They were dying. *No, we're being slaughtered.*

Trex's mind raced. She wasn't reacting fast enough. They weren't ready for this.

"Grenade!" Scox's voice was barely audible over the din.

Trex turned just in time to see Scox load a high explosive grenade into his XLi2's underslung launcher as August and Reaper dropped to the ground. The grenade arced into the writhing mass of hulking arms and tentacles.

The explosion threw Trex back into the wall again. Ears ringing, her vision blurred by dust clouds, she coughed and tried to gather her bearings.

The gunfire had stopped. The calls of her guards had stopped. The thumping, crashing, and rampaging had all ceased.

Silence.

Reaper, coated with thick chucks of translucent blue goo, emerged like a ghost through the dust. Trex gripped his outstretched hand and Reaper pulled her to her feet. Chunks of blue goo dripping off her too.

"The octo-apes are gone," Reaper said.

"Scox and August?"

"They'll live."

"Squads report," Trex wheezed into her chin microphone.

"Bravo. We're fucked up but we're all here."

"Charlie. Two KIA. Badger and Stevens. Two walking wounded."

"Delta. One KIA. Lopez. The rest of us are still in the fight."

"Zulu. One KIA. Johnson. Three badly injured, but not out of the game. Those monkey motherfuckers ran past us. They're heading to the lobby."

Fuck! Four down and we've only just started. "Let's push the advantage," Trex said to Reaper.

"Right!" Reaper barked. "Get your shit together. We'll come back for our fallen brothers and sister. We're moving. Now!" Reaper lifted August to his feet by his drag straps and pushed him out into the corridor. Trex helped Scox up and dusted the young man down, dried blood trails ran from his ears to his chin.

"Sorry, Cap," Scox said with a cough and an apologetic smile.

"No, you did good. Now let's go even the odds."

The team formed up in the corridor, checking each other and their weapons. She passed the bodies of her fallen guards and forced a wave of regret down into a hot ball of rage, silently promising each of them vengeance.

Trex took point, moving at speed. The single corridor led straight to the first lobby that connected B3 to B2. Trex desperately wanted to get her guards into that part of the level. With a cache of heavier ordnance, wide open spaces, and clear arcs of fire, it was a shooter's paradise. There, she'd own a commanding advantage over the monsters. First, they needed to clear the twisting labyrinth of labs, offices and storage rooms.

Trex raised her fist, stopping the guards' outside the next set of doors. "Right," she said. "We're going to roll up this corridor to the end. Fast and efficient. Groups of two. In the room, call it. Get out. Only stop if we have contact. Otherwise, grenade the room, lock the doors and keep moving. Clear and move. Clear and move. Let's get it done. Go."

The first calls came quietly over the team's radio.

"Clear."

"Clear."

"Clear."

Trex maintained her position at the front of the column, moving quickly towards the end of sub-level B3. Reaper, as ever, executing her orders in the thick of it.

"Five rooms to go," Trex whispered into her chin mic.

"Rene here. I've got a blind spot in this room. Wait one."

"Negative. Grenade the room and get out," Trex ordered.

The corridor's lights flickered, died. Darkness swallowed the team again. Rifle-mounted lights snapped on, illuminating small patches of the corridor.

"Contact! They're in the corridor!" The part-shout, part-scream came from the back of the column.

"Tentacles are coming through the fucking vents!"

The artificial lights snapped back on. Long, sleek tentacles protruded from every wall, floor and ceiling vent. The harsh light whipped every obsidian limb into a frenzy.

Snake-like tendrils wrapped around legs, arms and bodies. Guards were hurled in every direction, smashed into walls, floors, and each other.

A shout turned into a scream as the tentacles mercilessly dragged Inkster into a vent. His torso jammed in the narrow vent opening, and the scream morphed into a spine-chilling screech. The crunch of bone, then the screech died as his body dropped to the ground like a bag of wet meat.

"Fire into the ducts! Fire into the fucking ducts," Reaper roared.

Muzzle flashes erupted in all directions. Bullets thumped into every surface. Metal shrieked. Geysers of blue goo spurted from the bullet-riddled ducts.

Trex hacked off a tentacle with her combat knife, freeing Morloss. She dragged the young man to his feet and stared into his sheet-white face and saucer-wide eyes. "You and Briggs clear the path to the lobby," she yelled. "Get the auto turrets in here now. If anything stands in your way, you grenade that fuck square in the face. Do you understand me?" She shoved him forward.

Rene's voice emerged in Trex's ear. "They're in the room with me. I'm—"

An ear-splitting explosion cut short his transmission. Dust, debris, blue goo and a red mist erupted from the room.

"Rene's gone!" Reaper reported from the bent and warped doorway.

"We're moving! On me," Trex shouted into her mic, grabbing the nearest guard and dragging him after Morloss and Briggs.

Weapons up and firing at anything that moved, the team double-timed as quickly as those with leg injuries would allow.

Trex slowed the column at the sound of grenades crumping in the near distance. The roars and howls had now shifted ahead of them. "Morloss!" She shouted to be heard over the continuous fire of the guards behind her. "Report. Over!"

Fuck! Have I just sent two more to their deaths? Trex sped up, desperate to get to her men. Her vision tunnelled; her mind focused. She turned a corner and leaped over the faceless corpses of two octo-apes.

The tac channel crackled in her ear. "Trex. Morloss. The lobby is clear. Repeat, the lobby is clear. Auto turrets are up and will cover your approach."

Morloss's voice filled her with relief. The two auto turrets would target anything not wearing smart armour... if they behaved as they should. Leading eleven guards past activated auto turrets, in close quarters, at speed, covered in body parts of other creatures wasn't best practice. But she had no choice. It was either that or hang around to be sucked into a vent or thrashed to death by a bio-engineered super gorilla with octopus parts stuck on for good measure.

Two football-sized orbs flew past Trex and her team. Seconds later, buzzsaw sounds filled the corridors. The howls and roars turned to squeals of pain. Trex couldn't stop her smile.

Trex turned the last corner and saw Morloss and Briggs waving her in. She powered the team over the last twenty metres.

Sprinted past Morloss and Briggs, turned to count thirteen guards, then collapsed onto the lobby's cold, hard floor.

* * *

After switching to heavier ordnance, Trex led her fourteen-strong team up to sub-level B2, Reaper taking rear-guard position. She chinned her mic to the private link she shared with her 2IC. "Reaper, was that an ambush back there? Did they set us up?"

"Captain, who knows what those mad scientists cooked up. They've created super creatures and weaponised them for warfare."

"Was there anything in the bio-security reports about the creatures being resistant to 5.56mm rounds at point blank range?" she asked.

"Those reports aren't worth the shit they're written on, Captain. They've never taken our security protocols seriously. That's why we're in this mess. " He paused. "External blast doors are still sealed and electrified."

As they passed the crumbled remains of the internal doors, Trex heard a soul-piercing screech, accompanied by muted roars. The sound was unsettling enough to slow the advance of the team but far enough away to make its origin impossible to pinpoint.

"What in God's name was that?" Scox whispered.

"God had nothing to do with whatever made that sound," Briggs replied.

"Something worse than the octo-apes." Reaper's response was more of a question than an answer.

"Sounds like all of them," said Trex as she upped the team's pace towards the mauled door at the end of the long corridor.

"Fighting each other?" Scox said.

"Na, Scox. Fucking each other." Soft chuckles rippled from the guards, masking the fear worming into their minds.

As if on cue, the corridor's lights flickered and died. Thin beams of torchlight lit the way, probing the darkness.

"So, what fucked up monstrosity are we up against now?" Briggs said.

Trex didn't answer. Not because the information was classified, which it was, but because she didn't know.

Reaper must have sensed the awkward silence. "I don't give a fuck what it looks like, if you see Yogi Bear munching a picnic basket, you light the fucker up."

"Room's up ahead," Trex said, exhaling slowly.

"Kappie. Morloss. You're up," Reaper motioned.

The first door slid up. The lights flickered back to life and four octo-apes exploded through the walls and into the corridor.

The acoustics of the heavier XLS1s were deafening. Like a chainsaw in a shower cubicle, and just as messy. 7.62mm rounds thumped into the attackers, shredding them into chunks of blue meat. It was over as fast as it started.

"Take that you ugly bastards! How you like me now!" Kappie roared at the four lifeless bodies heaped on the floor.

"Everyone's accounted for," Reaper told Trex.

Moving deeper into sub-level B2 they continued to clear rooms. The new XLS1s were long and somewhat awkward in the confined space but Trex couldn't argue their results. The boost to moral was unmeasurable.

Trex started to entertain the idea the octo-apes had killed the other breached creatures as a T-Junction loomed ahead. She stopped the team and a few beats later Reaper's voice sounded in her ear. "Right. Left is a dead end."

Trex was astonished at Reaper's supernatural ability to read her mind. She had the deepest respect for the man. He was un-killable, the first ever BSS guard and one of the complexes founding members. His intimate knowledge of the subterranean maze was unrivalled. His service record was one of the most impressive she'd ever seen. Including the parts the public would never see. He'd put down several breaches in the complex's ten-year history. But never a full one hundred per cent breach. Nothing like what was happening now.

Howls reverberated down the narrow corridor, washing over the team like a wave, tensing their muscles and eroding their sense of safety. These howls sounded different however, full of anguish. Like those made when the auto turrets buzzed through the octo-apes down on B3.

Suddenly, the T-junction was filled with a mass of black fur and flailing tentacles. Then just as suddenly, the monsters stopped, turned, and ran in the opposite direction.

"That's not good," Trex whispered.

A roar was viciously cut short. Then another. And another.

"That ain't either," Kappie muttered.

"Fuck! Contact!" The call came from the back of the stationary column, followed by a short burst of heavy gunfire.

"Report," Trex called over the radio.

"Shorty is dead," Reaper replied.

"Morloss. Kappie," Trex said. "Take point. Find out what's happening up ahead."

Trex reached Reaper at the back of the column and found Shorty in two pieces. His body cleanly severed from shoulder to hip, crimson pooling between the body parts.

"Was that a tentacle?" asked Briggs.

The question was met with silence.

"Captain," Kappie's voice came through the comms. "You're gonna want to see this."

"Keep it together, people," Reaper ordered. "Stay close and watch each other's backs," he said, following Trex to the forward position.

They found Kappie and Morloss standing over the decapitated mess of body parts that looked like two or possibly three octo-apes. Each chunk was cleanly severed, not ripped, torn or pulled to pieces. Cut, just like Shorty.

"Contact rear!"

The deafening report of an XLS1 flooded the tight space. Trex spun, weapon raised, but saw nothing.

"Report. What's out there?" Trex demanded.

"It's gone," August said, his voice shaky. "It was there, I swear."

"What was there?" Reaper demanded.

"It's... ah... fuck, I don't know," August said.

"Was it another damn monkey?" Reaper asked.

"No. It… was carrying a… a scythe," August whispered.

"Are you fucking shitting me?" Briggs blurted. "What's down here, Cap? What the hell have these whitecoats made?"

Trex remained silent. The eyes and expectations of her team drilled into her. She had nothing to offer because she didn't fucking know.

"Right," Reaper snapped. "This changes nothing." The lights overhead flickered, punctuating his point. "Power is failing, and we've still got the rest of B2 and all of B1 to secure. We've got to move. Add Farmer Jack to your list of supernatural monsters that need a bullet to the face. Jones. Tracy. Clear the last room. Kappie, Morloss scout up ahead and report back."

Trex moved with the team, but on muscle memory alone. She felt detached from reality. Useless.

"Conta—" Tracy's words were cut short.

A burst of heavy gunfire then nothing but eerie silence.

Trex shoved guards out of her way and stormed into the room. Ribbons of what used to be Jones and Tracy lay in bloody heaps, pools of blood glistening on the floor.

"Fuck!" Trex roared. Her head spun; her stomach dropped. The room was empty. The threat was gone but she couldn't drag her eyes off the two guards.

Kappie's voice crackled over the channel. "Reaper? Corridor ends with a room full of lab spaces. Lights are out, red emergencies are on. But no sign of any movement."

"Copy that. We're inbound your location. Secure it and stay put," Reaper replied.

Trex flinched as Reaper firmly grabbed her shoulder.

"We're not done, Captain." She caught his eye, his expression softer than she'd seen in the twelve months of working together, but it was full of urgency. She got it. Whatever she was experiencing – guilt of blindly leading her team into hell, remorse or whatever the hell it was… she wasn't helping her team. She wasn't effectively leading them.

Trex nodded at her 2IC and sped to Kappie's position.

● ● ●

A quick look into the darkened room revealed no sign of any movement. Trex stopped and inspected the shredded tatters of the doors. With the muzzle of her XLS1, she nudged chunks of blue gore from the angry, metal barbs.

The metallic stink of death drew her into the room, the largest laboratory on B2. The space was considerably darker than the lower lobby, illuminated by the emergency red lights around the walls. The silence in this space was its own beast.

The lab space was large but split into arrays of smaller cubicles. Each with their own half-height stud walls. *Large enough to manoeuvre the XLS1s but still small enough to be ambushed.*

"Looks like something is hunting the octo-apes," Kappie whispered, her XLS1 pointing at the remains of two mangled corpses. Dismembered tentacles were scattered nearby.

"Defensive line," Trex snapped. "Expect anything. August, Scox, you're with Reaper on the left flank. Kappie, take Briggs, Jamieson, Morloss – right flank. Cummings, O'Neil, and Wesley, you're on me. Eyes sharp. Slow is smooth, smooth is fast."

The progress of the team slowed, fatigue setting in. Chatter on the comms had returned to simple reports confirming their areas had been cleared. Trex could feel the tension of all her guards. Facing down creatures bred to kill was stressful enough, knowing you were walking into an ambush was something else entirely.

The massive black form of an octo-ape stalked into the room, thirty metres ahead of the team's advance. Trex tensed, her three guards mimicking her battle-ready posture. All eleven guards shouldered their XLS1s.

The nightmarish creature instantly spotted Trex, its merciless eyes narrowing into what Trex swore was a knowing stare of revenge.

The creature, bathed in the eerie red glow of the emergency lights, released a godless howl that flooded the room. The beast thumped its chest. Its tentacles extended to their full length, tripling the monster's size. The thing charged, shattering the cubicles, hurling objects at the team.

"Fire!" Trex roared. The rage in her voice matched that of the beast smashing its way toward her.

The line of XLS1s flashed. Blue spurts of ichor exploded from the creature's body. Its rabid howl turned to one of pain as the team fired off twenty-two rounds per second of death and fury.

A louder smash sounded to Trex's rear, tugging at her attention. Flying chunks of metallic debris peppered the back of her neck, cutting into her exposed skin.

Trex turned to see three more octo-apes had exploded into the room.

"Contact rear!" Trex roared.

Before she could engage, green blurs dropped onto the beasts, forcing them to the floor. Bellows and ear-splitting screeches fought to dominate the air.

The green blurs materialised into a towering mantis-serpent hybrids that must have been responsible for the deaths of Shorty, Jones, and Tracy.

"Light 'em up," Trex shouted.

The octo-apes wrestled to their feet, flailing wildly and shifted their attention to the bladed serpents. The massive creatures consumed the tight space. The two monsters couldn't be more different. The sleek iridescent green scales of the bladed serpents shimmered as the creature jerked, seemingly anticipating the thrashing limbs of the octo-apes. Its bony quills, accentuating its slender form, made it impossible for a hand or tentacle to find purchase.

"Cease fire," Trex ordered, and the team responded, ducking out of the way.

The battle for supremacy between these two monsters had sprawled across the room, crushing and destroying anything that got in their way.

Lightning-quick, the scythe-like forearms of the bladed serpents sliced through muscular arms and tentacles with ease. The octo-apes erupted with rampaging fury, and the serpents seemed to feed off the rage. The more desperate and enraged the octo-apes became, the less the serpentine figures moved.

After several perfectly-aimed swipes, the bladed serpents reduced the octo-apes into a mess of blue-goo.

In the dying moments of the monsters' battle, the realisation that the bladed serpents had dropped from the ceiling hit Trex with a cold chill.

Her gaze shot upwards.

The entire ceiling was a writhing sea of iridescent green tails. The white beam of light from her gun glinted off razor sharp blades.

"The fuckers are on the ceiling!" Trex screamed into her chin mic.

As if awaiting her words, three of the bladed serpents dropped onto Cummings, O'Neil and Wesley. Trex cut loose the cumbersome XLS1, giving her the agility to sprint and weave through the devastated lab spaces.

Dropping nightmares missed her by millimetres as she ran. Dodging as best she could, Trex's foot slid across chunks of blue gore. She smashed, hard, into a cluster of destroyed lab equipment.

Kappie's defensive line erupted with bright flashes of gunfire as the four XLS1s went cyclic. Rounds smashed into every surface behind and above Trex. Geysers of tar-like purple fluid shot from the iridescent surfaces. The putrid-smelling substances caused Briggs and Jamieson to gag, buckle and vomit. The din of ear-splitting screeches had Morloss drop his weapon, opting to use his hands to shield his ears from the painful sound.

More of the bladed serpents continued to drop from the ceiling.

Reaper pulled Trex to her feet, aimed and thumped powerful 7.62mm rounds into the nightmare creatures. Reaper had helped her up yet again, now she was determined to press what little advantage their superior firepower provided.

"I'm pushing to the upper lobby!" Trex shouted over the excruciating screeching of the serpents. "I'm coming back with the auto turrets. Gather the guards. Firing withdrawal to the upper lobby. Got that?"

"Copy," Reaper replied.

Trex's world spun and her head thumped but she wasn't slowing, not with some many of her guards' lives on the line.

The lights in the upper lobby were on, barely. Trex gave a cautionary glance upwards and scanned her surrounds. The carpet-lined floor provided much needed traction and a welcome change from the slick floors of the labs. This lobby was as sparsely populated as the last. A couple of desks and sofas, but more importantly, the massive main exit door to the surface was still intact.

The cyclic sound of heavy weapons was replaced by the crumping of high explosive grenades. The doorway into the lab space flashed with each percussive blast.

Trex ripped away the wall panel to reveal the cache of weapons and the sentry system control interface. Working off its own battery power, she furiously called up the commands to activate the sentries. A few seconds later and two spherical auto turrets dropped from the ceiling and hovered a metre above the floor. They blinked, then zoomed into the labs.

"Reaper. Trex. Turrets inbound. Evac. Now!"

● ● ●

Reaper was the last guard through the door. The team encircling Trex were panting and exhausted. But with weapons raised, they were not out of the game.

The glorious buzzsaw sounds of the auto turrets whirled non-stop for forty seconds, halting only when the screeching turned to shrilling, then to silence. They floated back into the lobby, viscous purple ichor dripping from their spherical bodies.

"I love those fucking floating bots," Kappie said, breaking the tension.

The seven guards broke their defensive stance, hit the weapons cache and started reloading.

"Jamieson?" Trex asked.

Reaper simply shook his head. "Right. Listen up team. We're at the main entrance but we're not done. Stock up, we're clearing sub-level B1 in two minutes. Kappie, what's in that cache?"

"XLH1 50 cals, XLV1 rockets, a fuck tonne of 7.62mm rounds. HE grenades. Hell, we even have bayonets and flares," Kappie replied.

Trex studied her watch. Any minute now the power would go off, permanently and her reinforcements were still miles away.

She watched her remaining six guards as they exchanged ammunition and tended to each other's injuries. Covered in dust, blood, gore, putrid purple gel and dried chunks of blue, they looked like shit. They'd been through hell. Correction, two levels of hell. Non-stop, nerve-shredding hell, yet here they were. Getting stuck in. United. Digging down. Staying the course. She'd lost thirteen guards since this began. Seeing the last six stack up at the entrance into sub-level B1, her next order was clear.

"We're last standing right here," she said.

Six sets of eyes locked on to her.

"The exit is right there," Trex pointed to the massive metallic wheel behind her, the words *Lock Down. No Exit* scrolling along the top. "We've suffered enough. I don't know what's hiding beyond that door." She pointed to the large doorway leading to B1. "But I can promise you it'll be one hundred times worse than everything we've faced so far. This is the line. If hell wants to get to the surface, they'll have to come through here. Through us. I don't know about you, but I'm sick of being fucking ambushed. We fight on our terms now."

"Let's give 'em hell, Cap!" Kappie cheered.

"Kappie, August, Morloss – stack those tables and sofas into a sangar facing the labs. See if you can't get those ceiling cannons online. Reaper, Briggs, Scox – let's lure those fuckers out of B1."

Reaper's lip twitched in what only Trex knew to be a smile. "Right! You heard the captain. 50 cals stay here. Advanced squad gear up with the XLS1s. Load-up with extra grenades and explosive rounds. Let's end this!"

* • •

"Auto turrets in position at your six." Kappie's voice was clear and calm through the comms.

Trex glanced back up the corridor and saw the two spherical weapons hovering just below ceiling height. Whatever they found down here, they'd fall back, luring the monsters into the kill box. The turrets would stay where they were, just outside the lobby; she wanted as much firepower covering the dash to her last stand position as she could afford.

"Great. Another dark room," Scox said.

"This door did not have a good day," Briggs said with a chuckle.

Trex regarded the doors for a second, typical slicing and tortured steel ripped apart. The same signature-breaching methods seen down on B2 and B3. They had a tasty influx of serious fire power, but Trex couldn't help wondering what these *demons* the shit-scared scientists spoke about at the briefing were capable of. Trex's team had paid a high price to get this far, to keep humanity above safe. *What will I have to sacrifice to bring these monsters down? Everything. Fucking everything.*

She stepped quietly out of the bright corridor and into the chilled darkness of B1's labs, the promise to exact revenge for her fallen guards like a hand at her back.

This darkness felt alive. It chilled Trex to her very soul.

"On the ceiling, other end of the room," Scox whispered, weapon raised.

Trex followed the white beam of light from Scox's weapon to the writhing mass of iridescent green scales and bony quills.

"Cap... we've..." Kappie's voice faltered through static.

"Kappie. Trex. Come back. Repeat your last. Over."

Only static.

Trex tried once more. Whispering into her mic.

Nothing.

The only reassurance was the lack of gunfire. *Maybe they never had the chance to fire a single shot.* Trex nixed that thought and refocused. "Right. Stop here. We cut the fuck out of these bastards. Get their attention. Then led them back down to the sangar. Rinse and repeat. Got it?" Trex whispered to her three guards. "Pick a target. Fire."

Bullets thumped into the ceiling. Brilliant flashes lit the room like a fireworks display. Agonised screeches filled the air. Trex clenched her teeth, grinding her jaw to endure the pain spiking through her ears.

Shimmering green bodies dropped from the ceiling, smashing into the furniture below.

"Cease fire," Trex called. "Wait until they see us. Then we—"

"What the fuck is that!" Briggs shouted.

All around the room, pairs of red-gold eyes flicked open.

Trex spun, her light searching. Whatever was connected to those demonic eyes were too quick to be caught by the light. The darkness felt more intense. Alive. Suffocating.

Demons.

"We're surrounded," Reaper called out.

A short burst of gunfire erupted in the distance. *Kappie's position.*

"Fire and move towards the doors. Stay together," Reaper ordered.

Scox and Briggs launched a deadly barrage of explosive-tipped rounds into the tightest concentration of the bladed serpents rushing towards them. Trex and Reaper flanked the two guards, trying but failing to hit whatever was behind those demonic eyes.

"Running low. Reloading in zero five seconds," Briggs roared.

"Go. I'm halfway through mine!" Scox replied.

Halfway to the door the team's weapon-mounted lights began to flicker and die. Muzzle flash and the glow from the corridor were now the team's only source of illumination. The short bursts of light provided Trex with blinking images of a live-action horror scene. Swarms of bladed serpents were moving closer. The two XLS1s doing little to slow the growing horde's advance.

Trex lost her footing on a viscous lump and crashed into an office desk. The impact sent wicked spikes of pain into her ribs despite the heavy body armour.

She scrambled towards the light of the corridor, the thick darkness threatening to consume her. Unable to find her footing, she rolled to avoid the crushing force of the bladed creatures as they continued to drop from the ceiling. She watched helplessly as gleaming, eyeless heads tilted towards her team. Squirts of fluid shot from the tip of their conical faces. Backlit by the corridor's light, Trex watched in horror as the grey liquid wrapped around Scox's, then Brigg's head, congealing around every orifice.

Both men dropped their weapons. Their screams were stifled, unable to draw breath. In seconds their heads melted, their bodies dropping into lifeless heaps.

A blood-curdling growl erupted from her.

Only one of the bladed serpents remained. A skeletal hand clamped over the creature's head. Undeterred by the bony quills, the fist clenched tightly. Pungent purple tar oozed through sharp, angular fingers before the carcass was tossed aside.

Two blood-gold eyes glared at her. Framed by the glow from the corridor, Trex stared into evil.

"Demon," she muttered.

Pairs of those blood-gold eyes began to wink into existence again within the undulating darkness of the lab. *Reaper. Where's Reaper?*

The nearest set of eyes seemed to burn through her chest, setting her soul on fire, and she hoped like hell her 2IC had made it out alive.

Trex thrashed as she was plucked off the ground.

"Captain. We gotta go. Now!"

Reaper dragged Trex to her feet and pulled her into the corridor. "What the hell was that?" he shouted as they fled.

Trex's mind raced, trying to piece together what she'd seen of the demon. "It looked like some sort of... dragon, I think," Trex yelled, panting hard. "Reaper, it's face was bone. It's face, arms and legs were bone. It had no skin!"

The ceiling and wall lights immediately behind them started dying. Trex and Reaper ran, and the darkness gave chase.

That same demonic growl nipped at their heels. Growing louder. Closer.

Trex glanced over her shoulder; scores of blood-gold eyes flooded into the corridor.

High explosive rounds whizzed past Trex. They thumped and exploded mere metres behind her. She kept close to the right side of the corridor, offering the hovering auto turrets the clean lines of sight they would need to keep the demons off her and Reaper's backs. At least for as long as it would take for her to get behind a XLH1 and use its firepower to cut these bastards into chucks.

"Captain!" Kappie's voice cut through a blast of static. "Captain. Do you copy? Over." Kappie's voice grated with static.

"Kappie. This is Trex. We're coming in hot."

"We lost comms with you earlier. The auto-suppression turrets are red on ammo. One zero seconds left. When you enter the lob—" Kappie's voice was cut off by a blast of static.

"Fuck!" Trex yelled, ripping the comms receiver from her ear. Were the demons creating the electronic interference? Lights and comms always went dark when these things were near. It couldn't be a coincidence.

The first auto turret stopped spitting its life-saving ordnance. The second one would be dry in seconds.

Trex's blood ran cold, her peripheral vision catching the skeletal snort of a demon as it tried to grab her. The final auto turret used the last of its ammunition to destroy the demons nearest to Trex. Spurts of black mist coated her as she fought to resist the lactic acid burning through her legs.

The skeletal demons closed the gap, Trex and Reaper at the front of the stampede. The monsters' growls were hot and putrid on the back of her neck.

Metres away from the end of the corridor, Kappie and August materialised, weapons raised.

"Fire in the hole!" Kappie roared.

Trex heard the thuds of two high explosive grenades leaving their underslung launchers. The explosives arced over Trex and Reaper, smashing into the horde at their backs. The percussive force propelled Trex and Reaper into Kappie and August, and all four guards flew out of the corridor, smashing hard into their makeshift sangar.

* •   •*

"There's some weird fucking dragon thing trying to get through that door!" Morloss shouted to Trex and pointed towards the doorway leading down to the labs of B2.

Trex took Reaper's outstretched hand once more and pushed to her feet. "Wonderful," Trex replied. "Tell that bitch there's a queue. August, grab that box of flares."

"Everyone back on the XLH1s," Reaper ordered. "Shit's about to get real."

"Briggs and Scox?" August asked.

Trex could only shake her head.

She attached the 50-calibre weapon and dropped behind the long v-shaped sangar that provided all-round protection but faced the two entry points – the corridor that led into B1 and the doorway that led down to B2. She was furious at losing Briggs and Scox. They'd barely made it five hundred metres, and she'd lost half of the advance team. *I hope to heaven this wave is the all of them.*

Pushing that thought aside, Trex rose into the eerie stillness and joined the remaining four guards. They were alone in the lobby facing two entry points. She knew better than to think two HE grenades had destroyed the entire demon horde of B1. *This respite wouldn't last long.*

"The ceiling cannons," Trex said. "Do we have ceiling cannon support!"

"We did," Morloss said. "They kept that fucking dragon thing away. It stopped working just before you flew through the door."

"Black on ammo?" Reaper asked.

"Nope. The digital controls just died," Morloss replied.

Trex rubbed her hand over her face and through her hair, her fatigue showing. *Maybe it's over.* She hated to admit it, but holding this area was suicide. There was no victory to be had here.

"No auto turrets. No cannons," Kappie said. "The damn exit doors won't open. 'Bout to be attacked by the spawn of hell, on two fronts. Just the way I like it."

The remaining lights in the corridor of B1 leading to the lobby started flickering and dying.

"Here we fucking go again," Morloss muttered.

A deafening chorus of merciless growls burst from the blackness.

"August. Flares. How many and what type?" Trex asked.

"Thirty. Cyalume. Five minutes. Intense light," August replied.

"Pop those flares. Six at a time. Wide arc around the sangar," Trex ordered. "All right, guards. Twenty-five minutes of wonderful life-saving light. Then this shit gets real interesting."

"No retreat, no surrender, you motherfuckers!" Reaper yelled.

● ● ●

Ten sets of blood-gold eyes burst out of the inky black corridor. Using their powerful back legs, they launched into the air and arced towards the sangar. Teeth, claws and bony spikes first.

Like an anti-aircraft battery, the guards matched the arc of the airborne threat and filled the air with high-explosive, 50-calibre rounds. Chunks of black, bony body parts and viscous inky gore rained over the five guards as the creatures slammed to the floor. The threat eliminated.

"Fuck yeah!" Kappie roared.

"Keep your shit together," Reaper said. "Next wave. Get ready."

Twice as many demons rushed into the lobby, staying grounded and swarming the sangar. Darkness continued to ooze from the entrance to B1, swallowing the room's white lights. But it was enough to give Trex her first clean look at the demons.

The creatures were in a whole different category of horrific. *The white coats must have been proud of you, you motherfuckers.* Trex pumped out round after round towards the encircling demons.

Moving at unfathomable speed the bipedal creatures were almost impossible to hit. Their long, skeletal frame providing little to aim for and a lot to miss. The things must have been ten metres long from the tip of their bony, crocodile-like snout to the end of their long-barbed tail. These things weren't demons, they were more dinosaur or dragon than a crocodile. But the maw was unmistakably reptilian. She raked her weapon from side to side, covering her sector of fire. As far as she could tell, no-one had landed a direct hit much less dropped any of the things.

"Fuck!" Trex cursed. *Only a matter of time, you fuckers.*

"Target their legs!" The shout came from Reaper.

Trex dropped her aim and let rip. Chunks of carpet and concrete leapt into the air. Seconds later,Trex had blown off clawed feet and shattered legs.

"Reloading!" The call came from behind Trex. She glanced at the ammo counter on the side of the weapon. *Half empty.*

"More inbound!" August yelled.

Ranks of demons continued to pour into the lobby, willingly filling the voids left by their fallen brethren. Within seconds, the sangar became an island, isolated by a sea of jet-black death. The tide seemed endless. If retreating was ever an option, it had long passed. The guards were now in the eye of the storm. And the storm was ever-expanding. Hitting one of the abominations quickly became harder as the creatures started twisting, turning and changing direction.

"They're testing our defences. Watch your ammo levels," Reaper shouted over the song of battle.

"Test this you ugly bastards!" Kappie yelled.

Trex felt the force and heat of three explosions push at her from behind.

Darkness had totally consumed the lobby, the eerie green glow of the flare sticks now the team's only source of light.

Fifty-cal rounds spat out in every direction. With overlapping fields of fire, Trex had no idea how the creatures were still alive, let alone mobile. Not just mobile but getting closer. Targeting was becoming problematic as the storm of black death surged. Demonic skeletal maws snapped at their faces but stopped short of attacking. *Are they calculating our angles and rate of fire?*

"Reloading!" Morloss called to Trex's left.

Trex's fears were instantly confirmed. The temporary drop gave the creatures the opening they were waiting for. One of the demons lunged into the sangar, directly at Morloss. Teeth, claws and spikes smashed into Morloss, and sent the other guards sprawling to the deck.

Their defensive circle had been breached.

Morloss' scream was the worst sound Trex had ever heard but it was short lived. His face was ripped off, and the demon feasted on the blood and flesh that came with it. Reaper, the first to regain his feet, used the end of his weapon to smash the creature in the face, stunning it, then 50 calibre rounds at point-blank range ended the creature before it could continue its meal.

Trex and the others furiously re-engaged, closing the gap. The creatures were upon them. Skeletal maws snapped ferociously. Trex alternated between smashing faces with the butt of her weapon then thumping high explosive rounds into the small spaces she created. Adrenaline, panic and training gave the guards enough space to survive. For now.

"Keep those flares coming!" Trex shouted.

Beaten back but far from destroyed, the remaining demons howled, heralding a new wave entering the battlefield. The green glow from the second set of flares cast malformed shadows over the area.

The air was filled with gunfire, cordite and death. The four remaining guards fought back to back. Ammo was quickly running low for the 50 cals. It wouldn't be long before they had to resort to the XLS1s – smaller magazines, less stopping power.

The beginning of the end. But hope rose within Trex as the seemingly endless tide of demons slowed – the storm began to thin.

"Pour it on! They're wearing down!" Trex roared.

A demon snapped forward and bit down on Trex's forearm before she blew its head off in a spray of black mist.

Excruciating pain ripped through her limb. *Fire. I'm on fire.* She tore off the body armour covering her wrist.

"Cover me!" Trex called. The gunfire slowed as the attackers evaporated into the ethereal darkness. Distant growls told her this was far from over. She needed to tend to her wounds while she had time.

An ugly bite mark ringed her arm, right through double helix insignia. The armour had absorbed the bulk of the blunt force trauma, but the demon saliva was eating through her skin like acid. The fingers of her right hand tingled. It would soon lose strength and dexterity. Adrenaline surged, and she fought through the urge to scream. Dropping what remained of her sleeve, she rejoined the fight.

"Flares," Trex ordered through gritted teeth.

August complied. Reaper and Kappie fired sporadically at the few remaining demons in the room.

The low growling rose to a roar. *Both entry points.*

"Ammo check," Reaper ordered.

"One full mag of 50 cal. Then I'm on the XLS1," Kappie reported.

"I'm on the XLS1 now," August muttered. "But suited and booted with enough mags and HE grenades. We have more flares than ammo."

Trex tossed her now useless XLH1 and shouldered her XLS1. Reaper did the same. Trex's arm flared hot and blistering.

"When the time comes," Trex said, blinking back the pain. "We use the XLV1 rockets to drop the ceiling over those two doorways." She gave it one last glance before the thumping of Kappie's XLH1 drew her attention to the entrance to B1.

"Incoming!" Reaper shouted.

Fresh waves of demons surged into the room. The green glow from the flare showed this wave was just as large as the previous one.

"Reaper, August, aim high!" Trex roared.

Within seconds the sangar was surrounded again, the demons opting for a full-frontal assault this time. Jet black, razor sharp maws chomped dangerously close, only to be filled with lead and sent tumbling back into the dark sea of chaos. *Getting desperate, are we?*

Trex sensed the monsters wanted to finish this, now. *End game, motherfuckers.* Time to ramp it up.

"Reloading!" August roared.

"Grenade!" Reaper shouted. With three thuds from his grenade launcher, the landscape around the sangar blossomed with brilliant blasts of white and yellow.

"Fix bayonets!" Reaper yelled. Trex glanced at her 2IC, and she saw a mass of destroyed bony demons lying in front of him. The man periodically switching from launching grenades into the near distance and stabbing those who were lunging and biting at him.

"I'm running low on ammo," August shouted. "I'm going for the rockets."

"Covering you! Go!" Trex shouted.

She increased her arc of fire. Her own ammunition indicator flashed with an amber warning light.

"Fuck you!" Reaper yelled.

Trex spared a glance behind her. Reaper stood over the now screaming Kappie, one of the demon's long barbed tails in one hand whilst he smashed 750 rounds per minute of pure hate into the owner's face. With the creature thoroughly dead he pulled two grenades and tossed them into the horde.

Muffled crumps, then body parts were hurled into the air. Reaper climbed to the top of the overturned sofa. Elevated, he fired relentlessly into the nearest creatures.

Trex had only seconds to admire her 2IC. Deadly claws, barbed tails and vicious jaws were landing dangerously close.

August rose with the XLV1 resting on his shoulder. "Fire in the—"

A demon clamped its teeth around August's head and

yanked the guard into the horde, the XLV1 launcher dropping from lifeless fingers.

Trex spun, firing wildly. Turning. Firing. Reloading. Firing. Turning. Firing. The horde was thinning, but so was her team.

Kappie rose, blood bubbling from the gashes in her face, hefted the launcher and aimed. Claws sliced down her back as she fired, the explosion taking out the entrance into the labs of B2.

Deadly showers of steel, concrete and scorched demon parts showered down.

Reaper turned and destroyed Kappie's attacker as Trex stepped back to give herself some space. The demons crawled over their destroyed kin, pressing over the sangar to get to Trex and Reaper.

With a mangled cry, Kappie rose again, holding the last launcher. Pain twisted her partially melted face into a tortured mask.

One doorway permanently closed. One to go. Roars and growls from beyond the corridor to B1 was the harbinger of the next wave. They couldn't survive another. Humanity couldn't survive if they didn't.

"Do it!" Reaper roared. Trex and Reaper stood sentry over Kappie, firing in every direction, making sure the next clawed swipe or barbed tail would hit them before Kappie.

The rocket blasted from the launcher, right on target. The ceiling inside the dark corridor exploded.

The shock wave blasted everything around the sangar to the ground.

Trex rose first, and her heart sank when the smoke and dust cleared. The ceiling was still intact. The blast hadn't been enough to collapse the corridor. The ammunition indicator on her XLS1 flashed red.

A heinous howl rumbled up the corridor. Louder, stronger, angrier than any she'd heard thus far. Trex felt as much as heard the sound.·

Reaper emptied the last of his magazine into the remaining demons. He unslung his XLS1, its ammunition light flashing red. He stomped on the heads of demons trying to crawl into the sangar.

Kappie's one remaining eye stared lifelessly towards the ceiling. Trex dropped her XLS1, the crippling pain in her lower arm returning with vengeance. She slumped to the ground, aching and exhausted.

Darkness began reclaiming the lobby, creeping over everything in its path. The flares blinked out one by one.

That baleful howl drew closer.

A loud clunk sounded behind them. The sign above the exit read: *offline.* She had failed. Her team was dead, the demons were still coming, and nothing would stop them from breaching the complex and attacking the city above.

"No. Not this time," Trex said, refusing to take Reaper's outstretched hand. "You need to get to Colonel Jack Humphries at the UDR barracks." Trex flinched at the growing pain. "You need to get outta here."

She placed her hand on Reaper's shoulder and smiled sadly. He stared at her for a moment before nodding. He unsheathed three grenades from his rear pouches and handed them to her. He nodded one final time out of respect, and without another word, turned and ran towards the exit.

Trex dragged her beaten body to position herself between the demons and the exit. Propping herself against the doorway, she sat quiet and alone in the diminishing light of the lobby.

A pair of blood-gold eyes emerged from the corridor and entered the dark lobby. This one was bigger than all the others.

With her right hand, now numb and almost useless, Trex awkwardly pulled the pins on all three grenades.

The last flare flickered and died.

"Come and have a go," Trex whispered into the darkness.

CANUTE

R.P.L. Johnson

illiam Briggs looked out from the battlements, searching for any sign of the returning patrol. In the distance the nanomite colonies rose like a forest of cathedral spires above the ruins of Heathrow airport.

He checked his watch and raised his binoculars to scan the muddy track that wound through the cratered ruin of no man's land. When he finally saw the battered Land Cruiser leading the returning patrol, he let out a breath he hadn't remembered holding and started the long climb down.

The old country manor dated back to the 17th century, and its turrets and crenellations were originally decorative. They had been pressed into service in a war that its builders could never have foreseen.

Briggs ran down the ornate timber staircase to the main hall. Ditton Manor had once been home to the first Duke of Montague before being taken over by the British Admiralty. In the Second World War it had been reborn as a research station. The fledgling science of radar had been born within its stone walls. Later, the addition of a high-tech business park – joined to the old manor house by a tree-lined boulevard – had continued the manor's second life as a technology hub.

As far as Briggs knew, the manor had played no part in the development of the nanomites, perhaps that was why it still stood rather than being ground zero for the plague that had consumed the rest of the world.

Its high-ceilinged rooms were now dormitories. Its galleries were packed to the ceilings with crates of canned goods and vacuum-sealed tubs of legumes. The corridors were lined with bookshelves and the scavenged relics from half a hundred libraries. Art saved from the ruins of the Tate Modern and the National Gallery decorated the walls. Briggs himself had a Turner and a frieze from the Parthenon Marbles in his quarters. The end of the world had its benefits, it seemed.

Outside, Briggs walked the gravel path between what had once been ornate gardens and which were now high-yield vegetable beds. Tented Mylar greenhouses held other crops that would see them through the English winter. Or, at least, that was the plan. He looked up at the anthracite clouds. They churned in the chill westerly wind looking more like vast flocks of birds than any meteorological formation.

Briggs carried a pistol on each hip, making him look like a gunslinger straight from the Wild West. On his right was an old but serviceable Browning. On his left, an EM pistol, a sleek frame of black composite, glass, and high capacity rare-earth batteries. He checked the charge on the EM pistol. It was full: enough for twenty or so shots before it began to lose effectiveness. The nanomites themselves were vulnerable to electromagnetic pulses, but the microscopic machines were also capable of combining into autonomous colonies billions strong. These constructs – semi-organic creatures with nanomites instead of cells – were big enough to shield their innards from all but the strongest EM pulses.

He passed the first ring of defences, nodding at the teams manning the mortars and howitzers. In turn he received a smattering of nods and salutes from the quasi-military militia stationed there. Further out, a ring of earthwork berms studded with roughly concreted pill-box machine gun nests looked out onto no man's land. A bristle of scavenged weaponry stood sentry at their perimeter: a mismatch of tanks and armoured vehicles dating back to the Cold War. Centurions and Chieftains desperately pressed back into service, with a couple of M1 Abrams scavenged from the American base at nearby RAF Croughton, were all that stood between humanity and extinction. There were even a few Russian T-90s on the line. The world had contracted in those last days as desperate nations sent what men and materiel they could before they fell.

The best of the armour was still mobile. But the majority, rendered immobile either through damage or lack of parts, had been towed into protective pits so only their turrets appeared above ground.

A pair of Challenger 2 main battle tanks flanked the tech-gate. Fuel was scarce, and only one was running. The low rumble of the engine was a fluttering pressure against his chest. The 120mm main gun tracked the small group advancing up the path. Above the barrel a powerful electromagnetic cannon was mounted atop the main gun as if the tank had been fitted with an oversized telescopic sight.

Briggs waited just inside the tech-gate. The huge circle of humming magnets encased within a white plastic torus looked much like the MRI scanner from which its technology had come. It stood incongruously on the front grounds of the Manor about three hundred meters from the house like some giant techno-logical donut dropped from the sky. The muddy track that led down to the remains of the M4 motorway passed through the gate.

With the patrol so close the main guns were no longer effec-tive. The tank crews climbed warily out of their mounts and stood atop them, rifles to their shoulders.

Briggs shifted his gaze back to the patrol and tried to ignore what a sorry bunch they looked like. They were tired, that much was obvious from the way they slouched as they tramped up the muddy path to the gate. The Land Cruiser at the head of the column sagged on its axles. Briggs wanted to believe this was because it was heavily laden with supplies, but some suspension failure was more likely.

"How'd it go?" Briggs asked as the Land Cruiser pulled up before him.

Rachel, the leader of the rag-tag column, rubbed her eyes. She looked exhausted. It had been a long run, three days away from the Manor, and Briggs guessed there had been precious little time to sleep outside the estate's defences.

"Oh you know. Shit as usual," she replied. "But I think we're clean. Can we just do this so I can go take a shower?"

Briggs nodded. He signalled to the guards at the gate and then waved Rachel forward. He drew his EM pistol and aimed it at his friend and second in command as she walked through the gate.

Nothing happened.

"Told you." Rachel smiled, relief washing over her face. "We saw a cloud of mites around Heathrow. Looks like most of the airport is gone now, but they didn't seem interested in us."

"That's good to know," Briggs replied, sheathing his pistol. "I wonder if they've given up?"

"That's not exactly their nature."

Briggs signalled the rest of the patrol, and they started to walk through the gate one by one under the watchful eyes of the guards. The Land Cruiser had to be pushed through. Although most of its electrics were shielded, the strong magnetic fields inside the iris of the gate would still be enough to fry any active circuits.

Chloe Hepburn was the first to follow the Land Cruiser through the gate. Briggs was looking right at her as she stepped across its threshold and her leg crumpled underneath her. Flesh, bone and cloth disintegrated in the magnetic field. Without support from the leg, Chloe stumbled forward, pitching through the gate. Briggs had a single lucid second to recognize the expression of pure shock on her face before everything Chloe Hepburn had ever been was reduced to a drift of dead nanomites. As her body crossed the invisible threshold at the centre of the gate it disintegrated, blackening and crumbling as the electromagnetic forces tore the nanomite construct apart.

At the back of the column a man screamed as the quad bike he was riding dissolved under him. Steel and plastic turned to black tar that raced up his legs. His shouts of terror turned rapidly to screams of pain as the nanomites began to eat into him, ripping him apart cell by cell, his flesh broken down to its raw materials and rebuilt as offspring of the tiny self-replicating machines.

"Help me! Help!" he cried.

He waved his arms uselessly, wanting to reach down, to pull himself from the mass of nanomites, but afraid to touch the seething mass for fear of losing his hands to the voracious machines.

The guards fired their EM pistols, blasting dead nanomites out of the mass in handfuls of black sand, but it wasn't enough. The man's screams turned to frantic gasps, then just a dry whisper as the mites consumed his lungs. His panicked stare fixed on Briggs as questing tendrils of mites reached up and closed over his head.

Their prey consumed, the mass of nanomites burst outward in a spray of black spines, seeking new flesh to corrupt and convert.

A guard standing on the tank screamed as one of the spines burst through his chest, the living weapon melting into a swarm of nanomites that flowed over his body in an almost desperate hunger. His limbs changed, becoming longer and thinner, morphing into mantis-like chitinous blades of black glass. His head peeled apart, skin sloughing off his skull into the central mass of his former body. Blood-slicked bone glistened briefly before that too was consumed by the mites. More spines burst from the thing's body, impaling a neighbour. Whip-like cilia, hair-fine and sharp as a cheese-wire flailed in all directions, slicing effortlessly through flesh and steel, even cutting cleanly through the thick barrel of the tank's main gun.

Another spine jabbed toward the gate, toward Briggs, who still stood on the other side of the aperture.

He flinched instinctively, but the spine disintegrated in the magnetic field. Its fierce momentum was still enough to pepper his face with windblown sand.

The mites began to combine: the thing that had once been a guard merging with the remains of the former patrolman and his quad bike in a vaguely bipedal mass nearly three metres tall. It charged at its former comrades.

One of the tank crew fired their rifle in panic at the thing. The rounds punched straight through, as ineffective as firing at a swarm of bees. It grabbed the guard with one huge hand, lifted him off the ground and squeezed. The man's screams died in a gruesome crunch of crushing bone and tearing cartilage.

"EM weapons, dammit," Briggs shouted, drawing and firing his own EM pistol at the nanomite construct.

Rachel joined him, firing the powerful EM cannon slung under the barrel of her rifle.

The construct fell under the withering blasts of half a dozen EM weapons. It had only taken a few seconds, but it had left three people dead, not including the unfortunate Chloe Hepburn.

Briggs ushered two survivors through the gate. A third man lay trembling on the ground, and Briggs wracked his memory to remember the man's name. "It's okay Jarrod," he said. "It's over, you can come through."

Jarrod looked up at him, eyes wide with shock, his breath coming in short pants. He didn't look injured, just panicked. "I can't," he said eventually. "I can't go through."

"Of course you can. It's over now. Just walk through the gate and we'll get you looked after."

"What if I... What if I'm like Chloe?"

"You're not infected. The nanomites are all gone." Briggs fired his EM pistol at him without effect. "See."

"Chloe didn't know. I was talking to her all the way back. It was still her. She didn't know."

"You're not like Chloe," Briggs said. "If you were, you'd be dead already. But they might have left other things: shielded constructs. We need you to walk through the gate."

Jarrod began to work his way, crab-like, around the side of the gate. "You're right. I'm not infected, I can't be. You can just let me come around."

Briggs sheathed his EM pistol and drew the heavy Browning automatic. "You know we can't do that. We have to follow protocol."

Jarrod looked at the gate and then the razor-wire-filled ditch encircling the manor's grounds.

"Don't do it, Jarrod," Briggs warned. "We have to make sure you're clean."

Jarrod made a run for it, sprinting around the side of the gate, trying to breach the perimeter of razor wire rather than risk annihilation in the vortex of magnetic fields that whirled within it.

Briggs fired once with his Browning and Jarrod crumpled to the grass a couple of meters from the perimeter fence. Briggs looked closer, hoping to see some sign of infection, but the blood that flowed from the ruin that once been Jarrod's head was bright, human red.

* * *

Briggs sat quietly in his quarters, holding a small chest in his lap. It was made from dark wood and inlaid with walnut and a spiral design of some still lighter veneer. It was obviously antique but Briggs wasn't sure if it had been rescued from a museum before the fall, or had come with the manor house. Now it just held his memories.

Briggs opened the lid. Inside were dog tags, scraps of bloodied clothing, coins, jewellery and a child's plastic digital watch, its screen cracked and dead. Carefully, Briggs placed a plastic card on top of the pile: Jarrod's drivers license. One more reminder of all the people Briggs hadn't saved.

He gave himself a minute to grieve and tried to remember everything he could about the young man he'd been forced to kill. Then he closed the lid. One minute a day. That was all the time he could spare for the dead.

There was a knock at the door and Rachel entered without waiting for a response. "We've replaced the damaged tank at the tech gate with one of the Abrams and I've doubled the guard at the perimeter," she said. "I just hope that's enough."

She was still wearing the same clothes from the patrol, and even though she'd pulled her long hair back in a ponytail, Briggs could tell it was greasy and unwashed.

"When's the last time you slept?" he asked.

"I feel like I'm asleep on my feet right now." She slumped into an overstuffed leather armchair.

Briggs placed the chest back on the mantelpiece, found two crystal tumblers and half-filled both with whisky. He handed one to Rachel and took a seat opposite her.

Rachel waved her glass towards the chest. "Are you going to put me into that box of yours, one day?" she asked. "I'm curious... What would you keep? You could take a lock of hair I guess, provided the mites don't get me."

Briggs thought for a while. "You remember the convoy from London?"

"How could I forget?"

"At the hotel outside Heathrow... You found that room."

Rachel sipped her whisky and nodded. "It was a suite," she corrected.

"All of London on fire and you find the one suite that hadn't been looted."

Rachel closed her eyes and threw her head back. "Those sheets!" she said. "Egyptian cotton. I can still feel them."

"I still have a bottle from the mini bar," Briggs admitted. "Couldn't bring myself to drink it. Maybe I'll put that in the box."

"That was a good night." She smiled mischievously, suddenly looking younger and less tired.

"Yes... Yes it was."

"Makes a girl wonder why you never wanted another." She sipped at her whisky, watching him over the rim of the glass.

"And then what?" Briggs asked. "A relationship?" He sipped his drink. "Just one more thing to lose."

Rachel kicked his leg playfully. "We still have a relationship, asshole. It's called being friends."

"You know what I mean."

"Yeah, I suppose I do... Get the bottle."

Briggs leaned over and took a miniature plastic bottle of Smirnoff from a drawer. He handed it to her.

Rachel cracked the bottle open and swigged half of it down. She handed it back. "To old friends," she said, "and new memories."

"New memories," Briggs repeated and finished the rest of the bottle.

They drank in silence and Briggs refilled their glasses.

"Just what the hell happened out there, Ray?" he asked.

Rachel sighed. "I don't know," she said. "It seemed like the perfect run. Quiet. We managed to find some diesel at a petrol station outside Stanwell. Didn't see any nanomites, 'cept at a distance. I never even saw what took over Chloe."

"Did she seem right to you?" Briggs asked. "Jarrod said he was talking to her on the way back."

"Yeah, I heard them. She seemed fine."

Briggs took a sip of his whisky. He hated the medicinal iodine taste. But they had nothing else, and he felt like killing a few brain cells. "Do you remember John Bailey?"

Rachel shuddered theatrically. "I've been trying not to," she whispered.

John had walked knee deep into a pool of nanomites. Within seconds the mites had started dissolving him. He'd screamed as if he was being fed feet first into a woodchipper whilst he died.

"It wasn't like John," Rachel said. "They must have taken her over slowly, replicated her cell by cell. So slowly she probably didn't even notice."

"Can they do that?"

"I guess they can now."

"But her brain? Her... mind? That's more than just cells surely. How could they copy that? I was looking right at her, Ray. When she stepped through the gate, she wasn't expecting to die. She thought she was human."

Rachel's hand tightened on the glass. "Well, she wasn't. And if she'd got into the camp she'd have tried to kill us all. That's all these things do. They just eat. And if you get in the way, they eat you first."

"They're not mindless, Ray."

"I know, I know. But they're a weapon, Will. Like a smart missile or a drone. They've got just enough smarts to achieve their objective, but simulate a human? I don't think so."

Briggs felt his hand stray towards his chest, to the breast pocket where he had kept his cigarettes before they had run out.

"I know what I saw."

"But how?"

Briggs sat forward in his chair, the leather creaking beneath him. "I don't know. I mean, they're a distributed network right? A hive mind made up of trillions of individual nanomites working together."

"So?"

"So they were designed to act in colonies of a few trillion mites, maybe a couple of hundred kilos delivered as one payload. Now there must be megatons of mites just in the South East. Who knows how many worldwide..."

"You're saying their intelligence is scalable? More mites equal more brainpower?"

"Maybe."

Rachel drained the last of her whisky. "Just what we need."

"I need you to keep the patrols short. No more overnight trips. Don't give them time for the slow takeover."

"That's not going to work, Will. We've exhausted all the supplies within a day's travel. We need to go further, stay out longer."

"We can't."

"And then what? When we run out of fuel for the generator. When we can't power the gate or the EMP. What then? You just going to hold up your hand like King Canute and expect the tide to stop?"

Briggs didn't have an answer. "It's just for the short term until we figure this thing out. Let's just get through today," he said. "We can worry about tomorrow tomorrow."

"If you say so."

"And charge the EMP. I want it ready to fire around the clock. Take charge of the trigger yourself. If we're not using fuel for patrols you can take it to power the generator."

Rachel sighed again and set down her glass. "Come on, Will. It's not that bad. We'd just be burning fuel for nothing. Anyway, the EMP is kind of a last resort. You'll take out a lot of mites, but also every unshielded electrical circuit within a hundred clicks.

We'd be lucky to rebuild before winter. And that's if the mites leave us alone."

"Humour me."

Rachel grimaced. "Okay, you're the boss. But we're going to need fuel sometime. This strategy of yours won't work forever."

Briggs thought about the contents of the walnut chest above the fireplace and Jarrod's blood seeping into the mud of no man's land.

"Nothing is forever," he whispered.

• • •

Chloe Hepburn came back the next morning.

Briggs woke to the sound of alarm bells screaming across the manor. By the time he reached the gate, the lone figure tramping up the muddy trail was close enough to recognize as the woman he'd seen disintegrate the previous day. Behind her, a sludge of nanomites flowed across the landscape like a slow, grey tide. It stopped when it was still several hundred metres away and without any other targets to track, the tanks' turrets swivelled and followed the young woman as she trudged alone along the track to within an arm's length of the humming gate.

"Hi, Will," she said. She sounded just like Chloe. Looked like her too, down to every smudge of road dust and every tuft of insulation poking through half a dozen tiny tears in her dirty jacket.

"What do you want?' he asked, his mouth dry and raspy.

"It's me, Will. I know this seems weird, but it's really me."

She smiled – nervous, hopeful – another mannerism Briggs remembered from the woman he had once known. For a moment he believed her. What if the thing that had disintegrated yesterday was not a corruption, but a copy? Could this be the original Chloe, still alive?

"If it's really you, walk through the gate."

Chloe's smile disappeared. "I... I can't."

"I know." Will reached slowly towards his EM pistol. "What do you want?"

"I'm still me, Will. Despite... despite what happened. It's different now. I can hear them, Will. They say they can do the same for you. They have to keep growing... they can't stop. I mean they literally can't. Like a car rolling downhill with its brakes cut. It's not their fault, Will. It really isn't. We made them that way."

"What do you mean, 'they can do the same'?"

"You can be like me. All of you, even the Manor if you want. You can be unmade and then remade. You won't even know the difference." Another self-conscious smile. "I didn't."

It was almost tempting. "How do I know it isn't a trick?"

"They're building a new world, Will. Ask Rachel; she saw it. They're not a plague anymore. They've changed."

"Ray told me about Heathrow. What are they doing?"

"I don't know, not really. I told you, I'm still me. They're something else now. Something... more. I don't really understand what they're doing"

"Mom?"

Briggs turned to see a teenaged girl running down the path from the Manor.

"Sarah?" said Chloe. "Oh my God, Sarah!"

She took half a step forward, then seemed to remember the gate and halted, eyes glistening, wringing her hands.

Sarah was about to run through the gate when Briggs caught her.

In his earpiece the tank crew were asking for permission to fire. Briggs looked down the hill towards the mass of nanomites. They weren't advancing. Yet.

Chloe hesitated, swaying backward and forward between her desire to reach out for her daughter and the knowledge that to cross the threshold meant instant destruction. She started to scream: a high-pitched keening that swiftly rose out of any human register: longer and louder than any human lungs could have produced.

Sarah's sobs turned to her own terrified cries at the inhuman noise coming from her mother.

Chloe tore at her hair in some misapplied nanomite emotion. A mother's desperation seen in the distorted mirror of the mites attempt to recreate a human.

Her scalp came away in chunks.

"I need you," she screamed. "Sarah... Sarah! Come to Mummy!"

Sarah's knees buckled.

Chloe couldn't help herself any longer and reached towards her daughter. Sarah was still in Briggs's arms, no longer trying to escape, just digging her fingers into his clothing and clinging to him like she was drowning.

Chloe's fingertips passed the invisible barrier of the gate and disintegrated. She didn't even notice and walked forward losing fingers, hands, forearms. The cross-sections through her severed arms were dark circles as if she was made of clay. No blood, no bone, nothing even remotely human apart from her grief.

She collapsed backwards and sat on the ground, staring in shock at her ruined arms as if reminded of what she now was.

Briggs became aware of movement behind her as more nanomites massed in the distance.

Chloe opened her mouth wide until the flesh of her cheeks tore. The thing masquerading as Chloe didn't seem to notice and opened its jaw like a snake while its breathless scream rose in pitch and volume like a jet turbine heard across a mile of broken glass.

The mass of nanomites at the edge of no man's land started to boil. All along the edge of the mass, figures rose, growing up from the grey sludge like swimmers returning to shore from some terrible dark tide.

They were all Chloe, and they were all screaming.

The tank crews clambered back into their vehicles, guns already tracking towards new targets.

Briggs unsheathed his EM pistol, Sarah held tight in his other arm. The little weapon was not much good for anything beyond ten meters and its field of fire was woeful. But it was all he had.

He aimed at Chloe and pulled the trigger. There was a tiny whine of electromagnets and the side of Chloe's head spilled across her shoulders. She started to stand and Briggs fired again as fast as he could. The pistol needed a few seconds between shots to recharge its capacitors. It seemed to take forever.

Chloe started to walk around the gate: slowly with faltering steps as if she was not fully in control of herself. She and Briggs took on a bizarre rhythm. One step and Briggs fired – the imprecise beam of electromagnetic energy blowing a hole through Chloe's shoulder. Another step and Briggs blasted away the remains of her head. He started to aim for her legs, and her process became a painful crawl. She ignored Briggs and somehow, without eyes or ears, crawled doggedly towards her daughter as he shot her legs out from under her. She was just the stump of one arm and a disembodied torso until Briggs blasted even those into a drift of dead nanomites.

In the distance, the army of screaming figures sank back into the boiling sludge of nanomites.

Briggs held Sarah close and spoke into his radio. "Ray, tell me that EMP is charged."

"My finger's on the trigger," Rachel replied. "Just give the word."

"Stand by. Wait for my order." He switched channels to speak to the tank commanders.

"Weapons free," he said. "If anything gets within range, take it out."

The big tanks flanking the tech-gate rumbled to life with a rising, electronic whine as their powerful diesel engines charged the capacitors of the electromagnetic cannons mounted above the main guns.

The boiling tide of nanomites started to advance. Giant structures rose from the sludge, trillions of microscopic machines recombining and building with manic creativity.

Creations as big as buildings stalked from the mass on stiff legs the size of telephone poles.

Pulsing tubes oozed forward, projecting tendrils that dissolved everything they touched before being reabsorbed like a snail retracting its antennae.

Things like giant tumbleweeds bound from razor wire pulled themselves forward on barbed tendrils, while others – spider-like with bladed limbs – charged forward, spinning like pinwheels.

The mites had never mastered flight, but built huge contraptions that leapt like fleas. They fired themselves forward, crushing whatever they landed on.

The guns of Ditton Manor thundered in response: an angry, defiant roar. Artillery shells burst within the mass of mites, shaking the ground in a concussive barrage like the footsteps of an oncoming giant.

Tank crews fired into the wavefront of oncoming destruction: armour-piercing, fin-stabilised rounds of depleted uranium lanced into the constructs at hypersonic speed. High explosive ordinance tore them apart in giant fireballs of smoked orange flame.

Electromagnetic cannons raked the exposed mites with invisible cones of destruction and nanomites crumbled to black sand in drifts.

But still they advanced.

The mites scarified themselves by the trillion, the ones behind taking up the inert material of their dead brothers and refashioning their corpses into conductive plating to shield themselves from the deadly electromagnetic assault. An individual nanomite could never shield itself, they were too small to give up enough of themselves to form any effective barrier. But a plate built from dead mites a million thick would stop almost anything.

The first of the giant flea-like constructs reached the human lines, smashing into a self-propelled gun like a hammer from the heavens: sheer mass and speed transforming on impact into a destructive shockwave that ignited the gun's stockpile of ammunition in a series of vicious secondary detonations.

Those mites that survived the impact started to multiply, converting the twisted wreckage of bloodied steel and torn scraps of flesh into more of their kind. Nearby gun crews raced over to stem the infection: fanning the recombining mites with hand-held EM weapons like firefighters hosing down the flames of an advancing brush fire.

Briggs saw survivors of the initial impact desperately crawling away: clawing at the dirt, pulling themselves forwards even as the mites consumed them. He saw one man, from the waist down his legs were as black and withered as burned match-sticks. The man rolled onto his back and drew an EM pistol and fired desperately into his own body, trying to stem the creeping corruption that was steadily consuming him. Finally he gave up and switched his EM pistol for a sleek semi-automatic. He put the barrel in his mouth and pulled the trigger before the mites could take even that final act from him.

"We need to get you back to the manor!" Briggs screamed at Sarah as mites screeched and humans died around him. He dragged her past the smashed gun emplacement and up the path towards the house, barking orders into his radio.

Behind them a trio of the fast, bladed pinwheels smashed through the tech-gate: slicing it apart with spinning, obsidian limbs.

"Will!" shouted Rachel over the radio. "We've lost the gate and three tanks. We need to fire the EMP!"

Briggs looked back. In no man's land the mites' advance had faltered. Dunes of black sand built up, marking the effective range of the electromagnetic weapons. The huge projectors fired microwaves of low frequency radiation. Just like a flashlight, the strength of their beam dispersed with distance. At close range they were just too intense. As each new construct burst through, the tank crews focussed their fire, blasting it apart with conventional munitions while the gunners tried desperately to strafe its innards with electromagnetic energy before the mites could complete their armour.

One spider-like construct as big as a building collapsed in a shower of black sand under one such barrage and Briggs heard the cheers of the gun crews over the radio. But there was no end to the black tide and the dead mites were soon rebuilt into even thicker armour to plate ever more nightmarish engines of destruction.

"Not yet!" yelled Briggs into the radio. "We'll only get one shot, and we need to make it count. I've got Sarah Hepburn, and we're heading back to the Manor. Meet me at the North entrance."

By the time Briggs was in sight of the North entrance he could see Rachel waiting for them.

"Stay inside the manor house," Briggs said as he sent Sarah on ahead. "It'll be all right. Rachel will look after you." He wished he felt as confident as he sounded.

Briggs gave Rachel a mock salute and turned his attention back to the front line. It was holding for now, but only at a terrible cost. Although the tide of advancing mites had been halted, there were skirmishes all along the front line.

A huge millipede-like construct with segments as big as SUVs charged forward on a hundred clawed legs. One of the tanks, an old French Leclerc, fired on the construct, blasting it in half with a high explosive shell. The front half continued its charge and the Leclerc rose to meet it, powering out of its defensive tank scrape and into no-mans land. It rammed the construct at full speed, the 120mm main gun spearing into it and the furiously whirring treads grinding the millipede's flailing legs to powder.

The construct's ruptured innards flowed across the ground, bogging the tank down in a morass of seething nanomites, mud and leaking oil. Briggs saw the hatch on top of the turret flip open as the three-man crew tried to escape. The first managed to jump clear, but the second man was caught in mid-air by the whip like antennae of the crippled construct, tearing him into bloody ribbons.

The last of the crew, seeing the mites closing in, pulled the pins on two grenades and dropped back inside the turret. The muffled detonation of the grenades was followed a split second later by a tremendous explosion that tore the millipede construct apart as the Leclerc's remaining ammunition cooked off inside the doomed tank.

The ground suddenly shook.

Briggs struggled to keep his feet as the whole northern wing of the Manor House lurched, the ground around it turning black with nanomites.

Between Briggs and the Manor House a huge mass of mites burst upward from the ground, a rising black column metres in diameter like a pillar fit to hold up the heavens. It caught Sarah as it shot skyward. Briggs could see her arms flailing, legs embedded in the monstrous tentacle of megatons of nanomites that rose higher and higher until it towered above the Manor itself.

More tentacles rose around the Manor as if some subterranean leviathan was rising from the deep to drag down the ancient building. For a second they hung in the air, and then slammed down into the building, crushing brick and stone as if the ancient building was fashioned from spun glass.

Briggs threw himself to the ground, choking on a cloud of dust and pulverised stone as it radiated outwards from the destroyed building. He bled from a score of cuts from flying glass and masonry, and one fragment was embedded in his thigh. He pulled it out, crying in pain but also relieved to see that the shard was a ruby red sliver from one of the Manor's stained glass windows, not the obsidian black of a nanomite construct.

He stood tentatively and hobbled towards the ruins of the Manor. "Rachel! Rachel!"

The gothic stone arch above the heavy frame of the north entrance still stood along with some of the buildings facade, but behind that the entire north wing was in ruins. Briggs could see through to its central courtyard where a pool of nanomites swirled like a maelstrom.

They'd come up through the ground: tendrils of mites absorbing soil and stone and spreading unseen under their defences.

Then he saw her. Rachel lay half buried by rubble, her long hair grey with dust.

He called out to her and she struggled to one elbow. Half her face was red with blood, the other half was black with swarming nanomites.

She managed a smile. "Nothing is forever," she said, and threw him something as the mass of mites closed over her.

Briggs looked at the EMP trigger that lay in the dust at his feet.

He picked it up. A red LED showed that the trigger was armed.

"I'm sorry Ray," he said. "I really thought we could make it."

He held up the safety with his thumb and squeezed down on the trigger.

Nothing happened.

He tried again. The trigger seemed to be functional but the EMP wouldn't fire.

He ran desperately around a spreading pool of nanomites towards the East Wing that housed the EMP. A pile of rubble was all that was left of the Manor's once proud main entrance, but the tower that housed the EMP looked intact.

He clambered over the rubble to the exposed splintered timbers of the Manor's first floor.

Rachel was waiting for him inside.

The nanomite copy was perfect in every way, even down to the copy of the EMP trigger she held. She was squeezing it over and over again as if the nanomites had only captured her last wish and were replaying it on a loop. She looked up as he walked past.

"It won't work, Will," she said. "I keep trying, but it won't work."

Briggs ignored her and limped past as fast as he could, ignoring the pain and the blood that seeped from his thigh. The effort and dust that still caked his mouth made him cough, and his spittle was speckled black with nanomites.

He came to a steel security door embedded incongruously in the wood panelled wall of the stately gallery. The door hung from its frame. Inside, the room that housed the EMP was just gone: the floor collapsed in on itself. The stone walls still stood as a giant empty shaft showing the fractured stumps of timber beams like rotting broken teeth in a huge stone mouth.

Briggs started to climb down into the darkness.

The stone walls were black with what looked like mould but Briggs knew it wasn't. He didn't bother avoiding the mites anymore. They were in him now. It was time for speed, not caution.

Figures grew out from the walls: Rachel, Chloe, Sarah...

Some faces he remembered from the tank crews and a dozen others he didn't. They were all talking: a bedlam of jumbled valedictions, pleas and sobs from which Briggs plucked only the familiar to torture himself with.

It won't work, Will...

You can be unmade, then remade...

Nothing is forever...

We can worry about tomorrow tomorrow...

Old friends and new memories...

Forever... is... nothing... is...

Unmade, then remade...

Forever...

They were in him now. He could feel them working their way in from his extremities: searing pain followed by numbness as if he had plunged his limbs into ice water. He tried to ignore it, tried to force his paralyzed hands and feet to do his bidding. He felt separate from his body, as if it was no longer his own, but something else. A vehicle, which for now was still obeying his commands but was no longer *him*. He concentrated on the task at hand and pushed down the terror like a child fearing to look at the monster in the shadows as if even that glance would give it strength.

The pain he could ignore; the numbness he could work around. What really terrified him was when the sensation came back to his leaden feet. Had the mites better integrated his quisling limbs? Or worse still, were they now in his brain? Could he feel his fake limbs because he was also an imposter?

He reached the bottom of the shaft and the shattered remains where the rooms above had collapsed together into the basement.

There!

The EMP was about as big as an oil drum. One end of the cylinder was exposed and Briggs could see the moulded plastic of a heavy-duty electrical connection. The cable had come out in the fall. Briggs plugged it back in, hoping that somewhere under the rubble the capacitors were still intact.

"If you do that, then it's all over."

Briggs looked up and found himself staring at a familiar face.

The other Briggs stared back at him. "It's too late," it whispered. "We're part of them now."

Briggs started at his doppelganger. Jesus, did he really look that tired?

"If you're here then that means—"

"The mites are already inside your mind," his doppelganger finished for him. "Our mind, I guess."

"I can't hear them yet."

"You will."

It sat down on the rubble and scooped up a handful of nanomites. They rearranged themselves in its hand until it was holding a pack of cigarettes. From somewhere it conjured a lighter, took a cigarette out of the pack and lit it.

Briggs tried to remember his last cigarette. They had run out months ago.

"The war's over," the construct said. "They're all here now... Not just Rachel and Chloe, but everyone. Whatever's left of them anyway."

The stone walls around them ran like wax. The remains of the Manor House that had stood for five hundred years sank peacefully into a black sea that stretched off for kilometres in all directions.

There was no sign of the tanks, or the outbuildings and dormitories that had once held all that remained of humanity. Even the trees were gone. Only the vague contours of the Manor's grounds still remained to show that they were not, in fact, floating on mirror-smooth sea of nanomites.

They stood on an island of churned earth and broken timbers. A pair of unlikely King Canutes, holding back the tide that had submerged the rest of the world.

"It's not real," Briggs said. "I talked to Chloe. She looked real at first, but she wasn't. The mites don't understand us. There are... errors." He remembered Chloe screaming until her flesh tore, ripping out her own scalp in some twisted machine's analogue of grief. He wondered what it would be like to be trapped inside that cage. If there was any part of the real Chloe in that thing, then no wonder it was screaming.

"Not real, maybe," said the doppelganger. "But still something more than a memory. Isn't that worth saving?"

"You tell me."

His doppelganger took a long pull on the cigarette. The tip flared orange, but there was no smoke. Nothing really burning, nothing to inhale and no lungs to inhale it with. He remembered Chloe's severed fingers and the solid grey clay of her exposed insides.

"Is Rachel there?" Briggs asked.

"She's here."

"Are we... I mean, are you together in there?"

It took another fake smokeless drag and shook its head.

It stood and walked towards Briggs.

Briggs brandished the EMP trigger at him. "No closer." He wondered if he tried to squeeze, would his fist still do his bidding?

The doppelganger held out the cigarette.

The tide around them stirred.

Briggs accepted the offered cigarette and took a long drag. It tasted like a stick of chalk.

The doppelganger put its hands around Briggs's on the EMP trigger.

"Nothing is forever," it said. "On three. One... Two..."

OF MEAT AND MAN

Jason Fischer

f it flies, it dies.

That was the first rule of operation in this new war. Everything that went up, every plane, drone, and missile, the enemy brought down hard. The satellites and the ISS were in cinders. They were the first things to go. Now, the military had resorted back to beach landings, arguing over maps, and clocking up casualties not seen since World War One.

This is how Tara Bachmann found herself in Johannesburg, her company deep in enemy territory with no air support. No support, period. She hadn't slept in over twenty-four hours, and she couldn't remember a moment where she wasn't shooting or being shot at.

They'd been cut off. Desperate. One numb part of her brain poked through long forgotten tactics lessons trying to parse how others had survived the Battle of the Bulge, the Battle of Aleppo, the Second and Fourth Battles of Tikrit, whilst the other numb part resigned itself to death.

There's nothing in human history that can help us, she realised. This enemy was not afraid. This enemy threw lives away. They were relentless, uncaring.

Tara fought on because she was a good soldier. Every movement had been drilled into her until it was instinct and muscle memory. She was able to move through this nightmare because of it. To keep her weapon charged and to bark out orders. She hauled terrified men and women back up on their feet and pointed them towards the enemy, screaming homilies of slaughter, shocking her people into fighting on.

Tara was a good soldier, but her resolve was now paper thin. She stepped over the dead, both hers and theirs, and tried not to see them.

Meat, and more meat. And that's blood, and you don't have time to lose it, Bachmann.

More of them were coming. She heard their cries, that horrible voiceless sound, and crept to the top of the barricade. The dead were so thick here they'd made a wall of them, and soon Corporal Tara Bachmann was crawling across cold meat, some shocked part of her mind registering that she was resting across the rib cage of a zebra.

She poked the snout of her smart-gun over the withers of the dead animal, and the scope camera fed through to her HUD. Tara painted targets, and she pulled the trigger. The firing solution emptied her clip in a fraction of a second. Flechettes, solid slugs, and neurotoxin shots.

As she scrambled for a fresh magazine, the team AI pinged her, telling her in a monotone that Sergeant Olds was dead. She was now the commanding officer on site, and several icons blinked into life on her HUD. The AI gave her a battlefield promotion, and she was now officially Brevet Sergeant Tara Bachmann.

"No, no," Tara mumbled, biting her lip, too busy to grieve Olds. She had control of the squad mechs now, and she felt a stone twisting in her stomach as she saw how few they had left.

Two Tarantulas, leaping from cover to cover, all guns, spinning blades and attitude. A trio of battered WarDogs, and one Bear class that was drawing most of the enemy's fire. This side of the barricade, they had the Merlin working on a fall-back trench while its forest of upper limbs built another barricade of dead flesh. Behind this, the auto-mortars were running hot, and they had one ammo fabber left, the unit struggling and showing initial signs of failure.

That was all the help they had. All their vehicles were gone. The rest of the 75th Ranger Regiment was held up at the coast, too busy fighting for the beachhead they held by a fingernail. Tara and her company were on their own.

Ellis Park Stadium sat behind their position, right in the middle of Johannesburg. The once proud structure now looked like something built by insects. The 70,000-seat venue resembled a vast nest that reached up to the heavens. The walls were now encased in something like rock, like gristle chewed over and turned into mortar. This was the material headquarters referred to as Meatstone.

It was diamond hard. Almost nothing could get through it, and the enemy even used it as a munition.

Yesterday, one drone had survived long enough to send back a signal to the invasion fleet. People bound in long lines, animals both wild and domestic, anything with a pulse, all being fed by the invaders into the black hole of that nest.

Under fire, the drone had stolen into the nest just long enough to capture the now infamous footage. People, half-starved and wailing, bound into little honeycomb cells. Sinewy straps pinned them flat against the walls and floor. Most of the prisoners were missing limbs, and most had scars to show where their organs had been removed.

Even more terrifying was the menagerie of beasts kept inside. Every type of animal still found in Africa, a raging Noah's ark of caged creatures. Almost all of them had been mutilated, and the footage of lions reduced to mewling torsos had haunted Tara worse than anything else she'd seen in this war.

Even as humanity fought to hold the African coast, Sergeant Olds had led their surprise strike on this nest, quickly overwhelming the token defence. The enemy hadn't expected them to attack so deep into their territory, but even as the company secured the site, the enemy retaliated.

All of them. All at once. As if someone had rung the dinner bell. Near as Tara could tell, they'd barely left enough troops behind to hold the invading force on the coast. The enemy wanted this site back, and they wanted it bad.

Tara felt panic start to rise, but clamped down on it through willpower alone. Scrolling through the Medinet, she noted most of the other rangers had their sedation packs dialled up. She fought the temptation to wash away the panic – right now, she needed her edge.

These were her people now, all of them, doomed where they

stood. Everyone knew the score, of course. They weren't grunts, they were rangers, and suiting up for lost causes was in their collective DNA.

Readily will I display the intestinal fortitude required to fight on to the ranger objective and complete the mission, though I be the lone survivor.

She took a minute to walk down the line, to look her people in the eye. Two rangers were sharing a nervous smoke by the ammo-fabber, watching someone else tinker with the sputtering unit. Teasing out a few more minutes of life from the machine. The auto-mortars were firing out of rhythm now, the firing program doing a morbid kind of reverse-triage – how could it kill the most things before the guns ran dry?

She saw one man staring up at the perfectly blue sky, making peace with the universe. Five were in a prayer circle. Everyone else was just a pair of eyes and a gun, watching the barricade, too amped up to think about eternity.

Gravitas. The nobility of the outnumbered warriors preparing to meet their fate. So of course, there was one dickhead to ruin that perfect moment.

One of the rangers was racing up the pile of dead bodies, grinning goofily, eyes glazed over. He'd dialled up all his meds, all at once.

"What the hell are you doing?" she shouted.

"Hooah!" he shouted, and then stood above the barricade, gun blazing. For one second he was the picture of glory, the very image of a final stand. If they ever made a movie of this disaster, Tara thought that would be the money shot. Then a second later he caught an enemy shell, and he simply vanished from the waist up.

The nanites in the dead ranger's bloodstream did their best to contain the trauma, and for one second Tara could see a grotesque map of his missing veins and arteries, the blood spurting out from his arteries clotting and trying to fill in the gaps. Then it all fell down, and so did he. Shaking her head, Tara summoned the Merlin, who took up his body with great care and stacked him with the other glorious dead.

"Nobody else do that," she shouted, and hit the CO override on the medpacks. Ensuring that only the badly wounded were at stoned levels, she hustled along the line, yelling until she was hoarse, pulling the scared fragment of her company into some sort of order. They were down to four fire teams, and a handful of mechs.

Tara pinged for a demo expert, and the AI hooked her up with Specialist Pollard. Her command access showed a précis of disciplinary charges, mostly to do with blowing things up on his own time. This was her guy.

"Ma'am, shall I send up the Wasps?" Pollard radioed. His inventory showed a full canister of the nasty drones, hunter-killers that fought in packs.

"Save 'em," Tara grunted. "If it flies, it dies. I need you to set charges at the entrance to the nest. We might have to fall back inside, and I want it to seal behind us."

"*Inside* the nest? Sergeant ordered us to hold it. We need to wait for the medics, for the – for the damn xeno team."

"Set the charges, Specialist," Tara barked, and cut the link.

More shells were falling. Tara watched through the company feed as the Tarantulas were overwhelmed, their metal limbs bent and twisted out of their bodies. Next it was the Bear who fell, its tank-like body riddled with holes.

Tara called the WarDogs back to the barricade, noting that most of their systems were now in the red. They waited like good dogs, alert, noses pointed at the empty sky beyond the barricade. Three perfect canines realised in chrome. Each unit was a killer, and their carapaces were filled with munitions. When those were gone, the dogs had tasers, and then steel jaws, titanium fangs. Claws that could tear through an engine block.

Tara wished she had fifty more WarDogs, and then realised that wasn't enough.

The survivors made ready to move into the fallback position. She put the Merlin between her little group and the outer barricade. Beyond the wall it was all misting plumes of meat and dirt, the cacophony of the enemy screeching, hooting, even trilling with that laughter which had no business falling out of a mouth.

A random chunk of meat flew over the barricade, landing at Tara's feet. Thick and red, striated muscle fibres, seared and sizzling on one side. Not human. It was mystery bushmeat, but not even the most grizzled survivalist here would eat this. When times were really tough, anything goes into the ranger pot, but this meat was just as likely to fight you from the inside of your own asshole.

"Boys and girls," Tara looked around at her troops. "The powers that be made a shitty call. We're going to die. Questions?"

"Did the rest of our people get through?" Pollard asked.

"Yes," Tara said after consulting the feed. "This cluster-fuck has bought them a beachhead. They're on their way. The Chinese, Australians, everyone. They've all landed."

"In time to save us?"

"Soldier, we may have just won the war. All of the poor bastards in that nest have just been saved."

"Big deal. We're screwed."

"Your point?" she barked, giving the man a friendly helmet bump. "Sometimes you have to lose in order to win."

The mortar rounds were landing closer, closer, just shy of the barricade now, the sheer concussive force hammering on Tara's armour. The enemy was about to make their final push. The seconds of Tara's life were falling closer to zero.

The ammo-fabber died with a smoky fart. A few moments later, mortars fell silent. No more prayer now, nothing but eyes and guns.

The Merlin stood up like a meerkat, sensors twitching. It was single-minded in the building of the meat wall, and it knew that more material was coming its way. A lot more. "Get ready! Hold fast!"

One last awful moment, and then the first enemy cleared the wall. A mad chimera, a lion's body merged with gorilla limbs, eight in all. It had a trio of fleshy tubes writhing around on its back. Guns, alive and deadly accurate. Before it could bring them to bear it fell, screeching, as Tara's crew riddled it with bullets.

Next was a hippopotamus with hundreds of tusks protruding from its body. It soaked up bullets as it charged, shrieking alien hatred as it came for them. The Merlin gave itself up to stop the thing, tangling it with dozens of servo limbs and grapples before it dragged the beast to a halt and slowly strangled it.

"Pollard, are the charges ready?" Tara shouted.

"I need one more minute. It's gonna take everything I've got to bring this entrance down."

"You do not have that minute, Specialist! We are coming inside in the next thirty fucking seconds."

The horrors kept clearing the wall. There was an elephant covered with thousands of snakes, giraffes converted into cannons, and cattle that were now tanks.

Worst still were the things that had once been people.

Fighting down a bubble of hysteria, Tara ordered the fall back. The enemy was a wave of twisted meat, howling and cackling and screaming, and Tara's orderly fighting withdrawal turned into a rout. Monsters tore her people apart, and Tara wasn't a good soldier then, she was just a terrified woman running for her life.

She made it into the nest itself, pushing and shoving alongside a handful of soldiers and only one of the WarDogs, limping and dribbling oil from a dozen places. Taclites danced as the survivors ran deeper into the nest. Specialist Pollard slammed one last charge into place behind them, and dropped the rest of the pack on the floor as he, too, ran for his life.

"Hit it! Blow the door!" Tara screamed.

Pollard paled visibly. "We're too close!"

"That's an order!" she yelled, firing behind her at a full run. The first wave of monstrosities were entering the nest now, cautiously. Almost with respect. Or fear.

Pollard fumbled for the remote, and then hit the switch. The shockwave sent the soldiers sprawling, and tonnes of Meatstone fell from the ceiling. Soldiers cried out as chunks of the alien material punched into them.

After that great rush of noise, they were in silence, save the shifting of dust and the cracking of the Meatstone as it settled. The screaming cacophony of the evil zoo outside was gone, and the difference in the sound was jarring.

Tara got to her knees, shaking and numb as the clouds of dirt and ash blew past her. A distant part of her mind was grateful for the enclosed tac-suit, the air-filters and membranes that kept all that poisonous shit out of her lungs. One by one the survivors turned on their suit lamps, waiting for the dust to settle. A thicket of guns pointed at the entrance to the nest, shaking.

The dust finally cleared. The entrance was sealed over.

The survivors relaxed briefly, and then the cacophony began. Human prisoners, in the thousands, begging, pleading, and howling in pain. Animals joined the chorus, bleating, roaring, and screeching in terror.

There were other noises, too. Distant… unrecognisable. Tara shivered, and saw the fear on everyone's faces. It had taken certain death outside to bring them inside this godawful place.

Tara tried to access the Company feed but it was gone. They'd been bouncing a signal from the landing fleet, who'd sent up a comms balloon off the coast. No satellites meant that people had learnt to make do. She quickly set up a line-of-sight network with the survivors and scrolled through the Medinet. Two soldiers had died in the cave-in, and she had one badly wounded and one walking wounded. She restored full access to meds, dialled down everyone's audio input, and then checked on the WarDog.

WarDog 'Bruno' was in a bad way. He was down to less than five percent munitions total. Ammo-fabber was offline, he'd lost an eye, and one of his legs was struggling to flex. The mech was walking with a marked limp, but still he looked up at Tara with his cartoonish dog face, tail wagging hopefully.

"Good dog," Tara said, patting him on the head. She opened up a channel, speaking quietly to the survivors.

"We have to move deeper into the nest," she whispered. "They're probably trying to dig through that rubble. Pollard, you still got those Wasps? Let's get a survey done, at the very least."

Nodding, the Specialist let out the whole canister, and hundreds of the murderous little drones lit out into the tunnels.

The cloud of mechs divided at each junction, leaving members of the swarm behind to bounce a signal back to the entrance. In a matter of seconds Tara and her crew had a 3D map of the facility, growing before their eyes.

"It's laid out like an ant's nest, Sergeant," one of the privates muttered, and Tara nodded.

One set of Wasps reached a large gallery, and then fed back a combat warning. They bounced back a brief image of movement, more of the same horrors that were outside, trying to kill them. These ones were fresh, emerging from amniotic sacs and dripping with fluids, fleshy guns already blazing. The next second, the Wasps were simply gone.

"Holy shit, they're making them in here," Tara cursed, flagging the larger galleries on the map. "It's not a prison. This place is a factory, a – a fucking hatchery."

One of the privates yelped. "We're trapped in here with those things!"

Tara hit the man's sedative up a notch and shook him by the shoulder. "Keep it together, man! We're not done yet. Pollard, any more charges?"

"Used 'em all on the door," the Specialist replied.

"Okay, we need to find a place to dig in." She looked at the 3D map, flagging an area. "Here."

They hustled into the nest, squeezing through Meatstone tunnels that were lined from floor to ceiling with screaming prisoners. The captives, both human and animal, were pinned to the walls like butterflies. It was chaos, and Tara saw most of the survivors muting the external noise, falling back to radio only. Tara struggled to concentrate in the cacophony, but kept her own audio inputs on. Sound always gave her an edge. A footfall could be the only thing alerting you to an enemy.

They reached the point Tara had chosen, a hatching gallery with signs of disuse. The floor was scattered with bones and rotten flesh, the fused leftovers of chimeras that didn't survive the process.

The AI ran a quick calculation for her – even if they could block off all entry points into the hatching gallery, they would run out of oxygen within twelve hours, and that was with their suit scrubbers. Not enough time for rescue to arrive from the beachhead.

Choking in the dark was not how Tara Bachmann wanted to go out.

"If they're going to come at us, we need to make it on our terms. We fight hard and take as many of the fuckers with us as we can. You two, I want frag rounds at these weak points." Tara flagged the entrance to the gallery behind them, painting the tunnel roof and two support 'pylons' in AR. The soldiers spent a clip each weakening the roof before it finally fell.

Only two entrances left. One, a main entrance that led to the other hatching galleries. Another leading to more prisoners – a supply route.

"We're digging in," Tara growled. "Use those dead things as a barricade. Locust Jam on the floor."

The soldiers looked at each other in shock as she gave authority for each of them to unlock their canisters of 'Locust Jam', nanites so caustic that they ate through just about anything. Rumour had it the Chinese were so free and easy with the stuff that they had nanite sinkholes all over their country, replicating out of control and eating into the Earth's mantle.

The US Army only let Locust Jam out in desperate circumstances. Tara dictated the area of effect, hollows deep enough to hold a kneeling soldier, after which the kill-code on the nanites kicked in.

Only one soldier lost a hand during the process, which Tara counted as a success. One knucklehead in her Basic course had burnt off his feet with the stuff, and there was a solid rumour around the water cooler that an unpopular officer in another company lost his genitals in his sleep with the stuff. Jamming was the new fragging.

Tara and her crew knelt in the dusty holes, part dead nanites and part ground-up Meatstone. They rested their guns across the walls of dead flesh and rot, waiting. There was nothing to Tara's world but the shallow sound of her breath, a tic in her eye, the information crawling across her HUD.

We are boned. What a strange place to die.

One by one, the surviving Wasps bounced contact reports back to them and died, as a stream of monsters homed in on their location with frightening accuracy.

The enemy movement on the HUD map became less detailed as they smashed every Wasp they found into dust. Some of the men and women around Tara started to openly weep, and she felt their terrible situation stretch to breaking point.

"Listen," she said over comms, taking back some control. "These things are the enemies of the human race. You kill as many as you can, as fast as you can. Your rifle goes dry, you take out your sidearm. Your sidearm goes dry, you use your knife. If that breaks, you have fists and teeth. Use everything. If some fucking scary thing eats you, I want you punching that asshole from the inside. Do you hear me?"

"Yes, Sergeant," they muttered back, either stoned or terrified. Frowning, Tara scrolled through her media files, and then sent out a song across the network. It was old, something she'd picked up during her history major, and she smiled as the guitars wailed, the drums smashed, and the singer chanted.

She saw the pulse rates rise in her team. Helmeted heads bobbed up and down, in time with the thunder of drums. A fist raised in defiance, and then another.

In the fox-hole next to her, Pollard smiled, and reached over for a fist-bump. "We've had some fun," he said.

For a final treat, Tara completely unlocked all of the remaining Locust Jam. They might burn a hole down to the centre of the earth, but damn if it wouldn't take a few more of the bastards out.

"No turning back now," she said.

Drums. Footsteps. Screeching. The vocalist, the band, chanting. Then a monster came thumping into the hatching gallery, still dripping with amniotic fluid, lion's teeth set in a boy's face, writhing on the end of a giraffe neck.

The chatter of guns tore it apart. Then another unholy thing, and another. A gorilla-thing tore one of her rangers apart like a rotisserie chicken, even as it absorbed enough bullets to kill ten men. Pollard panicked and lobbed a canister of Locust Jam, instantly burning away his gun hand, droplets falling all over the others as the deadly little jar splashed across a rhino's head. It was like a tube of meat and muscle, moving snake-like, unable to charge but bearing down on them, hoping to suffocate them with its weight.

"Argh! Gimme the nano kill code! That shit is burning right through me!"

"No! Let it eat up the damn rhino first!"

One man died, and then another, screaming as the Locust Jam burnt them up from within, even as the rhino roared defiance at their bullets, crushing a ranger to death in her foxhole. Then its enormous armoured head collapsed inwards like a smashed Easter egg, pulling monster and dead ranger deep into the ground.

Monkeys with knife-blade hands. Broken people twisted into enormous furred spiders. These aberrations came by the dozen, endless and hungry, soaking up bullets, but their neighbours got that much closer, and then they were plucking men from foxholes, murdering them with stingers, fangs, claws, or what was once a bare human hand.

Pollard was a vision of fury, gun chattering in his one hand, and then a hyena on elephant legs clattered forward, stoving in his helmet, face and skull with a gorilla's fist. Still the rifle fired, dead hand locked down on the trigger, carving divots in the ceiling. *Bang bang bang* went the gun. *Boom boom boom* went the drums. Everything else was the wet sound of feeding, the screams and moans of those warriors who were being eaten alive.

"You bastards!" Tara screamed, tossing aside her dead rifle, flinging out the last of her Jam, and then she was up and moving, emptying her sidearm, and then it was her knife, and she was fury and human defiance, fighting for as long as she could.

They'd gotten most of the way through AC/DC's 'Thunderstruck' before their guns fell silent. By the time the song ended, everybody but Tara was dead.

* .*

A pair of monsters hauled Tara deeper into the nest, and she hung between them, senseless and numb. At least three of their Meatstone 'bullets' had punched through her liquid armour, the Kevlar and thickening fluids barely slowing the rounds. Some hybrid of gorilla and lion had destroyed her helmet, caving in the toughened faceplate and savaging everything from the left eye down.

Blood ran down her nose and spattered onto the tunnel floor. Her left forearm flopped painfully, even as the familiar tickle of medical nanites tried to fuse the shattered bone together. There was just too much for the microscopic workers to do, and her life was leaking out of her by the second.

"Kill me, you fuckers," she managed, thrashing weakly in her captor's grip. An eagle talon and a handful of tentacles shook her into submission, and she cried out as her broken bones grated together.

The beasts continued to drag her into the depths of the nest, winding through the sinuous tunnels and ignoring the screams and cries of the prisoners fastened to the walls. They soon reached a vast chamber in the centre, a cathedral-sized hollow fed by hundreds of other tunnels. The floor was the old turf of the stadium, still marked with faint chalk lines and sponsor logos. The once green grass was long dead from lack of sunlight. Every few yards, a 'torch' had been driven into the ground, humans bound into an awful rictus, flesh melted like running wax. They were phosphorescent, so bright after the darkness of the tunnels that it hurt to look at. Tara's captors hauled her into the centre of the playing field and dropped her into the dirt.

Through the eye remaining to her, Tara looked at her shattered HUD. Only a quarter of the screen remained intact, the film barely transmitting an image. Even as she lay huddled on the ground, she regrouped, examining the options left to her.

No firearms, ammunition, or knife. No combat nanites or droids. Her armour was compromised, and her suit's battery was running just above the red. She reconfigured her HUD to display on the remaining screen, and flicked through her medical diagnostics.

She upped her painkillers and triaged her medical nanites away from her head injuries and into her bullet wounds. Tweaking the liquid armour, she hardened the sleeve around her broken forearm, making a crude field splint. Gasping as the bones ground together, Tara climbed slowly to her feet, making a fist with her good hand.

"Energetically will I meet the enemies of my country," she recited, eyeing off her two guards. "I shall defeat them on the field of battle, for I am better trained and will fight with all my might."

The creature that was a man fused with dozens of sea creatures stared at her blankly, while the warthog-man with the eagle claws snarled at her.

"Surrender is not a ranger word!" Tara yelled. She raised her hands and squared off in a Krav Maga pattern, looking for an advantage.

As one, her captors looked over her shoulder and withdrew past the living candles, chittering and loping into the nearest tunnel. Something was coming. Something with a heavy tread.

She turned and saw the elephant. Not an animal merged with another, just a standard bull elephant, if a little the worse for wear. The animal had scars all over its face and flanks, its ears torn into strips. Tara dropped her attack pose. The elephant seemed as much a prisoner as she did, and there was nothing she could do to harm it anyway.

"It's okay," she said soothingly. The creature came up to her haltingly, trunk raised, and she held out her good hand as it snuffled at her, as if questing for something to eat.

"Sorry fella," Tara whispered. "I'm all out of peanuts."

The next part happened faster than she could track. The elephant seized her wrist with its trunk, and then another trunk wrapped around her neck, another around her waist, and another around her legs. The elephant had dozens of trunks falling from its face now, spiralling out like an unplaited rope. Its eyes burned with intelligence, and it warbled in some strange tongue, a song somewhere between victory and anger.

A trio of finer trunks shot out, wrestling with the fastenings of her helmet, tossing it aside. Tara struggled and cursed, but she couldn't resist as these fine tendrils seized her jaw, prising it open.

Another trunk came forth, this one as fine as a hair, and jammed into her ear, sending Tara into a tsunami of pain. It passed through tissue, and *pushed*, and then Tara was hearing another voice in her head.

YOU ARE NOT MEAT, the elephant-thing growled, YOU ARE... SUITABLE. YOU WILL BEAR US WELL.

Tara sobbed. She pissed herself, screaming as the creature pushed another tendril deep into her brain. She kicked and twitched, her nerves firing as the monster tinkered with her insides.

YOU ARE A VESSEL AND SERVANT AND SLAVE, the voice thundered into her mind, the words shaking her to the core. SUBMIT NOW, AND ALWAYS.

"No," she groaned painfully, limbs twitching. With the last of her will she raised the broken arm and punched the elephant in the face with her makeshift cast. One, two, three times, and then the pain in her arm broke through the hypnotic fugue the monster was driving her into.

With one motion, she wrenched the thin proboscis out of her ear, and yanked back on it, hard as she could. The elephant-thing cried out in rage, then pain and confusion. It shook her around, crushing her ribs with one of its trunks, but Tara wrapped the thinnest one around her hand, and pulled on it like an errant hair, doing her best to rip it right out of the creature's face. The mind-probe limb proved sensitive, and the creature fell into a rage, yowling with pain as it beat her.

Another entered the great cathedral, walking to a rhythm like a horse's canter. The elephant stopped thrashing, winding its trunks back into one main limb, almost swallowing Tara's hand until she let go of the thin proboscis and fell to the ground in a heap.

She looked up to see an alien standing above her, regarding her coldly through a bank of eyes. This was not a mad hybrid of human and animal, but a true extra-terrestrial. An invader, responsible for the death of billions. Responsible for the near destruction of the planet.

The alien looked like a spider walking on a bed of tree roots. It pounced on Tara, hundreds of prehensile hairs unfolding from its head and seizing her. She was wrapped up tight, the hairs easily lifting her up to the alien's maw.

This close, she could see the creature was diseased. Its flesh was dotted with necrotic sores. Just like their spaceships, which were crumbling apart in orbit. The invaders who'd climbed out of the landing craft five years ago were rotting, dying.

It regarded her, eyes nictitating as a series of thicker hairs emerged from its face. They brushed across her broken face, almost as if tasting her.

VESSEL, it said into her mind, the word leaping across the hairs like a static shock. NOT MEAT.

It was desperate, this thing. This whole bizarre race was having its own last stand, but this time on an intergalactic scale. Find a new planet. Fight or die. Get a new body. Repeat.

"F-fuck you," Tara managed, and then the creature jammed thousands of hairs into her mouth, gripping her jaw, prying her mouth wider. It opened its own mouth, and a tongue emerged, something like a dirty root. It twined around her own tongue, scraping at the skin, intimate and horrifying and vile.

Tara howled until the darkness took her.

＊ ＊ ＊

A company of German engineers found her three days later. They cracked open the alien nest with construction equipment, and it took them many hours to sift through the ruined entrance. They sent in clouds of little drones to map the layout, survey gnats that were little more than wings and sensory gear. The robots noted the dead American soldiers, the residues from their final stand.

They found Tara Bachmann in the centre of the nest. She was near death, her medical nanites stretched to the limit. She was huddled up to an elephant, another prisoner covered with scars. Tara raved when the medics came for her and fought anyone that touched her. She broke two noses and one arm before she was tasered and sedated.

She was dubbed the Angel of Johannesburg. She claimed to remember nothing after her failed last stand, and her suit's recorders were completely destroyed. Command brought her home with the first wave of wounded, and she laughed and cried the whole way, even as something cold and foreign grew within her skull.

They told her she was getting a medal. That the President would pin it to her, and the parasite hiding in her brain meat pilfered through Tara's memories, translating this title as *Leader/ Master/King*.

Tara's passenger adored her idea of a reverse triage, designed to inflict the most damage one creature could, and the more it learnt from her about the Battle of the Bulge, the Battle of Aleppo, the Second and Fourth Battles of Tikrit, the more it liked the concept of a last stand.

Tendrils grew on the end of her fingertips and across the palm of her right hand. Invisible to the naked eye, but sharp enough to pierce steel. Her fingers could unlace now, five fingers unplaiting into ten, fifty, a billion tiny fibres. A spiral of meat that would take the handshake of this President and turn it into something much more useful.

Sometimes, you have to lose in order to win.

JAWBREAKER

Justin Coates

Lieutenant Riley Hark lost her rifle on the third day of the siege. The sturdy M25 service weapon, having saved her life so many times on the desperate retreat to the Vegas Containment Line, disappeared down the slavering maw of an alien bioweapon.

"Bastard!"

Hark drew her pistol. The beast roared and heaved toward her. She emptied the magazine. It bought her enough time to pull her saber from the still-twitching corpse of a squid clone at her feet. The psychoreactive runes on the blade glowed bright red as

writhing psuedopods shot toward her. She cleaved through half a dozen before being snared by the bioweapon. Hark snarled, accepted the embrace, and drove the saber into its squealing mouth. Its lamprey teeth shattered on the enchanted blade. The runelight grew until it illuminated the horror from within.

The bioweapon blew apart, the blast knocking the air from her lungs. She tumbled to the ground, covered in gore and landing hard next to fragments of her rifle.

Hark was down for only a moment before Tally reached her. The adjutant, one of countless refugees now serving in frontline combat, smiled through bloody teeth.

"Not much of an example for the enlisted, ma'am," she said, grunting as she hauled Hark up. "The PL can't be seen laying down on the job."

Hark spat alien filth from her mouth. "Fuck me. I lived through Arlington, Chicago, and Salt Lake, just to fucking die in Vegas."

Tally turned and stabbed a still twitching squid corpse with her bayonet. "You're not dead yet, ma'am."

Hark was too tired to laugh. "Let me look at you, shithead."

The girl's weak, pale frame was whole all over. Hark hid her relief behind a hearty slap on the back. "Not a scratch. Vegas is working out for you. We should stop in at Caesar's Palace to place some bets"

Tally smiled weakly, then sighed. "God hates me too much to let me die." Tally hesitated. "The next push..."

Hark looked over her shoulder at the alien corpses tangled in the perimeter wire. The rampart was six meters high, so the bastards had thrown themselves at the guns until their corpses had formed a ramp for those that followed.

"It'll be the last one," Hark murmured. "They'll roll right over us."

Before Tally could respond, the enemy bombardment recommenced. Hark didn't have to give the command. Her soldiers all but hurled themselves off the battlements and retreated into the relative safety of the trench-and-bunker system as balls of roiling plasma hammered the line's defenses.

Two of her squad leaders, Staff Sergeants Barker and Engels, waited for her in the cramped command bunker. A weary-looking Specialist was there in place of Sergeant Willow.

"Report," she barked, allowing Tally to wipe alien filth from her body armor as she reloaded her pistol.

"We're black on 40mm," Barker said. "I'm having the grenadiers switch to bayonets like everyone else."

Hark grunted her assent. "You got any grenades left, Engels?"

Engels nodded wearily. "After cross-loading, we've three HEDP per grenadier. Enough for the next assault. Nothing more."

"Rifle ammo?"

The two NCOs glanced at each other. The specialist said, "We're winchester. Nothing but pistol ammo and bayonets."

"Cross load with the other two platoons, Specialist..." The warfighter's nametape was obscured by alien gore.

"Specialist Morris, ma'am," he said, straightening.

Once not knowing his name would've made her feel guilty.

She'd abandoned guilt, along with hope, long ago. Fear, the edge of stark, raving madness, was her only companion.

Fear, and Tally. "Good man, Morris. We'll fight with what we've got."

The single lightbulb in the ceiling flickered as plasma rained down from above. Dust and dirt fell from the ceiling. The private manning the comm station looked up.

"Ma'am? Hammer Actual is asking for you."

Hark took her pistol from her adjutant and snapped it back into her holster. "Tell Captain Anders I'm on my way."

* * *

The Hellraiser Tactical Operations Center (H-TOC) was a sandbag bunker in a crater that had once been the California Casino & Hotel. It was stiflingly hot inside. Staff worked in Army issue T-shirts or shirtless, buzzing around radios and field computers. Maps with markers of the Containment Line stretched across repurposed blackjack tables.

Captain Samuel Anders was at the center of the chaos. He'd been Lieutenant Anders just three days ago, but the near-rout at North Vegas had opened up a plethora of promotion opportunities. Hark had barely avoided one herself.

She didn't recognize the man at Anders' side. His tattered black uniform was covered in strange symbols daubed in red paint. A necklace of rusted nail hung low on his chest, and the faint smell of spoiled meat emanated from gleaming chrome plugs jutting out the base of his shaved skull.

He smiled at her and Tally's approach. His teeth were yellow headstones against the tomb of a too-wide mouth. Tally tensed. Hark caught the girl's eye, and shook her head.

"Lieutenant Hark." Anders sucked on a cigar. "Glad to see you're still in one piece."

"That makes one of us. What can I do for Hellraiser?"

Anders gestured at the map on the table between them. "The impossible, as usual."

She eyed the map. The lines were different from those she

remembered. Green poker chips were arrayed in a series of scything arrows, punching through the enemy fortifications to the north.

Hark snorted. "He's really going through with it?"

"Colonel Fitz thinks the best defense is a good offense. Colonel Young tried to talk him out of it, but…"

"…Fitz is a saber-swinging lunatic," Hark finished. Tally stifled a giggle. "He's commiting the entire brigade?"

"What's left of us." Anders wearily jabbed at the map with a fat finger. "Three spears, each a battalion strong, to break through the squid line. If we can take and hold the North Vegas ruins beyond the alien reef, we'll be ready to support 3rd brigade as they push in from the west."

"We lost three thousand men trying to hold those damn ruins. What's gonna make it different this time?"

Anders jerked his thumb at the man beside him. "Lieutenant MacLeod arrived late yesterday." He hesitated, then muttered, "From PSICOM."

Tally swore and spat onto the ground.

"Whole lot of good your scryers have been doing us," Hark said, glaring at her adjutant. "No offense."

MacLeod smiled again. "None taken." His voice was a soft rasp; the rustle of a corpse, sliding into a mass grave. Anders moved a half-step away from him. "Predicting the future isn't part of my job description anyway."

"You'll be escorting Lieutenant MacLeod to destroy an enemy HVT," Anders continued, sneaking a wary glance at the witch. "The assault will be mounted; Colonel Young has personally re-assigned several technicals to your platoon."

"What kind of high value target?"

"That's classified. We can't—"

"One of their idols," MacLeod said. "The reason they're so coordinated, and why our scryers can't see a thing."

"You better know your way around a block of C4. The last demo-qualified trooper in my platoon died yesterday."

"I don't need explosives. Just get me close. Urkhar will do the rest."

The cherry on Anders' cigar went out. His muttered curses left a vapor trail in the sudden cold. Hark's hand strayed to her pistol, with the certainty that some terrible, unseen thing had joined them in the bunker.

* ● *

The three technicals assigned to Hark's platoon had seen better days. Their tires sagged from the weight of scrap armor crudely welded to doors and engine blocks. Bench seats on extended beds brought carrying capacity to nine troopers each, plus one heavy machine gunner standing behind the cab.

Doing the impossible for the ungrateful, Hark mused, selecting the truck with the least amount of plasma scars. She picked a driver by similar criteria. "Private Jones! Get in, you're driving." The young man hastened to obey. She clapped him on the shoulder, then pulled herself up into the truck bed. Hark ran a quick check on the gun, an ancient and sturdy M2 Browning, then turned to her assembled platoon.

"All right, dickheads. There's a ton of squid between us and our objective. According to Lieutenant MacLeod..." She nodded to the PSICOM witch. He squatted in the dust, apart from the unit, tracing strange figures in the dust with a long, pale finger. He looked up. Grinned. "...the objective itself will probably try to eat us. Our primary mission is to get the lieutenant there so he can destroy it."

"And our secondary, ma'am?" Sergeant Engels murmured.

"Not get eaten."

Their laughter was edged in panic. She could see the terror in all of them, even Tally. It made her look like a child. She was a child, after all; a sobbing orphan from the Battle of Spokane, transformed into a warfighter by Hark, who had rescued her.

We're not dead yet. We can still come out of this alive.

"I won't lie to you. I'm scared shitless."

Outgoing bombardment began as she spoke. The main assault elements had started the push north fifteen minutes prior. If successful, they would crack open the squid reef and establish a beachhead in enemy territory, giving follow-on elements like

Hark's a chance to avoid running into the teeth of the enemy guns.

If they failed...

Vehicle and personal radios crackled. The battalion commander spoke calm over a net filled with screams and curses.

"All elements, this is Falcon Actual. Standby for greenlight."

"I'm scared shitless," she repeated, strapping on her helmet. "But I'm still gonna go out there and make some fucking calamari."

They cheered, her brothers and sisters, her children, clambering into the trucks, shouting orders and insults and unit mottos and desperate prayers to whatever god might be listening. Larger transports carrying the remainder of the brigade's heavy infantry pushed past them in support of the spearhead. Thirty Apache helicopters began their sorties, proceeded by flights of pugnacious A-10 Warthogs with noses painted to resemble the maws of predatory whales.

Macleod lurched into the bed of the truck. He looked at the platoon, the nails of his necklace clattering like dry bones. "Glorious," he whispered. "Oh, joy."

Hark chambered a round in her M2. "First platoon!" She bellowed, hoping none heard the tremor in her voice. "Kill for the Earth!"

Tally's voice cut through the rest.

"And all Her children!"

Hark smiled down at her. "Ready, kid?"

Tally's eyes glittered in the bloody light of her bayonet runes. "Born to kill, lieutenant."

"GREENLIGHT" echoed across the net, and they accelerated up the assault ramp, over the ramparts and into No Man's Land. The truck's chained tires burst alien corpses and clawed at the ash for purchase. Jones sang from the driver's seat. The wind tore at Hark's goggles. Beside her, Private Pankhurst yelled, "Gory, gory, what a helluva way to die!" Lieutenant Macleod grinned until thin trickles of blood ran from the sides of his mouth. He licked his lips. Hark spat, wondering if his flesh had always looked so thin, his teeth so sharp.

The alien reef came into view as Hark's element roared down the remnants of Las Vegas Boulevard. A furious battle raged in the breach formed by the first spearhead. A massive M1 Abrams lay on its side, burning with green fire. Hark caught glimpses of its titanic kin, heard their savage voices in each cannon blast beyond the barricade. Wounded and dying warfighters staggered through the hot dust, away from the battle, turning vacant eyes toward her as she hurtled past.

800 meters. Hark planted her feet and twisted the grips of the machine gun. Medical evac choppers flew overhead, trailing thick, stinking smoke. Closing fast.

Violet light bloomed behind the reef. A Bradley Fighting Vehicle (BFV) disappeared in a rapidly expanding mushroom cloud. Particle beams whipped through a cluster of guntrucks too near each other to maneuver. One detonated, and the other two collided, pinwheeling end to end before slamming into the wall of a smoldering high-rise.

Hark opened fire. Half-inch rounds punched through dozens of squid pouring over the reef, ignoring the breach in favor of this new threat.

600 meters.

Sergeant Barker's truck took a hit from an enemy rocket. The flash singed Hark's exposed flesh. She pounded on the cab roof. "Keep going, Jones! Don't you stop!"

A-10s screamed in hot and low, Vulcan cannons shredding the horde with depleted uranium rounds. They banked hard and accelerated, pursued by cackling alien abominations resembling gigantic airborne stingrays. One of them swooped over a troop carrier, carving it in half with a belly-mounted laser. The air stank of scorched flesh and burning ozone.

300 meters.

An Apache helicopter smashed into the ground to her left. The blastwave kissed the blistered skin of her neck. Heavy 25mm chaingun fire from the remaining BFVs brought down one of the stingrays. MacLeod howled with laughter. "Yes!" He shouted to the sky. "Yes! The flesh is mine!"

100 meters...50 meters...survived all this shit, just to die in Vegas.

The BFV's and up-armored MRAPs took the lead. The tanks smashed two abreast through the breach. Hark's truck raced through the gap and into a writhing sea of black tentacles, microwave guns and vicious, vivisecting blades. There were squid everywhere, scuttling down from jagged hive structures and up from tunneled labyrinths of stinking coral, an ocean of horrors swarming over armor and hasty infantry positions filled with screaming, bleeding soldiers.

She fired into the shrieking mass, just for the gap in the unliving carpet to be filled by more and more aliens. Jones flattened them beneath their wheel. Tally shouted, "Pick your shots!" but there were too many. Too goddamn many. The things caught beneath the truck and snagged on the engine block, fouling sight lines and clogging muzzles with their corpses.

Some made it past Hark's fusillade and clambered onto the roof, beaks snapping against the red-hot barrel, one of them raising a crude projectile weapon. Hark ducked, as razor-sharp slivers of coral turned Pankhurt's head into a pincushion, his brain leaking onto the bed as he fell. Tally and two other soldiers lunged forward to drive bayonets into the skulls of the horrors as Jones swerved, screaming that he couldn't see. Hark lunged for the gore-slick M2A1 and opened up again, splitting soft, hateful bodies the way they'd split open Pankhurst.

They hit something.

Hark slammed into the back of the cab. She fell to a knee, the air ripped from her lungs, and saw a leech twice the size of the one they'd killed at the Containment Line with its mouth around the truck hood. Jones screamed at her from the driver's seat, trying to crawl out the back window.

"Come on!" She grabbed his arm. The truck tilted forward, rear wheels lifting off the ground. Her head struck the roof. The hood disappeared into the leech's mouth, metal shrieking as rows of circular teeth carved it apart. Jones shrieked, too, until it swallowed him, leaving Hark holding an arm severed at the shoulder, staring down into a gulping alien throat.

She fell as it whipped the truck back and forth. Sergeant Engel's vehicle screeched to a halt nearby, fire from his heavy gunner forcing a tortured squeal from the giant leech. Engel fired his pistol from the window, his face a mask of raw horror.

Hark's surviving soldiers fought the horde of squid closing around them. Tally and Morris were right next to the leech, trying to pull a still-laughing MacLeod out from beneath a section of the engine.

They stood their ground. It ignored their weapon fire and advanced, pausing only to vomit out the rest of Jones and the truck.

MacLeod cursed the leech before Hark could reach them. The black magic tasted hot and hard on her tongue, all copper, saffron and shit, full and rich and vile enough to make her stomach clench and mouth water. MacLeod's cry of "Hail Satan!" quaked in her bones and filled her lungs with bloody phlegm. There was something else within and behind his scream: the sound of tattered wings casting a shadow across the face of the Sun, and a choir of sibilant voices screaming the flesh is mine the flesh is mine Anzunna-kyras!

Things leaped from pools of blood and turned ravenous claws on the leech. They burst into ash the moment the alien stopped moving. Hark struggled not to vomit as she helped Tally and Morris drag a babbling MacLeod toward Engel's truck.

"Anzunna lives." He clutched his left hand to his chest. Blood flowed from the stump of his left ring finger. "Anzunna-kyras. Hail... hail Satan."

"Crazy bastard cut it off." Tally's face was pale. Her eyebrows were singed. "Ma'am, what were those—?"

Attack helicopters roared overhead. Brass casings poured down like hot rain around them as their chainguns opened fire. Some of Engel's soldiers helped Hark and what remained of their crew into the back of the truck. The beachhead was strewn with corpses, human and alien alike, but the spearhead pushed onward, deeper into squid territory.

Hark hammered her fist on the roof and gave the order to move out.

* * *

The Voidborn had not rested after taking North Vegas. Squid crawled through towers and hives of coral. Monstrous polyps blasted A-10s and Apaches from the sky with steaming bioplasma. Holes in the towers turned the wind into a chorus of piping screams. The squid joined their voices to the wind, forming scuttling choirs that fought to the last to hold back the human assault.

There was truth inside their music. Terrible, hideous truth, that Hark knew better than to heed.

Engel's truck brought them to the nascent frontline; five hundred infantrymen, supported by a company of Abrams tanks and self-propelled artillery. Hark dismounted with Tally and MacLeod and headed for the command vehicle. Outfitted with gigantic armored plates, it formed the core of the position. Its name, Tyrant of Hope, was painted in black and gold lettering next to an image of Saint George slaying a tentacled horror. Colonel Jack Young stood behind the giant, examining a series of images on a holoscreen with his adjutants.

He looked up at their approach. His eyes narrowed. "I take it the technicals I assigned you didn't make it."

"Just one," Hark said. "We're grateful for it."

He looked MacLeod up and down. "And I take it you're our PSICOM asset. MacLeod?"

"Yes, sir."

One of the adjutants jumped at his voice. Tally hissed, and spat. Young's face paled, then turned bright red as he set his jaw and pointed at the holoscreen.

"See that?" A series of glowing red runes moved away from the human lines, growing nearer to each other as they fell back. "They're regrouping past the range of our guns. Their coordination is fast. Damn fast. They're gonna be swarming back this way in under an hour, and they'll roll right over us."

"Our objective is why they're so coordinated," MacLeod said. "It's...an antenna. Buried deep below the nest."

"An antenna with eyes and teeth, no doubt." Young scowled. "I'll assist you, Lieutenant, as much as the tactical situation allows. Right now, it doesn't allow for much. The recon teams we sent into the tunnels didn't come back."

"I can get us to the target," MacLeod said.

"And then?"

MacLeod smiled, and spoke with the thing (bloody wings blotting out the sun) that lived in his soul. "We kill it."

Tally snarled and went for her pistol. Hark slapped her hand down, even as a wave of nausea washed over her. One of Young's adjutants staggered back, puke splashing over her boots. Young cursed, staring livid at the ever-smiling PSICOM witch, then shifting his gaze to just beyond the line of his troops.

"We'll send you in with Charlie Company. I'll radio Captain deSol, let her know you're coming." He turned to MacLeod; took a halting step forward, teeth grit like he was walking into storm winds. "These are my men and women you're taking in there. I'd appreciate it if you're well away from them when you do whatever it is you plan to do."

"I'll—"

"I mean it." Young drew himself up. Hark had the sudden image of a man waving a torch to ward off some terrible animal lurking just beyond the firelight. "I was at Tacoma. I saw the things some of you PSICOM freaks are playing with, and what happened when they get out of control. I don't care if you want to let Old Scratch wear you like a cheap fucking suit, but if your 'assets' harm even one of my troopers I swear I'll have your skinned hide hanging from Captain deSol's guidon before dark."

Something old and cold giggled in Hark's ear.

So fierce!

Yes-yes, so fierce, so loyal, Anzunna-kyras...

Then a growl, far away, but coming closer. The wind whispered a name... Urkhar, and the voices scattered.

Hark realized Young was staring at her. "Understood, Colonel. I'll take full responsibility for Lieutenant MacLeod. We'll rendezvous with Captain deSol immediately."

• • •

Tally broke the silence on the way to Charlie Company. "Why the hell would the Devil want to fight the Voidborn?"

"I don't know if it's actually the Devil," MacLeod said. He'd smeared his blood into the shape of an inverted cross on his face before Young's medic had patched up his finger. "Maybe it's what inspired the myths."

"Whatever. Why is it helping us?"

"Sergeant, imagine that you've…" He paused. Looked over his shoulder, just behind him; shook his head, and whispered something Hark didn't catch. He turned back to Tally and smiled. "You are a sergeant, yes?"

"I don't have any rank." Tally's hand on the butt of her pistol again. This time Hark didn't move to stop her.

If MacLeod noticed, he didn't care. "Ah. Well, regardless, imagine you've put a lot of time and energy into making a fine meal. It's—"

"A burrito. That's what I'm imagining."

He wrinkled his nose. "Fine. This… burrito, is the most wonderful and perfect thing you will ever make; your magnum opus. In fact, you've been making it for almost a million years, since the ingredients first evolved sentience and stopped swinging from trees." Tattered wings across the Sun; hunger as old as the stars behind those grinning headstone teeth.

Now picture when the burrito is almost ready. You take a seat at the table. You hold it in your hands. You open your mouth wide, to take that first bite, to savor, to finally devour, and then—"

"—an extradimensional squid demon comes along and tries to fuck it."

"Yes! Wouldn't that infuriate you?"

"So our choices are 'get eaten' or 'get fucked'?" Hark asked.

"Better the devil you know." MacLeod picked at the dead skin peeling away from the base of his skull implants. They'd turned a dark red, and were growing larger.

Charlie Company's ops center was a filthy tent pitched inside a muddy crater. Hark motioned for MacLeod to enter, but grabbed Tally's arm before she could follow.

"You'll hang back."

Tally stared at the hand on her arm, then jerked away. "No. I'm going with you."

"This isn't up for debate. There are going to be some survivors from our platoon. Rally those you can, and put yourselves under the command of Bravo Company's CO."

"Fuck you. You think we're all gonna die down there, and you don't want me to go."

"No." Yes. "You need to be a point of contact for the platoon. Engels will need—"

"Fuck Engels. Fuck the platoon. They'll merge with other units. It's what we've done a thousand times."

Tally stepped close. So small. "Do you remember what you said? In Tacoma?" Blue eyes filled with tears, tiny fists shook. "You promised. You…"

"That's an order, Tally."

She set her jaw, gave an absurd salute, and stomped away. Hark watched her go. It wouldn't be safe with Bravo Company, but it was better than certain death. She hadn't forgotten her promise to Tally; she'd just known she'd break it from the moment the words left her lips, as she held the girl who would become her only friend in the ruins of Spokane.

"All this way," she muttered, stepping into the ops center. "Just to die in Vegas."

*　.*

The men and women of Charlie Company were exhausted. Filthy, ragged, clutching weapons scavenged from the battlefield, they fell into assault formation without a word. To her credit, Captain deSol insisted on commanding from the lead platoon, keeping her XO near the center to guide the rest of the unit. The guidon bearer, a teenager no older than Tally, stayed close to her side, his eyes wide and vacant.

"Lieutenant MacLeod will get us to the objective," Hark told deSol before they moved into the mouth of the hive. "It's up to us to fight our way out."

The inside of the structure was a combination of stinking coral and remnants of the old world. The trunk of a car stuck out a nearby wall. Rusted rebar poked up from the floor. Human corpses, still rotting and covered in alien mites, hung limp from the ceiling. The unit passed mindless polyps secreting foul resin, slowly adding to the strength and thickness of the coral walls.

MacLeod had given deSol a rough map of the hive. He had sketched it with his eyes rolled back into his head and, when he had emerged from the trance, could remember nothing of the last five minutes. His skin pulled tight against the bones of his jaw.

She called for a short halt in a large junction. Hark and MacLeod joined her, taking a knee in the mist.

"Where to?" deSol asked.

MacLeod pointed down the widest corridor. "It burrowed in there."

Hark looked up at the multiple tunnels in the walls and ceiling. "Anybody else wondering where the hell they are?"

deSol checked her rifle. "I'm sure we'll find out soon."

Soon turned out to be half a kilometer down the tunnel. A sudden cacophony of screeches and screams smashed into Charlie Company, as squid boiled out of the adjacent corridors. The first wave was met with the steady pop of automatic weapons fire, then shredded by the echoing roar of M240L machine guns. Platoon and squad leaders shouted orders as more squid appeared. The company contracted, forming a circle of fire to face the coming threat.

For a moment Hark dared to think they might withstand the ambush. That hope died when deSol abruptly disappeared into the mist. She came back into view seconds later, hoisted up to the ceiling by a hair-covered tentacle the width of her torso. The infantry officer hacked at the stinking limb with her combat knife. It slammed her back to the floor with a wet crunch. The psychoreactive runes on the blade glowed white-hot, then snuffed out, reducing the blade to rust and ashes.

More tentacles whipped out from beneath the company's feet. Confusion, then panic, came with them. Hark killed two more squid before feeling something cold and thick wrap around her leg. She fell hard, smacking her head onto the ground. MacLeod shouted her name.

Glowing pustules lined the walls. The air in the chamber at the end of the corridor was rank and humid. In the half-light, crouched beneath piles of desecrated corpses, the objective regarded its captives with growing hunger. That hunger echoed in Hark's mind like the screams of the still-living soldiers it dragged down into the darkness.

A flash of grenades and small arms fire lit up the nest. The surviving members of Charlie Company attacked from the rear of the platform, at the very mouth of the tunnel. The abomination's vast tentacles smeared one to stinking paste. Others were plucked from their feet and fed to the quivering fronds of loathsome anemones growing from the horror's armored bulk. Hark saw one of the parasites pierce a screaming trooper in a dozen places, skewering him, dragging him slowly into a chattering mouth that dripped with bile.

Hundreds of squid worshipped around it. Their hateful ministrations before the Great One drowned out the dwindling sound of gunfire. Soon their praise was all Hark could hear; their worship of this Void-thing, the embodiment of what really waited for Humanity out in the darkness between the stars.

She reached for the machete on her hip.

I'm sorry, Tally. This was always a one-way trip.

"Lieutenant."

MacLeod lay next to her. He bled from a fracture on his forehead. He smiled. His teeth were fangs.

"My arm is broken, or I'd do it myself." The chrome implants on his skull had turned crimson. They rose, slowly curling into what Hark knew would be horns. "There is no victory without sacrifice. Mine is… comparatively small."

Hark nodded. She raised the machete from where she lay, bringing her arm across her body.

"Good luck, soldier," she said.

He smiled weakly. "See you on the other side."

She hacked the machete into his neck. Blunted by war, swung at an awkward angle, it carved into his windpipe and stuck. Hark yanked it free. Blood from severed veins and arteries sprayed over them. She swung it again, and felt the blade bite into the bones of his neck.

Impossibly, MacLeod laughed. The Fallen Thing… Urkhar… laughed with him, until its laughter was all she heard. MacLeod's wild grin split his cheeks, the skin of his face peeling back as the Fallen reached up from his throat and pulled itself out into reality.

Hail, the Sacred-Martyr Thomas MacLeod! Anzunna lives!

Hark pissed herself. Urkhar shook its great saurian head. Cloven hooves split the earth with great bursts of steam. It brayed with wild, triumphant laughter, boundless and free.

Like you could be. Forked tongues flickered in Hark's ear. Its bulging eyes regarded her with terrifying familiarity. Like you all could be...

The Fallen stooped to pick up MacLeod's severed head. Flesh ran like wax down the creature's muscled arm. It took the blackened skull and added it to the crown of rusted wire on its horned brow.

Six hands gripped a flaming sword longer than Hark was tall. She recoiled from the heat. The flames screamed, and from them came dozens of lesser horrors, all of them wearing MacLeod's face and chanting the praise of their loathsome god. The monstrous Great One gibbered and shrieked, rising out of the nest it had dug for itself.

The squid charged. Urkhar thundered with laughter. Flames burst from the empty sockets of its saurian skull. Wings of stitched human flesh erupted from its back. It went for the Voidborn demi-god, which rose from its divine sloth, snapping with claws large enough to shatter battle tanks. The shadows grappled with the squid in the light of the Fallen's blade. It swung at the Great One, trailing great archs of howling flame that smashed into the abomination's shell. The Voidborn demi-god drove its crustacean limbs toward Urkhar. It boomed again with laughter. Winds that stunk of sulfur washed over the nest as the Fallen took flight, flayed flesh wings straining above its tremendous bulk.

Anzunna lives!

It fell like a red thunderbolt on the Great One. The alien monster gave a pained, throaty howl.

The sound of heavy machine gun fire drowned out the clash of demons. Engel's truck careened into view. Tally stood on the gun, firing at any squid that made it past the red-skinned imps. Specialist Morris hurled smoke and frag grenades from the bed.

"Let's go!" Tally shouted.

Hark stumbled to her feet. A giggling, long-tongued demon scampered to make way. Go, Hark, go. We are with you, we are always with you.

Morris pulled her into the truck. They spun around, heading back toward the surface. Flames blasted from the tunnels and corridors. Black ropes of contagion arched through the coral, rotting it from within.

The hive collapsed as they raced out into the beachhead. Cackling laughter echoed in every mortal mind for a hundred miles. Hark collapsed onto the truck bed. She laughed, too, to keep from sobbing, to keep the visions of their grim patrons at bay.

Tally embraced her. The truck shuddered around them. Outgoing artillery howled overhead.

"All this way," the girl whispered. "All this way…"

Hark shifted. She thought of her promise ("we'll kill them, together, I swear it") and somehow, despite it all, managed to smile.

FINAL HARVEST

Justin Bell

Even through three layers of air filtration in her battle helmet, Talia Sorace could still smell the stink of the final city on Earth burning to the ground. Pedestal cities had once stood tall to allow humanity's survival as climate changes ravaged the planet at large.

"It's done," she said in a low voice, the tenor of her words metallic as they echoed from her helmet into the surrounding forest.

Weber drew in a long breath, his layered composite battle armor heaving with the motion as his padded gloves clamped around the handle of the automatic rifle. The air had that same tinny taste as the recirculated air of the pedestals, and looking at the trees around them, Weber had the urge to rip off his filtration mask. But he knew he couldn't, as much as he longed to take a lungful of fresh, non-artificial air, it would be the death of him.

He gripped his military-style weapon tighter; it was thick and rectangular, the embedded scope on top slender and metallic. Underslung the main body of the weapon was a cylindrical flashlight with an extended mag drawing out from the weapon's handle. "So that's it," he said. "We failed."

"Not yet," Yanez barked, his voice sharp and angrier than he intended. "We knew we were going to lose the last Pedestal City when we launched yesterday. That's not what this operation is about."

"Easy for you to say," Weber replied, glaring at him. "You were a glorified engineer. A scientist more than a soldier. My main responsibility was security and protection."

"Soldiers, engineers, what's the difference these days?" Yanez replied. He ducked under a thick tree branch and moved left, weaving in and out of the trunks that stretched up from root systems toward the slate gray sky above. "Ever since our primary enemy became the planet itself, the military and R & D have become mostly the same thing."

"Right?" Sorace scoffed. She was taller than both Yanez and Weber, nearly seven feet with broad shoulders and thick, rippling muscle made even larger by the layered armor she wore. "No wonder these bastards eviscerated humanity as quickly as they did. All of our combat training was replaced by fucking climatology."

"We adapted," replied Moldano. Like Yanez, his battle suit was brushed metal without the ornate camouflage, the dull metal sheen looking just as bland as the sky above. "Just like humanity always has."

Sorace shook her head, her eyes narrowing within the semi-translucent material of her battle helmet. She shifted her shoulders as she walked through the trees, angling the cylindrical mini-gun so she could cut between two thick trunks. Her massive boots thudded with metallic sounds, crushing one of the roots extending from a particularly large oak. "We adapted so well we made it easier for them to wipe us out," she growled. "Now what? There are only a few of us left."

Weber glared through his own visor. "That's what this operation is for, Sorace. We're going to fix that."

"Fix it?" she barked back. "With three soldiers and a bunch of glorified biologists?"

"Bah, we got you and me, sister," Otela replied, her own voice a metal twinge. She wore similar armor as the other more combat-oriented members of the squad, her own triple-barreled shotgun held tight in both hands.

"What am I, chopped liver?" asked Moldano, holding his hands out.

"Fine," Sorace replied with a smirk, "you can be a sister, too." They tapped fists briefly as Moldano's synthetic chuckle flowed from behind his rebreather.

Every member of the group wore the slender, rounded

helmets, looking almost insectile as they moved through the woodlands. Nearly every surface of the planet was covered in thick forest these days, it was an environment they were mostly accustomed to, though even the soldiers hadn't spent much time outside since the atmosphere had become nearly unbreathable.

"Hold up," Jeremiah hissed from point position, single gloved-fist raised.

"You hear them?" asked Weber in a low, quiet voice.

"Oh, man," Rinder murmured. "Oh, man, oh, man. I fucking knew I should have stayed at the Pedestal."

"Yeah, and if you stayed there you'd have been burning to death right now," spat Dalon. A winged shield glistened on his armor as he twisted and scanned the surroundings. He felt totally out of place not behind the joystick of his dropship, but Weber had asked for all hands on deck, so he'd volunteered.

"Northeast," Jeremiah said quietly, pointing through the trees. "I think there are some also coming from the north—"

Rustling shook the trees to their north, leaves shifting menacingly in the quiet. Two of the thinner trees tilted as some unseen thing moved rapidly through the upper branches.

"Shit!" shouted Dalon. "That's them! Fuck!"

A low and rattling chitter cascaded through the thick leaves of the surrounding trees.

"How did they find us so quickly?" Dalon yelled, lifting his rifle and turning, looking for targets.

"Same way they brought down the Pedestals!" barked Sorace. "These shitheads are fast and smart. Way too fucking smart!"

Leaves exploded to her left, a gray smear of motion leaping from one of the trees in a dart of mottled flesh.

"Three o'clock!" shouted Jeremiah, whirling around. Moldano moved left, turning and firing his weapon before he could even aim it, composite rounds smashing through wood and leaves and passing just over the creature's head. It landed in the dirt on all fours, knees and elbows contorted into odd angles as it caught its own momentum. Its vertebrae seemed to deny structure as its slender, sloped skull whipped around, luminescent eyes glaring over a sneer of jagged incisors. Its skin was a pallid gray, pulled tight over twisting muscle and bulging bone structure. Three-toed claws dug hard into the dirt for purchase as it adjusted its glare, looking hard at Moldano.

Weber grunted and shifted his weight, twisting his armored body around and zeroing in on the creature. His rifle spoke, and the creature's head exploded in a wet splat of shredded bone and torn flesh.

As Weber's rifle fell silent noise exploded all around them, leaves thrashing as the blurred forms of charging bodies leapt from tree to tree.

"They're coming!" screamed Sorace, stamping her metal boot down for purchase as she swung her minigun around. Her finger slammed on the firing mechanism as she hefted the weapon into an upward angle. A hundred rounds per second screamed up into the leaves, chewing apart branches like matchsticks. Sorace roared as leaves and twigs rained down on her and the others.

"We need to keep moving!" Jeremiah yelled, adjusting the aim of his own rifle and firing a swift burst. "Yanez, you know where we're going, right?"

"I think so!" Yanez said just as another creature burst from the trees to his right. He shouted and stumbled backward, but Otela was there, bringing her triple-barreled shotgun around and blasting the beast in the ribs with sharpened buckshot that nearly tore the creature in two, throwing it hard to the dirt.

"You think so?" replied Weber. "Did you say you *think* so?"

"Yes!" Yanez clarified. "Yes, I know where the caves are!"

"I've got his back!" Jeremiah interjected. "Yanez knows what he's talking about. We should listen to him."

Three more gray-skinned creatures leapt, mouths filled with fangs open and hungry.

Dalon fired, and one of the creatures pitched into a clumsy forward roll, limbs flailing. A second one hit the ground, roared, and then launched itself through the air at him.

"Dammit, Dalon, look out!" screamed Weber, desperately trying to adjust his aim.

The creature plowed into Dalon, claws slashing at armor, teeth gnashing at the helmet. Its long fangs punched through his visor and dug hard into the flesh beneath. Dalon screamed, his blood splashing inside his helmet.

"No!" Weber charged forward. He drew within a meter of the beast, which now had Dalon pinned to the ground. Weber fired a sustained burst, the rifle jostling in his grip. The volley struck the huddled gray-skin and ripped it from its prey.

Otela charged forward and knelt to check on Dalon. His gasping breaths could be heard over the cacophony of the battle around them.

"Dalon's down!" Otela shouted. Behind her, Sorace adjusted the aim of her minigun and fired again, scattering leaves in the distance. A sigh broke from Otela. "His breathing appliance is shredded, there's nothing we can do." She looked into his eyes, wide and afraid. His lips parted, desperately mouthing words she could not understand.

She shook her head softly. "I'm sorry," she whispered. Tears streamed down the young man's face, pale and fully visible beneath the shattered visor.

Dalon's eyes widened then darted over her shoulder. She whirled from her kneeling position, brought up her shotgun and fired. The blast struck the leaping gray-skin in the chest and neck, ripping its head off and throwing the lifeless corpse to the ground. She winced as dark blood scattered over her visor and sprayed her armor. With her gloved hand, she wiped a thick smear of it from her faceplate then turned to thank Dalon but he was gone. She threw herself into a run to join the rest of the squad.

"Move, move, *move!*" yelled Weber as he charged through the trees, following Yanez, who was running as fast as he could. Metal clanged as the group raced between tree trunks and ducked under branches, moving as swiftly as they could to shake the enemy. The deeper into the forest, the larger and more menacing the trees became.

"Those assholes could be anywhere in here," Rinder hissed. "Can't believe Dalon is down!"

"I hope we don't need an evac," Moldano replied. "Our only pilot just suffocated on his own blood." As he moved through the trees, he rotated one shoulder, adjusting the cylindrical pack strapped to his armored back, thankful for the light sloshing within.

"I think we need a plane before we get an evac," Otela replied.

"I got plenty of spare fuel for it," Moldano said, gesturing to the pack he wore. "These things move too damn fast for the flamethrower."

"A place to evac to would help, too," said Rinder. "No plane, no headquarters. Nothing but these fucking trees and some mythical cave to save humanity. No pressure, right?"

"Hey, look at the bright side," Sorace said, moving up next to the group. "We fuck this up, none of us will ever know."

"That supposed to make us feel better?" asked Rinder with a chuckle. "You're a shit motivational speaker, you know that?"

"This shit's all the motivation I need," she replied, lifting her massive weapon as if it weren't a six-foot-long slab of metal. Leaves continued to move and rustle around them as they double-timed through the thick trees and brush.

Jeremiah pulled up next to Weber, silently issuing advice, clamping two fingers together, pointing north. They moved forward in quiet crouches, every step watching the meter on their internal air quality metrics. As they moved through the trees, the leaves continued to rustle, the movement and sound of creatures milling about. Suddenly, the sound ceased and the entire world was soaked in a crisp and physical silence; tension in the air around them a solid presence. Jeremiah held up a hand in a sharp, abrupt halting gesture and the team stopped, muscles tense, armored battle suits rigid in anticipation of inevitable attack.

Weber's eyes met Jeremiah's, which were surprisingly calm and collected, analytical as always, darting from leaf to leaf, evaluating.

Softly, the rustling continued, above them and around them and Sorace twisted on her plant foot, the long barrel of her weapon sweeping around. Otela pressed against her, back-to-back, shouldering the shotgun and desperately trying to cover the real estate Sorace wasn't. Rustling stopped. Silence returned. It was such a pervasive quiet that Weber could almost swear he heard the low and rhythmic heartbeats of the other team members around him. Looking from trooper to trooper, he glanced at their eyes, the alertness or calm, noting any trickles of nervous sweat or pale flesh.

He blinked as the salty trickle from his forehead creased down his furrowed brow and dipped into the wells of his eyes, temporarily fogging his vision.

In the trees above, a blurring shadow leaped from one tree to the next, scattering leaves and sending broken twigs down around them. Weapons clacked as they swung upward, but the sound had already ceased.

"We need to keep moving," whispered Jeremiah, his voice narrow and tinny from within the synthesized air filter. Weber could see the team around him, cautious and apprehensive, bracing themselves, waiting for what they envisioned was the inevitable attack, not just from the trees around them, but from the front, the back, and above. Rustling came again, and a large rock hurtled through the clearing from the left, prompting Moldano to lurch forward, swinging his automatic around, his finger tensing between the trigger and the guard.

Jeremiah moved swiftly, stepping forward and placing a gloved hand on the side of Moldano's weapon, and the infantry man looked at him, eyes wide, pupils dilated. Moldano's finger jerked, but released, moving further away from the trigger, his weapon physically trembling in his firm grasp as the movement of the leaves slowed, then finally stilled.

"What are we doing out here?" Otela snarled. "This is fucking nuts. They could be anywhere."

"Everyone," Weber hissed, his voice rising slightly. "Calm down. They're playing with us."

"Calm down?" Moldano replied. "We can't even breathe this air, and there are gray-skinned nasties crawling about in the damned trees all around us. How the hell are we supposed to stay calm?"

Sorace patted him on the shoulder. "Preach, brother Moldano, fucking preach."

"Moldano," said Weber, holding up a hand. "Get your head on straight. This mission is too critical to lose our focus."

"It would help if we knew what the hell we were dealing with," Sorace interjected. "Moldano may be overdramatic, but I agree with him."

"Jeremiah, you're the historian of the group," Weber hissed, nodding toward the short, squat man who drifted a bit ahead of them, "What's the deal with these things?"

Jeremiah looked back. Even through the opaque visor over his eyes, Weber could see the long, brown hair gathered up within his helmet.

"What, you didn't pay attention during biological history class?" he asked.

Weber shook his head. "Man, I joined this Army to be a soldier not a glorified engineer."

"You actually had a choice?" Moldano asked. "Over on Pedestal Seven it was mandatory. Once the planet became our chief threat there was no need for human-on-human combat training. For the first time in history, people actually got along."

"Yeah, and see how far that got us," Weber replied. "Now we do have a threat, and nobody knows how to deal with it."

"We are dealing with it!" shouted Yanez, looking back over his shoulder. "Jarheads back there yapping about shooting all your problems in the face while the engineer is up here leading you to the solution."

"I'll believe that shit when I see it," replied Sorace, shaking her head.

They continued through the trees, the low crackle of moving leaves growing somewhat fainter around them. Moldano's eyes darted left-to-right as he pushed through a thick cluster of branches.

"You hanging in there, Moldano?" asked Sorace twisting

around to look at him. Her long-barreled mini-gun moved with her, knocking at the thin branches as they moved.

Moldano shook his head. "Honestly?"

"No, tell me a lie."

Moldano chuckled then glanced to the right as more trees moved. "Not really." A wave of fluttering leaves cascaded, a clear sign of something going right-to-left, moving alongside them, matching their pace. "I wish they would just attack for fuck's sake," the growled. "Get this over with."

"It's in their nature to hunt," Sorace said as a vague shape lurched overhead, jumping from one cluster of leaves to another. "I think they're pack animals."

Jeremiah fell back in alignment with her, walking slowly, his boots softly crunching the leaf-litter. For one brief snatch of time the woods around them were quiet again.

"You're on the money," he said, looking at the tall woman. "They hunt in packs. That's the way they've evolved. How they've adapted to this world."

"We've spent so much time cooped up in artificial air that we haven't," Moldano said, slowing his pace and turning to look at the trees to his left, which had started moving again. "Adapted, I mean."

Jeremiah turned away from Moldano for a moment, stepping closer to Yanez and tilted his head slightly, listening to the trees again. A light rustle moved the leaves, but there was no sign of the gray-skins again. Everyone froze, waiting for his word. Eventually he nodded and moved forward.

"The Harvesters just kind of appeared," Jeremiah finally replied as he led them forward.

"Harvesters?" asked Yanez, turning to look at him. "I don't think I've ever heard them called that before."

Jeremiah nodded. "That's what they were called back in the day. The first human sighting like sixty years ago. Since then they've continued growing. At first they seemed to be friendly, or least just observant. Then, a few years back, they got a little more hostile."

Weber shook his head. "Tearing our Pedestals down, slaughtering the inhabitants, and setting fire to them. Yeah, I guess that qualifies as hostile."

"Now, we're all that's left," Rinder said.

"Not all," Yanez corrected. "Look, there are other survivors out there, I'm sure. But we're the ones with the best chance—"

A low, rattling hiss echoed in the trees. At first it was just one, then others joined, then a chorus of them.

"Should have known it was too fucking quiet out here," Sorace swore, turning and levelling her minigun.

Moldano covered her back, stepping forward and shouldering his rifle. Whenever things started falling apart, he always made sure to have Sorace's back – she'd saved his ass too many times to count.

Otela moved next to her, shotgun raised and ready. "These motherfuckers are everywhere in here," she said. "How can they breathe in this shit?"

"Like us," Jeremiah said softly. "They adapted. Evolved. Did something, I don't know."

Just ahead Sorace saw two of the gray-skins clawing their way up a particularly thick tree, glaring at her with glowing eyes. She wasn't sure what was worse – the painful silence, or the dead-eyed glare of the creatures as they looked down upon them.

"Two of them, twenty meters ahead," she whispered.

The trees suddenly exploded with movement.

"Oh, shit!" shouted Weber, stumbling back and whirling, bringing his automatic around and opening fire as two of the gray-skins burst from the long grass next to him. His sustained burst tore them apart, but two more were just behind them, lunging and snapping as they lurched forward.

"Weber, drop!" shouted Otela. He complied, and Otela unleashed with her shotgun. Buckshot ripped through flesh and bone, spattering the undergrowth.

"North side!" screamed Moldano, firing his weapon into a small group of the creatures bolting from the trees. Rinder lay down cover fire.

Moldano saw blurs to their right, and tried to swivel in time, but Rinder was hit by two gray-skins and thrown hard to the ground. Claws and talons slashed through the layered armor covering his chest, tearing ragged strips of metal away. Teeth clamped on the flexible material at his elbow and ripped. Moldano watched, numb, as the gray-skin severed Rinder's arm. The creature threw its head backwards, tossing the lower half of the soldier's limb high into the air as Rinder screamed beneath it.

His screams were cut to a gurgle as the second creature found his throat and tore it out.

"Pull back! Pull back!" screamed Yanez, his voice cutting through the sounds of gunfire and chittered roars.

"Pull back where?" Weber yelled. He stepped back, narrowly avoiding the slashing claw of one of the attacking animals, then fired a quick barrage into the back of the creature's head.

"Didn't you say the cave was around here somewhere?" Jeremiah yelled at Yanez, firing his own automatic rifle as he spoke. He took two of the approaching animals down, then moved forward, reaching over his shoulder. A third creature charged, and he swept a thick blade from a sheath on his back, swiping hard and cleaving the leaping creature in two.

"Damn, kid, who still uses a sword these days?" Sorace asked, shaking her head as she unleashed another volley of lead into the trees.

"A weapon for a more elegant age!" Jeremiah replied, lunging forward and swinging again, lopping off the head of a second creature. Two others converged on him, and he twisted, bringing the sword close, moving with a sort of brutal calligraphy, his body acting as a pen, the ink dark sprays of gray-skin blood. Contorting left, he wrapped both hands around the extended grip of the blade, then swung in a swift upward arc, cleaving another creature from hip to shoulder while ramming the sword almost hilt deep in the chest of another. In a flash his automatic was up in his hands and unleashing a furious torrent, blistering another monster's face, shredding flesh and pulverizing the yellowed bone beneath.

"Cave should be close I think!" Yanez shouted desperately as he gunned down a creature.

"Tell me that motherfucker didn't just say 'I think'!" Sorace said, firing her weapon again as more and more gray-skins leapt from the trees and hustled from the surrounding grass.

"Sounded like it," Otela confirmed. Her shotgun blasted a ragged hole in another group of creatures as they circled for an opening.

"I found the map in the Pedestal Four archives!" Yanez snapped. "It was already half-charred, okay?"

"He's on the right track," Jeremiah said. "I know you grunts like to solve everything with your fists and your guns, but sometimes the brains know what they're talking about."

"We're all gonna die," Moldano hissed, shaking his head as he fired into the leaves above him "They're everywhere. In every tree, behind every bush. They're just toying with us!"

"Calm the fuck down, Moldano!" Weber shouted. He adjusted and fired again, knocking another prowling creature from the tree above Moldano's head.

"Keep moving west!" Yanez barked, leading the way as the others moved to fall in behind him.

The creatures suddenly withdrew, the forest falling silent as the haze from the fight cleared. Jeremiah placed a foot on the ribs of the dead creature at his feet and ripped his blade free with a snap, then rubbed the blood off the blade on his pants and rammed it back into the sheath.

"You move pretty quick in that contraption," Weber said, shaking his head as he strode past. "This armor weighs like a hundred pounds."

"I'm stronger than I look," Jeremiah replied, darting forward after Yanez, his thickly armored boots moving over the ground far quieter than Weber thought possible. Weber struggled to keep up, and Moldano came up beside him, shaking his head.

"Man, I'm a freaking geneticist for crying out loud. I'm not a soldier."

"You're in the Army," Weber barked back. "You can do this, all right?"

"No, not all right," Moldano replied quickly. "Not all right by a fucking long shot, okay? This is not what I joined the army to do. I barely know which end is the shooty end!" Moldano adjusted the metal backpack, wincing slightly at the straps digging into his shoulders.

"That's why I love you," Sorace said, patting him playfully on the shoulder. "You're the toughest, dumbest scientist I ever met!"

"Uh—thanks?" Moldano replied, looking at her with a half-smirk. "Did you just tell me you loved me?"

"Just keep moving, okay?" Weber said, looking at Moldano through his visor. "Yanez might need your help. We all might."

The group scrambled after Yanez, and they picked up the pace and raced like armored ghosts through the trees.

"This way," Jeremiah said, then his eyes flitted quickly to Yanez, who nodded his agreement. They were off again, the gray-skins now ominously silent.

After running for what seemed hours, the group stopped to rest and check their gear. They hadn't seen or heard anything since the last attack, and that alone had them all on edge.

Weber was crouched near Jeremiah. "How do you suppose they communicate?"

Jerimiah grunted. "Some sort of wordless telepathy, maybe. A hive mind of sorts."

"That's horrifying."

"It would explain some things about this magical cave we're supposedly looking for," he said as the squad regrouped.

They moved off again, walking through the jungle instead of running. Weber and Jeremiah fell in near the rear, Moldano, Otela, and Sorace walking in a trio just ahead of them as Yanez prowled forward on point.

As always, the air felt thick even through the layers of their ballistic armor, as though they were pushing through gossamer spider's webs, the predators all around them, just waiting for them to be fully snared.

Jeremiah spoke softly as he scanned the forest around them. "Legend has it this cave contains a way to end the threat."

"Grasping at straws," Weber replied.

"We're all humanity has left at this point," Moldano interjected, looking back over his shoulder. "What other choice do we have?"

"No choice," Weber nodded grimly. "No choice at all."

The trees around them were still and silent as they marched. A disturbing and pervasive silence that seemed too muted to be real.

"Weber," a hushed voice barked from the head of the group, breaking the quiet. Weber looked up and his eyes met Yanez, who was gesturing him forward.

Weber moved to the head of the line and looked to where Yanez was pointing. Through a gap in the trees, out over an expanse of long, green grass, the foothills of a mountain thrust its way up from the forest like a stone giant.

Along the ridge of the gray stone was a huge, darkened opening. It looked carved out, hewn.

Weber and the others finally smiled.

Scratches and chitters cut into their hearing, and the smiles faltered. The scratches were strange sounds, pockets of it emanating from several different directions.

Then they saw them.

The Harvesters melted down from the vegetation like shadows, slinking along the edges of the rocks.

More and more of them appeared, converging into a barrier of teeth and flesh between the trees and the cave. This was why they'd pulled back. The entry.

"No bueno," Yanez whispered, shaking his head. "This is some bad mojo, boss."

"How many are there?" Sorace asked, moving up behind them, careful with her mini gun.

"Thirty?" Weber said, looking left to right. "Maybe fifty?"

"Damn, man," Moldano whispered. "Ten of them were handing us our asses before they ran off. How the hell we gonna take down fifty?"

"We just need to get to that cave," Yanez said quietly.

"Then what?" Moldano replied. "It's not like there's a door. Say we get inside, you think they're just magically gonna leave us alone? What fantasy world you living in, man, 'cause I want to go there."

"Hate to say it, but I kind of agree with the chicken shit here," growled Otela.

"Yeah— hey, wait," hissed Moldano.

"We have no other fucking options," Weber grimaced. "The human race has been nearly wiped out. Our civilization is burnt to the ground, and these bastards are the cause. We can either sit here in the trees finding all the reasons why we can't do this, or we can suck it up and try to find a way that we can."

Sorace shook her head, but beneath her helmet a thin smile creased her smooth features. "I got seventeen ammo canisters, boss," she said. "Burned through twenty-three to get here. Might as well use 'em all up, right?"

Moldano swore, then sighed in resignation. "I haven't even started with my flamethrower yet," he said. "They cluster together much tighter and I could whack a bunch all at once."

"I like the way you think, bro," Sorace said with a nod. The two of them bumped fists again.

"How confident are you the caves are safe?" Weber asked Yanez, whose eyes widened at the inquiry.

"Not confident at all, Weber, now that you mention it."

"I feel confident," Jeremiah replied. "If the history books tell the story, they don't like dark, dank places. They prefer the fresh air and trees."

Weber remained crouched by the tree line, looking out over the sea of grass toward the rock ahead. The Harvesters clustered around the entrance, the rest of them filtering out over the grass. Some lowered their heads to eat.

"You look like you've got an idea in your head," Sorace said.

Weber nodded. "I just might. No promises that it's a good idea, of course, but it's an idea, just the same."

* • *

The Harvesters by the cave entrance made no move toward the trees; didn't seem to realize the humans were even there, too focused on the vegetation, on feasting, doing what they were born to do.

Weber motioned for the squad to spread among the tree line while he studied the cave. There were a good thirty-odd Harvesters milling outside the rocks; more hidden up in the mountain trees, he was sure.

Weber and his team were outnumbered five-to-one, but as he rested a hand on the cool metal of the container sitting on the ground in front of him, the nuggets of a plan came together.

If they were going to pull this off, they'd have to do it the old-fashioned way.

Weber checked his rifle one more time, then set his foot on the surface of the rounded cannister and counted the Harvesters, slowly assembling the next several minutes in his head.

Even the best plan is only effective until first contact. He'd had that crammed into his skull during his leadership development course at Pedestal Two. There was truth in it. The next minute would dictate the entire operation. Could decide the fate of the human race.

Like Sorace said, no pressure.

He kicked the cannister, sending it rolling out over the grass. Momentum and its curved surface kept it moving, even over the rough terrain. The sound of metal on dirt drew the attention of the Harvesters. Even the ones busy chewing grass halted to watch, glimmering eyes narrowing at the intrusion on their meal.

The container rolled quickly at first, then slowed as a small group of creatures converged on it, chittering quietly as their clawed feet dug at the dirt.

"Come on, come on," Weber whispered. "Curiosity killed the Harvesters, right?"

They took cautious steps closer, surrounding the item as it finally rolled to a stop near the rocks and cave opening.

Weber shouldered his rifle, aimed, and fired.

His single shot was crisp and loud in the relative silence of the clearing, a muzzle flash splitting the darkness of the wood. Harvester heads whirled around and nostrils flared as a metallic *ting* signaled the bullet's impact. A brief spark. Then the fuel tank exploded in a roiling ball of flame and smoke.

"GO!" screamed Weber, throwing himself from the tree line, charging toward the charred crater where the fuel tank had been. It was a blackened wreck, the metal surrounding it ripped into shreds; the burnt and broken husks of a half dozen Harvesters scattered around it. "Cave entrance!" Weber headed straight for the blackened hole in the center of the rock wall.

To his left, Jeremiah burst from the trees, yelling wildly and drawing the interest of several other Harvesters. They dropped to all fours and broke toward him, legs pumping and claws digging, throwing dirt behind them as they charged. To Weber's right, four other Harvesters turned toward him, but a sudden echoing roar of consistent fire shattered from the trees, splintering wood and tearing grass apart. The ground around the Harvesters chewed up into rooster tails of dirt and flesh as the creatures were torn apart. Sorace marched from the trees, her minigun barrel smoking as she shifted her aim, directing more relentless fire at another small group of approaching creatures.

Yanez launched from the tree line, running full tilt, Sorace gave him heavy cover as he galloped toward the cave mouth, keeping his head low. He didn't even worry about his weapon.

"Cover, give him cover!" Weber shouted, twisting at the waist and adding his own firepower to Sorace's volleys. He grabbed a Harvester midair and slammed it into the ground before it could leap on Yanez. As he stood and scanned for more targets a loud thrashing and roar emanated from the trees behind him, and he looked over his shoulder. "Fuck me…" A wave of Harvesters advanced from the trees, at least a hundred of them dropping down and barreling forward.

"FUCK! Into the cave! Everyone into the cave!" screamed Weber, firing his rifle and throwing another creature against the stone, staining the hard surface with its dark blood. Yanez hurdled a charging Harvester, landing clumsily, but still moving forward as the creature turned back toward him. Otela was on it, blasting the back of the beast with her shotgun and tearing it open. Moldano had her back, using his own rifle as cover, though the grass was growing congested with the charging beasts.

Yanez plunged into the mouth of the cave, and Weber's legs pumped as he tried to match the other man's swift pace. He looked right and saw Otela blast another Harvester in the face, then turn just in time for a second to leap from the rock and land on her, driving her back, shotgun spinning up into the air as she screamed just before the creature's claws tore her to shreds.

Sorace hesitated for a moment, glancing toward Otela.

"Keep moving!" Weber roared.

Ahead he saw Jeremiah duck a Harvester attack, bury his sword into another beast, then gracefully hurdle a third. He didn't see the swift advance of yet another, coming in from his blind side.

"Jeremiah!" Weber screamed. The Harvester slammed hard into him, picking him up and throwing him violently. The armored body struck the curved wall inside the cave hard enough to pop the helmet release, sending the protective headpiece spinning out onto the grass. Even from this distance, Weber could hear him gagging, could see his shrouded form clawing at his throat and his face. Weber knew it was too late, the smallest exposure was enough to kill any human.

Shifting at the waist, he sighted in on the attacking Harvester and pulled the trigger, pumping a volley of fire into it and dropping it where it crouched. Sorace reached the mouth of the cave turning with her minigun and unloading a seemingly endless barrage of fire just to Weber's right. The ground exploded next to him, grass and dirt flying high in the air as a Harvester he had not seen was torn apart and thrown back, its dismembered body striking two others and slowing them as well. Weber accelerated, charging harder, reaching the mouth of the cave and throwing himself inside as Sorace continued her onslaught.

"Moldano, come on!" Weber shouted. The man nodded, running hard and reaching the edge just as Sorace's minigun clicked on empty.

"Dammit!" She threw the weapon inside, balling both fists. "Get in!" she screamed at Moldano. "I'll punch the taste outta their mouths if I have to!"

Moldano ducked his head, lunged forward, and slammed into Sorace.

"Hey—!" she shouted as the unexpected force struck her, knocking her on her ass and deeper into the cave. For a moment Moldano stood there, framed by the cave entrance. He looked at them all and smiled crookedly as Weber's eyes drifted to his hands. Moldano held two grenades, plucked from his backpack and with a curt nod to Sorace, he triggered them both, closed his eyes and exploded into a blinding white flash of hot light, the air itself splitting with the impact.

The explosion shattered the walls of the cave entrance, collapsing the opening in on itself and blocking the cavern from the horde of Harvesters lurking beyond.

"Holy shit... holy shit... holy shit..." Sorace whispered, rocking slowly back and forth on the smooth floor of the cave. The crumbled rock wall had cut off much of the light from the cavern, but there was still a lingering pale luminescence. In the dim light they could hear the relentless scratching and clawing at the other side of the rocks.

● ● ●

"Down here." Yanez's voice emanated from a dark corner, and Weber turned away from the collapsed entrance, passing Jeremiah's crumpled form. The room they were in was large and dark, but the ground was so smooth there was no way it was natural. The quiet echoes told him the walls were smoothed as well. This wasn't a normal cave.

A quiet snap in the darkness, the click of a switch flipping, and the lights along the ceiling exploded to life, a machine gun chatter of electricity illuminating the room.

As large as Weber thought the room was, it was far larger.

A circular chamber, the walls a combination of sharply carved rock and embedded metal consoles. Computer screens and keyboards flashed around him, and cables snaked between rock and man-made material. Against the far wall sat an even larger screen. It wasn't illuminated, but it was connected to a series of smaller consoles below. Gathered in a group to the left of this incredible construct was a series of glass tubes standing upon more complex technology, coils of rigid cable winding from the platforms down into the rock and metal floor.

"Is this... some sort of lab?" Weber asked, eyes wide as he inspected the chamber. Yanez had already made his way to the far wall, and was activating power switches on the console, bringing some of the smaller monitor screens to green-hued life.

Behind them more claws scraped on rock. The collapsed entrance shifted slightly.

"Whatever we're going to do, we need to do it quick," Sorace said, glancing over her shoulder. She hesitated for a moment, then looked back at the consoles. "What are we doing, exactly?"

"I'm, uh… I'm not real sure," Yanez replied with disturbing honesty. "The reports I found in Pedestal Four right before its collapse weren't that thorough. They called this the 'fail safe'."

"Fail safe?" Weber asked. "Fail safe against what?"

More rocks shifted by the entrance and Sorace looked back again. "Fail safe against them?"

"I don't understand," Weber replied, shaking his head. "How does a place like this possibly help us against a planet full of rabid inhabitants?"

Yanez stood by the computer terminal, fingers clacking the keyboard. Diagrams began flicking to life on the screen in front of him, and he was making strange, quiet noises.

"What do you see?" Weber asked, taking a few steps toward him. He carefully stepped around the fallen form of Jeremiah as he walked forward.

"Holy shit," Yanez said quietly. "The Harvesters."

"What about them?"

Yanez looked back at him. "I pulled up some genetic mappings and DNA constructs of the creatures."

"Okay?" Sorace murmured, trying to look over his shoulder as if she would understand what she was seeing.

"Genetically, the Harvesters are ninety-five percent human."

The room was silent except for the quiet hum of machinery and the occasional clunk of shifting rocks by the entrance.

"Say that fucking again?" Weber asked, confusion masking anger.

"The Harvesters aren't some sort of indigenous species. They're genetically modified human beings."

Weber looked around the room, his eyes focusing on the large glass tubes. They looked like test tubes, only large enough for… "So, they weren't researching them here. They were—"

"Growing them," Yanez replied quietly. "Cloning them."

"Okay, this is some science fiction bullshit," Sorace said, shaking her head. "Seriously. What are we even talking about here?"

"They made some subtle genetic improvements to them. Those small changes made big differences. Their claws enable them to dig better and defend themselves," Yanez said, focused on the screen before him. "The teeth are perfect for mashing up and grinding meat. Their lungs and nostrils have built-in filtration systems that allow them to survive in this air."

"So, basically, everything humans don't have to survive in this wasteland, the Harvesters do?"

Yanez nodded. "They even have a modified jaw and ear canal system, allowing them to communicate sub-sonically. They can speak with each other without us even hearing them. And depending on how many of them are involved, they can relay messages to each other—"

"Like a genetically engineered local area network," Weber interjected.

"Holy fuck," Sorace said. "So what does this fail safe do?"

Yanez didn't reply at first, persistently hacking away at the keyboard, accessing folders and sub folders, bringing up documents. "Looks like there was some fear the Harvesters might get out of control… so they built in this 'fail safe' as I said."

"What is it?"

"Looks like some kind of sub-sonic frequency generator that—"

A thick serrated blade cut through his words and through his chest, thrusting up and out, splitting Yanez's sternum and spraying blood in a wide arc across the terminal in front of him. Yanez choked and gasped, trying to catch his breath, trying to form words, but the wide blade shifted, then ripped free with a metal scrape, and Yanez slumped to the ground.

"What the fuck?" Weber screamed, lifting his rifle and turning. Sorace turned as well, fists clenched.

In the dim light of the terminals mounted on the wall, Jeremiah stood, sword in hand, his eyes narrow and fierce on a face unobscured by his protective helmet.

"Slaves," he spat.

"Jeremiah?" Weber asked, involuntarily looking over to the spot on the floor where his body had been laying.

"You created them to be slaves," the young man repeated. His long, brown hair was slick and matted to the rounded contours of his face. His mouth was a crooked sneer, the peeled back lips revealing just the hint of sharpened canines.

"What the hell is going on?" Sorace asked.

"How did you think you all survived in those Pedestal Cities?" Jeremiah asked, glaring at them both. "Who do you think maintained the pillars? Helped gather food for processing? Did all of your dirty work?"

Weber took an uncertain step backwards.

"Who do you think died by the thousands while mankind partied up in their clear glass domes, free from worry? Relying on the relentless, endless manual labor of people grown in test tubes simply to serve them."

"Please, Jeremiah," Weber said, holding out both hands. "We had nothing to do with that, okay? We don't even know what you're talking about."

"For two generations my kind served humans. Answered your beck and call. Lived in this untamed wilderness. Every flash flood, every severe winter. We were the ones drowning and freezing. We were the ones who died. What did your scientists do? Just grew some more."

Weber and Sorace glanced at each other, then looked back at him.

"That's right," Jeremiah replied. "I'm one of them. Twenty-four years ago there was a bad batch of clones. Reproduced material that was simply too human to use. So they disintegrated all of it." He paused for a moment, letting his words sink in. "Well, not quite all of it." Extending his arms, he held them out as if proof of his outlandish claims. "My lungs still allowed me to breathe. I could still communicate with them. But I didn't have the claws or the eyes or the teeth." He ran a thick pink tongue over the slightly sharpened incisors.

"So you acted as a double-agent on their behalf," Weber said.

"There were rumors the humans had a fail safe. Even as I helped coordinate the attacks that burned the Pedestal Cities to the ground, I tried to find out where this facility was." He kicked Yanez's body. "Finally, his big mouth spouted off about it."

"So you worked your way into our group," Weber whispered.

"I knew you'd lead me straight to it."

Weber's eyes darted to the console, looking over the keys and screens.

Jeremiah laughed, and it was all too human a sound. "What? You think there's just going to be some big red button? Some huge plunger you can just slam down to wipe us all out? Not that easy, and the one man who might have been able to figure it out is now dead."

There was another series of clawing at the rocks, and two large boulders broke free, letting in twin beams of light; scant movement of gray-skins just the other side.

"Another few minutes and my brothers will be in. Your final stand… humanity's final stand, is over."

"Like fuck it is," Sorace growled and lunged at him. Her massive, gloved fist slammed into Jeremiah's bony jaw, snapping his head to the right and sending his long hair flying. He stumbled and she pressed forward, throwing a second fist hard into his stomach, doubling him over and blowing air from his genetically enhanced lungs. Recovering, he swung his blade in a tight arc as Sorace barely slipped under the swing, the blade slicing just over her helmeted head.

"Activate it!" she screamed, looking back at Weber.

"How the fuck am I supposed to do that?" he barked back, shaking his head.

A hand clutched at the terminal, leaving a streak of crimson across the brushed metal. Weber looked down and saw Yanez slowly picking himself back up. The hard, pale crust of what looked like medicinal foam collected at the fringes of the wound, the armor's desperate attempt to close the gaping hole, an attempt that was far too little, too late. The healing foam was pink with blood puckered around the puncture in his armor, but he pushed himself to his feet, struggling to make it to the console.

"How could you possibly survive that?" he gasped at Yanez as the man lurched forward toward the terminal.

"Prototype. Self-healing… medicinal foam." Yanez struggled to speak. "One of the benefits to being in Research… and… Development." The words choked out. "Two more months and there… would have been enough… for everyone."

A bang at the entrance as rocks separated, collapsing inwards, half of the wall still blocking them. A tightly clutched group of Harvesters pressed against the opening, trying to move past each other to get inside.

Sorace darted right, the sword clattering hard against the curved metal to her left, leaving a sparking streak of blade against plate.

Yanez whacked at the keyboard, bringing up a terminal screen and he started typing in commands. Weber nodded, patted him on the shoulder and lifted his rifle, lurching toward the door. As he got halfway there was another shattering crash and the rest of the rocks piled in the way collapsed inside, opening the doorway completely.

"For the human race!" Weber shouted. He shouldered his weapon and opened fire, the rattling explosion of gunfire punching into the crowd of Harvesters, tearing open skin, showering blood, sending them back from the entrance.

Jeremiah side-stepped a swing by Sorace and brought the sword down, the blade burying itself in her left collarbone, driving her down to one knee. He stood above her, blade clutched in two hands, his mouth twisted into a tooth-filled snarl.

"This ends here," he hissed.

From ten yards away, Yanez's eyes widened. His fingers hovered over the keys. The Harvesters finally burst in, charging into and over Weber and filling the room, legs pumping, claws clacking, teeth snarling —

Yanez thrust his finger down on the enter key and closed his eyes, embracing whatever might come next.

CONDITIONING

Patrick Freivald

Richards turned toward Alice's position, a high-pitched scream in his throat, silver-black death crackling across his eyes. He and Waldeis stood guard next to the Asp transport, using it not so much as cover but backdrop — she couldn't shoot them without risking damage to their only ticket out of Merkes 2 and back to base. That made the screamers smart, but not too smart.

With a gesture Alice sent Mahmood right, careful not to make the slightest sound through the COM. Her former squadmates could hear her every bit as much as she couldn't shut off their incessant wailing, which sent sharp daggers through her mounting headache. She counted down on her fingers once Mahmood got into position, and on three they charged.

Waldeis spun and swung the plasma rifle like a club. She slid underneath it, her feet impacting his left shin. Clumsy, at least for the first few minutes after takeover, he stumbled. The barrel of his weapon dug into the dirt, one leg of an unsteady tripod, and as she spun to her feet, she kicked it out from under him.

His arm stretched into something inhuman, a wiry rope of knotted, barbed hell that yanked her off her feet. She landed on her back, helmet softening her head's impact with the hardpack sand, and jerked her foot away from his slavering mouth.

Gnashing, he dragged himself toward her, still screaming that endless shriek of madness and hate. Looking into his silver-black eyes, she shot him point-blank in the forehead. The depleted uranium kinetic-kill bullets punctured his skull, traveling through his body to disappear into the ground. Bright red blood gushed from the wound, wiry filaments erupting with it. Alice crawled backward to avoid their deadly touch.

Rolling, she swept up Waldeis's plasma rifle and came to her feet.

Mahmood ducked a clumsy swing and kicked Derek in the chest. The screamer stumbled back, screaming, always screaming. Alice shot him. Their former squad-mate's torso evaporated in a cloud of white-hot plasma and hissing steam. Derek's arm pawed at her foot, and she kicked it across the sandy ground, twisting her boot back and forth to look for contamination. Tiny dark strands twisted and clawed at the ground from the ragged wound at Derek's shoulder, but her eyes caught no movement on her body.

While Mahmood incinerated the bodies, Alice scrambled up into the turret and swiveled the twin cannon toward the unseen enemy, sweat stinging her eyes. The HUD tracked them by their screams, red blips pulsing in time with the sound.

So many.

"This whole thing is FUBAR. How the fuck did they get in here?" She pulled the trigger.

If Mahmood replied, his answer got lost in the sizzling fusillade from the vehicle-mounted weapon that evaporated a dozen approaching screamers right through the wall of a resident building. Autodarkening saved her eyes, but despite the helmet the flashes left spots across her vision. The building shuddered but held, most of its lower story now molten slag.

"Delta, check in," Fahim said over the COM, his breathing hard and fast. Relief flooded through her, a near-physical thing, at her lover's voice.

"Derek's gone," Mahmood said. "Waldeis and Richards, too."

"Alice?" he asked.

"I'm here, baby. Get your ass back to transport before they attack again."

"On your nine. Got some company." He grunted.

"I'll cover—"

A blast of static cut her off, and her HUD flickered, but the hardened circuits withstood the EMP without apparent damage. She swiveled the plasma cannon leftward while Mahmood jumped into the driver's seat.

"Babe?"

Fahim bolted into view, no sign of his rifle, a grenade in each hand. He tossed one down the alley, followed by the other, and ran for his life toward them. Twin explosions rocked the Asp as their engine whined to life, lifting half a meter off the ground. Fahim scrambled for the back while she aimed over his head.

A crowd of screamers surged from the alleyway he'd come from, once-human faces twisted in rage, throats constricted in a ceaseless keening wail. The silver-black filaments reinforcing their muscles and controlling their nervous systems drove them at inhuman speed toward the truck. As the Asp lurched forward, twin blasts from the cannon ionized the air over Fahim's head and turned a dozen former settlers into so much smoking goo. A dozen more followed, and more behind those.

Fahim leaped to the assault ramp and pulled himself aboard as she fired again. Then an EMP tumbled from the back into the closing throng, and the silent blast ripped static through her COMs. Screamers fell in a twenty-meter radius, twitching, their screams now more human as spasming... whatever-the-fuck-they-were, shredded their host bodies from within.

The "Whoop!" died in her throat as another mob emerged from the north.

"They got the whole fucking town," Alice said. "Time to jet."

"Fall back to base." Fahim prepped another EMP.

She dropped down to help him, steadying herself with the wall harnesses when Mahmood hit open ground and let loose the throttle. A kick sent the bomb out the back but she didn't detonate it, waiting for more of the things to reach it. Breathless, she turned to her lover.

A ragged hole in his armor exposed a burn-blackened patch of his right forearm. Silvery tendrils wriggled beneath, insinuating themselves into his nervous system. It wouldn't be long, and Fahim wouldn't be Fahim.

Her heart broke as he removed his helmet, soft brown eyes full of apologetic tears. He reached for but did not touch her.

"It... babe... I'm sorry."

She swallowed her gorge, forced herself by sheer will not to throw up. "I told you not to go after them." Her anger at his stupidity held no candle to the despondent fury she felt for the biomechanical creature killing him. "And you shouldn't have come back."

"I wanted to say goodbye." He gritted his teeth, and a high-pitched squeak erupted from his throat. Fighting it down with a grimace, he dropped to one knee with the strain. "And tell you that I love you. Give my love to Timothy."

A sigh escaped her lips, lost in the rushing wind.

"I love you, too. And I will." She kicked him square in the chest.

His body tumbled down the assault ramp, disappearing into the dusty backwash of the Asp's engines. She set the rifle to burn and washed the floor of any contamination he may have left behind.

* * *

Raqiya scowled at the thin streak of dust racing across the desert, and the wall of dust behind it. Her HUD tracked the closer trail at one hundred forty kilometers per hour, top speed for an Asp unconcerned about conserving fuel. The men next to her fingered their rifles and shifted their feet but did not break position.

"Fahim, report, over." She tapped her helmet. "Tony? Alice? Anybody out there? Over."

Static shot through her COM, the third distant EMP detonation in as many minutes.

"Commander!" Mahmood's voice, high with panic.

"I read you, over."

"ETA four minutes. Merkes 2… it's just… gone. They got through." Belatedly, "Over."

"How many?"

Mahmood choked back a sob. "All of them. We killed maybe a couple dozen, but the whole damned settlement's turned."

Her soldiers scrambled for battle stations without her having to give the order. Behind Raqiya, the power station's deep hum became a whine as turbines kicked into overdrive. Plasma crackled from tips of emplaced guns brought up to full power.

Martin grunted. "How many in Merkes?"

"Three thousand."

"Shit," Martin said, face hidden behind the mirrored visor. "I guess this is it. We're dead."

She sighed. "Yeah." And then, into her COM. "Control, evacuate the children to the skyhook, and get me a time-to-takeoff." Fantastically more efficient than preparing a rocket, the electromagnetic space elevator still took enormous amounts of energy to carry a heavy load into orbit, and they hadn't charged the capacitors in anticipation of such a catastrophe.

"Roger that, Sir. Uhhh… twenty-nine minutes. Roughly."

Clapping Martin on the shoulder, she knocked her helmet into his.

"No problem, then, Captain. You only need to survive another half-hour."

He patted the side of her helmet. "Good knowing you, Sir."

* * *

Dusty sweat in his eyes, Lionel approached the Asp as it coasted to a stop just inside the gate. Plascrete and titanium-fiber doors slammed closed behind it, something to buy them a little time. Enough, maybe.

He helped Alice down without a word — with nothing to comfort her grief, he said nothing — then turned to Mahmood, wrapped his brother in a wide hug.

"You made it."

"Always, little brother. Where's Taniya?"

His heart jumped at his daughter's name. "With Bhavana and the others, at evac."

"Good." Their children would live, if they could hold off the screamers long enough.

They climbed the ladders together, taking positions on the wall. In the distance, another wall spread across the desert, huge gusts of sand and dust obscuring the terraced mountains and their abandoned biohabs, an aborted attempt at terraforming this cursed rock, a hollow promise laced with poison and death.

Gouts of white-hot plasma streaked overhead, the big guns firing blindly into the dust cloud in a panicked attempt to thin the herd. They watched the billowing clouds of plasma wobble into vortexes of violets, yellows, and reds as the gasses cooled on impact. He imagined a diminishment of the approaching screams.

But no. The army of screamers ran at the wall full speed, the inhuman sounds erupting from their throats only growing louder, thousands of voices slicing through the air like a force of nature. Lionel dropped his visor and set his rifle on sure targets. Wasted ammunition might cost them everything.

The first shapes resolved at the front of the cloud, legs and arms breaking free of dust revealing humans, or human forms, covering the open ground impossibly fast. Red outlines shifted to orange on his HUD. His throat dry, he took a sip from the reclaimer straw in his helmet and pulled the trigger when the first outline turned green.

Recoil against his shoulder turned him, but the shot streaked across the open space to vaporize the right half of a screamer's torso. More shots flashed from the left and right, silent, sun-bright death ionizing the air as two hundred tried to ward off thousands. The screamers closed the distance, and he switched his rifle to burn.

They hit the wall at a full sprint, ropy masses streaking from their limbs, adhering to the plascrete like desert lizards running up the side of a building. Someone screamed through the COM, deep and throaty, and another cried out for his mother, but for each casualty, they took out dozens of screamers. Hundreds died in seconds, and the stink of cooked bodies and boiling shit made him want to puke.

Mahmood laughed beside him, blasting away into a crowd impossible to miss. Lionel washed a slow gout of flame across the second wave clambering up the wall. Hair and clothes caught fire, armor and flesh melted, dozens of screaming wails cut short as oxygenated lungs cooked from the inside. And he thought, for one shining moment, that maybe, just maybe, if the wall held, then another drop-ship—

His visor darkened as a white-green ball of plasma streaked from the cloud toward them, vaporizing every screamer in its path. Lionel had just enough time to shove Mahmood from the precipice before he and the wall beneath him evaporated in an explosion of atomized mist.

* • *

Shielding her eyes from the brilliant green light that obliterated the wall, Alice fired several bursts into the gap.

"On me!" she said, forming her troops in a dispersed line, spitting death and destruction at the alien things that had once been farmers, craftsmen, mothers, lovers, dreaming of a better place than the polluted squalor of Earth. She paced backward, firing with every step. Each meter of ground cost the screamers dearly, but they advanced without the slightest hint of fear, without the slightest acknowledgment of casualties.

Behind her the ground rumbled, the nuclear furnaces burning hot, too hot, to power the weapons they never thought they'd need and the electromagnetic engines of the skyhook that would take their children back to Earth, to safety. The countdown on her HUD read four minutes to liftoff.

A screamer hit Jones at a dead sprint. He exploded, body rupturing in a spray of red gore. Hot and sticky, it splashed across her armor, trickled down her neck and into her gloves. She burned his killer, and the two behind it, then rolled right to take shelter behind the plascrete bricks of her favorite coffee shop.

A trio of screamers bolted from her left. Whirling, she blew the legs off the first. The second ran straight into her gun, spinning it and her wide. She pulled the trigger point-blank and it stumbled back, a two-inch hole glowing red through its chest.

Mahmood appeared, helmetless, an avenging angel awash in brown-red, his eyes glowing with the reflected orange-green blaze from his rifle. He sprayed across the street, preventing the rest from following, backing away from an inferno of his own creation.

The third screamer slammed her sideways into the wall, clawing at her armor, digging in to find a patch of bare skin and deliver its fatal, parasitic bite. She elbowed it in the face, twice, and as it stumbled back she snarled in hate and despair. The thing that had been Fahim shook its head to recalibrate, eyes no longer brown but silver-black, infected, inhuman. Bone jutted from its right arm, and half its face had stripped off on impact with the desert sand, but otherwise he — it — looked intact.

It reached for her as a pile of screamers rounded the corner behind them. They charged.

She tugged off her helmet, stepped in for Fahim's deadly embrace. He grabbed her face as if going for a kiss and a thousand pinpricks announced the infection, silver tendrils of nano-whatever-the-fuck stealing her body and will to its own ends. With her left hand she pulled the pins from the three grenades on her bandoleer.

"For Timothy, baby."

* • *

The explosion threw Mahmood forward, over burning bodies and into a mass of screamers. He didn't let up on the trigger, drowning them in fire as hot as the sun. His armor melted and somewhere part of him smelled cooking meat and burnt hair, but he didn't stop.

Sharp pain pierced his savage rage. He looked down to a hand, or something like one, gnarled fingers shot through with silver-black filament. Drenched in blood, it protruded from his abdomen, having torn a hole right through his armor. It pulled out and took with it his will to continue.

He fell to his knees, and then onto his face, his last thoughts on his daughter and niece.

* • *

Another explosion shook the ground near Raqiya's position at the base of the skyhook, snaking up into impenetrable clouds far above to the asteroid that anchored it. Behind her, frantic technicians scrambled to disconnect the power cables from the elevator carriage. Her HUD read ninety seconds to liftoff.

"We're not going to hold them."

At Martin's pronouncement, his soldiers shifted around him, twenty faces hidden behind mirrored visors, their body language a mess of nervous terror.

Raqiya grunted. "We don't have a choice, Captain. We hold them, or everything we love dies with us." Her nod directed his gaze back to the front. "Here they come."

She fired at the first to appear, a fully-automatic salvo that cut down dozens before her power cell clicked dry. Martin fired with her, and his men as well, pummeling the unstoppable horde that poured through the streets like shrieking water through a shattered dam. When she drew a long knife from her belt, he did the same and her heart filled with pride.

These men, her men, would live in the halls of honor forever.

Thirty-eight seconds. It would be close.

"Give the order, Captain."

He swallowed, spoke without inflection. "Charge."

They broke across open ground, a stuttering jog at first, then a sprint, twenty against a multitude, twenty men and women screaming their last defiance at an unstoppable force that couldn't hear them over their own insane wailing.

As the press of bodies swallowed the last of her forces, she sheathed her knife and waited for the end.

At six seconds they bolted around her, buffeting her and knocking her over to tear apart the remaining technicians and clamber aboard the skyhook's elevator even as it lifted from the ground.

"Fuck," she mumbled.

None lived to hear her curse.

A screamer reached for her. She slapped its hand away, furious. Turning, she stalked to the hovering platform, shoving screamers out of her way to get to it, twisted and pulled to open the airlock hatch.

A giant screen filled the far wall of the otherwise-empty room. On it, General Oreto sat in his command console, his bulging, grotesque body hard-wired into the zero-gravity harness that allowed his mind to control the screamers from orbit. His throat wobbled up and down, but his voice came from the elevator's speakers.

"Well done, Commander. Your forces outperformed Battalion 4481 by three-point-four-zero percent, and even 3707 by one-point-one-eight."

She scowled. "They all died, and I lost. Sir."

"By only three seconds. No one has ever come that close, and it only cost us a few thousand civilians. Your casualty numbers… most impressive. What did you do to the soldiers?"

"I hacked their personality matrices in the growth tanks, made them believe they were protecting their own loved ones. I… I made them care, Sir."

"Interesting. We'll have to try that on the next batch. These incremental improvements are critical to the war effort."

"This batch should have—"

He cut her off with a flabby wave. "You did an excellent job, Commander, just excellent. Five hundred thousand credits have been transferred to your account for beating the five-second mark. Would you care to try again?"

She grinned. "How many settlers at Base 217?"

"Nineteen thousand," the general said.

"And how many soldiers?"

"Eight hundred, mostly conscripts. And you can bring another four hundred from the vats."

"A million credits if I beat three seconds, ten if the elevator makes it off-world."

He chuckled through the speakers, loud and low, and spoke to someone.

"Breach the perimeter on Base 217, probing strikes only for now. Make the civilians nervous enough to request High

Council support. I'm sending Raqiya Ngige to condition the troops there."

Thanks for reading SNAFU: Last Stand.
We hope you've enjoyed it as much as we did putting it together.

It was a great honour to have Tim Miller read the entire volume and write the foreword for us. We sorta feel like Bill and Ted, and we're not worthy, but Tim is a great guy, and very humble considering all his achievements. Even though he stated he was honoured to be given the chance to work on this, the honour is all ours.

Please consider leaving us a review if (and anywhere) you see fit. Any and all reviews are gratefully accepted.

If you have any questions, or want to quote from the book, please contact us at any time.

I would ask please, if you DO review online, send a link to Geoff via editor@cohesionpress.com or via our Facebook page messaging system. If you review for a magazine or paper, let us know and we'll buy it.

Thank you.

+ + +

Geoff Brown - Director, Cohesion Press.
Mayday Hills Lunatic Asylum
Beechworth, Australia

Amanda J Spedding - Editor-in-chief, Cohesion Press
Sydney, Australia

Matthew Summers - Editor, Cohesion Press
Sydney, Australia